Cupid F*cks Up

PAULA HOUSEMAN

Title: Cupid F*cks Up
Author: Paula Houseman
ISBNs: 978-0-6482836-0-7 (paperback)
978-0-6482836-1-4 (epub)
978-0-6482836-2-1 (mobi)

Publisher: WildWoman Publishing,
Sydney, Australia

Connect with Paula Houseman
Website: https://paulahouseman.com

Social Networks
https://www.facebook.com/PaulaHousemanAuthor
https://www.goodreads.com/PaulaHouseman
https://www.linkedin.com/in/paulahouseman
https://www.pinterest.com/paulahouseman
https://twitter.com/paulahouseman

For Jasper, Bailey & Remy

Eros: The Greek god of love | *Cupid: His Roman counterpart*

'*His arrows are of different power: some are golden, and kindle love in the heart they wound; others are blunt and heavy with lead, and produce aversion to a lover.*'

(Ov. Met. i. 468; Eurip. Iphig. Aul. 548.)

CONTENTS

PART THREE
Waking Over the Coals

PART ONE

A TABOOBOO ROMANCE

PROLOGUE

The mirror. The goddamn, bloody mirror. A 'transportation system' like no other. Looking at it could be a moving experience, but too often it had taken me down. Not so long ago, it took me into hell. Then it brought me back.

Today, though, as I stood in front of it, turned this way and that, it was forgiving—generous, even. I loved what I saw. *Yeah, baby!* I was a sizzling hot tamale in my heavenly, wicked, ruby-red dress!

Maybe demure in its knee length, but its plunging neckline exposed a good amount of cleavage. Teamed with the dress was a pair of red patent, barely there high-heeled sandals with slender toe and ankle straps.

For a long time I'd kitted out in wishy-washy colours to blend in, to disappear. No more. I wasn't a 'mistake' like my parents had said. I was meant to be here, I was meant to shine! And right now, I felt like a princess. A shameless one.

My hair hung loose, covering half of my half-bare back. The wild curls would start to drop once I left the air-conditioned room and was outside in the humidity that was rare for an Adelaide summer. Not much I could do about the weather.

I faced the mirror now, leaned in and checked my make-up. It could have passed for a professional job. I'd taken extra care applying it, especially around the eyes. I looked into them.

Uh-oh. A short-sighted move.

Thank God for my contact lenses, those water-loving, plasticky discs that meant I didn't have to wear glasses. But they hardly shielded my eyes from the memories pooling beyond them—the fearful and ridiculous sequence of events that led to my present niggling concerns. Made me wonder ... all in all, was I ready to put myself out there again? Was I ready for a date (with destiny)?

I moved away from the mirror and sat in the easy chair in the corner of the room, my thoughts drifting back in time to that momentous night three years earlier, when it all began.

Although, realistically, the signs—implicit in dreams and in desires—are there long before something manifests for anyone. As a child, I'd fantasised about a fairy-tale prince. I grew up and found one, but he wasn't the man of my dreams. Turned out I wasn't the woman of his. It was okay. We had two terrific children, an amicable divorce and a solid friendship. I was okay.

Then just when the wish for happily-ever-after had lost its sway over me, just when I'd stopped looking—when I felt that maybe *I* was 'The One' for me—it happened. I was in my forty-sixth year.

It was a balmy Saturday evening when the handsome, silver-tongued prince rolled up in his shiny bachelor Mercedes convertible. He professed his undying love for me and claimed it was written in the stars that he and I were destined to be together forever.

I told him to fuck off.

CHAPTER ONE

Once Upon a Bloody Time

'I think I need to be alone,' I'd said. It was a politically correct way of saying fuck off. So he left. But his revelation had roused the fire-breathing dragon in my psyche, and I spent the night doing battle with it.

In fairy tales, this was the handsome prince's job. He was supposed to rescue the damsel in distress. And much as I'd worshipped his character, hers kind of pissed me off. As a child, I didn't know the meaning of 'grow some balls', but by God, I had 'em! I wished she did. Still, what she lacked in moxie, she made up for in gentility. I couldn't identify with that. It bothered me a little, because I was a girl. And girls were supposed to be all pink and meek and froufrou. I didn't play by the book, though.

When my mother, Sylvia, started reading fairy tales to me in the late 1950s, they'd been scrubbed clean of all the scatological stuff of their earlier versions. If they hadn't been, she would have Ajaxed my books and hung the authors out to dry. But try as she might, while I was under her roof she couldn't scrub my mouth clean.

When I got used to the taste of soap, she relied on words to shame me into moral purity. *'Tu es possédé par le diable lui même!'* (You are possessed by the devil himself!). It didn't work. And it was a bit harsh coming from someone who wasn't all that ladylike. Also, saying it in French didn't soften the delivery any, just because it's a romance language (the main one of several languages she and my father, Joe, spoke). Anyway, did having a dirty mind mean I was possessed? *I* didn't think so. I just had a kinship with the raw stories—the ancient myths. I assumed it was because my life had felt like a Greek tragedy, and because the female characters had more substance than the milquetoast maidens of those fluffy, bullshit fairy tales.

My prince—the one I'd told to fuck off—had loved me, potty mouth and all, his whole life and most of mine (I'm a week older than him). But it wasn't like he'd carved 'Ralph Brill ♡ Ruth Roth' on a tree trunk. No. That would have been creepy, because Ralph Brill, my best friend, was also my first cousin. His mother, Norma, was my mother's older sister by seven years.

'We *used* to be cousins,' he'd argued that night, before I sent him on his way. It was a daft comment. Just because he'd accidentally discovered six months earlier that he'd been adopted, I couldn't merely stamp out the deeply etched imprint that said we were blood related. Like that—*poof!* Be that as it may, once I'd slain the dragon, I unearthed some very strong feelings for Ralph. And that imprint was being challenged by the image of getting naked with him ... *Mmm, mmm, oh ...*

Well, my insistent prince returned the next morning. Dishevelled, looking like he'd ridden in on horseback, he appeared more pauper than prince. But schlumpy didn't eclipse his six-footness of sexy gorgeousness. It didn't hide his roundish face with its chiselled jawline, his subtle chin dimple or his Cupid's-bow lips. Schlumpy didn't mask his sturdy physique (all these features had lent themselves to his previous profession as a model, before he became a psychologist). And schlumpy didn't veil my lust. So, I confessed my feelings for him.

Ralph cupped my face in his hands and kissed me, softly at first, then passionately and feverishly, then softly again. He led me to the bedroom, where he planted scorching butterfly kisses along my neck as he deftly hooked his fingers under the spaghetti straps of my nightie, and pushed them down over my shoulders. The nightie fell to the floor. Ralph feasted his eyes on my semi-nakedness, and with the utmost reverence, he removed my panties.

'My God, Ruthie, you are so incredibly beautiful.' His voice was husky with desire as he stroked my breasts, teasing each nipple with his thumbs.

I lifted up his T-shirt and he took it the rest of the way. As he dropped his jeans and briefs, I gasped at the size of his throbbing manhood. Although, from an unfortunate extended family gathering in his backyard when we were fifteen, I already knew that my prince was hung like the horse he rode in on.

Zooming around on his father's Bantam motorbike, the vibrations got Ralph all excited. His excitement fell out of his hand-me-down, oversized shorts and too-loose Y-fronts. This, in full view of a whole bunch of relatives and friends.

Now, with his junk intentionally exposed, Ralph tilted his head ever so slightly at my reaction. A bemused half-smile crossed his lips. It seemed to say, *You've never let me forget the incident. How could* you *forget the biggest part of it?*

He became serious again and moved in close. In one smooth motion, he scooped me into his arms and placed me on the bed.

He lay down next to me and slowly and deliberately mapped the contours of my body with his hand. Next, he was above me, lowering himself onto me. We melted into each other, our kisses becoming hungrier and more desperate. He paused and looked into my eyes, then he moved south, his tongue snaking down my stomach and coming to rest at the Promised Land. With practised precision and broad strokes, he explored, and didn't stop until I arched and shuddered, crying out in pleasure. Ralph slid back up my body and pressed his hips against mine as he plunge—

Blah, blah, blah ...

It was the stuff of romance novels—those fabulous, sexed up fairy tales. It didn't happen, though. And it had never been my reality.

If my issues with the fairy tales of my childhood had been limited solely to an aversion to the damsel, then this romantic interlude might have unfurled like Rapunzel's hair, and the prince would have mounted *me*. But, questioning the credibility of these fantasy couplings from when I was very little undoubtedly set up blocks: At best, I'd experienced the odd fleeting impression of the fairy-tale.

I was four when my father read *Sleeping Beauty* to me for the first time. I went to sleep happy, but there was no prince next to my bed when I woke up. Confusion. Joe read stories to me every night, but I only got to hear *Sleeping Beauty* once a week. It was the Monday night special. One night a year later, when Joe was out, Sylvia read it to me. Cognition. A light came on. Suspicion.

'Why would the printh want to kith Thleeping Beauty?' I asked Sylvia. 'If she'th been athleep for a hundred yearth, her breath would thtink and she'd look like shit.'

She slapped me for swearing and switched the light off. The question went unanswered.

It was a reasonable one, though, based on fact, not fantasy. Two nights before, I'd stared with wide-eyed fascination as Sylvia applied her make-up for a dinner dance they were going to. The next morning, I climbed into my parents' bed. Again, I stared at my mother with fascination as she lay there with panda eyes. Her pillowcase smeared with lipstick and foundation, she was snoring, drooling and blasting me with rhythmic swooshes of breath as foul as pre-treatment at a sewage plant.

After that, I had trouble imagining anyone wanting to come close to a hundred years' worth of this nasty pong. And when Joe had rolled over and farted, I thought, *Really? This is it? This is the prince?*

Sylvia was hardly the damsel, though. She may have started out as one, but this damsel in distress had become embittered. Through a fairy-tale lens, I saw her more along the lines of the wicked stepmother, the evil queen, the witch. From the depths of my ancient survival consciousness, I experienced her as a harpy—in the old myths, the harpies were foul-tempered nasties with the face of a woman and the body of a bird. They swooped, stole food from plates, took a dump on the remains, and left their victims starving and deprived of nourishment.

Despite all this, I believed in the prince because I had a role model for him in Ralph. Ralph always had my back. He was my hero. But ... my low opinion of the fairy-tale blueprint aside, and notwithstanding the difficulty in getting my head around the fact that Ralph and I weren't biologically connected, 'it' most likely didn't happen because the bottom line is this: To have a prince, you have to be princess material. And I was never made to feel like one at home.

So, what *did* take place when the prince came back that morning?

CHAPTER TWO

The Balls in His Court

Ralph had been so concerned about losing me—about losing *us*—he was prepared to remain just best friends. He apologised for his ill-conceived declaration of love from the night before, then added, 'I hope it doesn't change anything between us.'

'I hope it does,' I said. Not exactly a confession; more a suggestion.

As that sunk in, he cried. I took a step towards him and we hugged. It was a long hug. Ralph hung on tightly and released a sigh of relief. Or ... was that a sigh of pleasure?

Oh God ... Please, please *don't try to kiss me!*

The memory of Sylvia's vomitous morning breath had not diminished over four decades. And with Ralph's rheumy eyes, rumpled clothes and mussed hair—which I couldn't see past—I imagined he hadn't given any thought to brushing his teeth before leaving home.

But he kept hugging, didn't push it, didn't attempt to kiss me.

Why not? Why aren't you at least trying *to kiss me?*

I'd just woken from the single hour's sleep I'd managed to get. Was only one hour of snoring enough to cause bad breath? I surreptitiously brought my hand down, cupped it over my mouth and nose and blew into it. My breath seemed okay to me. But even if it stunk to high heaven, would Ralph care? Sleeping Beauty's halitosis was not a deal-breaker for Prince Prototype. He didn't give a crap about her rank air. And if he'd been a womaniser, he would have cared even less.

Ralph had been a womaniser. He'd had an oversupply of raging adolescent hormones that hadn't started to mature until a few years ago. And womanisers don't just hug you. Womanisers slip their hands under your nightie. They fondle your breasts and then they slide their fingers inside your panties. *Oh God.* Womanisers caress you between your legs ... *Oh my. Oh, mmm.* But first, womanisers cover your mouth with their mouth and probe it with their ... furry morning tongues—

Shit!

I shot my hand up and locked my fingers around the back of his neck in a death grip. He misread it. I felt him growing hard.

Shit!

'I want to court you,' he said.

Huh? *'What?'* I whispered into his chest.

'I said, I want to court you, Ruthie.'

'"Court" me?'

'Yes.'

You're shittin' me!

I wasn't all that surprised, but I still felt like laughing. 'Court' sounded so seventeenth century, but then ... my Don Juan had his mother tongue tied to the same era as the original fictional philanderer. Ralph hadn't heard this kind of lingo in his working-class home environment. Maybe his biological parents, whoever they were, were bluebloods. Or not. I always just thought he'd over-identified with the chivalrous heroes of his adoptive mother's many period romance novels (which he'd sworn blind he never read—*liar, liar, pants on fire*) to further distance himself from his boorish, pit bull-like father and siblings. It had only served to make him stand out like a swashbuckling dog's balls.

I disengaged from the hug and took a step back. The earnest look on Ralph's face said, *Really, I do want to court you.*

Okay, then. First things first. 'I need to brush my teeth,' I said. 'You can use the main bathroom. There're new toothbrushes in the top drawer.' *Subtle.*

I went to my en-suite and Ralph went to fix himself up a bit. When we met up a few minutes later in the hallway, I had a panic attack at the thought of having sex with my cousin (who wasn't really my cousin and who had yet to start courting me). We pretty much started off the morning the same way the previous evening ended: Ralph clamped his hand over my mouth and said, 'Just breathe. *Breathe!*'

My breathing slowed and regulated itself, and we eyed each other like a pair of self-conscious teenagers. Grunge had not been a fashion trend in our adolescence, though. And Ralph's spruce up from the neck up was in sharp contrast to his grunginess from the neck down.

He cleared his throat. 'Can I borrow your iron?'

Shit. Our bond was such that he often 'heard' my thoughts.

'Uh, why?' *That's it, play dumb.*

'My clothes are wrinkled.'

'Oh ... I hadn't noticed.' *Dumber.*

He gave me a quizzical look. I reddened.

'Anyway, I feel unkempt.'

Ralph used to feel unkempt when a hair was out of place. It wasn't just vanity. He had obsessive-compulsive personality disorder. It came on (and was self-diagnosed) not long after his backyard expo. He'd been in a state of remission for quite some time, but he lapsed when he felt vulnerable. I felt vulnerable too. He needed to iron. I needed to eat.

I set up the ironing board in the laundry and came back into the kitchen, where he was still loitering. I inclined my head and raised an eyebrow. 'You hungry?'

It was a rhetorical question; Ralph was always hungry. But as a psychologist, he fancied himself as an expert on body language. Even so, he filtered my question through his skirt-chasing alter ego, which refiltered it through its lizard-brain. Ralph inclined *his* head, raised an eyebrow, gave me a lustful smile and edged closer. I felt a stirring down under.

Oh God. I need to be more specific. 'Uh, d'ya want some breakfast?' As in ... not crumpet, not muffin.

Ralph backed off a bit and nodded. 'Mm. I could eat. Mm. I could eat.' Repetition repetition— another OCPD symptom.

'Okay, but I'm gonna have a shower before I make it.'

Again, he misread it as an invitation and he fixed me with a rakish smile. Again, I felt that little quiver. *Shit.* Blood was rushing to the wrong place. I needed that shower; I needed to stay alert.

I marched across to the hallway linen closet, grabbed a fresh towel and shoved it into his chest. 'Here ya go.' *Make sure yours is a cold shower.* I held up a finger. *I'm not done yet.* I went back to the closet and fished out a pink Gillette Daisy disposable from an open packet (it gave me silky legs. It could give him a silky face just in case he wore me down and I let him kiss me). I put the razor on top of the towel. 'There's aftershave in the drawer under where you found the toothbrush.'

A bewildered expression crossed his face. Understandable. I was sending mixed signals. I left him standing there staring after me as I disappeared into my en-suite and locked the door (and double-checked it was locked).

I finished before Ralph did. I threw on a loose, stretchy cotton T-shirt dress and gathered my wet hair up into a ponytail. I was pfaffing around in the kitchen when he came out wearing just the towel around his slim waist. His damp, medium-length brown hair was slicked back and starting to curl up at the bottom as it dried.

With ripped biceps that bulged, but not in a steroidal, sinewy kind of way, and broad shoulders, Ralph was the pinnacle of perfection. He used to wax his torso in his modelling days, but when he switched vocations and his psychology practice grew sufficiently for him to knock back modelling assignments, he stopped his hair removal. His well-developed pecs were now covered with a light smattering of soft, downy hair that tapered down his toned abs and disappeared under the towel. I snuck looks as I took stuff out of the fridge.

His state of undress unnerved me. Even worse, I sensed him ogling me. I turned around and was alarmed by his proximity. He'd moved in a little closer. His face was smooth-shaven and gave off the woodsy scent of Joop! Homme. *Dear God.* Our eyes locked. Without looking down, I saw his nipples become erect— I have the wide peripheral vision of a goat—and I swear I could almost hear the *whooshing* of his brain flooding with endorphins, and the *lub-dub-lub-dub-lub-dubbing* of his heart rate increasing.

I about-faced to avoid his intense gaze and to stave off another panic attack. I inserted four slices of bread into the toaster (one for me, three for him), cracked and beat the bejesus out of the eggs, and brewed the coffee.

Telepathic bucket of cold water. I felt him watching me for some time before he padded away to press his unkempt clothes.

He didn't bother to put them on before he sat down for breakfast and tucked into his food.

Watching his guns coil and uncoil with the movements of sawing with his knife, and weightlifting his loaded fork, was getting me hot. But Ralph was oblivious to my heavy breathing. He was too busy making love to his omelette: *'Mmm, nom nom nom, mmm.'* Ralph sometimes moaned while he ate, usually when he was nervous. It was one of his many quirks that I mostly ignored; I was so accustomed to them.

He had a voracious appetite, like Fat Bastard, Dr Evil's obese henchman in *Austin Powers: The Spy Who Shagged Me* (if he had the same metabolism as Fat Bastard, he wouldn't be sitting in my kitchen half-naked—*ecch*. I have cacomorphobia, a dread of the morbidly obese). Ralph's relationship with food was a typically Jewish one just like mine (but he could eat me under the table ... and had earlier looked like he wanted to). His healthy appetite probably wasn't encoded in his DNA, though (Norma and Albie—Ralph's st-t-t-tuttering, bully-boy German father—assumed his biological mother wasn't Jewish: They'd have known if she was; nothing stays secret for long in the Jewish community. They converted Ralph when they adopted him). His love affair with food was probably influenced by childhood circumstances. Having grown up relatively poor, he was often hungry as a child, but once he started working and was earning a good living, he overstocked his fridge and pantry.

I stopped eating, and watched him as he *mmmed* and *nom nommed* and polished off his breakfast. Then, with meticulous care, he lined up his cutlery so that it pointed upwards to twelve o'clock, but he turned the fork upside down so the prongs were touching the plate. He once told me he'd heard this practice was The European way and it was Euro-chic for a man-about-town. I told him I'd heard it was *de rigueur* for a wanker. I smiled at the memory.

Ralph looked up. He caught me watching him and smiling. He returned a crooked, closed-mouth, flirtatious grin, cocking one eyebrow questioningly. Then his eyes caressed my body—

the parts he could see above the breakfast bar—read ... 'tits' (I am much shorter than him). It was clear his shower had restored order and his confidence. My shower had washed away my defences. *Shit.* I wanted to yell at him to stop thinking with his dick, but I couldn't form the words. My bean was sprouting again! *No, no, no. This cannot happen. I haven't waxed my bikini line. I look like an African bush pig. And, and, anyway, you're my cousin!* I focused on my food and unconsciously started shovelling it into my mouth. I made a mental note to google 'stages of courtship'.

Ralph and I made polite small talk over our coffee. It was as if I'd been on a first date with a stranger I'd picked up, let him spend the night, then couldn't wait for him to finish his breakfast and leave. That kind of thing had never happened to me; I was only going by what I'd seen in movies. It was uncomfortable. I imagined it was how the female movie character would feel if she were really at one with her role. But I was disturbed that I felt this way with my best friend.

I assumed that as a psychologist, Ralph understood. Although, expertise in human behaviour or not, it probably would have been hard for him to get some distance from an experience he himself was immersed in.

He helped me clear up, then said, 'I think I'll get dressed now.'

Thank God! But ... what about the underpants? You're not going to wear the undies you had on last night, are you? So, how do I say this without being offensive? 'Uh, Casper's got a jockey three-pack in his drawer. One's still in the packet. It's yours.'

Casper is my son (real name Jake, nicknamed Casper because my GP at the time said my pregnancy was a phantom one). At fifteen, Casper was built more like Ralph than like his father, Reuben, who was medium height and frame. Already standing at five feet ten inches, Casper was a good-looking boy-man. Like his dad, he had thick, wavy black hair, brown eyes, and an almost perpetual tan. Casper and his older sister, Hannah, were at Reuben's for the weekend. Reuben and I had been divorced for fifteen months.

'It's fine. I'll just go commando,' Ralph said.

What? Freeballing? Oh boy. After that fateful afternoon thirty years ago, Ralph had imprisoned his 'boys' in tight jocks. Now they were gonna hang l-l-l-loose—a pair of nuts escaping the insanity of years of restrai—

'Ruthie?'

'Huh?'

'I said it's okay, I'll go comm—'

'Yeah, yeah. Whatever.' *Just make sure the barn door stays closed.*

He started heading towards the laundry where he'd left his clothes, when a loud *thunk* on the front door startled him. 'What was that?'

'Oh, just the paperboy. I swear, one of these days he's gonna deliver it straight through the lounge room window.'

Ralph looked at the window, looked back at me, looked at the front door and walked past the laundry.

Oh shit! You've overshot. 'Where are you going?'

'To bring in the paper.'

'No-no-no! I'll get it!'

Ralph turned and stared at me, a perplexed expression on his face. 'I'm already here.'

Fuck. The butterflies in my stomach were going to revert to the pupa stage. I exhaled noisily. 'Ralph. You *cannot* go out there with just a towel.'

He didn't twig at first, but then shook his head. 'Ruthie ... you gotta stop worrying about the neighbours.' He opened the door, took a few steps out and retrieved the paper.

Crap.

'Neighbours' was a catch-all term for 'everyone'. (Sylvia had an unhealthy obsession with the need for people's approval. Except mine. If she had, she might have treated me a little more kindly; not been so critical.) My torturous night ended with indifference to what the neighbours would think, but not so much to what the neighbours would say. Specifically, Olive Portnoy, the flap-jawed pisspot who lived across the road from me.

I looked at Ralph with a sense of resignation. 'Go get dressed. We need to talk.'

CHAPTER THREE

Portnoy's Complaint

'You've changed your mind, haven't you? This isn't going to happen with us, is it?' Ralph looked frightened and forlorn.

'What? Oh. No-no-no.' *We need to talk* had been a poor choice of words, a hope-dasher. 'I meant, we need to talk, you know, to get things out there instead of tiptoeing around each other.'

He breathed a sigh of relief. 'Yeah.' He stared at me, waiting for me to initiate the conversation.

I looked down at his towel. *Like ... hello!* He got it. He ducked into the laundry, collected his clothes and made for the bathroom.

I walked over to the living room window and adjusted the angle of the plantation shutters enough for me to be able to see Portnoy's place.

It had been a year since I'd moved into my home. A relatively new, single-storey, three-bedroom duplex, it was located on a quiet street. It had been advertised as a townhouse because it looked like it was part of a boutique block of eight—four identical pairs of homes next door to each other. The realtor must have thought that 'large townhouse' had more pulling power than 'small duplex'. The realtor also drove a really, really big car and carried a really, really big briefcase. Ralph had said this man's preoccupation with bigness compensated for smallness elsewhere, and that his 'pulling power' might stretch the truth, but little else.

Each pair of duplexes had a mirrored floor plan. Viewed from the street, my duplex was on the right. My driveway and my neighbour's, separated by a narrow bed of dwarf Agapanthus, led to abutting single garages. At the rear of the garage and partitioned off from it was the laundry with two access doors—one leading into the garage, the other leading into the lounge. Behind the laundry was the U-shaped kitchen with island divider. The main bathroom was behind that, then the master bedroom, with its en-suite on the left behind the bathroom and a walk-in closet on the right. French doors opened out into a courtyard. On the front right side of my duplex was a long living area, then Hannah and Casper's bedrooms. The duplexes had grey slate roofs and glossy, fire-engine red front doors. The exterior walls were rendered and painted in an oatmeal colour.

The rest of the street had similarly configured housing. Most, mine included, had no front fence; the boundary line was where the lawn met the footpath. It gave the street a sense of openness, which extended to the neighbours—friendly people who minded their own business. The only blot on the landscape was the scandalmongering Olive Portnoy and her ramshackle cottage.

Her front yard looked like the suburb's central waste facility. Many of the neighbours had complained to the council, who sent their people out. These pen pushers had to be seen to be doing something, but nothing changed.

I ran out one morning when I saw a short, dumpy, whiskered, white-haired inspector surveying her house. He held a clipboard against his protuberant belly and was writing something on an official-looking form when I approached him. I told him what I thought. He agreed that the yard was extremely cluttered, but in his opinion nothing really constituted a fire hazard—not even the odd weed poking out through the broken concrete that was littered with car parts, an upended birdbath, flowerless flowerpots, rusted-out appliances, newspapers, and plastic crates.

Yeah, well, what about the army of garden gnomes? I'd asked him. Of the twenty or so of these little bearded fuckers with their red pointy hats, seven held guns—one even had a bazooka! What about firearm regulations? I'd asked him. I wasn't being serious but I didn't much like that he'd snorted his disdain and eyed me with contempt.

Oh, yes. Go ahead and disparage me and my concerns, I'd thought. *You ... you fat, jollyless bastard with your gold-plated pension just around the corner. Maybe you could don a red pointy hat and retire in her garden as Bad Santa. And I hope that when you don't deliver, the others shoot you with their clay weapons. In the balls. Maybe then you'll have more respect for gun laws! Ho ho ho.*

I thought back to about eight months before that ineffectual exchange, when I'd made an offer on my place.

The agent called me the next day and tried to squeeze me for another twenty thousand as a counter-offer to a fake counter-offer to my original one (which the vendor had already accepted). I refused. He came back to me two hours later. The fake counter-offerers had reneged. 'What luck,' he said. 'It's yours,' he said. 'Indeed,' I said, and counter-offered ten thousand dollars less than my original one. The vendor accepted.

In hindsight, I could see that they'd capitulated because whatever the place was marketed as—duplex, townhouse, castle, Wonderland—Portnoy's shithole was going to make the surrounding properties hard to sell. I didn't feel so complacent on the day I moved in. I hadn't thought to question the strategic placement of four vans parked across the road in front of the shithole whenever I met with the agent.

In the months since, I conceded that the only way things would change was when the old woman snuffed it. Odds-on it wasn't going to be anytime soon. She was like the Hydra, the nine-headed water snake of ancient myth. Cut off one head, it just grew another two. People like Portnoy live forever.

Now, standing here staring at the snake's dump, I felt grateful that my bedroom didn't face the god-awful view. I wasn't so grateful that this woman was a snoop. A malignant mole of the Jewish community, she had a direct link to my mother.

Sylvia had never met the spinster Portnoy. Nor had I. (In fact, I knew of no one who had. Spies need to operate incognito.) But mommy dearest had finagled the hag's number from a friend of an acquaintance of an acquaintance of an acquaintance. My smothering mother was thrilled to have an association with someone who stalked and talked. She was unaware that I knew Portnoy was her informant. How naïve. Gossips gossip to everyone, and about everyone.

I momentarily regretted buying this place, but then as I turned away from the window and took in the soothing pastel décor of my living area, as I glimpsed my off-white, state-of-the-art kitchen, as I thought of my spacious bedroom and of having my own bathroom, I turned back to the window and thought, *No—I'm not going to let you drive me out!* Maybe I could plant a tall-growing privacy hedge. Would I need council permission? Would they send out the Kris Kringle troll again? I needed to speak to Phoebe and Zac, who owned the adjoining duplex. I was certain they'd be open to the idea of having something to screen out the eyesore across the road.

My musings were interrupted when Ralph came back. He was wearing his perfectly pressed, Fabuloned T-shirt and jeans.

Why have you ironed creases into your jeans? Should a man iron creases into his jeans? I didn't recall seeing them before, not in his jeans. His OC behaviour had amped up.

I had a pair of large two-seater, pale mushroom-pink leather sofas in my lounge room. Facing each other, they were separated by a heavy travertine and jarrah coffee table. Ralph sat on one sofa, I sat on the other. We held each other's gaze for a moment before he prompted me. 'I'm listening.'

Noooo! Seriously? You're using Frasier Crane's by-line? I had the urge to laugh again. That had always been my problem—wanting to laugh at the wrong time. I'd had little self-restraint as a child, and it hadn't improved much over the years.

Think disturbing thoughts, think disturbing thoughts. I did, and the urge passed. But then Ralph crossed his legs. *Think disturbing thoughts.* I did, but they turned to dirty ones—*Ooh. How does that work when you go commando? Does it chafe? Does the rubbing turn you on? Oh God, I wanna come back in my next life as a man so I know what it's like to have balls.* The dirty thoughts turned back into disturbing ones: *I did have 'balls' as a child, but they'd become like undescended testicles over the years. Man! I was convinced I'd regrown them last night, but—*

'Ruthie?'

I looked up at him. 'Mm?'

He was eyeing me expectantly.

Oh. Right. You're listening.

I pulled my knees up and hugged them against my chest, dragging my shift down over my knees at the same time so my knickers were concealed. I took a deep breath, blew out audibly and said, 'What is *wrong* with me?' I was about to say more when the phone rang. I checked my watch. It wasn't even eight o'clock. I launched off the couch and made a dash for the kitchen. I don't like early-morning calls, or late-night ones. Sylvia had me believing they were bad omens—'Whorebringers of doom,' she'd said. I was all the more anxious now that Hannah had her licence.

I almost dropped the phone. 'H-hello?'

'Have you got a man there?' Sylvia didn't mince words and her tone was accusatory.

Crap. Must get Caller ID.

The old bag across the road probably had Sylvia's number on speed dial. Her living room window overlooked the street. The venetians covering the window had a permanent diamond shape between two of the slats as a result of prising them apart too many times. It often felt like I was under surveillance. It often felt like I'd never left my childhood home.

'I'm waiting!' Sylvia's grating voice penetrated my thoughts.

Well, you can wait a little longer. I walked back into the lounge with the cordless flip phone and plonked down onto the sofa.

'Hello, are you there?'

'Yeees, I'm here.' I mouthed *'Sylvia'* to Ralph. He nodded like he'd already figured it out. My perfunctory attitude was no doubt a dead giveaway.

'Then answer my question!'

'What makes you think I have a man here?' I looked at Ralph, smiling. His eyes had widened.

'Uh, uh ... the children are at Reuben's. When they're with Reuben, you usually go out. You're not married anymore. You might bring someone home.' Her hesitant tone had turned into a cold clipped one.

'And what if I did?'

'Well, you need to think of your children!'

I lay down. 'Oh, I know. I do.' I yawned loudly; it conveyed my ennui. 'But like you said, they're not here.'

'B-but they'll come home soon. And it's not good for them to find a strange man in the house!'

'True.' I let her stew for a bit before adding, 'Who said anything about a *strange* man in the house, though?'

'So there *is* someone there, I knew it!'

I didn't respond. I could hear her mind ticking over in the silence. Then ... *ker-ching!*

'Is it Reuben?'

Reuben? 'Well, that wouldn't make much sense, would it? If the kids are there, why would he be here?'

Several seconds passed as she tried to process this. Before she could respond, I said, 'Anyway, why don't you just ask Portnoy?'

Her telltale, involuntary sharp intake of breath left me feeling smug. There'd be plenty of time to wallow in guilt later on. For now, I was on a roll. Toying with Sylvia was like an extreme sport that caused an adrenaline surge. I expected a hot-tempered response, and got one.

'How would *she* know?' If Sylvia were wooden, her nose would have been growing right about now.

'Well, let's seeeeee. I can't think of any other reason why you'd think there's a man in my house unless you heard it from her.'

'Uh, I-I'm your mother. I know you like the back of my hand!' she snapped. 'Who's there?'

'Why don't you ask the back of your hand?'

'*Oeuf!* Always with the smart mouth. I'm asking *you. Pest!*'

For as long as I could remember, Sylvia had regularly full-stopped our exchanges with *pest* and prefaced them with *oeuf. Oeuf* is French for egg. *Oeuf!* meant she was, well, eggy. For Sylvia, *oeuf* was the well-bred equivalent of *fuck*. I'd never heard the relatives or anyone else use it, so it seemed original. But because Sylvia tended to speak in clichés, I assumed it was commonly used in her homeland, Egypt. I'd never been there, so I didn't know. I never bothered to ask.

'*Oeuf!* WHO IS THERE?' Her yelling dragged me back up into the present again. 'Answer me, *pest!*'

The game had become tedious. Time to put her out of her misery. 'Ralph's here.'

'Ralph?' Another moment of silence passed while she digested this. *Tick-tock, tick-tock—*

'Why has he only got a towel on?'

And there we have it. This reminded me of when I used to play hide-and-seek with a three-year-old Hannah. When she was the hider, she'd remain in front of me but she'd cover her face. Sylvia wasn't even hiding her face. And she sure wasn't covering her arse. I turned to Ralph and smirked as I answered my mother's question with another one. 'What makes you think he's only got a towel on?'

Ralph's eyebrows shot up. His face wore a stunned but knowing expression that seemed to say, *How can someone so predictable never cease to amaze you?*

'Uh, I, uh ... never mind, just answer the question, *pest!*'

'And what if my answer to your question is no?'

'Then I'd say you were *lying!*'

I imagined Portnoy had provided Sylvia with just the bare bones, which would have left her in a tortured state. Even if she'd had all the facts, though, Sylvia fleshed things out however she wanted to. But it kind of worked in my favour. If I let her come up with the story, she couldn't blame me for pissing her off.

'Well, I guess you've already decided what the answer is, so why bother asking?'

'He had a shower there, didn't he? Did you have sex with him? You did, didn't you? I just know it! I can tell something's been going on with you two since he found out he's adopted. I've seen the way you look at each other. I'm not blind and I'm not stupid.'

No. You're not blind.

'And Norma says the same thing.' These backup words dripped with censure. My aunt might have made the same observation, but she was not a disapproving sort. 'So. *Did you have sex with him?*'

I looked at Ralph, rolled my eyes. 'Yeah. We had sex.'

The sarcasm went over the top of her head. She gasped and slammed the receiver down hard.

'Ow!' I pulled the phone away from my ear, stared at it with irritation, and flipped it shut forcefully.

'Still think something's wrong with you?' Ralph quipped.

'*Hmph.* Not so much.' I sat up, closed my eyes and rolled my head around on my tense shoulders. 'Frasier' was smart enough to keep mum while I tried to calm my breathing. We sat in silence for a full minute before the phone rang again. My eyes flew open.

'Round two,' Ralph said. He knew my mother well. He favoured me with a sympathetic smile. It didn't help.

I let it ring out. But when it rang a second time, I didn't want to ignore it in case the call really was a 'whorebringer of doom'.

It was Joe. Things must have been bad for Sylvia to skip a couple of steps. 'I don't know what you said to your mother, but you better get over here. She's threatening to kill herself.'

CHAPTER FOUR

A Novel Whopper

'And?' I scoffed at my father's half-hearted plea. 'You're using *that* to make a case to get me there!'

Joe snickered. He had a lot to answer for, but he also had a sense of humour. It helped him survive the marriage.

I asked why he couldn't just deal with it. He said it was between my mother and me. 'Leave-me-out-of-this' was Joe's anthem.

I hung up and looked at Ralph. 'I know you're adopted, but please don't tell me you got the short end of the stick.'

He groaned. 'Now what?'

'She's threatening to kill herself.'

He laughed out loud. 'Does she need a hand? I know some people.'

'I'll ask. I gotta go over there. You know, damage control.' I traipsed into the bedroom, slipped on a pair of espadrilles and grabbed my bag. 'Won't be long,' I said as I headed for the front door.

He called after me, 'D'you want me to come with you?'

I spun around to face him. 'Hell, no! We'd be looking at collateral damage. Anyway, I caused this, I gotta fix it.'

Ralph gave me a long, hard look. 'You did not cause this.'

I stared back and slowly nodded. 'Yeah. You know what? You're right.' Sylvia had pegged me as the designated, unremitting thorn in her side. Over the years, she'd crafted a whole bag of tricks to make me feel responsible for her misery. When one, or ten, didn't work, she'd pull another out of the hat. I didn't always see it for what it was.

I felt more positive as I walked to my car. I'd left it in the driveway overnight. Before climbing in, I waved to Portnoy's spyhole. I detected some movement there. Probably in retreat—the sleuth avoiding being caught out.

I should have been at my parents' place seven minutes later—why did I buy a place so close to them?—but I didn't feel an urgency. Sylvia never made good on these kinds of promises. Besides, let Joe sweat for a bit. I drove around for about twenty minutes rehearsing what I'd say.

When I let myself in, I found Joe in the lounge. Lolling in his easy chair with one leg draped over the arm, he was vegged out in front of the tube. He was still in his mustardy waffle-knit Holeproof pyjamas. The middle island patch of grey hair on his baldish head was usually slicked back. Now it stood upright, strands of hair facing every which way. He looked like he'd just collapsed after beating a hasty retreat from his hotbed. He was cooling down with a bowl of ice cream.

I shook my head. 'It's not even nine o'clock and you're eating ice cream? On a health kick, are you?'

He looked at me with tired eyes. 'You sound like your mother.'

This did not help my mood. I shuddered. He pointed backwards with his thumb. 'In the bedroom.'

Where else?

Sylvia was stretched out on her bed. Its centre had yielded to her tall, fleshy frame as she lay in what had become her martyr position—on her stomach across the bed, head at nine o'clock, toes at three o'clock. Her gronde (grey + blonde) boofy hair was mussed, used tissues were strewn all over the bedspread, and a Harlequin romance novel lay open, face down on her pillow (Sylvia's bedhead bookcase could have passed for a Harlequin or Mills & Boon outlet). I tilted my head to read the title: *Hidden Rapture*. I sniggered at the irony. She heard me and sat bolt upright, her double chin wobbling from the sudden movement. She gave me a blue-eyed, same old, same old black look that was in sharp contrast to her wan complexion.

'How could you do this to me?' she screeched.

Huh? 'W-what have I done to you?' I was incredulous.

'You're sleeping with your cousin!' she shrieked.

'No. I'm not.'

'You said you had sex with him.'

'No-no-no. *You* decided I had sex with him. I just went along with you. There's no point arguing with you when you claim to "just know" something. But here's what *I* know. He is not my *blood* cous—'

'He *is* your bloody cousin! He's my sister's child, the fruit of her tenderloins!'

Oh God, a Harlequin cock-up of the first order. Ralph sprung from someone's 'tenderloins', but certainly not your sister's. And he is no fruit, baby! He's a choice cut of gorgeous rump—

'*Oeuf!* Wipe that smirk off your face, *pest*! I know there's something going on with you and your cousin. I'm not blind. What you two are doing is ... it's voodoo!'

'Voodoo?'

'Yes. Don't pretend you don't know what I mean. It's voodoo, it's forbidden!'

I snorted. *That would be 'taboo'.* Stupid.

She shot me daggers. 'God's going to punish you for this!' she spat out her righteous indignation, then started wailing again. 'How could you do this to me?'

Again, 'Exactly, what am I doing to you?'

'You are going to make me the laughing stock of the whole community.'

Newsflash. With a husband who social farts like Big Bertha, you're already there. My father's unchecked tendencies had earned him such a reputation (and nickname), people actually believed his last name was Blow, not Roth. But here and now, my mother's martyr complex had worn thin.

'How is this about you?' I shrilled. 'How is *everything* always about you? What about ME?'

I stormed out.

'You'll be sorry when I die!' she squawked after me.

Whatever. You'll-be-sorry-when-I-die had lost its charge, I'd heard it so often.

Joe was still in front of the TV. I stopped short and stared at him, partly because he was sniggering, partly because he was now stuffing his ruddy face with chocolate cake. I yelled, 'You deal with her!' He stopped sniggering. I slammed the door on my way out.

Slow, measured breathing had helped me centre myself in the past, but sitting in my car inhaling and exhaling to the count of five didn't make much of a dent this time. I thought back to what had worked when I was a child, trapped in that oppressive environment.

An image of Sylvia as a horse sustained me. An old blonde mare on rickety legs, whinnying—*nei-ei-ei-ei-eigh, oe-oe-oe-oeuf, nei-ei-ei-ei-eigh*—snorting, baring big pink gums and big yellow teeth, massive lips retracted and flapping away through the nickering.

I drew on that image now. I drew a blank. *Zippo. Nada. No horse, not a frickin' dicky bird.* So, I seethed all the way home. I was a grown woman with a good, well-paying job working as a feature writer for one of my two closest girlfriends, Maxi (Maxine Mayer-Rose), who was editor-in-chief of a popular women's magazine. I'd survived a divorce, owned my own home and had two well-adjusted children. Yet, whenever I went to my childhood home, I shrunk back into the posture of a petulant child.

I startled Ralph out of his brooding state as I burst back into the lounge. He was where I'd left him, but leaning forward with his elbows on his knees, his chin resting in his hands. I screamed at him, 'Next time you wanna go out there with just a towel, *don't.* Lose the towel, go naked!'

I plopped down on the sofa opposite and exhaled noisily, exasperated.

He leaned back and scrunched up his face. 'So ... I take it, it didn't go too well?'

I told him what had happened. He was all ears *(I'm listening)*. He didn't comment, though. He left me to get the rest off my chest.

'I don't get it. Last night—well, no, only a few hours ago—I had all these epiphanies. I thought I'd let go of a whole lot of fears. And everything was so clear. I even understood Sylvia. I mean, I really, really got her. I actually felt compassion for her. *Pff!* Imagine?'

Ralph gave me a worldly-wise smile.

'But now ... I dunno. Now, it's like it's all threatening to go down the crapper, you know? Like everything's changed but nothing's changed.' I looked down, stared at my knees and shook my head. I looked up at Ralph. He was watching me. I gave a helpless shrug.

He leaned forward again, rested his forearms on his thighs, clasped his hands, and spoke. 'How does that leave you feeling?'

I jerked my head back like a pigeon. I couldn't conceal my amusement. 'Seriously? Are you ... ge*shhhhh*talting me?' (I didn't know how the hell gestalt therapy worked, I just loved the pronunciation. It was one of those neat-sounding words, like *flapdoodle* or *shilly-shally*.)

Ralph responded with a sheepish grin, and then gave me puppy face—head tilted down, eyes up. It made him look less psychologist, more human. It made him look irresistible ... *mmm, mmm—*

'It was a bit therapeutic-ish, wasn't it? Is that even a word? Uh, anyway ... Look. It's hard for me to be detached. I'm one of the players in this psychodrama—'

More psychologist, less human.

'And I do feel kinda responsible for this. I mean, not for your mother's reaction—that's a whole new ballgame,' he muttered. 'But I forgot about Portnoy. Under the circumstances, I shouldn've gone out there wearing just a towel.'

'True. But I shouldn've goaded Sylvia.'

Ralph the now-detached psychologist just nodded, and resisted saying something. A wise move.

'It wasn't nice, was it?' I was looking for validation. Although, was it validating to have someone agree that what you did wasn't nice?

Again, he didn't answer. Another wise move.

I screwed up my face. 'I'm feeling a bit like a lousy daughter.' I wasn't sure what was worse—to have a default feeling of guilt or to feel nothing, like Joe. Joe was emotionally shut down. 'I know she's unhappy with my father. With life, I guess. Why can't I be a little more tolerant? Why can't I just be the bigger person?'

'So ... you're asking why can't you be the parent to her child?'

Ralph's question had just put it in perspective. 'Thank you, I needed to hear that.' I smiled at him, but then raised an inquisitive eyebrow. 'Was that a ge*shhhhh*talt technique?'

He laughed at me. 'Nah. A client-centred one.'

Whatever ... it had worked. We sat in silence for a short time. I watched as he rubbed his chin and looked skyward. Ralph was 'ralphulating'. It was a term Maxi had coined years earlier because Ralph did this so often. *Ralphulate* was a hybrid of 'to ralph' (slang for 'to vomit') + to speculate, which added up to throwing up an idea he'd chewed over. He introduced these with, 'Hmm ...'

'Hmm ... seems a lot of your upset is because, as you said, everything's always about her—'

'Oh, always—'

'Well then, let's stop talking about her and make it about you.' He softly added, 'And me. Let's talk about us.'

Shit, in other words, you wanna talk about having sex with me!

CHAPTER FIVE

More D & M, Less S & M

'Just breathe. Juuuust breeeathe,' Ralph said.

I did as he instructed, I felt more relaxed, and I started talking. 'Okay. First up, can we please drop the psychologist-client thing and just talk like *normal* people?'

Ralph smiled and nodded. He sat upright, crossed his legs, rested his hands in his lap like a psychologist, and waited for me to talk like a normal person.

I wrung my hands. 'I feel like I'm bouncing off walls. Doesn't it bother you that we're cousins? I mean, I know we're not related by blood, but still, we've grown up as cousins.'

'No. It doesn't bother me.'

I stared at him, mystified. 'How can you switch it off, just like that?' I said, clicking my fingers for emphasis.

'Oh, I didn't do it "just like that". You've no idea how much I wrestled with it. And with my feelings for you. For months.' Ralph gave me a wistful smile. 'I think I probably unconsciously wrestled with my feelings for you for years.'

'What? *Years?* How many?'

'Ooh, probably ... close to thirty.'

My mouth fell open.

Ralph stared down at his hands as he flexed them. 'Okay. Here we go,' he mumbled. He looked up at me with an embarrassed smile. 'D'you remember when I avoided you for a couple of weeks? When we were seventeen?'

'Uh-huh. Yeah. I remember it well. It was after that day at the beach. And you never did tell me why—'

'Yes, well ... that day was the first time I'd seen you in a bikini.' He squirmed in the chair, his face reddening slightly. 'Man, I got so turned on it scared me. You were my cousin!'

Wow. *Wow.* I felt better, not so ashamed of those not so platonic feelings I'd had back then, when Ralph shot up, filled out, shed his coke-bottle glasses in favour of contacts, and transformed from borderline ugly to studly. I'd looked at him differently, entertained some unholy thoughts about him (which wouldn't have been unholy at all if we lived in ancient times when everyone bonked everyone and everything—parents, children, siblings, the west wind, beasts, gorgons, gods). But I'd squashed the thoughts and feelings until the long, apocalyptic night before.

With his face aflush, he added, 'Anyway, that night I, uh, thought of you while I was, uh, you know ...?'

I stared, uncomprehending. Still a little thrown off balance after my encounter with Sylvia, I was slow on the uptake.

Ralph was determined to clear the air. He cleared his throat and soldiered on. 'You know, that thing that hormonal teenage boys often do.'

'*Ahh.*' I got the picture and gave him a wicked grin. 'Choke the chicken; slap the salami; flog the log; beat the meat; jerk the gherki—'

'Yes, yes! All of the above.' He laughed at me.

This kind of interaction was how we used to relate (until this morning). It helped neutralise the hoo-ha that had started brewing in my lower belly, whipped up by the image of Ralph taking himself in hand.

'I couldn't face you.' Then, or now, it seemed. He briefly averted his eyes before continuing. 'I felt so guilty about it, especially with our mothers telling us that God punishes. Anyway, I waited for the warts to sprout, but,'—he held up his hands and examined them—'nothing.'

I examined them. There wasn't much that I didn't know about Ralph. But it was as if I were seeing his hands for the first time. They were large and strong. Wide palms, long fingers with manicured nails, slightly bulging veins that extended into his forearms. *Oooh. Sexy hands moving greedily over my bare ski—*

'But, cultural taboos and all, I shut down those feelings. Tried to, anyway.' He gave an apologetic half-shrug. 'Thing is, like I said to you last night, we're Twin Flames. Twin Flames instantly recognise each other. You and I did. That spiritual connection's been there from the beginning, and we've had an undeniable emotional and mental connection our whole lives.'

'Mm ...' I nodded.

Even before last night, I already knew that Ralph subscribed to Plato's 'split-apart' theory: each of us is supposedly part of one soul—one half of it. The two halves split apart, incarnate into two separate human forms and then they search for each other. Once circumstances bring them together, their bond is unbreakable and unconditional and they're meant to spend their lives together. Sounded very pie in the sky, I'd said to Ralph. Lots of people find their soul mate and they end up hating each other's guts. No, no, no, Ralph had said. You can have lots of soul mates, but you only have one split apart—he or she is your Twin Flame. Ralph's shock discovery about his adoption had sent him plummeting into a dark night experience. It was there he realised he'd been in love with me for years, and he became convinced I was his Twin Flame. It followed that he was mine.

He continued. 'And now you know, the physical attraction to you kicked in for me at seventeen.' He paused before asking, 'So, when did it happen for you?'

I was struck dumb. 'Uh, uh ...' Ralph had caught me unawares, but there was no point denying it. He would see through it. I gave him a reticent smile. 'Also seventeen.'

He flashed me an impish grin and bedroom eyes.

Oh boy. 'Anyway, you were saying?'

'What? Oh, uh ... so, yeah. I blocked the feelings—Hmm. Maybe that's why I slept around so much.' He rubbed his chin and nodded. 'Hmm ...' Ralph was lost in space. I brought him back.

'You blocked the feelings—'

'Yeah. But as you get more and more real, you can't squash what's heartfelt. Not without suffering. I think it became a struggle because I resorted to rationalising the feelings away.' Ralph frowned. I could tell he was berating himself. 'Rationalising!' He harrumphed. 'It's exhausting. Reasoning didn't give me any comfort when I found out I was adopted. Getting stuck in my head just made everything worse. There was so much pain around the whole issue ...' His voice faltered, a shadow crossed his face. 'It meant I had to spend a lot of time in my heart. And for someone as analytical as me, well ... you know how tough it was.'

'Mm-hmm.' I remembered.

He went silent. Looking pained, he was no doubt reflecting on that harrowing time. I recalled his many crying jags, his despair, and how all I could do was hold him.

Finding out he was adopted was bittersweet for Ralph. Bitter, because he felt betrayed by his adored and adoring adoptive mother, who withheld such important information from him. But sweet, because it meant he wasn't swimming in the same shallow, fetid gene pool as the other idiots in his family—

his father, his younger whiney sister, Louise (Louwhiney), and his two brothers, george and simon (who, according to Ralph, had no brains, miniscule penises, and were too common to be worthy of majuscule letters at the beginning of their names).

He shook himself out of his trance state and seemed to rally. 'A lot of good came out of it, though. I started trusting my heart, listening to it instead of my head.' He paused to gather his thoughts. 'In the beginning, one of my rationales was, well, if I take away the word *cousin*, would it still be wrong if I just saw it as being in love with my best friend? Like a childhood sweetheart. Nobody considers that wrong. It's a great romantic story. So, logically, the answer would be no. But ... knowing something that way isn't the same as knowing it in here.' He touched his chest. 'Intellectualising isn't the same as understanding. And you can't get that understanding, that deep, secure kind of knowing in the heart unless you go into it.' He gave me an omniscient smile before turning more serious. 'And once you do, once your heart opens up, you can't close it. You can't deny its needs without paying a price.'

His words touched a raw nerve. I was happy for him but I teared up. I felt sad that I was still hostage to my intellect. Ralph read me (he usually did when he was thinking above the waist).

'Give it time, Ruthie.' He was sensitive enough to leave 'also seventeen' alone.

I wiped my eyes. 'I guess. But I need you to know I meant what I said early this morning. I do want this to happen.' *I think.*

Ralph looked relieved and pleased. He was about to say something but we were distracted by a car horn as Hannah pulled up into the drive. She had her own car. Before Joe retired six years ago, he had a used car yard and service station. He'd sold the business, but kept four small cars, one for each of his grandchildren for when they reached driving age. Three were in use (my brother, Myron, had nineteen-year-old twin boys, Rory and Robbie) and the fourth was housed in Joe's garage for when Casper turned seventeen.

Hannah burst noisily through the front door with her overnight bag and Casper in tow. Even at seventeen, Hannah was still a little dynamo. A couple of inches shorter than me, at just over five feet one she was well proportioned (in a miniature kind of way), and, like me, she had olive skin, a smallish, oval face, and reddish, mid-brown hair. Where mine sat a few inches below my shoulders, hers extended halfway down her back. Where mine was straightish with a bit of a kick in it, hers was a thick mass of curls. And unlike my hazel eyes, Hannah's were a deep blue like Joe's.

Both Hannah and Casper were happy to see Ralph. The three of them chatted animatedly. Ralph was very involved and very much a permanent fixture in my kids' lives. He'd attended Casper's soccer matches, Hannah's ballet recitals and their school assemblies when he was available. And he'd been available often when they were little because as a model, his hours had been flexible. I wasn't sure they'd be too happy to know his involvement with their mother was cranking up a notch.

I left the three of them to their catch-up, moved across to the window again and scoped out Portnoy's place.

What? What was that?

Was I imagining movement in her ratty, wooden letterbox? I leaned in and narrowed my eyes to get a better look. A spy cam, maybe? Or not. The rat probably had a pet rat living in her letterbox. Pity the postie. I envisaged him scratching away at the bite from the parasitic flea that was riding shotgun on the rat's bum. I envisaged an outbreak of bubonic plague—

'Ruthie?'

'Huh?' I turned around. 'What?'

'Are you going to tell the kids now?' Ralph whispered.

The kids? I looked past him. Both had disappeared into their rooms. Ralph's question had stirred things up. I groaned and plodded back to the sofa, my thoughts skittering here and there. They stopped on this one: maybe the she-devil over the road hadn't called anyone after telling Sylvia? *As if.* Muckraking was her lifeblood.

It hit home just how much Hannah and Casper's world would be turned upside down once they found out.

Then again ...

CHAPTER SIX

Truth or Dare

I answered Ralph's question with a question. *'What's to tell?'* I whispered. *'Nothing's happened.'* Denial.

'Uh, plenty has happened. Maybe not physically. Yet.' He smiled; I shallow-breathed. *'But let's not forget it's out there.'*

I drew in a sharp breath. *'My mother!'*

'No, no. Sylvia won't say anything.' He hitched his chin in the direction of Portnoy's place. *'But you know what* she's *capable of. It's just a matter of time before an ugly version of the truth comes back.'*

'Yeah. I s'pose. But I could always deny it when it does.' Denial.

'Nuh-uh. You could deny the story, but not the basis for it. And Hannah and Casper won't leave it alone till they get it out of you.'

Ralph knew my children well—both were precocious, nauseatingly inquisitive and in possession of fertile imaginations. How would I explain why their adored and adoring godfather had been semi-naked in their house in the early hours?

'Mm.' I gnawed at my bottom lip. Sylvia's fear of what the 'neighbours' would think had her by the short hairs. My fear of Portnoy's furphies had *me* by the short hairs. *'Oh God, I do need to say something, don't I?'*

Ralph nodded. *'Do you want me to stay?'*

'No. I think I better do this on my own. I'll wait a bit, though. At least until I feel brave enough.'

I still didn't feel brave enough ten minutes after Ralph left, when Hannah appeared in the lounge with her mobile phone in her hand. Her face was ghost-white. 'Is it true?'

Feign ignorance. 'Uh, is what true?'

'That you and your ... *cousin* were naked together?'

Ralph was now nameless. He was just my cousin. She'd spat it out like it was a dirty word, and that's all I heard. I got defensive. 'He's not my cousin!'

Her eyes widened.

Crap. It was the wrong answer and it was too late to recover lost ground.

'So you *were* naked!' Hannah was shouting now.

'Who was naked?' Casper had come out to see what the commotion was about.

'Our mother and her cousin were parading around the front yard together ... *buck-naked*!'

Casper gawped at me. I gawped at Hannah. 'Do you have any idea how ridiculous that sounds?'

'But you're not denying it!'

I exhaled a long-suffering sigh. These back-to-back skirmishes were draining and I was running out of steam. 'Nobody was naked. Ralph had a shower here and he had a towel around him when he went to get the newspaper. And he only took a few steps outside, he wasn't "parading".'

'Why did he have a shower here? He lives five minutes away. Why couldn't he have a shower at his own place?'

Oh no, my daughter is turning into Sylvia. Oh God, anything but that!

I didn't know how to respond. Hannah was glaring at me. But Casper gave me the benefit of the doubt. Sort of. He was circumspect, unlike his sister. And where Hannah took things at face value, Casper was more inclined to read between the lines. 'Mum? Is something going on with you and Ralph?'

Shit.

At seventeen, Hannah was just starting to outgrow that stage where I was a horrible embarrassment to her. At fifteen, Casper had yet to reach it. He was a few years overdue, so I thought and hoped he'd bypassed it. If he had, he was about to enter it in a brutal way.

'Um, I, uh, we ...' *Just say it!* 'Ralph and I really like each other.'

'Yeah, I know. So what?'

'No, I mean we, um, we more than, uh, like each other.'

'Oh my God, you're having *sex* with him?' Hannah was getting hysterical.

NOW you start reading between the lines? 'No, we are not having sex!' I was getting angry.

Casper maintained his softly-softly approach. 'Hmm. So, if you more than like each other, I take it it's on the cards?' His tone was cool-headed. (Reuben used to say that if Ralph and I weren't cousins, he'd swear Casper was Ralph's son. Like, duh, as if cousins couldn't get it on. Reuben's form of logic was black and white. He was a little like Sylvia in that respect.) But it was a strange question coming from an offspring for whom the concept of a parent as a sexual being was beastly.

I opened my mouth to say something, but nothing came out.

Hannah jumped in. 'What? *What!* You're actually *considering* it? That's incest, that is DISGUSTING!'

I felt myself shrinking back from her piercing glare.

'I HATE YOU AND I HATE YOUR COUSIN, I AM SO OUTTA HERE!' She stormed off, grabbed her still-packed bag from her bedroom and left, slamming the front door so hard the living room window rattled.

Casper just gave me a disappointed look, went to his bedroom and silently closed the door. Somehow, that felt worse than Hannah's reaction.

I slumped onto the sofa. It all seemed too much. But then there was more.

I was still staring at nothing when Reuben rang twenty minutes later.

'You and Ralph?'

'Yes. *No!* We have feelings for each other, but we're not cousins. And we're not having sex!' A pre-emptive strike.

'Mm.' A heavy silence followed before he asked, 'Was this going on when we were together?'

'What? No. Of course not! And nothing's going on!'

He told me of Hannah's anguish, we discussed possible ways to deal with it, then I hung up, called Ralph and whined. 'It feels like the whole world's against me, or about to turn against me because of our taboo relationship.'

'It is not taboo. It's ... "voodoo".'

I laughed. 'Ralph, it's not funny.'

'I know. But we're not cousins, either.'

'Mm.' I was distracted. Still stuck on the thought of everything going to hell, my shoulders sagged with defeat. But then ... 'Actually, if the whole world is about to turn on me, it's not because of our relationship. I'll call you back in about ten.'

I hung up the phone and charged across the road.

CHAPTER SEVEN

Eye Spy with My Little i

The hairs on the back of my neck stood up as I stepped onto Portnoy's front porch, which was guarded by one of her gnomes. Lazy little bastard was reclining on his left side. He held a pipe in his right moulded hand and stared at me with cold, hard eyes. I stuck my middle finger up at him, but then thought better of it. I gave him a horn hand gesture—the index finger and pinky up, the thumb holding the two middle fingers down. It was to ward off the evil eye.

Dear God, I am turning into my crazy, superstitious mother!

The gesture seemed fitting, though. I felt like I was approaching the threshold of Hades. I rang the doorbell, which made a long *bzzzt* sound loud enough to wake the dead. Also fitting. There was no answer. I rapped hard on the door. Still no answer. I turned to leave. My breath caught as I knocked over an old broom propped up against the wall. *Jesus! Try parking your fucking vehicle in the driveway like a normal person!*

I stepped off the porch and looked left. I noticed one of the narrow casement windows on either side of the main fixed one was open a crack. I edged closer. She was there all right. I heard her shuffling around in the lounge. I crept over to the big window, stood on tippy-toes and peered through the rhombic venetian spyhole. As I took in the dark, squalid room, she came out of left field, the side of her face smack bang against the gaping maw. I gasped. She started turning towards the sound. I jumped back, and squatted down so I was out of sight.

It wasn't entirely true that I'd never seen Portnoy. Even though I often worked on my laptop in the dining room, I'd never seen her during the day. But I'd caught a glimpse of her one night while I was watching TV. I'd heard a noise outside, so I ran over to the window and opened the shutters a fraction, just enough to snatch a furtive glance. Illuminated by the streetlight, Portnoy appeared as a silhouetted figure. She was making her way to her letterbox with the teetering gait of someone who was sozzled. Drunk as a skunk, she was just like this nocturnal creature that creates a stink from the shadows.

But now that I was so close to her, I felt cold and clammy and feared I might pass out. I dropped my head down between my knees and the lightheadedness started to abate. I considered aborting the mission, but I'd come this far, and needed to look the enemy in the eye. First, it was imperative that I map my trajectory just in case I had to flee. I turned around to take in the positions of all the earthenware cretins dotting her front yard.

I gasped again. Directly behind me, one of Portnoy's gun-toting figurines had his weapon trained on me. *Bugger off, hard-arse! She's always loaded; your gun is not.* I looked past him and inspected the yard. Jesus Christ! Portnoy was deranged. There in amongst her private army was a new gnome. With arms folded behind his head and sunbaking on his back on a green clay fringed towel, he was stark naked except for his blue boots, a red hat, sunglasses, a feather sticking out of his mouth, and a pubic hair fig leaf around his little stone penis—above it, not covering it. His cheeks were ruddy; probably sunburnt. Well, clearly, *someone* hadn't Slip-Slop-Slapped. *Serves you right, arsehole.*

I stood up, faced the window again and inched towards it. I heard Portnoy talking—the woman had a gravelly voice. She was either having a conversation with herself or she was on the phone. Once again, I craned my neck and peered through the gap.

Fuck.

The phone pressed to her ear—she was probably reporting in to Sylvia—she had her back to me, but it was still a spine-chilling sight. *Quelle* beast! A towering woman, she was shaped like a prize-winning pear, with a narrow upper body and a humungous derrière. A thatch of straggly, straw-like, DIY bleached hair sprung from her head and blended in with the mangy, skanky cat hanging off her shoulder. I sucked in a deep, shuddering breath. Portnoy heard and whipped around towards the window.

Aaaaaaargh!

Sweet suffering Jesus. I was about to shit my pants!

He who advocated looking the enemy in the eye must have been spouting from an ivory tower. Yet, like staring at a train wreck, I couldn't look away. This particular enemy was a bug-eyed monster. One of her peepers bulged like a giant orb.

Ice blue and surrounded by a mofo sclera—surprisingly, barely bloodshot—it was *this* that had been filling the space between the slats. It probably protruded permanently and to such an extent from favouring it too much during her stake-outs (just like that section between the venetians had ended up in a permanent, yawn-like form). *Oh man.* This was worse than when Sylvia had hung her evil-eye bead on my cupboard door to ward off the demonic spirits that might influence me to surrender my virginity. Or, to bare my boobs in the centrefold spread of a football magazine (like Maxi had done when we were seventeen). Only, where that 'eye' was glass, this was the real deal. Forget the Hydra. I was living opposite a Cyclops!

I was shaking. In fight/flight mode, I prepared to take flight, but not before putting up a fight in the best way I knew how—with words: 'You're a rotten person! You don't give a damn about all the people you hurt with your vicious gossip,' I yelled. *'Fucking freak,'* I whispered, then started backing away.

Her eye filled up the hole. *Shit.* I turned tail, hurdled the naked sunbaker and circumvented all the others without getting shot. I made it home, bolted the front door, closed the shutters and collapsed on the sofa, trembling. I wrapped my arms around my midsection and rocked back and forth. Portnoy was probably over there, hitting the bottle and getting stinko, while I was here struggling to vanquish the memory of a look that would forever haunt me.

Having a mother who was always on the offensive meant I was often on the defensive. It made me a little hypervigilant. And paranoid: *Oh God, Portnoy's going to avenge me.* I needed to be armed and ready. With what, though?

I called Ralph back and related the incident. He laughed. 'Well, it's more than likely she has exophthalmia. It's a condition where one eye bulges. Usually caused by a hyperactive thyroi—'

'What? Who the hell *cares* what she's got?'

Ralph had spent a lot of time at the library as a child, collecting a stockpile of bumf that he'd never use. And even when he did use it, like now, it was useless.

'Let me remind you that the Cyclops in *The Odyssey* had a tendency to eat people, Ralph. THEY ATE PEOPLE.' I enunciated and screeched each word. 'And we know that Portnoy's big bloody eye blows things out of proportion. I'm worried she's gonna eat me alive with her big bloody mouth!' I felt a headache coming on and kneaded my forehead with my free hand. 'Geez, could it be any worse?'

'Mm. Yeah. You could look like her.' He laughed again.

I got annoyed with him. 'You know, it's really pissing me off that you're making light of this whole situation.'

'No, I-I'm sor—'

'*I'm* the one copping the fallout here. And this is only the beginning.'

'I know. Ruthie, I'm sorry. It wasn't my intention to diminish what you're going through.'

I drew in a long breath and let it out slowly.

'D'you want me to come over?' Ralph asked.

'No. I'm gonna go. I just wanna sit with all of this.'

'Okay, but I'm here if you need me.' I was about to hang up when Ralph said, 'Oh, one last thing. Just remember, stories aren't only brimming with monsters.'

'Uh-huh.' I'd already switched off. I flipped the phone shut, sat with unhearing ears and stared with unseeing eyes at nothing. But then, Ralph's parting words came back and jounced me out of my protective, deadened state: *stories aren't only brimming with monsters.*

Sylvia's hostility had loomed large in the story of my life. And like Portnoy's frickin' eye, when that's what stands out, it can become pretty much all you see. But I'd thwarted baddies and nutjobs in the past. I may not have felt like a fairy-tale princess, but I'd been a little girl version of *Xena: Warrior Princess*, she who had journeyed through the ancient world and ... and ...

Yes, that's it! Of course, I am Xena!

The insight transported me to my high school days, and the person who introduced me to the ancient way.

Mr Zero Kosta was an exceptional history teacher. He had a fondness for ancient mythology, so it was a big component of his course. The other students saw it as another pointless topic in a pointless subject with pointless bites of information that had bugger-all to do with our future. I understood it as the philosophy of life.

Mr Kosta said that our present-day existence was really just ancient myth in modern dress. These old stories were ridiculous, but it wasn't such a ridiculous claim when you considered the crazy people and the crazy shit going down out there.

Mr Kosta said the deviant gods and spectacular heroes and monsters of mythology personified the many aspects of the human psyche and the human condition. Each one—good and bad—was respected and given embodied form in the classic tales. He told us that one of these characters in everyone, ergo, one characteristic, could dominate, but we were civilised so we managed to keep our base impulses in check, despite the fact that they were alive and well in the backwoods of psyche. Obviously, Mr Kosta hadn't met my parents—the harpy and the wind god.

And he was damn lucky he'd never met Portnoy. Although he himself was creepy looking—cadaverous, like he'd been raised from the crypt—even he was no match for Portnoy in the ugliness stakes.

When I started to see life through the same vibrant, symbolic lens as Mr Kosta—rather than take it literally and personally—and when I started to see that life was a series of rites of passage and initiations, it helped me cope with the daily idiocy I was up against, at home and out and about. And though I'd often forget, the seeds had been planted.

Remembering this, and reminding myself that stories were brimming with heroes too, inspired me. Also, I recalled what

Ralph had once told me about people being mirrors, that they reflected aspects of you ...

Oh shit.

The pumped-up feeling passed. I was like a balloon that had been blown up, then released. *FFrrrrrrrrrrrrr.* Deflated and breathless, I called Ralph again.

'What the *fuck* does Portnoy reflect?'

It was a monstrous thought. But the Xena-me was battle-weary. I was too tired to fight or think. I'd wrangled all night with demons, struggled to keep Ralph at arm's length, come to blows with Sylvia, had to defend myself against Hannah, and warded off Portnoy and her stone-cold militia.

'Hmm. You tell *me*. What does she reflect?'

'Christ, Ralph! Can you please just stop being my psychologist?'

He expelled a soft breath before answering. 'And what? Be your hero instead?'

Oh God. I was about to yell 'Yes!' until I realised I felt like Suzy Creamcheese, the hapless fair maiden persona I so loathed. I groaned.

'Look, Ruthie, I don't know what Portnoy's showing you. Just keep asking yourself the question. You'll figure it out.'

Ralph didn't try to rescue me. He did offer encouragement, though. 'You keep reminding yourself you're Xena. And don't forget, she blinded the Cyclops. She even told him he should get a new line of work.'

He said it with such seriousness, it made me see the stupidity of having mentally fenced with those garden ornaments. I started laughing. I laughed so hard my belly ached.

The lightness helped me understand that even though I'd perceived both sides of the story—villains and heroes—seeing in black and white wasn't enough. Seeing in warring terms of white versus black wasn't enough. All of me needed sustenance. That was the thing I so loved about mythical reality. It included and breathed life into the many, many colourful sides—bright and murky. And Mr Kosta's perspective had helped me uncover the character that had the whip hand in my life: Baubo, the ancient goddess of obscenity.

I remembered another titbit Mr Kosta had shared with us students. Life, he said, was a tragi*comedy*.

Sylvia had probably been right when she told me all those years ago that I was possessed. But not by the devil—Satan was a humourless sack of shit. There'd been many times when I felt bedevilled, when I couldn't find my Xena-ness. But Baubo always had my back. The dirty goddess continued to spurt or ooze from my lips, in my thoughts and in many encounters and situations. My spicy outlook may have landed me in hot water more times than I cared to remember, but it was also my salvation.

As Ralph and I talked about this, a sudden burst of music came from Casper's room, belching out of his boom box like a thunderclap. It shook the walls and it shook me out of my self-preoccupied state. I'd forgotten he was there. It was a sobering moment.

I said to Ralph, 'You know, I might be able to see the humour in my dealings with Portnoy, but I can't find anything funny in what she's done where my kids are concerned.'

'Mm. Well, firstly, let me just say that humour's *your* best weapon. They have to find theirs. They have their own journey.' He was right. And Hannah and Casper had humour as a dominant force in their lives. They were an irrepressible pair. I hoped all of this wouldn't permanently take the shine off that.

'Secondly, this is much bigger than Portnoy's mouth. Or her eye.' He was right on that score too.

He asked again if I wanted him to come back. Again, I said no. If anything, he needed to make himself scarce.

After we hung up, I was tempted to go and talk to Casper, but the timing felt wrong. I tried calling Maxi. I didn't want her to find out about Ralph and me through a malicious, one-eyed source. I left a voicemail message saying I had something important to tell her. When I still hadn't heard back from her the next morning, I called her office.

The war in my world was about to escalate.

CHAPTER EIGHT

Fifty Shades of Fray

Gossip is an important part of Maxi's job as editor-in-chief. It's profitable for the magazine. Maxi herself isn't a gossip, but like me, she isn't averse to hearing it. And I assumed she hadn't yet heard, because she would have called me back straight away.

'One moment, Ms Roth.' Maxi's secretary always called me by my maiden name rather than 'Mrs Gold'. I used it as my *nom de plume*, with 'Ruth Roth Rites' as the banner for my feature stories. I listened to some music on hold while the call was being transferred.

'I'm sorry, Ms Roth, Ms Mayer-Rose isn't available right now. I'm to put you through to the assistant editor. One mo—'

'No, this isn't work-related. It's a personal call and it's important.'

'Well ... she's in a meeting. I'll pass the message on.'

Strange. Maxi's secretary had always been courteous, but she sounded a little aloof this time. And even if Maxi thought the call was about one of my articles, editor-in-chief or not, she still liaised directly with me because of our close friendship. Why would she put me onto the assistant editor? Anyway, I hung up and called Vette.

Yvette Klein, Maxi, Ralph and I had been a foursome when we were growing up. Maxi, Vette and I had been inseparable since we became besties at kindergarten. We did everything together, even stopped growing at the same time, with them ending up around the five foot three mark like me. Ralph and I didn't get together with them as much as we used to, though. Because they were both so busy in their professional lives— Vette is a fashion buyer for Myer—it left them little time for a personal one.

I hadn't called Vette earlier because I knew she'd been on a buying trip and had only got back late last night. I assumed the news wouldn't have reached her. She reacted as I'd expected.

'Oh my God. Wow! Although ... I can't say I'm entirely surprised. You two have always been so simpatico. It's like you're the perfect couple!'

I relaxed a little. 'Thanks, Vette. It's a relief to get a positive response. It's been pretty awful.' I told her everything.

She was upset but optimistic. 'Your kids'll eventually see through the lies. Hang in there. And they'll get used to it.' Vette—my gorgeous, slim, small-breasted, green-eyed friend with her black corkscrew curls, Betty Boop lips and big caboose—always gentle, always sympathetic. And always perceptive: 'Your mother ... maybe not.'

She laughed when I recounted my experience with Portnoy. But she was just as surprised as me when I told her about my call to Maxi.

'Mm. I know she's been really busy, but still ...'

But still nothing had changed a week later. By the following Saturday, Maxi hadn't returned any of my numerous calls or responded to my voicemail messages, or Ralph's. Hannah stayed put at Reuben's. She only came home to pick up clothes she needed, but she ignored me. Casper spoke to me in monosyllables, Joe remained uninvolved (typical), Sylvia was giving me the cold shoulder (not a bad thing), but only after passing on a bitchy remark Myron had made about me. Ever the loyal brother. These were all hurtful, but Maxi's reaction was the most upsetting. I'd always been able to count on her being there no matter what. What could I have done that was so unforgivable, my ballsy friend, with her Jessica Rabbit attitude—'I'm not bad, I'm just drawn that way'—would shun me? I was beside myself. I rang Vette again.

'I still haven't heard from her. She's not returning any of my calls. Have you spoken to her?'

Vette hesitated.

'Veeeette. What's going on? Why is she ignoring me?'

'Honestly, I don't know. The most I got from her is that, um ...'

'Just say it!' It was a big ask of someone who was a peacemaker.

'Uh, okay,' she said with reluctance. 'These are *her* words, Ruthie. She said, um, she said ... "I don't want to know her". And she refused to expand on that. I'm sorry.'

I felt sick to the stomach. Sylvia and Joe had told me I was a mistake because I was born only eleven months after Myron. So, for me, rejection didn't just say *You made a mistake*. Rejection said *You are a mistake*. When it came from someone who really mattered to me, it cut to the quick.

'That's it. I'm going over there tonight!'

'Uh, I don't know if that's such a great idea. Why don't you just give her some time?'

'Because what she's doing, well, it's not fair!' To my own ears, it sounded like the plaintive cry of the put-upon child. I reined myself in and tried to be more adult about it. 'I'll take my chances.' The thought of taking my chances, though, was a lot scarier than going over the road.

Ralph and I had plans for an early dinner. I cancelled them. He said he'd come over after I finished at Maxi's, and offered to pick up a Gâteau Saint Honoré and a Gâteau Mont Blanc from my favourite French patisserie. 'It'll help with the debriefing.'

Bringing me the cakes I loved the most—an artful bit of foreplay? I'd googled 'courtship'. Maybe. *Nice move, stud. But you're not de-briefing me!* 'Great. I'll call you when I'm on my way home.'

Maxi always worked late when she had to put the magazine to bed. The current issue had hit the newsstands the day before. I knew she stayed in on the Saturday night after each magazine release date because she was so exhausted.

At six-thirty, half an hour after Reuben had picked up Casper, I was just about to leave for Maxi's when the phone rang. I rushed to it, hopeful it would be Maxi. It wasn't.

'Hey, sweet-cheeks. What's this I hear about you shagging Ralphy?' It was Iris, Reuben's sister.

Iris and I had been compadres from the get-go. She was a loyal sister to Reuben, but she also remained a loyal friend to me after Reuben and I split. We didn't speak all that often, but the connection between us had never waned.

'Spill,' she instructed. 'Leave nothing out.' So I did, and I didn't.

Iris was upset that I hadn't called sooner. I said I'd been distressed by the backlash.

'All the more reason to call!'

'I know. I should have. I guess after Maxi's reaction—'

'Ruthie, I'm not Maxi.' No, she wasn't. Her tone was stern, but I knew her anger was directed at Maxi, not me.

Iris was just as gutsy as Maxi. Probably gutsier. An Amazon woman both in stature and in attitude, she was a six-foot hellion who would never back down or away from anything (it was hard to believe she and Reuben were siblings). And unlike Vette, Iris endorsed my decision to confront my sidestepping friend.

I left twenty minutes later feeling a little buoyed by Iris's support.

I rang Maxi's doorbell. I thought I heard movement in her apartment but she didn't answer the door. I called her mobile and could hear the faint ring coming from inside, so she was home, all right! She ignored the call. It was an in-your-face rejection behind closed doors.

I texted Ralph when I got home.

> Don't come over.
>
> Going to bed.
>
> Don't wanna talk about it.

Even les gâteaux wouldn't help me tonight. He didn't push, just sent me a couple of xx's. I crawled into bed and cried myself to sleep.

When Ralph turned up early the next morning, I greeted him at the door with a stultified look and a wet tea bag dangling from each hand.

'Ooh,' he winced. 'What happened?'

'Nothing. She ignored the doorbell.' I answered the next question probably forming in his mind. 'I know she was home, I called her mobile and heard it ring.' I turned and trudged through the lounge, lay down on the sofa, covered each eye with a teabag and sighed. 'This is not gonna work.'

'No, no. It works well. Your eyes'll go down in no time.'

I blew out long and hard. 'I'm not talking about the tea bags, Ralph. I mean you and me.'

Silence.

The sofa dipped beside me as Ralph sat down on the edge of it. He removed the tea bags. His brow furled with concern, but he said nothing.

'I'm pissing everyone off.' Tears welled in my eyes.

He tilted his head back and eyed me with incredulity. 'You cannot be serious! Do you remember what happened the last time you let other people's opinions influence you?'

Ralph was right. The 'last time' had lasted about twenty years and I'd become almost as boring as squeaky-clean Myron. And it wasn't like my nearest and dearest had warmed towards me because I'd become a white sheep instead of the black one. Myron remained a sanctimonious pain in the arse, Sylvia was still always piqued about nothing and everything, and Joe continued to tune out whenever anything got too hard.

Whatever decision I made now wouldn't change any of that. But I felt confident that Hannah would eventually come home, and Casper would go back to exploiting meaning. The mother and child reunion, according to Paul Simon, was only a motion away. So really, when we got down to brass tacks, 'everyone' represented Maxi. I told Ralph as much.

'Maxi's a big girl,' he said. 'You can't let her play you like that. She'll eventually come round.'

'And if she doesn't?'

He looked at me sympathetically. 'Then you'll grieve and learn to live without her.'

The thought of losing Maxi was unspeakable. I started crying. Ralph held me until my sobs turned to hiccups. Pulling away, I looked into his eyes. And then ... it happened. He leaned in and very tenderly, he kissed me. Without any hesitation, I responded.

CHAPTER NINE

Slam Dunk

A*h-ha-ah-ha-ah-ha.* I started to hyperventilate. Ralph was a smokin' hot kisser, and just moments before, I'd surrendered myself to him. Until his hands started to wander.

'What if Casper had come home? *Ah-ha-ah-ha-ah-ha.* What if Hannah had come home? *Ah-ha-ah-ha-ah-ha ...*'

'Ruthie, just breathe. Breeeathe.'

'What if Sylvia decided to speak to me again and called?'

'She wouldn't be able to see you. Breeeeeathe.'

'What if the old bitch across the road has a camera with a telescopic lens in her lounge room?'

'Shhh. Breathe. Your shutters are semi-closed. But I *get* it.'

Ralph really did get it that he wasn't going to get it. Over the next few weeks, even the hint of an overture set me off. So, he backed off. It was a relief. But his laissez-faire attitude was a little disconcerting ... and a little sexually arousing. Plus, the memory of *that* kiss, and what it had sparked off in my 'tenderloins', had lingered.

We'd just finished Chinese takeaway at his place late one Sunday night. I helped him clear the plates away, then we retired to the lounge room. Ralph had a large two-bedroom apartment tailored to a man who lived alone, but tastefully decorated in a minimalist and contemporary style: blond timber flooring, off-white sofas, area rugs in shades of grey, ebony furniture, off-white walls, and recessed lighting.

I plunked down onto the three-seater sofa and lamented once again about no word from Maxi. Ralph, who had sat next to me (a respectful distance away), listened like a psychologist and regarded me like a mate. It bugged me. I turned my whole body towards him and tucked one bare leg under me with the other one dangling off the edge, kind of invitingly.

Nothing.

I jutted my chest out, flicked my hair with my hand and stretched catlike.

Nothing again.

I gave him a kittenish look.

Still nothing.

For crying out loud! Do I have to do all the bloody work here? 'You can kiss me, you know.'

Something.

Ralph gave me a half-smile and edged closer. He took my face in his hands, caressing my cheeks with his thumbs. He leaned in and kissed me, then he gently pulled me down the settee and covered my body with his, his tongue searching my mouth. I lost myself in the experience. Until ... my mind found me.

What ... here? You're going to take me here? You're not going to take me on the bed?

I'd always envied first-time lovers in movies, how they tore off each other's clothes as they made their way to the bedroom, oblivious to the vases and tchotchkes they knocked off the furniture en route, the blouse and skirt haphazardly discarded here, the bra and panties strewn there. That had never happened with Reuben—he was an accountant. And much as I hoped it would happen with Ralph, it was unlikely. Disorder didn't factor into the mode of existence of those possessed by his disorder. Still, I'd planned for it by thinking like an obsessive-compulsive. I wore a double exit-strategy garment—a loose, zipless, buttonless, hook and eyeless slip dress that could either be slipped over the head or slid down the body. But then ... would he neatly fold it? No point worrying about this because lying on top of me with his hardness pressed against my stomach, he wasn't in a position to remove and fold anything.

Might we remove to the bed, though?

It seemed Ralph could rough it. I needed my creature comforts. Unlike Xena, Warrior Princess —who slept in an ice cave for twenty-five years—I'd developed some pampered princess tendencies. I was now more Worrier Princess. Still, I wasn't asking for black satin sheets, just a smooth surface. The sofa was covered in a corduroy fabric, so I was going to end up with vertical stripe imprints all over my back, and two intersecting horizontal indents on my arse from the welts of the adjoining cushions. And now, my foot started cramping. It was painful. *Ow, ow, ow.* The toes were curling over each other. And then came the painful voice.

Ha—serves you right for sinning with the fruit of my sister's tenderloins!

Sweet, merciful crap!

The cramp didn't hurt as much as the spectre of my mother shadowing me at this most inopportune time. She was like a third party in a ménage à trois. *Eww!* Was her presence God's punishment? Maybe. Maybe not. It was Sunday, after all.

I used to suffer from Dimanchophobia (Sunday-dread) because lots of awful things happened to me on Sundays. I looked to Joe to protect me from Sylvia, particularly on this day when she was at her worst. Joe, with the God complex. Joe, who sought refuge from Sylvia's onslaught on Sundays by holding up in front of him *Saturday's* broadsheet as a screen. He, who couldn't even protect himself from her, passed the buck and taught me to pray to God when I was five years old. But it seemed that God was no more available on Sundays than Joe was. On Sundays, my prayers hadn't amounted to much more than fearful grovelling that yielded jack shit. I assumed God slacked off on this day. I assumed Sunday was His day of rest, not Saturday.

That cataclysmic night a few weeks earlier had yielded plenty. It helped diffuse this phobia because I saw the proverbial light in the early hours of a Sunday morning. So, I knew God didn't go AWOL; He was just a little laid back. God had attitude on Sundays, like ... *meh.* I also realised my belief that God wasn't available on Sundays was really the belief He wasn't there for me. And at some level, I hadn't expected Him to be.

Sylvia had convinced me I had no rights. To a mini-Xena, it was a hard sell. At first and for a while. But Sylvia was Sylvia. And, thinking I was a mistake was my Achilles heel. If you're a mistake, it follows that you have no rights. On that cataclysmic night, I started to get a sense that I was no mistake. And amongst the many rights I reclaimed was the right to have my prayers heard 24/7.

I, the warrior princess, exercised it now.

Dear God, where the fuck are You? I need to get laid!

The cramp got worse. I prayed harder.

Dear God, I really do not appreciate Your passive-aggressiveness. I'm taking a leap of faith by following my heart and risking the neighbours' disapproval. I pay my bloody bills. I don't cheat on my taxes—

I didn't know what part did it, but my cramp eased.

Ralph rolled off me and perched semi-sideways on the edge of the settee. He dipped his head, his lips grazing my neck as he pushed my dress up, slid his hand under it and around to my back until his fingers located the bra fastening. With minimal effort, he unhooked it, brought his hand back around and caressed my left breast, rolling my hardened nipple between his thumb and forefinger. Then his hand moved to my right breast.

Where the pain in my foot had all but disappeared, the pain in the arse in my head ramped it up. The inner monologue multiplied and divided into dialogue.

Shit. Please don't do things in pairs.

Shut up you idiot! He's not. You have two tits.

Thank God I have only one vagina. My mind wandered again.

Years earlier, Ralph had briefly dated a woman who had two twats—a condition called didelphys. Even though he shared everything with me, to his credit he never bragged about his many conquests. The most I got out of him about this particular liaison was that for an obsessive-compulsive who needed to do everything twice, it was like a Garden of Eden with two entrances.

Ralph's moaning brought me back. As he slid his hand down my stomach towards my one vagina, he whispered, *'Oh, Ruthie, your skin is like velvet.'*

What? Ye olde-worlde poetic shit? Why, oh why couldn't it be dirty talk?

There's something to be said for dirty talk during sex. Things like, 'Kiss me there, mmm, mmm. Lick every inch of me', or, 'I'm your slave for the night', or, 'Maybe you should spank me—I've been very, very bad'. But this? This was too much. I lost it. I started laughing.

Ralph's hand froze on my velvety skin just above my short and curlies. He looked up at me, flummoxed. I was laughing so hard, I could hardly breathe. He stared at me, shook his head. When my laughter died down, he sighed limply and said, 'And we were doing so well.'

I was a little taken aback. 'Oh. Uh, what's wrong with laughing during sex?'

'Nothing. But we're not actually having it.'

'Um ... isn't foreplay part of sex?'

'Some would say. But strictly speaking, no. Foreplay *leads* to sex. And we haven't got past second base.'

It was like being back in high school, partly because of his use of 'second base', partly because I could feel a biology lesson coming on. I didn't like biology when I was at school. Dissecting frogs made me queasy. I didn't want to dissect concepts now.

Propping up his head on his hand, he studied my face. Foreplay might not be part of sex, but an intellectual discussion was like foreplay for Ralph. How many times had I heard him say, 'The mind is an erogenous zone'? I felt bad. I felt I owed it to him to play along. But I changed the subject.

'Um, so, what law of physics governs shrinkage?'

A Cheshire-cat grin lifted the corner of his mouth, and I felt his semi-hardness growing hard again. He ran a lone finger down my body, skirting but teasing my other erogenous zones. 'Mmm. Let's see. That would be thermodynamics. It deals with expansion and shrinkage: I got hotter. I expanded. You threw a bucket of cold water. I contracted. But then ... there's also Newton's first law of motion; you know, every object in a state of uniform motion tends to remain in that state of motion unless an external force is applied to it. In this case, the external force was your laughter.'

I tuned out as Ralph got off on babbling on. I yawned.

He stopped babbling. 'You tired?'

'Yeah. And I've got an early start tomorrow. I think I'll call it a night.'

'Okay.' His response was ringed with disappointment, but I admired the man's patience.

Over the next two weeks, we had a number of false starts, and even though we made it to his bed, which was much more comfortable than the sofa, the gods conspired to stop it from happening before we even had a chance to get naked: phone calls, the doorbell, a fart, more laughing, more errant internal dialogue, fear, hyperventilation.

One night after another bout of laughter before we even got to first base (and we were still fully clothed), I got all philosophical. 'Maybe it's just not meant to be.'

He shrugged, rolled over onto his back and conceded: 'Maybe you're right.' He sat up and slapped his thighs. 'I'm going to make myself a sandwich. Want one?' he said over his shoulder as he walked towards the door.

What? Poor bastard had worked so hard to make it happen, and now ... this. *Really, Ralph?* Neutrality. Detachment. Resignation. Oh God. Then again ... Oh God, what a turn-on!

I bounded off the bed, met him at the doorway and threw myself at him.

The stunned look on his face was replaced by a self-satisfied one—the psychologist revelling in the glory of his successful reverse psychology manoeuvre. No matter.

As I kissed him and ground into him, he placed his hands on the small of my back, walked me against the wall and pressed his engorging manhood against me. He eased back and brought his hands around to my hips, grabbed a handful of the fabric of my shift dress, pulled it up over my head and dropped it on the floor. He kissed me passionately as he reached behind me, unhooked my bra and removed it. He looked at my breasts hungrily, ran his hands over them. Then he stripped off his T-shirt. He groaned as I lightly raked my nails down his chest.

I caught my breath when he teasingly traced the inside top edge of my panties with the back of his fingers, then, turning his hand, he slid it down until it rested between my legs. I moaned as he caressed me. I pushed my knickers all the way down to make it easier for him. He took a step back and surveyed my body with awe (the last time Ralph had seen me naked was when we were six and took a bath together). I had a good body, but like most women, I was self-critical. My waist was too high, my hips too narrow, my legs were long but too thin ... I felt a little self-conscious. Too bad.

I pushed his shorts and jocks down and gasped as he sprung to life. *Holy shit!* That day in his backyard when his moving parts dropped out didn't do justice to such a beautiful piece of equipment, now standing large, proud and upright, and boing-boinging unselfconsciously.

Oh man, you are gorgeous.

He mirrored my thoughts with his murmured words, *'You are gorgeous.'*

Ralph didn't see my faults. It seems guys are hardwired to ignore a woman's shortcomings when she's standing there naked, or maybe they just don't consider them flaws. And unlike women, men are uninhibited in their own imperfect nakedness. Even the nipple-twiddling Fat Bastard—'Um dead sexy. Look at ma sexy bo-day.'

Oh no. The urge to laugh threatened to derail me. *Bugger off, Baubo!* This intrusive, dirty bitch, who was also the goddess of sacred sexuality, was ruining my sex life. But Ralph's exploring hands and insistent fingers made it hard to remain distracted.

I wrapped my hand around his vital organ. *Oh my God!* My fingers barely met each other. I moved them along his length, eliciting another animal-like groan from him. He cupped my face and kissed me deeply, his tongue probing my mouth. Then his hands found my buttocks and with one smooth movement, he lifted me up. I wrapped my arms around his neck and my legs around his waist. He carried me to the bed.

He lay me down and lowered himself on top of me. Gently he parted my lips with his, our tongues exploring each other's mouths. He moved to my neck, then seared a path on my skin with his tongue and lips as they travelled downwards—nipples, stomach ... 'No!' *Don't go there.*

Ralph looked up at me. He didn't try to coerce or entice. He moved up, rolled onto his side and used his fingers where his tongue couldn't go. I didn't have to direct him and I didn't have to ask him to change the pressure or speed. Ralph instinctively knew. Pleasure coursed through me, sensations that had been dormant for too long erupted. The release was volcanic.

Ralph levered himself above me and guided himself inside. His rhythmic movement was slow to begin with, then it quickened. I could feel a second climax building up. Ralph's body tensed, a low growling sound came from his throat, and we both shuddered as we came at the same time. Sacred sex.

We lay there panting, our hearts pounding. Ralph raised himself up on his elbows and looked deep into my eyes. 'I love you so much.' His lips then curled into a content smile. 'I've never had anything like this.'

'Mmm. Same.' But where Ralph's breathing slowed, mine sped up.

You Jezebel! You have just had sex with your cousin. Pth, pth, pth!

CHAPTER TEN

Coming Together

'Ah-ha-ah-ha-ah-ha.'

Ralph rolled off me and covered my mouth with his hand. 'Breathe.'

I obeyed.

'It's the cousin thing again, isn't it?'

I tried to speak but my mouth was dry. I could only nod.

'Your mother's voice?'

I nodded again and wiped her non-existent spit from my face.

Ralph waited till my breathing was slow and steady before speaking again, his voice soft and even. 'We're not cousins, Ruthie.'

I eyed him with scepticism. 'Does that mean you're suddenly not Norma's son and that you no longer see her as your mother?'

That stopped him. 'Well, uh, no. I still see her as my mother, but as my adoptive mother. And you're my adoptive cousin.

We're not blood related.' He gave me a wry smile. 'What we're doing is not "voodoo".'

I laughed. Sylvia's image crawled back under her rock in my psyche. My unhappy mother had always felt threatened by my happiness, even when what I did was not in the least 'voodoo'. It was something I needed to learn to accept.

Ralph wrapped his arm around me and pulled me close to him. We lay on our sides looking at each other, legs intertwined. He stroked my face. I ran my fingers through his chest hair.

He spoke in a low, soft voice. 'I'm so happy. This is the sort of thing you read about in romance novels.'

Ha, sprung! From Don Juan to Don Quixote. I lifted a mocking eyebrow.

'I mean, *Playboy*. It's the sort of thing you read in *Playboy*.'

Sure it is. Because Playboy Bunnies are all about romance, as opposed to fucking like rabbits, right?

Don Whoever digressed. 'Soooo. You don't like oral?'

I felt my cheeks grow hot. 'Uh, no. I mean, yes. Yes, I do! But—'

'A bit too soon, maybe?'

'Yeah.' It was too soon, too intimate. And I also feared he would start *nom nom nomming* while he was eating me.

Over the next weeks, we couldn't get enough of each other. We were each in a constant state of arousal at the thought of the other. I went to his place every night and spent most of the weekend there, in his bed ... on the kitchen table, in the shower, on the breakfast bar ... And he showed me positions I never knew existed. One of the books he'd apparently devoured in the library all those years ago was the *Kama Sutra*. Maybe I'd misjudged when I said he'd amassed a cache of useless pap.

Ralph was a passionate, considerate lover. And I was breathing easier as he was looking less like my cousin and I cared less about others' approval. I wasn't going out of my way to upset the people in my life and I stopped feeling responsible for their discontent. To a point. I still wanted to keep our *affaire de coeur* underground. Ralph complied, even though he wanted to shout it from the rooftops.

Two months had passed since the shit had hit the fan, and Hannah was still sleeping at Reuben's. Our daughter had a short fuse, but it wasn't like her to nurse grudges. For her to be angry this long, I imagined she was wracked with crushing feelings of betrayal and humiliation. Over the years, I had been her confidante. And when she was angry with me, she turned to Ralph for comfort and advice, rather than Reuben, who had a hard time with emotions—his own and others'. Independent as Hannah was, she would have been feeling adrift. There was nothing I could do but let her work through it.

Seemed she was, though. She started spending more time at home. She now grunted at me when I asked her a question. And Casper was speaking in whole sentences. Joe rang occasionally and made the odd snide remark. I told him to put a sock in it. He did. Sylvia started calling and continued martyring herself, so things were back to normal there. Myron didn't give me the time of day (who cared). And though I still felt grief over my relationship with Maxi, I wasn't as consumed by it. I was powerless to do anything, and so be it. I'd written two articles for the magazine and noticed that both were published with hardly any changes. The first was about the challenge in following your heart even if it upset those around you. The second was about the painful process of letting go. Neither was a veiled attempt at manipulating Maxi. I was above doing that sort of thing (mostly). I wrote with sincerity about what I'd learned.

Another week passed, when Joe called on a Sunday just after lunch. I braced myself for one of his jibes, but he surprised me. He gave me his blessing.

'Ralph's a good boy. If he makes you happy, don't pass up a chance for that.'

It was nice to have my father's backing. It wasn't something I was used to. His words were poignant, though, because they also carried a sense of his own unhappiness, which I'd never given much thought to.

Ralph was due to come over in an hour, but I couldn't wait to tell him what Joe had said. I was about to pick up the phone when the doorbell rang. Even better, I could tell him face to face. I tore the door open, excitedly yabbering. 'Ha! I was just about to call y—' I stopped.

It was Maxi.

I was dumbstruck, just stared at her. She was uncomfortable: Uncharacteristic, but unsurprising. Yet, even as her Jessica Rabbit attitude seemed to have deserted her in this moment, she was still stunning, with her Jessica Rabbit bod and looks.

'Can I please come in?'

I didn't answer, just stepped aside.

I closed the door and turned to face her. With a hangdog look on her face, she said, 'I've been a bitch.'

You got that right. I crossed my arms, but didn't move, didn't answer. I didn't trust myself and I sure didn't trust her.

'I was jealous.'

Still dumbstruck—even more so. I didn't realise she carried a torch for Ralph. I found my words. 'Uh, I don't understand. You're the one who ended it with him.'

With Maxi and Ralph, everything had always turned into a game of one-upmanship, but he'd harboured a crush on her from when we were about nine. As we entered our teenage years, their competitiveness developed an erotic edge. And after Maxi posed bare-breasted for the footy magazine, Ralph mustered the courage to ask her out. She only agreed to go out with him because we'd heard that 'size matters'—and she'd been in his backyard the day his 'packed lunch' unpacked itself and went al fresco.

Ralph and Maxi devirginised each other after three weeks of dating, but a couple of weeks after that, when she thought his weirdness dwarfed his man-size, she dumped him.

'You could have had him, but you didn't want him,' I added.

'And I still don't. Not as anything other than a friend.' She frowned. 'I mean, *fuck*, don't get me wrong, I love Ralph, but he'd drive me to drink.'

I could understand that. But then, why this gorgeous, accomplished woman would be jealous of me had me stumped beyond speech or thought.

She gave me a doleful smile and continued. 'It's just that ... it's always been that I've had guys wanting to get into my pants, but you've had guys wanting to marry you.'

'Oh.' Her disclosure had caught me off guard. It was news to me. 'Um, it was only two guys. And look how well *that* turned out ...' I sneered. I thought back to the first one. Sylvia hadn't liked Glen Jones. At all.

'He doesn't measure up,' she said.

The hell he doesn't—seven and half inches to be exact! Remember when the tape measure went missing for a couple of days from your sewing box? Remember how you couldn't understand why I laughed every time you used it after that? Ha, ha, ha!

The little glint of amusement in my eyes, and my faint, derisive smile incensed her. She badgered me to end my relationship with Glen. I was still living at home, and at twenty, I was not yet officially an adult. I couldn't afford to move out and her threats and put-downs wore me down. Besides, Sylvia had rights and because I'd come to believe I didn't, I succumbed to her demands and dropped Glen.

Even though I picked up with him the next day and saw him on the sly for a while, he got sick of having to sneak around, so he dropped me.

After Glen, I dated several guys. After Glen, they all fell short. Even so, some were in it for more than just sex. But I wasn't. Then came Reuben.

Maxi jarred me out of my introspection. 'Well ... that's two more than I've had. I think I always envied you,' she continued, 'but I've only just admitted it to myself. And it's not a nice feeling.' Her eyes filled with tears. Maxi and I had shared everything over the years, and she'd talked about her vulnerability, but in a removed sort of way. This was the first time she'd shown it.

'Maxi, you've been married to your career. You never wanted domesticity.' And little wonder with the dippy, hippy style of domesticity she'd witnessed growing up.

'True. And you know me. I've fiercely defended every one of my choices. But now, with you and Ralph getting together—and you two are *made* for each other—I guess I'm starting to see what I've missed out on.'

I wasn't sure how to respond, so I settled for lame. 'It's not too late.'

'Maybe.' She waved it aside. 'Anyway, I'm sorry about these last couple of months, Ruthie.' Her forced smile conveyed regret over much more than these last couple of months. 'Are we good?' she asked, her voice thick and hesitant.

Again, I wasn't quite sure how to respond. I was stuck on her apology. Joe had often belittled me in public, then in private he'd say, 'I'm sorry.' I'd tell him it was okay. His were empty words. Mine were delusional ones. For too long, I'd remained mollified by the crumbs he threw me, but 'I'm sorry' had little currency, and swipe 'n' sorry had become a pattern because I never told him how I felt.

I narrowed my eyes at Maxi. 'No. We're not good. Not until you hear what I have to say.'

She nodded slowly.

'What you did, cutting me off like that, it really hurt me. Badly. I didn't deserve it.'

'I know, but I was asham—'

I held up my hand. 'I'm not interested in your excuses, Maxi.'

That threw her for a couple of seconds. Looking remorseful, she said, 'No. There's no excuse for what I did. I was wrong. It's not like me and I promise it won't happen again. Please forgive me?'

Unlike Joe, Maxi had humility and her apology was heartfelt. I nodded. 'Yeah. And yes, we're good.'

We hugged and both cried. I called Ralph and cancelled my plans with him—*Ralph, who does not fall short. Ralph, who measures up. And up and up ...*

Maxi mouthed, *'Can I speak to him?'* I handed her the phone. She apologised for snubbing him as well. Then she and I talked all through the afternoon and well into the evening. She said my articles were great and they'd made her think. I caught her up on the whole situation (although, I didn't say anything about my sex life. I wasn't ready to and she knew not to ask). We laughed about it all—the comedy in the tragedy. Maxi asked me to write my next feature story on the small-mindedness of people with big mouths.

'Hmm,' I said. 'Maybe I should call it "Eye Spy with My Little i".'

'Love it!' she said.

Not long after she left, Hannah walked in with her bag. She was back home to stay. She went into her room; I went into mine. I called Ralph and told him about Joe's call, my time with Maxi, and Hannah's return. He was elated.

'It was meant to be.'

Really? A Jungian psychologist and all you can give me is a cliché? Okay, I'll play. 'Uh-huh.' I threw him one of Sylvia's favourites. 'And good times follow bad times.'

His voice got a little deeper and all velvety (like my skin). 'So ... why don't you come over? I'll show you a good time. Or maybe a bad one.'

Ooh. Aye yai yai! Ralph was learning the art of dirty talk. A familiar heat stirred in my tenderloins. I told him I was tired, but I'd think of him while I showed myself a good and a bad time. When I crawled into bed, though, I felt a little too disquieted to feel me. Another one of Sylvia's banalities had impinged on my mind. 'All good things must come to an end.'

I wasn't being pessimistic like her. I just had a feeling in my bones that I wasn't quite done with the bad times.

CHAPTER ELEVEN

In the Dead of Night

The call came a few hours later and jolted me out of a deep sleep. Still fuzzyheaded, I squinted at the neon number display on my bedside clock radio: **11:53**. *Oh no.* Disorientation turned to panic, but then I remembered both kids were home and asleep. I also remembered my earlier sense of foreboding as I fumbled for the phone and answered with an anxious hello. It was Myron.

'Joe's dead.'

'What?'

'Joe's dead. I'd say it was a heart attack.'

Just like that.

'Oh, no. *No.*' I started crying.

Myron told me Joe had thrown up after a bad bout of indigestion, appeared to have staggered out of the bathroom and collapsed on the bedroom floor. It was where Sylvia had found him. She called Myron, who lived around the corner. He tried to resuscitate Joe, but it was too late.

As Myron was giving me the rundown, I reached for the lamp switch and turned it on, as if even a dim light would save me from the dark emotions that started to envelop me. But where the light didn't, Myron's delivery did. He reported the dry facts, presented them like a piece of unbiased journalese that left me feeling numb. I told him I'd be over shortly.

After calling Ralph, I roused the kids. They both cried. They were sitting sleepily at the breakfast bar when Ralph turned up.

'What's *he* doing here?' Hannah snarled.

'Hannah, back off!' I glared at her.

She backed down, but her rancour had stung Ralph—his pained expression was revealing. He didn't say anything, though. Instead, he cocooned me in a bear hug that dissolved the anger and made it safe for me to cry.

The kids and I threw on some clothes and, all a little punch drunk from the harsh wake-up, we piled into Ralph's car.

Sylvia's house was eerily quiet. She was sitting on the couch in a stupefied state with Myron on her right and his wife, space-cadet-Tammy, on her left. Rory and Robbie sat on the opposite couch like a pair of blobs, each one chomping away on biscuits. Nothing had changed since infancy (these two hadn't moved their fat arses until they were fifteen months old, when they went straight from sitting to walking. They never crawled because you can't eat and crawl at the same time). But I noticed significant changes in Myron from when I last saw him, none particularly flattering. His blue eyes had dulled, his mane of thick blond hair had thinned and darkened into mousy, like his nature. And Chubs had grown an extra chin. He'd always looked like Sylvia's son. Now he could pass for her younger brother.

Our differences dropped away, though, and we all hugged and cried, except for Rory and Robbie, who looked on as they continued snarfing their cookies. (If they'd tossed them occasionally, they mightn't have ended up so fat.)

I went into the bedroom to see Joe. He looked like he was just sleeping peacefully. Relieved, maybe. I knelt down next to him and kissed his cool cheek. 'Oh, Joe ...' I shed silent tears. Then I chuckled and whispered in his ear, *'The extremes you go to to get away from her.'* I stayed on the floor with him, lost in nothingness until I heard the irritating ding dang ding dong of the doorbell, a sound that seemed so disrespectful under the circumstances. I got up and went back into the lounge.

My parents' GP was crouched down in front of Sylvia. He held her hand in his and was speaking to her in a muted tone. Distracted by a soft rapping on the front door, he left Sylvia and moved to the bedroom. Ralph let in two men from the Chevra Kadisha (the Jewish Funeral Society). Sympathetic and sombre, they went about their business, but the whole thing felt clinical to me. Joe was now 'the body'. No longer a person, he was just a thing.

We watched in wide-eyed silence as, a short time later, they took my father away. The doctor had completed the death certificate, but hung back. Once again, he squatted down in front of Sylvia. As he plied her with platitudes, the cliché queen rallied a little, like a participant at an evangelist prayer meeting, but then she sank and started wailing like an air raid siren. It shook everyone up. The doctor murmured some 'there, there's' and rummaged through his bag until he located a blister pack of drug samples. 'Sedatives,' he said. He pushed two pills out, pressed them into Sylvia's hand and asked Myron to fetch her a glass of water. Doc watched her down them and then, in the conciliatory tone of an undertaker, he subjected all of us to his pedestrianism: 'It was God's will'; 'He's in a better place'; 'Be strong'; 'Time will heal' ... yada yada yada.

Dear God, whose will it was to take Joe, please take this man to his car so he can go home and hit the hay, snatch forty winks, go to the land of nod, recharge the batteries ... bore himself *to sleep.*

God complied. Sylvia pushed herself up off the chair and escorted Doc to the door. While they stood there swapping more clichés, Myron said to me, 'We're going to sit shiva.'

'*What?* Says who?'

'Mum and I.'

'Oh, *really*? Firstly, we're not religious. Secondly, I have a say too, you know!'

'Well, it's been decided.' He said it like a bossy pants in the schoolyard. 'And Dad would have wanted it.'

'*Bullshit!*' I hissed.

Myron was miffed. He sniffed his disapproval. 'It's not up for discussion. Anyway, Dad would have sat shiva for Mum if she'd gone first.'

Again, 'Bullshit!' I gave him the stink eye. He looked away.

Shiva meant the family members had to sit for seven days of formal mourning starting after the funeral. Joe could have easily gone seven days without shaving, not wearing shoes or jewellery and sitting on his arse on a low chair doing nothing. But shiva meant covering all the mirrors in the house. That would have suited me fine, but Joe couldn't have gone seven days without looking in a mirror. No way. Joe couldn't have gone one hour without looking in a mirror. He was vain. And also, he'd become no more observant than he was when we were kids—the extent of his religiousness back then included celebrating Christmas and Easter. That was not in any Jewish-way-of-life handbook that I knew of. Sylvia and Myron's decision to sit shiva *was* up for discussion, but it would have to keep for now.

Sylvia had let the doctor out. She was headed for the kitchen and told me to follow her. She closed the door behind us.

'I don't want Ralph here!' she fumed.

What? Well, those pills he gave you are fucking useless!

I glared at her. 'Why not? Ralph's not a stranger. Joe was his uncle.'

'Not his *real* uncle, he's adopted!'

Oh, really? So NOW he's adopted. Then I guess it's okay for me to be sleeping with him? Those sentiments would have to keep for another time and another place. But these wouldn't: 'You might not want him here, but I need him here. He stays. Your husband, my father!' Xena warrior, not so princess-like. Sylvia didn't argue but she got her wish. Only because I didn't even want me here.

Ralph dropped us home and offered to spend the night. On the couch. I told him I'd be fine, but mostly, I didn't want to provoke another outburst from Hannah.

I wasn't fine. I tossed and turned and only got a few hours' sleep before returning to Sylvia's.

Myron and I took her to the Chevra to meet with the funeral director. And we met with the rabbi. The funeral was arranged for two o'clock the next day. It gave us enough time to write a eulogy and to let relatives and friends know.

Making the calls was agony. People meant well but it was hard listening to more of *It was God's will He's in a better place Be strong Time will heal.* This was about the only time Portnoy would have come in handy. Although ... the goggly-eyed lush would probably have spread the word that *Sylvia* was dead. What that woman passed down through the grapevine might not have been so grotesque if she wasn't always pissed as a newt on its fermented fruit.

When I brought up the shiva issue, Myron tried a different tack. 'It'll give Mum comfort.'

Oh, come on! I zapped him with clichés. 'Whatever floats her boat,' I told him. 'I'm just not in the same one.' He wasn't impressed that I'd rocked his. It was a long day. The next one felt even longer.

The Chevra service was a blur. The only thing that shook me out of my subdued state was when the rabbi prefaced the eulogy with, 'Joe Roth's nickname was Joe Blow.'

Oh dear God.

'Although, he was anything but average.'

Oh Lord.

The congregation laughed, the rabbi was perplexed. It appeared our divine leader had his head in the clouds, but not far enough to see the truth about our father. If only Joe could have been a little more 'average'. If only the rabbi could have stuck to the script we'd given him.

My brother and I flanked Sylvia at the graveside. It was a clear, chilly day. My sunnies offered protection from the light, but not from the biting breeze that stung my cheeks and made my already damp eyes water even more. Tammy and her two slobs were on Myron's left. Hannah and Casper were next to me, and Ralph stood behind me as a 'supportive friend'. Standing on his right side and also offering me comfort were Maxi, Vette, Reuben, Iris, and Iris's husband, Joel.

The rabbi was about to start the service. He beckoned with his hands and asked for everyone to please come in closer. I turned around, picking out the familiar faces of relatives whom I'd barely noticed at the Chevra. On Ralph's left and directly behind Sylvia were her older brother, Isaac, his wife, Miri, and Norma and Albie. An assortment of first and second cousins stood a few rows back. I'd hardly had any contact with them over the years, especially Isaac and Miri's youngest daughter, endomorphic Zelda: *Fatarse*. Or maybe not ...

She'd lost weight. A lot. She was a third of the size she used to be (although, still a porker). But even in an insipid beige dress, she was hard to miss. With the fitted stretch jersey fabric clinging to and accentuating layers of loose skin folds, she resembled a Shar Pei. In spite of the weight loss, though, in my mind, Zelda would always be obese. I had to steady my breathing. Seeing her again tripped my cacomorphobia—she'd been the source of it.

> When we were kids, I'd been Zelda's punching bag right up until she bulldozed me at her own wedding. Fed up, I shot her down. She didn't speak to me for a long time after that, which suited me just fine. She tried to re-establish a relationship a few years back, but I was having none of it. It concerned me, though, that I was becoming like Sylvia the grudge-holder because I was unable to forget the sting of Zelda's barbs. Always my champion, Ralph put a positive spin on it: He said I was unable to forget because I had a well-developed hippocampus (the part of the brain responsible for the storage of long-term memory), and Zelda was just a well-developed hippo. Ralph had also once told me I had a well-developed cerebral cortex (the part of the brain responsible for higher thought). My well-developed cerebral cortex made me think that having a well-developed hippocampus was a double-edged sword—

'Yitgadal v'yitkadash sh'mei rabbah ...' The Kaddish, the mourner's prayer recited by the men, dragged me back out of the seedy side of memory lane, but it transported me to another dark place. A purer one of raw sadness. The Kaddish had always had that effect on me. It was supposed to ease the loss, but somehow, it exacerbated it. All the more now because it was a personal one.

We'd come to the end of the service and Sylvia was shaky and pale. She heaved a theatrical sigh and leaned on me. She was heavy, I nearly toppled over. Myron noticed this, put his arm around her shoulder and pulled her towards him to support her. Her blood sugar occasionally nosedived in the afternoon and she needed a glucose hit. Myron reached into his jacket pocket, pulled out a couple of jelly beans and handed them to her. About twenty seconds later, Albie's guttural whisper carried on the wind and assaulted my ears.

'When do we throw the l-l-l-lollies?'

I heard Ralph harrumph and whisper, *'And to think he used to call* me *D-d-d-dumkopf.'*

Throwing sweets is a custom when a Barmitzvah boy is called to the Torah. It symbolises wishing him a sweet life as he makes his transition from boyhood to manhood. And sweets are also thrown at a groom-to-be at his aufruf (his call-up to the Torah on the Sabbath before his wedding) after he finishes reciting his benedictions. It's also to wish him and his bride-to-be a sweet life, and a fertile one. Note: *life* is the operative word here.

But the award for unrivalled faux pas went to Sylvia.

The minyan—a quorum of ten or more men for a prayer service—took place that evening at Sylvia's home. With prayers done, Sylvia's cronies flocked around her.

'My son the doctor did all he could,' she told them. I didn't think it was the right time to correct her. (Myron was a dentist. He had fallen short of Sylvia's dream of him becoming a doctor, but she regularly cashed in on his title, *Doctor* Roth.) Chalky-skinned, she dabbed at her weepy eyes with a tissue. She regained her composure and continued. 'Myron tried to revive his father with artificial insemination.'

Oh no! It was all too much. I had to get out. I made a beeline for the front door, grabbed my keys from the key holder, threw on my coat and scurried out of the house.

I climbed into my car, which was parked two doors down, locked myself in and doubled over, screeching. I jumped as someone tapped on the front passenger window. Ralph was scrutinising me, his face a mask of concern. I fiddled with the central locking, unlocked the door and fell back into my bent position. Ralph slid into the passenger seat and put his hand on my shoulder making soothing noises until he realised I was howling with laughter. It took me a few minutes to get the words out. When I finally did, Ralph was laughing just as hard as I was.

'And even scari-scari-scarier is that the pe-people she said thi ... that she said this to ... didn't b ... didn't b-bat an eyelid. They nodded sym-sympathetically!'

Our hoots and shrieks misted up the windscreen. But my laughter died down as guilt seeped in. Or out. I started crying.

'What kind of a daughter am I that I would laugh at a time like this?' I whimpered.

'One who knows the difference between breathing and blowing.'

Ralph's empathic but firm tone combined with his droll words implied that he would support my grief, but not feed the guilt. It stopped me from further indulging in it.

I laughed again, then cried again. Ralph reached over, pulled me towards him and stroked my head. I cried harder, out of a mixture of sorrow, pain (the handbrake was digging into my hip), and another source of guilt—his proximity made me feel horny. Ralph cooed like a mourning dove as I alternated between laughing and crying.

In the end, it was the guilt that made me go along with Sylvia and Myron's decision to sit shiva. I was there early the next morning.

Shiva was short-lived, though. Shiva had turned into a shitfight. With the two of them sitting on their low chairs taking the moral high ground and potshots at me about Ralph, come lunchtime, I'd had enough.

'Right! I'm done here.' I put my shoes back on, grabbed my bag and headed for the door.

Sylvia wasn't happy. 'And just where do you think you're going?'

'Home. To find "comfort" with Ralph!' I drew air quotes and directed this at Myron.

I expected an admonishing phone call from my prissy brother, but none came. I'd heard that their shiva had come to an end after only two days. Seemed Mr Holier-than-thou couldn't go the distance. He used the 'life-goes-on' cliché on our mother as a means of copping out.

Over the next weeks, I cried a lot. And as the months passed, the painful episodes were just as keen, but they diminished in frequency.

It was a difficult time, compounded by Sylvia's demands. And her browbeating. Joe was gone; I was here to wear it. She was ringing three or four times a day, but then for two days, there was nothing. It felt like a holiday. It didn't last long.

I was at the dining room table late one afternoon working on an article about hypercritical parents, when mine turned up on my doorstep. Sylvia had often worn black when Joe was alive, but now it was her uniform. Today, she had on a black towelling tracksuit.

'You could have called me,' she accused. 'I might have been dead on the floor like your father was. I could have composted.'

What? As in, like, manure and chicken scraps?

'You think that's funny? *Oeuf, pest!*'

I think it's hysterical. 'No, but I think you meant decomposed.'

'Decomposed, composted ... what difference does it make? You wouldn't have even known I was dead!' She beat her chest and snivelled.

'Yes, I would. Myron calls you every day. He would have let me know.'

It was the wrong answer. She turned off the waterworks and threw me a dirty look. I was in no mood for this today. The article had got me all riled. I held her stare and threw her back one of irritation. She shifted uncomfortably and cleared her throat.

'Well, are you going to invite me in?'

Is there a choice? I held out my hand in mock formality and watched her as she shuffled into the lounge. With her shrunken posture and slow gait, she seemed to have aged. I felt sorry for her. I also felt guilty that I had little tolerance for my mother, so I willed myself to think positive. *Ah yes, this is research for my article.* It was the best I could do.

She sat on the sofa, picked at a loose thread on the seam of her trackie dacks and picked up the thread of our conversation. 'Anyway, *I've* been calling *you.*'

Her little dig dissolved the pity I felt. I didn't respond.

'Where are the children?'

In a lucky place. 'In their bedrooms. Hannah! Casper!' I called out. 'Come say hello to Nanna.'

Two bedroom doors groaned open. Both kids came out, dutifully kissed their grandmother and said they had to finish their homework.

What the—? I was about to say something but they stared at me with eyes like saucers. Sylvia was too self-absorbed to remember it was school holidays. I kept quiet, but I fixed my children with a look that implied, *You owe me.* They nodded relief. It was the closest I'd come to feeling appreciated in a while.

'There must be something wrong with your phone,' Sylvia said, as Hannah and Casper disappeared into their rooms. 'Like I was saying, I've been calling you and I keep getting a wrong number. It's always the same one that's got a message telling me about good times coming. I'm not in the mood for a good time. I'm a grieving widow.' She sounded affronted.

'Uh, you sure you're not calling the wrong number?'

'Of course I'm not! I'm a grieving widow. I haven't lost my memory!'

Pity. All those accumulated grudges. The slate could have been wiped clean.

I told her I'd look into it.

The grieving widow stayed for another hour of lamentation. When she left, I called my landline from my mobile. I gasped.

'Hannah! Casper! Get out here, NOW!'

CHAPTER TWELVE

Down the Rabbit Hole

The automated greeting had been delivered by a smoky female voice, but the message made it pretty clear what the nature of the business was. I'd had a little chuckle before trying to act like a responsible person. And I'd felt confident enough to summon them with a shout—they were beholden to me.

The two of them came into the kitchen. 'Okay, which one of you call-forwarded to a brothel?'

Hannah looked at me with a confounded expression. Then, eyes widening, she turned to Casper and both of them started laughing. They slapped palms.

Oh, just lovely. Great job of mothering you've done that your children think it's okay to do something like that.

I think it's quite creative. I wanted to palm-slap along with them.

What? Creative? Your children have no respect for you!

'It's not funny!' I yelled, mainly to block out my internal head-to-head than berate my kids.

My disrespectful children stopped laughing. Casper gave me a repentant look. 'Mum, Nanna was ringing a hundred times a day and moaning about being a widow *eeeevery* time I answered the phone. I know she's your mother, but ... she's a pain in the arse.'

No shit. 'I know, but it's not very nice to do that, is it?' *It's never too late to be pious.*

'Sorry. I'll call her later to apologise.'

What? No! Not too pious. 'Uh, best not. If she finds out what you did ... well, imagine?'

Casper reversed the call forward and Sylvia kept up her hundred-times-a-day calls. They were melodramatic. She was always symptomatic and dying. Ralph gave me some tools to deal with her. Not one worked. Sylvia's sole topic of conversation was Sylvia, except when she hammered away at me about Ralph. It took every ounce of energy not to go down the rabbit hole with her. Exhausted, I had Telstra add caller ID to my telephone service and I invested in an answering machine.

I mostly ignored my mother's calls, and let the machine pick them up. I returned them after dinner, but even talking to her just once a day felt like too often. I told myself she had Munchausen syndrome and my enabling her did her no favours. It seemed I'd become dispensable when I stopped feeding her woe-is-me-ness. A few months on, we were down to speaking a couple of times a week.

Phew.

My inner Sylvia took umbrage—*What kind of a daughter are you?*

I bit back—*You have to be cruel to be kind* (it had been one of Sylvia's pet clichés. She used to say it every time she walloped me when I was little).

Well, after the cruel upheavals of the last several months, the following month was kind to me. It was drama-free and I was relishing the status quo. If only the status could have stayed quo for a little longer.

Ralph, my anchor, my rock, started rocking the boat we were in together. *He* became demanding.

The rumour about us being an item remained, largely, just a rumour—those in the know kept it to themselves, either from embarrassment or good sense. But Ralph was relentless.

'I want to go out in public.'

'We do go out in public.'

'Yes, but only as friends. You won't let me hold your hand or put my arm around you.'

'I-I, uh, I don't want to give Portnoy the satisfaction of—'

'Portnoy? How the hell would she know?' Irritation crept into his voice. 'She doesn't even leave the house.'

'But, but she has tentacles, fer crissake!'

'Oh, spare me. *Please*.'

It was a stern rebuke that made me defensive. 'Anyway, I don't like public displays of affection.'

He narrowed his eyes at me. 'Is that right? Funny, you didn't seem to mind with Reuben or all the other guys you dated before him.'

Ralph, who'd got me through many anxiety attacks, was now becoming a source of them. He was often sullen, which was unlike him. His childish behaviour was a turn-off and his belligerence frightened me. Instead of talking about it with him, though, I started making excuses not to see him, which was just as childish. We'd gone backwards—I was engaging in the same push/pull dance with him that I did when we first hooked up. I hated myself for it, and he wasn't impressed. It came to a head one Sunday night when I dropped in on him unexpectedly. Ralph had been giving me a taste of my own medicine. I hadn't heard a word from him in a week.

When he opened the door, I could tell he had not long stepped out of the shower. His hair was damp and he smelled of musk and spice. He was wearing a muscle tee that accentuated his broad shoulders, and nylon cargo shorts with a military camouflage pattern. These did little to conceal his impressive bulge. My nipples instantly stood to attention. He looked so hot, yet his greeting was cold, his expression, po-faced.

'Hello.'

'Hey.' I stepped inside and put my bag on the entrance hall table.

He stared at me dispassionately before asking, 'Why are you here?'

I answered him with a playful smile. 'Is that an existential question?'

Normally he would laugh at this, but he gave me a glacial look.

'What's wrong?' I said.

'What's "wrong"? Oh, not a thing.' *Sarcasm.* 'Other than the fact that you're treating me like I'm your dirty little secret.'

'Uh, that's not true.'

'No? Then, what am I to you?'

Distant and churlish, at the moment. But sexy as hell. I moved in, wrapped my arms around his waist and ground into him. I slid my hands under his top, moved it across his taut stomach and downwards as I kissed his neck. He moaned. I felt him growing hard—

'No!' he snapped. He removed my arms and took a step back. 'Don't do that. It insults me.'

I felt like I'd been kicked in the gut. Ralph wasn't one to knock back sex. *You're just joking around, right?*

'I'm not your plaything, you know.'

'I-I know, but ...' *But I so wanna play with your thing right now.*

'Really? You think this is funny?'

Jesus, Baubo, get out of my face! This goddess in the control tower of my psyche had sucky timing. But then, Ralph didn't look so attractive anymore. He sounded like Sylvia.

'N-no. I'm sorry. It's just that ... it's just that I'm not ready to come out as a couple yet.'

'Oh, and just when will you be ready?' His eyes flashed. 'It's been a year!' He was right. It was exactly a year since he'd revealed his feelings for me. Birthdays had come and gone—none particularly cheerful because of the lingering tensions.

'It's ... I don't know. Look ... I'm still concerned about the kids, about what they thi—'

'The kids? Casper's fine. And Hannah, well, Hannah's behaving like a spoilt brat and you're allowing it!' It irked him that she barely grunted at him. It irked me that he was criticising my parenting skills. And he wasn't done. 'You know, she's just like her grandmother—holds grudges.' It infuriated me that he was comparing my daughter to my mother! He still wasn't done. 'More to the point, you're concerned about what everyone thinks. But you don't give a damn about what I think.'

I opened my mouth to speak but nothing came out.

'Well, here's what I think. I think you better leave.'

'Uh, *no*! I-I want to talk about this.'

'Oh, really?' He glared at me. 'Everything's on your terms, isn't it? Well, I don't feel like talking. I'm tired of the games. Go home, Ruth.'

Ruth.

With that, he picked up my bag and handed it to me.

My heart lurched. I was shocked and humiliated. And more than a little scared. Ralph and I had had the odd argument over the years, and other than that time when he'd distanced himself for two weeks (after seeing me in a bikini), there was only one other time that he had shunned me.

We were in our late teens and Ralph had a girlfriend called Monique. His pet name for her was 'Mons'. Maxi asked him if her last name was Pubis or Veneris, which pretty much summed up what Maxi, Vette and I thought of her. Vette

and I laughed; Ralph refused to speak to the three of us for
a month.

But he'd never rejected me like this. With my stomach
churning, I walked out and got into my car.

Breathe, Ruthie, just breeeeeathe.

But he doesn't want me anymore. Ah-ha-ah-ha-ah-ha.

It was just a fight.

*It was more than that. He didn't raise his voice. He was
cold! And, he knocked back SEX!*

I drove away. A sudden, heavy downpour and my tears
hampered visibility. I was unfocused, ungrounded and unable to
contain my rising anxiety. What would I do without Ralph? He
who rarely judged me, even when I told him I was glad Joe
didn't die just before dinner because it would have meant
delaying a meal. All the rejections and losses of the year gained
on me and I felt myself slipping into that dark, primitive space
inhabited by gods and monsters. It was the anniversary of my
apocalyptic night and I was commemorating it by revisiting it—
the monsters were assailing me and the gods were laughing! I
prayed, backsliding into the childish Sunday begging.

*God, please make them hold off for five more minutes till I'm
home and under the doona, where I can brace myself for the
assault.*

It didn't work. God had also lapsed into His old ways. The
voices in my head got louder. I felt like a sitting duck.

Ah, but wait. God must be there. A bright light.

Or, maybe not. A frightening screech.

Terror.

A loud bang.

Black.

CHAPTER THIRTEEN

Seeing the Light

*A*m I dead? No, nooooo! I'm not ready to die, God, I'm not ready to leave my kids, I'm not ready to leave Ralph! On second thoughts, screw Ralph. Wait ... this can't be right. You're supposed to feel love and forgiveness and all that. Well, I don't. And aren't your dead relatives supposed to form a welcoming committee? Why isn't Joe here, then? Then again, why would I expect him to be? So maybe I am dead. But isn't there meant to be light at the end of the tunnel? This was arse about. First, there was the light, now it's just dark. Or semi-dark. No, wait ... a bright light getting closer. Oh God. I must be dead! But everything hurts. Isn't the pain supposed to go when you're dead?*

'Ruth. Ruth. Ruth. Ruth.' An angel's voice was reaching me from the other side. It got louder. 'Ruth. **Wake up ...**'

Ow! Why are you yelling? I thought angels spoke softly.

The light was eclipsed. A shadow hovered over me.

Oh no, I've gone to Hell! Sylvia was right. Punishment for being a difficult child.

'Am ... I ... dead?' I whispered. It was an effort to speak—I had a thumping headache.

The shadow said, **'No.'**

'Ouch. Shhh.'

'Oh. Sorry, <small>sorry.</small>'

'If I'm ... not dead ... then ... how do you ... know ... my name?'

I blinked a few times and the shadow became more defined. I discerned a young woman in a uniform. She had a kind, smiling face—no horns, no pitchfork. Not Lucifer. She answered my question: 'From your licence.'

'My ... licence? Where ... am ... I?'

'You're in an ambulance. You've been in an accident. Looks like you knocked your head on the side window when the Pajero hit you. Lucky the impact was short of your door. And lucky the guy wasn't moving fast. Anyway, your vitals are good, and we're at the hospital now, just pulling into Emergency.'

I groaned as they unloaded the gurney from the ambulance. They wheeled me into an ER bay and closed the curtains on either side. My head and right shoulder hurt like hell. A doctor approached, introduced himself and shone a light in my eyes. I winced.

A nurse spoke to me. 'Who can we call? Your husband?'

'No. Husband's away ... Ex-husband.' Reuben had taken Hannah and Casper up to Noosa for ten days and they weren't due back for another week.

'Your mother?'

Fuck no! I gave the nurse both Maxi and Vette's numbers. She said it was a good sign that I remembered them. I thought about the fine, the demerit points, the damage to my car and the other driver's (the driver himself wasn't hurt, they'd told me). My intact memory was a blessing and a curse.

Another nurse came in and took my blood pressure, temperature and medical history, and collected blood samples. Just as she finished up, Maxi and Vette burst in. Both were breathless. Vette took one look at me and started crying. Maxi clasped my hand and squeezed her eyes shut. I hadn't seen myself, but Maxi said I looked like a raccoon—I had two black eyes.

Both of them bombarded me with questions. In a hushed tone and unsteady voice I told them everything that had happened from the time I got to Ralph's, how I'd left in a foggy and agitated state, and hadn't noticed the Give Way sign I'd given way at countless times before.

Maxi was pissed off. 'Bloody Ralph! I'm gonna call him and give him what for.'

'No, don't!' *Ouch.*

The nurse came back, carefully removed my clothes and helped me into a hospital gown. An orderly then came in to take me for a shoulder X-ray and a CT scan. As I was wheeled away, I whispered, *'Maxi, please ... don't call him. Vette, please ... make sure she ... doesn't.'* Both nodded.

Both jumped up from their seats as the orderly brought me back an hour and a half later and closed the privacy curtain.

Vette asked, 'What did they say?'

I'd been given a strong analgesic for the pain and could speak normally now. 'I won't get the results for a while but the radiographer said there was no shoulder fracture and the CT scan looked clear.'

For the next half-hour, we talked more about what had happened and about other stuff, then Maxi tried again. 'Can I call him now?'

'No.'

'Isn't it a little bit late to be calling him, anyway?' Vette said.

'Really? Under the circumstances you're worried about waking him?' Maxi snapped.

'He's a night owl,' I said to Vette, 'and late-night phone calls aren't "whorebringers of doom" for him.'

They laughed. But then Maxi got serious. 'Ruthie, he needs to know. I'm gonna call him.'

'Then why bother asking?'

She shrugged and smiled. 'Token gesture.' No point arguing with her when her mind was made up. Besides, a part of me wanted him to know and wanted him to feel bad.

'Can I put it on speaker?'

'No! I don't wanna hear what he has to say.' *Unless he's tormented and wracked with crippling guilt.* But you don't need to put your phone on speaker for the person on the other end to be heard by those nearby. Ralph answered pretty much straight away. Maxi wasted no time on formalities.

'You're a real prick!'

'Well, hello to you, too, Maxi. Oh, and let me guess, Ruth called you.' His words dripped scorn.

'Yes, Ruthie did call me. And it's pretty telling that she chose to call me and Vette when something terrible happened.'

'Wow. She called *both* of you.' He harrumphed. 'But ... "terrible"? Come on. We both know Ruth tends to catastrophise. Sending her home's hardly a catastrophe.'

'No, but the fact that she didn't actually make it home *is* a catastrophe, you arsehole!'

'Uh, w-what? What are you talking about? What are you saying?' The scorn was gone. His response was suffused with a mix of impatience and worry.

Maxi waited a beat before speaking. 'She's been in an accident. She's in hospital.'

'Oh my God, oh my God! Is she okay? Is Ruthie okay?'

Oh, so now I'm 'Ruthie'.

'She'll live.'

What a bitch.

'Where is she? What hospital?' His voice teetered on the edge of hysteria.

'She doesn't want you here.'

Silence. Ralph's pain in that soundless space was almost palpable.

'Anyway, I'm only letting you know because it's the right thing to do.'

As if.

Then Maxi twisted the knife—'But she didn't want me to call you.'

This elicited a long whimpering sound from Ralph. Maxi's up yours was a low blow. I wanted to high-five her.

What a bitch.

Several seconds of what seemed like dead air passed before Ralph spoke again. His tone became querulous and demanding. 'Once again, Maxi, where is she? Which hospital?'

'It doesn't matter. Like I said, she doesn't want you here. You can call me; I'll keep you updated.' It was one of the few slugfests between them where Maxi had the upper hand, and she was enjoying it. Ralph wasn't. She hung up.

Her phone trilled ten seconds later. She sighed impatiently. 'What, Ralph?'

'Maxi, WHICH FUCKING HOSPITAL!' *This* was telling. Ralph rarely yelled and he never swore.

Knocked for six, Maxi spilled out the details. It couldn't have been more than about fifteen minutes later when he arrived, still wearing his muscle tee and shorts. He must have run reds to get here so quickly. His face turned white the instant he saw me.

'Oh, Ruthie ...'

I turned away from his gaze. He approached the side of the bed and took my hand. I pulled it away.

'What happened?' he asked in a strangled voice.

I didn't volunteer anything and Maxi stood steely and silently with her arms crossed. So, Vette did the talking. She told him a car had ploughed into me. She stressed that it was a four-wheel drive.

Bless you, Vette, for making it sound dramatic.

'Who was at fault?'

'YOU!' *Ouch.* It hurt to yell. And the sudden movement when I swivelled my head around to look at him made me feel dizzy.

Ralph opened his mouth to say something, but nothing came out, bafflement frozen on his face, like he was trying to get his head around how he could have caused an accident without being there.

Jesus, men are stupid.

The *whooshes* and *beeps* of the equipment measuring my vital signs seemed to grow in intensity against the fraught silence that followed. But the noise was drowned out by a voice belonging to the stupid species. He was issuing instructions on the other side of the curtain, which he then pushed aside. A doctor, probably in his early fifties, strode in.

'Hello ...' He looked down at the patient chart he'd removed from the end of the bed, and looked up again, '... Ruth.' He smiled. 'How are you feeling?'

'Awful.'

'Mm,' he nodded.

We all held our breath as he surveyed the chart. His head came up, and he smiled again. 'You're very lucky. All your tests are normal. It's just a concussion and a whole lot of bruising.' He pointed heavenwards. 'I'd say someone up there was looking after you.'

Uh-huh. After He threw me to the wolves!

'But we'll keep you in overnight for observation and you can go home in the morning if there are no problems. Do you have somebody who can keep an eye on you for the next few days?'

'That would be me,' Ralph jumped in.

As soon as the doctor left and before I could challenge Ralph, he added, 'And I'm staying here tonight.'

'No. You're not!' I shot him a black look through my black-rimmed eyes. 'I don't want you here.'

CHAPTER FOURTEEN

The (Pink) Elephant
in the Room

Ralph was undaunted by my bloody-mindedness. He folded his arms and stood firm. 'I'm staying.'

'Gee, if only *I'd* been so insistent a few hours ago, I wouldn't be here, would I?' There were kinder ways I could have said it, but I wasn't feeling too kindly. Even so, I felt bad—I sensed Ralph's hurt and I wanted to cry. Only my indignation stopped me.

Vette defused the tension in the cubicle. 'Um, did you let Hannah and Casper know before we got here?'

'Oh. N-no. What time is it?'

Vette looked at her watch. 'Eleven-thirty.'

'It's a bit late now. They'll get a fright if I call—'

'It's ten-thirty in Queensland. No daylight saving, remember?' Maxi said. 'And if they only find out tomorrow, well, it might inflame things.' She had a point. My relationship with Hannah was still a little precarious.

'My phone's in my bag.'

'Maybe text Reuben before ringing, you know, as a warning, so they don't get rattled.' Vette suggested.

I did, and he called me within seconds. I assured him I was okay, then I spoke to Hannah and Casper. Both were upset and wanted to come home. I told them what the doctor had said. When Hannah asked who would take care of me, I said, 'My cousin will be looking after me.'

It was bitchiness off the charts and I regretted the words as soon as they'd slithered out of my mouth. Hannah didn't say anything, but I sensed her gloating. And I noticed the tears forming in Ralph's eyes as he averted them.

Maxi and Vette left not long after. Ralph retreated to a chair to lick his wounds. His forearms resting on his legs, he sat quietly, head hanging down, and staring at the floor.

I lay there wondering how Sylvia could have made a habit of sniping. I felt I had good reason. Was that the way a spiteful disposition started off? Maybe the anger resulting from the good reason took hold and festered, and bitterness became a lifestyle. Then you'd rationalise that even the tiniest slight was a reason. Then you'd perceive everything as a slight. Was Hannah headed in that direction? I needed to set a better example for her. I needed to do something about thi—

'Can I get you anything, Ruthie?' Ralph was now standing a safe distance away from the bed, self-condemnation in his gaze.

'If I need anything, I'll use the call button.' *Miaow!* Yes, I needed to do something about this, but not right now. Right now, I was in survival mode. I was an injured animal.

I was moved to a two-bed ward and given a sleeping pill. It took me a while to drop off.

I woke with a start and in a sweaty, fearful state. I squinted at the clock above the entrance to the ward. Illuminated by the lighting in the hallway, it showed it was just after two-thirty. I hadn't slept long.

The tablet must have been the same drug as the one the doctor had given Sylvia the night Joe died. It was bad enough that it didn't promote sleep, it also hadn't kept the mythical beasts of the psyche at bay. It just made them launch a kind of slow-motion attack, like the walking dead—I was living out a frickin' zombie apocalypse! *Happy Anniversary.*

Ralph was fast asleep on the La-Z-Boy recliner next to my bed. He looked so sexy I wanted to jump him, but then I remembered I hated him.

I slept on and off for the next several hours and was discharged mid-morning with a script for Panadeine Forte and a patient instruction fact sheet. Ralph had the script filled at the hospital dispensary before taking me home.

I was jittery, quailing at the blare of car horns. Ralph offered gestures of support; I pushed them away as I seethed inwardly in the front passenger seat. He tried to help me out of the car. I rebuffed him. I shuffled towards my front door. Suddenly overcome by a wave of nausea and dizziness, I stopped and leaned my forehead against the doorjamb.

'Are you okay?'

'Dizzy,' I whispered.

The feeling passed and I tried to put the key in the door, but my vision was a little blurred.

Ralph took the key from me, unlocked the door, and slid his hand under my elbow. I didn't resist this time. He escorted me inside and helped me to my bedroom. I lowered myself onto the bed like a doddery old woman, huffing and puffing.

'Ruthie?' I looked up at him; his eyes conveyed remorse and shame. 'You have no idea how terrible I feel.'

'You have no idea how little I care.' I looked away. I didn't want to witness his pain again. *Later*, I told myself again. I would deal with my undesirable attitude later.

I called the kids to reassure them I was all right, then staggered into the bathroom and threw up. I sensed Ralph standing behind me, shadowing me. I motioned for him to move away. I didn't need an audience while I was barfing—while I was *ralphing*! After rinsing my mouth, I waddled to the bed and lowered myself onto it, groaning and clutching the sides of my head as I let it sink into the two pillows. *Please God, make the world go away. Please God, make Ralph go away.*

God heard me. Ralph left the room. But then he came back a moment later with a buttered SAO biscuit, a glass of water and a couple of Panadeine Forte. 'You shouldn't take the tablets on an empty stomach.'

He helped me sit forward and handed me the cracker. I nibbled at it, took the pills and washed them down. I lay back down and prayed again. I was more specific, this time: *Please God, make him STAY away.*

'I'll go home—'

Yes! 'Good—'

'—just to pick up a few things. But I'll wait till you're asleep before leaving.'

'Don't rush back,' I muttered under my breath.

Ralph flinched. I was enjoying this feeling of control I had over him. *Oh God help me, I am my mother's daughter.*

With that horrible thought, I fell asleep.

When I woke, my head felt muzzy. But I sensed a presence. I looked down the bed and saw a figure in white perched on the end of it. It was bathed in light. I blinked a couple of times. Was this one an angel? Was it God? Was I dead this time? I felt a little frightened. The figure must have sensed it. 'It's okay,' it said with a reassuring tone. It was a resonant male voice that had an attractive lilt.

Strange. He sounded like 'Jesus', the character from *South Park*. He spoke again. 'How are you feeling, Ruthie?'

Oh. Not dead. Not an angel. Not God. Not 'Jesus'. Just Ralph—still, a character from *South Park*: 'Mr Hankey the Christmas Poo.' Yes. A turd with a voice.

He repeated the question. 'How are you feeling?'

I moaned and mumbled, *'Got a raging headache.'*

'I'll get you some Panadeine.'

'Hmm? I just took two.'

'That was four hours ago.'

Had I slept that long? The doctor had warned me I'd probably need to sleep a lot for a while.

'Okay, yeah.'

He disappeared for a few minutes and came back with a plate of something. He helped me sit forward and handed me the plate. It held a cheese sandwich and a cinnamon palmier—a little scroll-like, flaky pastry—another one of my favourites from the French patisserie. I looked up at him.

'I picked some up on the way. I thought the gâteaux might be a bit rich at the moment.'

I grunted my thanks, pushed the sandwich aside, pecked at the pastry and took the caplets. He helped me lie back down and then disappeared again.

Thank you, God.

The tablets had taken effect when Ralph came back half an hour later. I lay staring at the ceiling. I had a sense of him standing in the doorway. He cleared his throat.

'Ruthie.'

I turned to face him. His gaze was unsteady, his voice, tremulous. 'Can we please talk?'

I looked away and closed my eyes. I had a bitchy answer at the ready, but bitchy wasn't palliative.

'No. I'm not doing this with you.' My response reeked of apathy, which was worse than anger. I'd found out just how callous it could be when he sent me away last night. Mine was not so much revenge as feeling too crappy to care about him feeling crappy. He knew to leave well enough alone.

For the rest of the day, he tended to my every whim. He made me cups of tea (which I drank), he made me an early dinner (most of which he ate), he called the insurance company (my car was a write-off). He tidied up, did my ironing, kissed my arse. In spite of myself, I was enjoying the attention. He didn't usually go into the practice on Mondays till the afternoon. He'd called work in the morning and had the receptionist reschedule his appointments for the rest of the week, which would probably piss off his co-dependent clients, but I didn't care. I accepted that I needed someone to attend to me. That night, I slept like a dead person, and not long after I woke, Ralph came in with a breakfast tray in his hands.

'How are you feeling?'

'*Groggy. Headachy.*' My words came out slow and slurred. I put my hand out. '*Panadeine, please.*'

'Mm. Okay. Have a bit to eat.'

I tentatively drew myself up and rested against the bedhead. Ralph placed the tray on my lap.

A bit? It was a breakfast fit for a king—a small bowl of hulled, quartered strawberries, a plate of fluffy scrambled eggs, two pieces of lightly buttered toast, a glass of freshly squeezed orange juice, and a cloth napkin. A single red rose picked from God knows where lay across the top of the tray (not between his teeth).

From thorny prick two days ago to this? Nice touch, Don Quixote. But I don't feel any warmer towards you today than I did yesterday.

On the plus side, though, my appetite seemed to have improved a little. I ate half the breakfast and managed to keep it down.

The day was pretty much a repeat of the one before, except I ate more, didn't hallucinate and Ralph didn't ask if we could please talk. Again, I slept through the night like a mummy.

On day three, having a shower didn't require so much effort. I was awake for longer periods, ate even more and started moving around a bit. Ralph ministered to my needs but didn't hover. That night, he gave me my two painkillers, switched off my bedside lamp, told me to sleep well, then left to take a shower (he showered twice a day). Half an hour later, he appeared in the doorway.

Backlit by the hallway light, his form, clothed in only boxer shorts, looked like a Mr Universe entrant, welterweight division. He approached the bed to check on me, bringing with him the scent of lavender, citrus, mint and pheromones. He was surprised I was still awake and asked if I was okay. I said yes. He asked if I needed anything. I said no. He said okay and turned to walk out the door.

'Wait ... Stay with me tonight,' a delusional voice said.

CHAPTER FIFTEEN

I Love You ... Now Piss Off!

W*hat?* Was Panadeine Forte hallucinogenic? Was it an aphrodisiac? Was I a weak woman at the mercy of my minge? Was it the fact that Mr Hankey was dead sexy— inasmuch as a turd can be? Whatever. I was now lucid and wanted to take back the words.

Too late.

Ralph wasn't dumb enough to say 'Are you sure?' He said nothing, just glided to the other side of the bed, lowered himself onto it, slid under the blanket and faced me. I rolled onto my left side and faced him—a gaze, not a glare this time. A little hesitantly, he stroked my face, mindful of the bruising. Sensing no resistance, he edged closer till our bodies were touching. He brushed my lips with his, then his kiss grew more impassioned, his tongue exploring my mouth. I closed my eyes and moaned. In a voice hoarse with desire, he whispered, *'I love you.'*

I hate your guts, but I'm horny.

He carefully pushed the straps of my nightie off my shoulders and pulled it downwards. He removed my undies, then he stripped off his boxers. With a silken touch, his hand roamed over my curves. He moved his head down to my breasts and teased my nipples with his tongue. He came back up, his soft lips grazing mine as his fingers slid down my belly and settled on the core of my womanhood. It didn't take long for my whole body to explode. I cried out in exquisite agony. Ralph looked at me with concern. My face was a twisted grimace of pain. The intensity hurt my head, but the hot tingling sensation right down to my extremities had an analgesic effect, and every muscle in my body relaxed. I let out a rapturous sigh.

A small gasp escaped his lips as I then reached down and applied the same feathery touch he'd used on me to his sensitive bit and pieces. Unable to wait any longer, he drew me close and eased himself inside. In a slow, measured dance, we moved against each other in sensuous harmony until one final thrust took him over the edge and he cried out in ecstasy.

My lust was quenched, but my anger had been kindled. I un-impaled myself, turned onto my back and closed my eyes. Ralph smoothed his hand over my cheek.

Sod off. I didn't want him touching me. I wanted to turn onto my side with my back to him, but I couldn't because of my tender, black and blue shoulder. Just as well. I didn't want him spooning me.

'Ruthie? Are you asleep?'

What kind of dumb-arse question is that? Do people really expect you to say 'Yes'?

I feigned the slow and steady breathing of sleep. I didn't want to engage in post-coital, deep and meaningful conversation with him. Instead, I engaged in shallow and meaningless conversation with myself.

I'm a weak, weak woman.

No, you're not.

Yes, I am.

You have needs!

In two minds, I fell asleep.

I woke the next morning with a splitting headache. I turned on my side. I forgot Ralph was there. He was awake. Leaning semi-reclined against his propped-up pillow, he was watching me. He looked like the cat that got the cream. I gave him a filthy look. The cream curdled, his face sagged.

He asked, 'Are you all right?'

'No. I am not all right. I'm bloody angry!' I spat out in disdain. Anything above a whisper hurt my head. I didn't care. 'I fucking hate you!'

His shoulders slumped. His flagging spirit was at odds with his pecker, which was as upright as a solid, carbon fibre tent pole holding up the sheet. It was at odds with what he said next. He Frasier-Craned me. 'I'm listening.'

Really? Firstly, I'm in no mood to go camping with you. Second, you're actually trying to psychologise me while you're lying there with a morning woody? Doesn't that qualify as unprofessional conduct? Isn't that akin to sexual harassment? Doesn't it breach a code of ethics? Or something like that? If I hadn't been so livid, I would have laughed at the absurdity. But he was listening, so I let him have it.

'Mr big-shot psychologist! You should've taken your own fucking advice—"we gotta communicate", nyah nyah nyah.' Granted, it was a nasally, childish taunt, but it wasn't like I'd stuck my tongue out at him. Still, I wasn't done. 'No. You had to send me away!' The yelling made my head feel like it would explode. Again, I didn't care. 'Well, it's all *your* fault. I wouldn't be in this mess if you'd put your bloody money where your mouth is!'

He was contrite: 'You're right. And I can't tell you how sorry I am.'

'You're a mean bastard, a horrible person!'

He looked crushed, but I didn't let up.

'You've ruined what we had and I hate you for it!'

'I know.'

I'd stooped to Sylvia's level; Ralph hadn't. Shame crept up on me. I tried to head it off with more anger. I was mad at him for not putting up a fight. When someone doesn't fight back, there's no war. When there's no war, there's no need for defences. When there are no defences, there's nothing to stop the raw pain from emerging. It swamped me and I started crying. Uncontrollably.

Ralph moved across and folded me into his arms. When I was done, the pain in my head and my heart had eased up considerably.

'I'm sorry. I didn't mean all those things I said.'

'I know. I know,' he said.

I lay still in his arms and he stroked my head. I could tell he wanted to kiss me, but I didn't let him. I still wasn't a fan of morning breath. He started kissing other parts that didn't give a rat's arse about woofy breath. I stopped him. My heart was more open, but I was more protective of it. Although I no longer hated him, I wasn't willing to ignore my emotions and give in to the urgings of my body. I told him so. He accepted and understood.

Ralph made us breakfast. I popped a couple of pills after I had something in my stomach. Both lost in our own thoughts, we ate in silence—not a strained one, though. Ralph cleared the plates away and I went off to have a shower. I almost lost my footing as I moved away from the breakfast bar. Dang flip-flops—I should have bought them in a smaller size. I grabbed my head. The tablets hadn't kicked in yet and the sudden jerking movement hurt. Ralph rushed over to me.

'What's wrong? Are you okay? What's wrong?' He was panic-stricken.

'What? Nothing's wrong.'

'But. But you stumbled.'

'Uh, yyye-ah. Only because my foot came out of my thong.'

He breathed out. 'I thought you had a subdural haematoma.'

Oh God. I so wanted to laugh—clearly, my brain injury hadn't cramped Baubo's style—but this was no time for bonhomie. I didn't want to lose the ground I'd gained. Still. A *subdural haematoma? Ha ha ha ha ha!* In my mind, I was peeing my pants.

Ralph had researched this condition in depth at the library when we were kids because it was a term we heard once a week. In every episode of Ben Casey, a TV hospital drama from the sixties, someone had a subdural haematoma. Doctor Ben Casey always tilted his head to the side when he delivered this diagnosis. And of course, he said it solemnly. But Ben Casey said everything solemnly, either because he was cast as a robotic personality, or he was a shit actor. Still, I had a huge crush on the head-cocking Ben Casey. When I was nine, I stuck a poster of him on my cupboard door and told Sylvia I wanted to marry him. With pursed lips she told me in no uncertain terms, 'You are not going to marry him. He's not Jewish.'

You're kidding, right?

Ralph also wanted to marry him because Ben Casey was his hero (superseding Noddy, Zorro, Tarzan, and Agent 007). And every time Ralph and I played doctors and nurses with Maxi and Vette, Ralph, who was always the doctor ('because I'm male'), inclined his head, assumed a mask of grimness and diagnosed one of us with 'ay sub-doo-rl heema-toe-ma', which he pronounced with an American accent. The first time he'd done this, I laughed, and he yelled at me.

'Stop laughing; it's serious! Don't you know this could be fatal?'

It made me laugh harder. It made Ralph cry. He ripped the toy stethoscope from around his neck and threw it on the floor. 'I'm not playing anymore!' Talk about precious.

'Who's gonna be the doctor then?'

'Nobody. You can all *die!*' Ralph stormed off in a sulk.

This worked a treat. The good Doctor Ralph had us over a barrel. Back then, until second-wave feminism gained ground, the medical profession was male-dominated. Other than Vette's mum, who was a widow and had a job out of necessity, our mothers were 'just' homemakers. So, in our make-believe world, our fate was in Doctor Ralph's hands. From then on, I had to quash the urge to laugh every time he diagnosed us.

Now, I was imagining us re-enacting our game of doctors and nurses: *'Um surry to tell you, Ruth, you haave ay sub-doorl heema-toe-ma es ay reesult of yer accident.'*

'Ruthie, are you sure you're okay?' Ralph's voice filtered through my reverie and dragged me back into the moment.

'Huh? What? Oh. Yeah, yeah.' I stared at him and made a wry face. 'A subdural haematoma? Really? And you reckon I "catastrophise".' I drew air quotes with my fingers.

His mouth fell open.

'She didn't have you on speaker, but I heard you.' I shook my head. 'Not nice, Ralph.'

He gave me a sheepish look. 'I'm sorry.'

The blow to my head hadn't caused bleeding under the skull, but it had knocked some sense into me and helped me see things more clearly. I waved away his apology and said, 'We need to talk.'

CHAPTER SIXTEEN

The Whole Ruth
& Nothing but the Ruth

There were those four words again—*we need to talk*. Not spoken so innocently this time. I'd been both Ruth, and ruthless. And that was okay with me.

Sylvia had wanted the perfect me. Again, I remembered that striving to be the shiny, fairy-tale princess was not my thing. I needed to keep reminding myself that my strong link with the raw stories meant I was compelled to live the deep life: light, dark, colourful, messy. It meant being real, which meant there was a good chance someone would be pissed off with me. Having too many someones pissed off with me at once had been overwhelming, so I'd relapsed. And the struggle to please this one or that one had taken its toll. This accident had turned out to be a blessing.

Ralph and I moved to the lounge. We sat opposite each other, the coffee table separating us. He sat forward and nervously raked his fingers through his hair. I expelled a deep breath and opened my mouth to speak, but he beat me to it.

'This is all my fault. Like you said, "big-shot psychologist". Fat lot I know. If I'd just—'

'Stop.' I held my hand up. 'Just stop. How about neither of us plays the poor-me card, hmm?'

Ralph nodded compliance. He squared his shoulders and let me have my say.

'First up, I didn't appreciate you telling me that Hannah's behaving like a spoilt brat and I'm allowing it. I'm doing the best I can with my kids. You might have an understanding of people's behaviour, Ralph, but when you don't have children yourself, it's easy to oversimplify things and to judge. And you don't have the right to criticise the way I'm raising mine. You don't have the right to decide what's best for them. And yeah, maybe my choices aren't always so great, but it's still *my* job, my call.'

With a pained expression, he closed his eyes and rubbed the nape of his neck. He then met my gaze. 'You're absolutely right. I'm sorry.'

I nodded. He looked down at his hands and I continued. 'But in fairness to you, what was happening with us ... well, it takes two. I know it was wrong of me to keep pushing you away like I did, and I apologise for that. I was feeling suffocated. You've been clinging and making demands on me, wanting something from me before I'm ready to give it. On top of that, having you constantly getting stuck into me, it scared me. It's a side of you I've never seen.' I softened my voice. 'And now you're being overprotective.' Then, I delivered an unmerciful blow. 'It all adds up to, well ... it's been like being in bed with Sylvia.'

Ralph inhaled sharply. I may as well have booted him in the nuts. He blenched as he crossed his legs—a protective move. I pressed on.

'You know, you ended a lot of relationships with girls when they became needy and clingy and demanding.'

With awareness kicking in, Ralph buried his face in his hands. 'Oh God.' His voice was little more than a murmur. He leaned back hard against the sofa cushion, looked up at the ceiling and blew out a protracted breath. 'I've become the kind of person even *I* run from.' He looked at me again. 'Why?'

'What?' I peered at him, nonplussed. 'You're asking me? You're the psychologist.'

Neither of us spoke for the longest time. Ralph looked fixedly at a space above my head, like he was waiting for a thought bubble to pop up with the answer in it.

The ringing of the phone shattered the quiet. I gave a start, but it seemed Ralph hadn't even heard it—he managed to tune out everything when he was in process mode. I let the answering machine pick up the call. There was the familiar beep, then Sylvia's jarring voice: 'You haven't called me. It's been six days. *Six days!* And I called you last. It's your turn. I'm all alone here. You could be a bit more considerate like your brother.'

And you wonder why I'm not calling?

No sooner had she hung up than Steve Winwood started singing 'Higher Love'. It was my mobile's ring tone.

The name 'IMA GRIEVINGWIDOW' flashed across the screen.

Ugh. If I didn't answer, she wouldn't let up. I grabbed the phone from the coffee table, left Ralph to his ruminations and went into the kitchen to take the call.

'Why didn't you answer your phone?' Before I could answer her question, she repeated the message she'd left on the machine.

How can I say this without alarming you? 'I was in a really, really bad car accident.'

Her voice registered alarm. 'What? Are you all right? Are you in hospital?'

'I spent Sunday night in hospital. I've got a concussion.'

'Sunday? It's Thursday today. How could you not let me know I'm your mother I'm a grieving widow I suppose you told all your friends but not me I'm always the last to know do you know how that makes me feel do you know how that *looks* whatwillpeoplethink—'

'Hello, hello. Are you there? I can't hear you.' I hung up. Note to Steve Winwood: *If this is your idea of bringing me a higher love, save yourself the trouble!* I put my phone on silent. For added insurance, I grabbed the phone book, flicked through it and found what I wanted. I picked up my cordless and punched in *21, the brothel's number, #.

You are such a bitch.

Amazing that I can hear your voice even after hanging up. I went back into the lounge room. Ralph was still in a cone of silence.

Yo, Earth to Ralph. The mothership is calling you home.

Ralph looked up. 'I just figured it out.'

And?

Nothing. Ralph often did this. It was like he was waiting for a round of applause.

God. Give me patience.

His expression turned sombre. Like Ben Casey's. He nodded to himself and once again stared out into the infinity of space. Ha. *'Man. Woman. Birth. Death. Infinity.'* These spoken words opened every episode of *Ben Cas*—

'It's never been like this with any woman,' Ralph said, his voice filled with emotion. 'I've loved a few women, you know that. But I think I'm like this with you, you know, trying to hold on so tightly, because I'm *in* love for the first time in my life. And it's more than just about being afraid of losing you. Although ... it's not lost on me that you could have ... that you could have ... died.' He pinched the bridge of his nose. Tears of self-reproach pooled in his eyes. He wiped them away. 'If you had, I wouldn't be able to go on ...' His voice broke. 'Wouldn't even want to. Especially knowing the last things I said to you.' He started crying. He doubled over, sobs wracking his body.

I held a space for him but resisted the urge to go hold him and break his fall. With my body. Which is what it would have led to. There's nothing quite as life-affirming as sex, and it had also just now hit me that I could have been killed. An unnerving thought, and not one I wanted to feed.

Ralph blew his nose loudly. The noise helped me shake off the frightening feeling. I watched him as, with eyes glazed over, he stared blankly ahead as you sometimes do after a big release. I let a couple of minutes pass before asking if he was okay. He seemed calmer as he looked up and nodded.

I said, 'You didn't finish what you were saying.'

He narrowed his eyes as if trying to recall what he didn't finish saying.

'You know. You started saying something about it being more than just a fear of losing me?'

'Oh. Yeah.' He collected his thoughts before speaking. 'The thing with a deep love, it touches you in deep places. And it uncovers anything hiding in there. For me, well, it's that original abandonment. And I guess I was clinging to you to stop myself from falling into the pain of it.'

I nodded.

'And I pushed you away for the same reason.'

'Uh ...' I gave him an uncomprehending shrug.

'Clinging, withdrawal—either way, it's defensive behaviour.'

'Ah.' I didn't need to know the specific names of defence mechanisms to get it. 'But what I don't get is why you didn't wanna fall into that pain. I mean, it's not like you haven't been there before. You went into it after you found out you were adopt—'

'And it's the same kind of pain. That primal pain.' His eyes misted over. 'Only this time, it was so much worse.'

I remembered Ralph dealing with the devastation of discovering he'd been given away by his birth mother. I remembered he told me that infants might not have the resources to understand what was happening, but at some level, they 'knew'. And the pain of the early rejection, for whatever reason, was imprinted on the psyche. He'd said that as an infant, there was no way your system could cope with that intensity of pain, so it got shut down and frozen. But it was frozen in its complete, crushing form that didn't lessen with time. Even so ...

'I know you've said it's just as painful every time you feel it, but you know what to expect, so, shouldn't going through it be getting easier? Why would it be so much worse?'

'It's different this time.' His voice became soft and strained. 'When I fell into it before, you were there to help me.' Ralph used his hands a lot when he spoke, but now he dropped them into his lap. The look in his eyes communicated profound sadness. They welled with tears again. 'I think because of our intense bond ever since we were babies, you've always had my back, you've always been my lifeline. But then, all those times you pulled away from me lately ... well, there was nothing to hold onto. And no one. The pain started to thaw and I was terrified of drowning in it.'

Oh God. I covered my eyes with my hand then moved it down to my mouth. I understood that, even worse than not being his lifeline, I was hurling him into the abyss!

Seeing it from the other side helped me understand his anger, and release mine. I got up, and went and sat next to him. 'I'm sorry.'

'I know.' He paused and wiped his eyes. 'It's frightening to go back to that space where you had no voice and no cognitive resources to process what's happening. But I think you have to relive that pain from your infancy so you can release its hold over you ...' He trailed off. 'Obviously, having a psychology degree doesn't stop you from going to hell,' he snorted. A worry line formed between his brows. 'But for the sake of my health and my sanity—for the sake of our relationship—I need to go there.'

I nodded. 'Well, for what it's worth, I'm here. Not as a lifeline. Just for comfort.'

He gave me a resigned but grateful smile. Then he spoke with resoluteness. 'I also need to know the truth, even if it is ugly. It's time I started looking for my birth mother.'

PART TWO

ALPHABET SOUP

CHAPTER SEVENTEEN

Adopting New 'Tudes

Sylvia came by the next morning. I answered the door. She gasped when she saw me, braced herself against the doorjamb and rested the back of her hand against her forehead in a dramatic almost-swoon, like a woebegone character in one of her old Mills & Boon historical romance novels.

'Hello, Aunt Sylvia.' Ralph emerged from the kitchen. His sudden appearance was like smelling salts. She recovered.

'Why is he here?' It was a reprimand. I felt a headache coming on.

'He's looking after me.'

Her lips thinned and tightened. 'I'm your mother. *I'm* the one who's supposed to look after you.'

'Supposed' being the operative word.

'Is he sleeping here?' she whispered.

'Yep.' *On top of me, normally, but side-on since the accident.*

'Well, I don't want to know!'

Bugger. I was so looking forward to telling you about my orgasms.

She stayed for an hour, belly-aching about the problems with my phone the fact that I'd kept her in the dark that it was unfair to do this to a grieving widow blah blah howtiredshewashowthe weatherwasgettingherdownblahblahblah ...

I yelled at her to STOP!

She yelled back about me being an ungrateful daughter, that she'd dropped everything to come and see me (a turtle's pace drop that had taken twenty-four hours), and *this* was how I was repaying her?

I asked her what exactly she had to drop to come and see me.

Her mouth dropped.

She stormed out. *Phew.*

She called me two days later and took me to task about the call forward. 'Myron figured it out. And he thinks it's truly disgusting that you would do that!'

'Oh, who gives a shit what Myron thinks!' I bit back. She slammed the phone down.

Ten minutes later, the prig himself called. Not even bothering to ask how I was after my accident, he tried lecturing me. I told him his tut-tutting was tiresome and that being a dentist and all, he should wire his own jaw shut. And then he should do the same to our mother. Like Sylvia, he slammed the phone down. I'd just bought myself an extended period of cold-shouldering. I offered up a silent prayer of gratitude.

Ralph stayed with me until Sunday morning. He left just before Hannah and Casper were due back from Noosa. Reuben and the kids had called me every day while they were away, and they'd been relieved to hear I was getting better. But when I opened the door to greet them, they were clearly agitated.

My bruised face had turned a yellowish-brown, with small splotches of red and purple here and there. Reuben struggled for words; Casper told me I looked like a *Kandinsky*, and yet, I was no oil painting; Hannah cried.

The bruising pretty much disappeared by the end of the next week, but Hannah's bruised ego persisted. Where Casper had become indifferent to my relationship with Ralph, Hannah continued to love-hate me.

Ralph and I were becoming closer than ever, although there were many nights when he didn't want to come over. He never hid his vulnerability from me, but apparently diving into 'no-man's-land' was a solo experience. 'I don't want anyone witnessing my returns to infancy,' he said. It evoked an image of him drooling, thumb sucking and shitting himself. I have a weak stomach, and with my highly developed hippocampus— the part responsible for the storage of long-term memory—it'd be hard to erase that image from my mind's eye, which meant it would be hard to get naked with him if I were to witness it. But it wasn't like this at all. It was so much more—something I would find out several months down the track from firsthand experience.

Meantime, Ralph shared the insights that came of his experience. And he wanted to talk about the night of the accident and everything leading up to it. He kept telling me how bad he felt, and while I repeatedly assured him that it took two, I secretly gloated a little. The voices in my head had their take on this, but at least one of these—my 'human rights advocate'— had built some muscle.

The inner bitch: *'You're SUCH a bitch!'*

The human rights advocate: *'No I'm not.'*

IB: *'Oh yes you are! What kind of person gets off on someone else's pain?'*

HRA: '*A normal one. Being spiritually evolved means loving and accepting all of me. And I love myself for getting off on his pain. So, fuck you!*'

I knew I was making progress because not only had I chosen to listen to HRA over IB, but HRA was now in the first person, and IB was a more distant third.

Meanwhile, Ralph's internal progress extended to his external world. Taking a first step towards searching for his biological mother, he contacted Adoption and Family Information Service (AFIS). He initially thought it would be difficult to locate his mother because he knew his adoption had been a closed one—one where the adopted child's original birth certificate was sealed, the adoptive parents got an amended one and the child got a whole new identity, which was why Norma and Albie were able to keep it a secret from Ralph. And because the whole process had been enshrouded in secrecy, they knew nothing about his biological parents. This was almost a relief for Ralph because then he didn't have to pump them for information they weren't privy to.

He no longer gave Albie the time of day—no love lost there—and his close and loving relationship with Norma had suffered a blow. He spoke to her occasionally, but he kept her at arm's length. I felt sad for Norma. Unlike Sylvia, my aunt was kind and forgiving. Her decision to withhold something so important had been a gross error in judgement, as had been her fear-driven choice not to protect Ralph from Albie's abuse. Ralph's alienation from his parents made it easier for him to push forward with his search.

He felt very optimistic after calling AFIS. They told him the *Adoption of Children Act* was changed in 1988, and all adoption files had been released, even the closed ones. They advised him to lodge an application and they'd get back to him after a 'Veto check'. The changed Act included a Contact Veto, which gave biological and adoptive parents the option to restrict the release of information, if they wanted. Norma and Albie weren't aware of the Contact Veto. The department needed to do a check to find out if Ralph's biological mother had placed one against him.

They said there might be a delay in processing his application if a large number of them came in at the same time, and there may be further delays if the necessary research was complex. How long? Several months. Still, it didn't look like it was going to be the bureaucratic headache he'd anticipated.

My non-bureaucratic headaches were slowly abating, and had completely disappeared after three months. But they were about to be replaced by an even bigger one.

A *mother* of a headache.

CHAPTER EIGHTEEN

Nobody Puts Baby in a Corner

It started on a Friday around eleven o'clock.

I'd taken a long leave of absence and was just getting back into writing my articles again. I was sitting in the dining room in front of my laptop when Hannah, who was in the second year of a Bachelor of Arts degree, came home after one of her lectures. She looked desolate and walked past me without a word.

'Hannah? What's wrong?'

She shook her head, ran the rest of the way to her room and slammed the door. I stared after her. Clearly, she wanted to be left alone. But then, after hearing her muffled sobbing, I jumped up out of my chair and made for her bedroom. I knocked. 'Hannah?'

She didn't respond, but her crying seemed to get louder. I cracked open the door.

'Hannah, can I come in?'

No answer. I went in.

Oh no. A stomach-churning déjà vu greeted me. Hannah was lying face down across her double bed the same way my mother did—head at nine o'clock, toes at three o'clock. The scary thought I'd had several months earlier that my daughter was turning into Sylvia, bolstered by Ralph's comparison between the two, was reinforced. It sent chills down my spine. But then I reminded myself that my gorgeous fireball was nothing like her grandmother. I sat on the edge of the bed and stroked her head.

'What's wrong, Hannah?' It was probably boy trouble.

She struggled to get the words out through her shuddering gasps: 'I-I-I-I'm pre-pre-pregnant!'

My jaw dropped. Words failed me. But then I managed to get out, 'H-how did this happen?'

Hannah stopped crying, turned her tear-streaked face up towards me, eyed me with distaste and said, 'Oh my God, you're turning into Nanna!'

Oh my God! Transference and countertransference? Screw that. Oh my God, my daughter is pregnant!

'Hannah, I-I'm stunned. I don't know what to say.'

She sat up and wiped the tears from her eyes, but said nothing. She looked down at her hands, dejected. A dense, uneasy silence seemed to widen the existing breach between us. I worried that our relationship would go the way of mine with my mother. No! I wouldn't allow it. Besides, my ties to Hannah weren't woven with guilt and manipulation.

'Who's the father?' The gist of a conversation I'd overheard Hannah having with one of her girlfriends a while back was that her mixed group of friends occasionally experimented sexually with each other. It wasn't the way things happened in my adolescence, but the sexual revolution was in its infancy back then. I assumed Hannah had fallen pregnant to someone in her group. I assumed wrong.

'Alex,' she replied.

'Who's Alex?' I knew all her friends.

'My boyfriend.'

'You have a *boyfriend*?'

She looked up at me, then looked away. 'We've been together s-six months,' she stammered.

'*What?* Why am I just finding out now?' Hannah had always been a bit of an oversharer, so this hurt.

'Well, you've been so wrapped up with your *cousin*—'

'Oh, *enough*. Stop with the "your cousin" bullshit!' I didn't want to be annoyed with her in this moment, but her pouting over my life choices was getting on my nerves. 'You've milked this to the nth degree. I'm not going out of my way to upset anyone, you know. But I have a right to be happy.'

She seemed to get that she'd overdone it. 'I'm sorry, Mum.'

I calmed down, reached for her and hugged her. She cried some more then pulled away. She wiped her nose on her sleeve.

Pregnant, but still a child.

She dragged herself along the bed until she was leaning against the bedhead, and crossed her legs yoga-style. 'I met Alex at uni. He's doing a Masters of Engineering.' She picked up a little as she spoke of him. 'You'd really like him.'

'Mm. Have you told him?'

'Not yet, I just found out. I've left a message for him to call me but he's got lectures till about four.'

Neither of us said anything for a moment. I massaged my temples, as if that would temper the million thoughts running riot in my headspace. I'd have to deal with how this affected me later. For now, though, I had to help my daughter. 'Look. These things happen. It's not the end of the world. I can call my gynaecologist and find out if he can take care of it, or if he can gi—'

'What do you mean, "take care of it"?' She cast me a dubious look.

'Um, a termination.'

'I am *not* having an abortion!'

'Hannah! You can't have a baby, you're only eighteen!'

'I would *never* abort Alex's baby. And I'm almost nineteen.'
She counted on her fingers. 'I'll be about nineteen and a half
when the baby's born.'

'But—'

'It's not your call!'

She was right. But sometimes I wished my kids were docile
like Myron's sons. I shivered, berated myself for the thought and
banished it.

'No, but it's not only yours, either. Alex has a say, too.'

'He'll want me to have it. Alex and I are in love.'

'Really? You've only known him for what, all of six
months?'

'So? So what? It was love at first sight for both of us. Alex
is the love of my life.'

I didn't want to say what would she know about love at her
age. The look on her face when she spoke about him shored up
the conviction in her words. It was hard to argue with that. So, I
tried a commonsensical approach.

'I'm happy you've found that; really, I am. But you can't
live on love. How's he going to support you?'

'He's almost finished his degree and he's had a couple of
fantastic job offers. Alex is a genius, Mum. He did a combined
degree: Bachelor of Engineering and Bachelor of Arts.'

I just nodded and tried to think of other important questions.
'Does Dad know about him?'

This one made her uneasy. 'Yes.'

It didn't do much for me either. Like I wasn't already feeling
forsaken enough.

'But he hasn't met him.'

Okay. A bit better.

'Have you met his parents?'

'No.'

Even better.

'And I'm not gonna tell Dad till I tell Alex. Please don't say anything to anyone.'

Anyone meant Ralph. I didn't mind so much because she started opening up. Her face softened and took on an ethereal glow as she told me all about Alexander Dion Agathe (pronounced a-GAHT).

Alex was twenty-four and of Greek and French descent. Again, I asked her how it had happened, meaning, wasn't she on the pill? She said she was but then she remembered she'd been sick several weeks earlier. I remembered she'd had a bout of vomiting and diarrhoea one Saturday morning. She remembered that it was just after she'd taken the pill—pity she didn't remember at the time. We remembered she'd felt better by mid-morning, then went out for lunch. A smile crossed her face. She must have remembered she'd had Alex for lunch.

I made us lunch. We took our sandwiches into the lounge room, sat cross-legged on the floor on either side of the coffee table and talked for the next couple of hours. She caught me up on the minutiae of anything and everything that I'd missed hearing about during our estrangement. Peppering a lot of her tales with 'OhmyGod', and weaving 'like' into every second sentence, she intoned as only a teenager could. For a while there, I forgot she was pregnant. It was nice to reconnect with my daughter.

Another half-hour passed before Hannah's mobile phone rang-sang 'Let Me Blow Ya Mind'.

'Oh my God, it's Alex!' She retrieved her phone from the coffee table and leapt up off the floor. 'Alex' was *dropping glasses, shaking asses, yeah bitch*, as Hannah hotfooted it to her bedroom.

She was back five minutes later flashing me a wide grin. 'Alex thinks it's super. He's majorly buzzed!'

Super. I was majorly buzzed that he was majorly buzzed, but I was also majorly concerned that the two of them saw this as just another super adventure.

Hannah told me Alex was on his way here. We talked for another half-hour until the sound of the doorbell interrupted our conversation. She raced to the door, wrenched it open and threw herself into the arms of one seriously good-looking boy. Or man. I stood up and waited, feeling awkward and trying not to listen to their whispers between fevered kisses.

'I love you so much, Ally baby.'

'I love you so much, Hanny baby.'

Young love—a good minute's worth before Hannah realised she had an audience. She drew her beau into the lounge.

'Mum, this is Alex.'

Alex put out his hand. 'Very nice to meet you, Mrs Gold.' He was soft-spoken but he had a firm grip—a favourable sign.

'Nice to meet you, Alex. And it's Ruth. You can call me Ruth.' Mrs Gold sounded old.

Alex had quite a presence. At around six feet tall, he towered over Hannah. He had thick black hair, olive skin and dark brown eyes. His tight, faded jeans and white, long-sleeved grandad shirt defined his lean masculinity. Alex's body, like his face, looked sculpted.

Hannah and Alex were a genetically blessed couple who would no doubt have a beautiful child. But watching my daughter as she clung to him and gazed at him like a wonderstruck groupie, I had trouble reconciling Hanny baby with Hanny 'n' baby.

'Mum!'

'Mm? What?'

'You are staring.' She said it through tight lips. Her expression conveyed, *Like, oh my God, like, you're creeping me out!*

'Oh, oh. Sorry. I, I ... Alex, would you like a cup of tea?'

He smiled at me. 'No, I'm fine thank—'

'We're going to my room.' Hanny baby had Ally baby by the sleeve. Hopefully, not by the balls as well.

'Uh-huh.'

'Just to talk, Mother!'

Like, what difference would it make if you did more than talk? Like, you're already, like, pregnant. 'Sure.' Then, as an afterthought I said, 'Are you gonna call your dad?'

'Oh yeah. I'll do it now.'

They disappeared into Hannah's room, and Reuben called me about five minutes later.

'So. We're gonna be grandparents!' He was really excited about it. He said he'd told Hannah he would come over after work so we could all talk, and he offered to pick up Thai for dinner. That was still a few hours away and I had work to do.

I sat back down in front of the laptop. Half an hour later, the word count hadn't advanced. I needed a change of scenery. I needed to focus. So I moved to the lounge room, sprawled on the sofa and focused on the ceiling.

I was still there when Casper got home from school.

He dropped his bag on the floor with a thud and followed the direction of my gaze. 'The tyranny of the blank ceiling, huh?'

'Yyyyep.' I sat up and took in my handsome son with his tie loosened and skew-whiff, and half of his shirt tail hanging out. 'How was your day?'

'It was ... action-packed. Fascinating,' he deadpanned.

'Good. It's about to get a lot more action-packed and fascinating.'

He raised an eyebrow just as Hannah and Alex emerged from her room. Hannah introduced him to Alex. They shook hands.

'Guess what?' she said.

'Ooh,' he shrugged, 'I dunno. You're pregnant?'

Hannah's face dropped. She turned to me. 'You *told* him?'

'No, I didn't *tell* him!'

'Huh?' Casper's eyes and mouth widened proportionately. 'I was just kidding. Seriously? You're pregnant?'

'Uh-huh.'

Casper whooped! He looked at Alex. 'Should I assume it's yours?'

'Jesus,' Hannah mumbled and rolled her eyes. Alex nodded.

'So ...' Casper smiled, 'I'm gonna be an uncle.' He turned to me. 'And you're gonna be a gran'ma. How cool is that?'

Real cool. Super cool. Majorly cool. I gave him a laconic 'Mm.'

The three of them left me there and moved to the kitchen. A cacophony of animated chatter, slamming cupboards, clattering plates and chiming cutlery reached me from a faraway land, and mingled with a disorderly jumble of thoughts.

'Mum!'

'Mm? What?'

'Alex is talking to you.'

'Oh. Sorry, Alex.' I gave him a thin smile. 'I'm still trying to process this.'

He sat down on the opposite couch. Nice move in terms of unseen power dynamics. We were now on an equal footing. 'That's okay. I understand,' he said.

Impressive. Had he majored in Psychology in his BA? Hannah sat down next to him. The two of them held hands.

'I just want you to know I'm in love with your daughter, Mrs Gold—Ruth.' The smitten pair gazed into each other's eyes.

Alex turned back to me. 'Hannah's "The One". She's my "Twin Flame".'

Holy shitballs, Batman! 'Twin Flame,' I repeated. I swallowed hard.

'Yes. According to Plato, a Twin—'

'Mm-hmm. I'm familiar with the concept.' I smiled at him. He and Hannah smiled at each other.

Hannah squeezed his arm with her free hand. 'Alex majored in Philosophy.'

Oh, joy. Just what this family needed—another Neo-Platonist. Wasn't Hannah supposed to look for someone like Reuben? What did it say that she'd found someone like Ralph?

'Are you planning to marry her?'

'Mu-um!'

'What? It's a fair question. You're expecting a child together.'

'Well, you don't need to get married these days.' Hannah had a hard time of it when Reuben and I split.

I looked at Alex. He looked at Hannah and then back at me. 'I would love to marry Hannah. But I'm happy to go along with whatever she wants.'

Yep. She had him by the balls. I smiled at him and said to Hannah, 'Okay, then. Let's wait till your father gets here to discuss the, uh, practicalities?'

'Sure. Anyway, we need to go to Alex's place so I can meet his parents and so we can tell 'em.'

I remained on the couch after they left, tuning out the music coming from Casper's room and once again, trying to get my head around all of it. I waited about half an hour before calling Ralph. I didn't think Hannah would mind, seeing as the immediate families now knew. I called work but he'd finished up for the day. I called him at home; he'd just walked in the door. He was stunned by the news, but also delighted. 'Hey, Granny!'

I seemed to be the only one not delighted or excited or majorly buzzed. It made me feel bad. But then ... it wasn't that I was unhappy about it. I just felt kind of sad. In one fell swoop, my daughter was about to leave the nest and build one of her own. It seemed like only yesterday I became a mum. My thoughts drifted back in time.

A three-year-old Hannah sitting on my lap imploring me, 'Mummy, pleath, *pleath* read the Bippolo Theed.' Dr Seuss's Bippolo Seed, her favourite story, was about McKluck the duck finding a magical, wish-granting Bippolo seed. He just needed to plant it and make a wish, which would sprout and grow out of a Bippolo tree. But McKluck the schmuck didn't think big. He wished for only a week's worth of food until an overambitious, money-grubbing cat persuaded him to wish for way more than he needed. The two of them got high on wishing for useless shit (like, seriously, who needs a thousand kangaroo-hair shirts or five million banjos?). In the end, greed—not wishing—was their undoing and they lost the seed. And that was the end of that!

I almost knew the story off by heart I'd read it to Hannah so often. And it was a good one. It taught her about different kinds of wishing, and how to apply them effectively. When she was five, she told me, 'I hate you so much! Sara's mummy lets her stay up really late and eat chocolate all the time. I'm going to keep wishing hard for a mummy just like Sara's.' *Wishful thinking*. When she was seven, she told me, 'Sometimes I hate you, but mostly I love you so, so much. You're the best mummy ever!' I let her stay up really late that night and eat chocolate. *Wish fulfilment*.

Hannah wished for a lot. She might have been a dreamer, but she was also a doer. If she wanted something badly enough, she went for it with dogged determination. I admired her tenacity. It was what I used to be like, and was becoming once again. I hoped that, unlike me, Hannah would never lose her feistiness. She must have wished hard for a great love, a good man. From what I could see, she'd got her wish.

Ralph's voice brought me back into the moment. 'Ruthie?'

'Huh? What?'

'Have you heard anything I've said?'

'Oh, uh ... sorry, I'm a little distracted.'

'I said it was always one of my fantasies to get it on with a grandmother.' His voice was thick and seductive.

I laughed. 'Always as in recently?'

'No-no. Always.'

Uh-oh.

I'd known about Ralph's fantasies in adolescence—French maids, cheerleaders, naughty constables, friendly skies flight attendants—but he'd never said anything about a babushka. Oh God ... what if he wanted to play dress-ups? Him donning a Big Bad Wolf mask; me wearing a twin set, pearls, orthopaedic shoes and a plaid woollen skirt covering crotchless knickers?

Fetishist.

Kinkies just weren't my thing. So, what would keep the wolf at bay? Ah, yes. An equally unpalatable thought. The she-wolf—she who needed to be told. *Shit.*

'Um, would you consider getting together with a great-grandmother?'

Silence.

'Hello?'

'W-what are you saying?'

'Sylvia.'

'Oh, *ugh*—that is beyond the pale!'

'Oh, *ecch*. No!' I switched on the simper. 'I meant, would you mind being the one to tell her?'

'Uh, yeah, I would mind. But I wouldn't mind watching you tell her.' I could hear the smile in his voice.

Voyeur.

Ralph psychobabbled about the need to assert myself, to show strength, empowerme—

'Gotta go.' Grateful for the *cltkty* sound of a key being inserted in the front door lock, I hung up.

Hannah came in. She was alone.

'Where's Alex?'

'He's just ducked over to his friend's place to get a copy of the notes from the lecture he missed this arvo. Won't be long. The guy lives a couple of streets away.'

'Okay. So. What are his parents like? How'd it go?'

She started laughing but kept on walking to her room. 'Oh, you are gonna love Alex's dad,' she said over her shoulder. 'And his mum's real warm and fuzzy.'

'Meaning?' I called after her.

'Chill. You'll be meeting them in a coupla weeks.' She was still laughing as she disappeared around the corner.

I got to her room just as she plopped down on her bed—the right orientation this time. She'd auto-corrected.

'What's in a coupla weeks?' I stood in the doorway.

'Alex's mum's gonna call you an' invite you over for Sunday week.' She laughed to herself again. 'She wanted to do it this Sunday but we've got Leah's engagement.'

Leah was my niece, Iris and Joel's daughter. I adored her and so did my kids. Like her mother, and like Hannah, Leah was spirited. But at least she was doing things in the right order. Engagement first. And it was going to be a long engagement because she was also very young.

'Fine, but what did they say? How did they react?'

She shrugged. 'Pretty much like you. Stunned, at first. And then they asked what we were gonna do about it. Well, I told them we're having it and it's not up for debate. They started warming to the idea, and by the time we left, they were thrrrrrilled.'

Hannah giggled again, but I read this as a dig at me seeing as I wasn't thrrrrrilled.

At the sound of the doorbell, Hannah almost sent me flying as she charged past me. Yet again, she threw herself into Alex's arms. Understandable. They hadn't seen each other for five minutes. I'd only ever experienced that kind of greeting in the years before I moved out of home. And it came from our dog, Mitzi the Maltese terrier.

Reuben rocked up half an hour later, bringing with him a mouth-watering mix of garlicky, aromatic, spicy wafts. Hannah introduced Alex and we all sat around the dining table digging into our Tod Mun Pla, Pad Si-iu, Phat Phak Boong Fai Daeng, Hor Mok Ma Prow Awn, stink beans and rice.

Alex's air of quiet self-assurance seemed to desert him. Unsurprising. He cleared his throat a lot —*ahem*—maybe from nerves. Or post-nasal drip. Or maybe he had acid reflux. But one thing was for sure—he had a good appetite. He did eat kind of delicately, though, like a girl, in contrast to Casper and Reuben, who shovelled their food like a pair of hoofed ruminants that had just taken a massive dump and needed to fill the void.

With dinner over, it was Q & A time.

How would Alex support Hannah and the baby?

'I graduate in a couple of months, *ahem*, and I have two very good job offers, *ahem*. I just have to decide which one I want to accept.'

Where were they planning to live?

'Hannah and I have talked about it, *ahem*, and we plan to look for a place once I start my job. I've been working part-time since I was sixteen, *ahem*, and I've got savings. But I'd prefer not to dip into them for rent. *Ahem*.'

Ahem was integrated into Alex's speech pattern, but he answered all our questions to our satisfaction, so I stopped noticing it so much.

By the time his mum, Rhea, called on Sunday afternoon to invite us all for afternoon tea the following Sunday, I'd warmed a little to the idea of becoming a grandmother.

Rhea seemed affable. We chatted easily like old friends, but I needed to cut the conversation short because we had to leave for Leah's engagement.

Iris and Joel were hosting the open house in their backyard for about eighty guests. The she-wolf would be roaming among them. My gut roiled at the thought.

CHAPTER NINETEEN

Sticky Situations

The weather was perfect. Waiters wove through the crowd with trays of drinks and hors d'oeuvres. I'd just finished an arancini ball, and picked up two mini banana cream pies. I stopped short of popping one in my mouth when I saw Reuben heading towards me. He had a wet, brown, Jackson Pollock-like splatter pattern across his shirtfront.

'What the hell happened to you?'

'Your mother sprayed a mouthful of Coke on me when I asked her how she felt about becoming a great-grandmother.'

Oh shit. 'Oops.' I gave him a forced smile. 'I was gonna tell her today. You know, in public where she wouldn't make a scene.'

'Sure.' Reuben looked past me. 'Aaaand, here she comes now. See ya!'

'No. Wait!'

Reuben raised his hand without looking back at me. 'You're on your own.' Nothing had changed.

I turned to see Sylvia advancing on me. She was wearing a black dress and a scowl. *Crap.*

She grabbed me by the arm, pulled me away from the other guests, and snarled, 'Just when were you going to tell me Hannah is pregnant?'

'Uh, she only just found out a couple of days ago and didn't want to say anything yet.'

'Well, *you* knew.'

'*What?* I'm her mother!'

'And I'm *your* mother,' she snapped. 'Even Reuben knows and you're divorced!'

'*What?* Divorced or not, Reuben is her father.'

'*Hmph.*' She narrowed her eyes. 'I knew that girl would get into trouble one day.'

Her reproof raised my hackles. 'She did not get into trouble. She got pregnant.'

Sylvia sniffed haughtily. 'Yes, and your father would be turning in his grave!'

A man of many talents.

'The boy is *Greek*, for God's sake.'

'Yeah. So what?'

Sylvia glowered at me. 'You know, your daughter is just like you,' she huffed. Her lip curled in disgust—the harpy preparing to swoop and befoul. 'No. I take that back. At least you married someone Jewish, and you remained a virgin till you were married. *Ta fille est pire que toi*—she's much worse than you. *Une pute!*'

'*Excuse* me? Don't you dare call my daughter a slut!'

Sylvia cowered under my glare.

'Maybe *you* need to have your mouth washed out with soap.' I could bare my incisors with the best of them.

She recoiled from the venom in my tone. I took advantage of the moment and threw in some bitchy, too. 'Oh, and for the record, I was not a virgin. Glen, remember him? He was my first. And there were many, many others after him.'

Her breath catching, Sylvia placed a hand over her heart. Without so much as another word, she slunk away, but not before giving me a withering look.

Although this stock response had lost some of its firepower, it got to me today. I stuffed both the banana cream pies into my mouth and fed my intractable inner bitch. It seemed to be my just desserts for that last little bite of spite.

IB: *'You contemptible person. You are so bad!'*

I whispered back, *'I know. I am tho vad, I'm good.'*

'Who are you talking to?' Ralph came up behind me.

'My vloody muver.'

I swallowed, and filled him in on my face-off with Sylvia. He clenched his fist in disapproval of her bitchiness, but then he fist-bumped me for mine just as Maxi and Vette were approaching us.

Maxi looked back and forth between the two of us. 'Yo, yo, Beeotch 'n' Homie. Wass goin' down?'

Ralph didn't miss a beat. 'You, tonight, most likely.' Maxi was going on a first date with a media mogul.

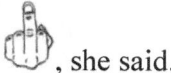, she said.

It helped dissipate my anger. I told them what had gone down. More fist-clenching, more fist-bumping. We moved on.

'Hannah's glowing. She looks so happy,' Vette said.

'Mm.' I nodded. 'She is.'

I'd told Vette and Maxi about Hannah's honeybun and bun in the oven when I'd spoken with each of them the day before. Like everyone else, they were astounded but ecstatic. I'd sworn them to secrecy.

The four of us now stood there observing the lovebirds. Stuck on each other and stuck to each other, they looked like

Siamese Twin Flames. They were talking to Leah and her fiancé, Ari, and another openly affectionate couple. It was like watching a touch-feely encounter group interact.

'Um ... why's Alex keep doing that thing with his shoulder?' Vette asked.

I looked at him again. 'Oh, yeah.' Until she'd pointed it out, I hadn't noticed that he shrugged his left shoulder every so often. I wondered if he was moving it to the beat of *ahem*.

'I do that when my bra strap slips down,' Vette said.

'Never happens to me,' Maxi said. 'My knockers are too big.'

'Mine, too,' I said. 'But it still happens sometimes. Just means I have to tighten the strap.'

'Mm. Mm,' Ralph said thoughtfully.

We often spoke like this in Ralph's presence. He'd always been more like one of the girls than one of the boys. But we still found it amusing when he contributed to our ditsy natter.

'What? You have that problem too?' Maxi teased.

Vette and I laughed.

Ralph smiled. 'Nah. I've got solid pecs,' he said, beating his chest like Tarzan. He pointed at each of us in turn—'You two have big fun bags; you missed out'—then he pointed to Alex—'and he's got a tic.'

I loved it when Ralph occasionally displayed average bloke tendencies. Maxi and I tittered; Vette gave him a gentle shove that nearly sent him toppling. (Macho, but still one of the girls.)

I stared at Alex again then looked back at Ralph. 'You think it's a tic?'

'Well, it's not a shoulder stretch. He's doing it every eight seconds.'

'And you're *timing* him?' Maxi made the wanker sign with her hand.

Ralph arched one eyebrow inquisitively. 'Practising for the date?'

Before Maxi could respond, I whispered, *'Hey? Isn't that Henry the First?'*

I nodded in the direction of a familiar-looking man standing several metres away behind Ralph. I'd noticed him earlier. He'd been circling us for a while, sneaking peeks at Vette. The three of them turned to look at him. The man snuck another glance, his cheeks flushing when he realised he'd been caught out.

'Henry?' Vette gave him a quizzical half-smile.

He smiled back. 'Vette? It is you, isn't it?'

Vette and Henry had been an item for several weeks when she was seventeen and he was twenty-seven. Maxi and I thought they were made for each other, mostly because they kind of looked alike. We'd nicknamed him Henry the First, not because he bore any resemblance to the English king, but because he took Vette's virginity.

He came over and they hugged. 'So, what's your connection here?' he asked Vette, spreading his arms out to indicate his surroundings.

'I'm friends with Iris. And you?'

'An indirect one. I came with my girlfriend. She works with Joel.'

Well, things were looking up because Henry the First used to come on his own.

If he had been like King Henry, who held the record for the largest number of acknowledged illegitimate children born to any English king, he probably would have left their mothers very unsatisfied. Henry the First was not much chop in the sack. Vette had guided him to her bean, but he didn't have the patience to pulse it. The earth never moved for her, she thought he was selfish, they argued and their relationship came to a sticky end.

'You haven't changed a bit, you know,' he said to Vette, his eyes lighting up. 'You're still beautiful.'

It's probably from the many, many orgasms she's had since she dumped you. So very many. And not just from solo performances. A hell of a lot. Good for the complexion.

'Thank you.' Vette blushed. 'You look good, too.'

She was right. His Afro fuzz had been sheared off into a number four buzz cut. His black hair had only a smattering of grey showing at the temples. He'd remained trim and his skin was still smooth (he must have also had many, many orgasms).

'Do you remember my friends, Maxi, Ruth and Ralph?'

Of course he did. He shook Ralph's hand and gave Maxi and me a peck on the cheek, then turned his attention back to Vette. We left them to catch up on almost thirty years' worth of news. Maxi resumed her verbal fencing with Ralph and I tuned in and out of the two conversations on either side of me.

'... career girl ... travel ... no time and energy for a relationship ...'

'Being an expert wanker, maybe you can give me some tips?'

'Why? After thirty years' experience, you're an old hand.'

'... I've also never married ... no kids ... none that I know of, anyway. Ha, ha, ha ...'

Ha! Henry the First and Last. He'd probably disseminated all over Adelaide, spawned a bunch of frizzy-haired sprogs and been responsible for an exponential increase in the sale of vibrators.

Maxi nudged me and whispered, *'What are those two talking about?'*

Just as I was about to answer, Henry walked away and Vette turned to us. 'We're having dinner tomorrow night.'

'What?' Maxi and I chorused.

'Hmm ... I didn't know you were into threesomes—you, Henry and his girlfriend.' Ralph had a wolfish grin on his face and a somewhere-else look in his eyes.

Please God, don't let him ask me to be party to one of these.

'Oh.' Vette reddened and fingered her necklace. It was quaint. 'I-I'm not! They actually broke up a couple of weeks ago. But they're still friends.'

'And yet, he made a point of saying he came with his girlfriend. Not friend, *girl*friend,' Maxi said.

'It didn't work with him back then, Vette,' I said. 'What if he hasn't changed?'

'People don't usually,' said Maxi.

'I don't agree,' Ralph said. 'People can chan—'

'Guys. Guys! *I've* changed. Back then I thought I needed a man.'

Back then, we girls all thought we needed a man. The fairy-tale prince and all. For Vette (and Maxi), it was a passing fancy, though. Her mum, her role model for a woman, had managed without one. A single mother after her husband died when Vette was two, she provided well for both her son and daughter. It was an exemplar of independence that had served Vette well. She might have the mien of the damsel, but she was no pushover. She didn't get where she was in her professional life by being meek. Yep, Vette could hold her own. And if it didn't work out with Henry, she said, then he could go back to holding *his* own.

The rest of the afternoon passed without incident. It was a fairy-tale party. Some loving speeches, an abundance of good food, genial chitchat, and the high point—Sylvia looked the other way when I passed her on my way out. My definition of a happy ending.

The next morning, Hannah stopped glowing. She woke me at six o'clock when she crawled into my bed.

'Mummy, I feel soooooo sick.'

I loved that she called me Mummy; didn't love that she had to go through morning sickness. But Alex came over every night to be with her. He tended to her many needs (just like Ralph had done for me after the accident). He *ahemmed* lots but his shoulder didn't get jiggy, not when I saw him, anyway. Maybe he just twitched in public.

Ralph, who wasn't regressing to infancy as often, was also over every night. He and Alex had hit it off from the get-go. Not many people in Ralph's world gave a shit about the Hellenistic period or Socratic debate. Alex did. Two nerdlingers, they had found each other. (Maybe Plato was a bit limited with his idea of Twin Flames. Maybe souls split into Triplet or Quadruplet Flames.)

In that short time, Hannah and Ralph's close relationship came back to life, but she wasn't too happy about him monopolising her man. I reminded her 'sharing is caring', and told her she needed to cut Alex some slack seeing as he was prepared to hold her hair back from her face while she puked.

I liked Alex and looked forward to meeting his parents. I was in no way prepared for what that Sunday afternoon would bring.

CHAPTER TWENTY

Hectoring

Hannah threw up once after she woke, felt a little seedy for the rest of the morning, but was okay by the time we were ready to leave. Ralph questioned the earliness of the afternoon tea—we were invited for one-thirty. I didn't give a crap. My gut's circadian rhythm had no respect for clock time.

Hannah and I went with Ralph. Reuben followed in his car with Casper.

Hannah was out of the car and running the minute we pulled up outside Alex's place. The front door flew open and he stepped out to greet her, lifting her up, twirling her in his arms and then kissing her passionately.

'Ahh, vicarious pleasure,' I said to Ralph as we watched them.

'It doesn't have to be vicarious.' He turned to look at me. 'I'd happily greet you that way if you let me.'

Sometimes it's just so much better to keep my mouth shut.

Alex's family home in Somerton Park was a triple-fronted, sixties house with a flagstone façade and a red tiled roof. A long concrete driveway to the left of the house led to a garage at the back of the property. The large front lawn was split in half by a gravel path leading to a wide, pillared porch. Our footsteps crunched over the coarse stones as we made our way towards Alex, who was waiting for us on the porch with one arm around Hannah. He shook hands with Reuben, Casper and Ralph, and gave me a hesitant peck on the cheek.

I'd already learned from Alex that his dad, Hector, who had a Greek father and French mother, was born in France. Hector's birth name was Ettore. His family moved to Australia when he was fifteen, and they'd anglicised his name. What Alex had told us about Hector made him sound very exotic. I expected him to be tall, dark and handsome like Alex, so I was surprised and disappointed when a short-statured, fair-skinned man appeared in the doorway. He was a sight.

His ginger hair was styled in a floppy Elvis Presley quiff (it was a coif that, in my opinion, had made The King of Rock and Roll himself look like a right dick, but at least he wasn't smote with red hair). Hector's long, bushy mutton chops framed a wide face with puppy-dog jowls. He had a Homer Simpsonesque three hundred and sixty-degree paunch—a muffin top straining against a button down, figure-hugging, retro sixties, paisley shirt in swirly pinks, greens and oranges. A mud-brown belt with a bronze buckle held up his low-slung jeans that were tucked into mud-brown, leather inlay rodeo boots. I feared we might be in for a rough ride.

Or not. Hector received us effusively. 'So nice to meet you all,' he said with the slightest trace of a French accent. As we introduced ourselves, he shook hands with the men and kissed me on both cheeks. I silently berated myself for judging him based on his appearance.

He ushered us inside as he said, 'Come in, come in, co-gwandpawents-to-be!'

What the fuck?

I stopped dead. Reuben ran into the back of me. Mumbling an apology, he looked like he'd been sucker-punched.

Had Bugs Bunny's archenemy Elmer Fudd ('I'm wooking for a wabbit') uprooted himself from the Warner Bros. lot and relocated to Somerton Park?

Ralph, who was behind Reuben, was straight-faced, but his eyes held a glint of amusement. I snuck a peek behind him at Hannah. She was trying hard to suppress a giggle. *Bitch.* She and Casper exchanged conspiratorial smirks. I planned to list them both on eBay when we got home.

'Hello, Ruth?'

Recognising that rich, throaty contralto voice from our phone conversation a week earlier, I turned towards the direction it came from. Rhea approached with an extended hand. 'I've so looked forward to meeting you.' We shook hands and kissed and I handed her a gift-wrapped box of chocolates. (Sylvia had drummed into me that a good guest never shows up empty-handed.)

I stared at her as Hector formally introduced 'Whea' to the others.

Several inches taller than her husband, she wore tight white slacks and a three-quarter sleeve, black and white-striped top that showed off her blocky, athletic build. She was a handsome woman. And I say 'handsome' because she was attractive, yet androgynous in appearance. Her ebony black hair, styled in a pageboy cut, framed her face with its solid square jaw, thin lips and a sharp, patrician nose. If you put her in a suit and tie and cut her hair a little shorter, she could have easily passed for a good-looking bloke. But it wasn't this so much that captured my attention. Rhea was über-hairy.

She had thick, close-knit eyebrows (not quite like Frida Kahlo's), which was no big deal because some consider lush brows sexy. But she had a soul patch—a small tuft of hair just beneath her lower lip. I knew a 'mouche' was considered a symbol of cool, but to my mind, only for a man. Rhea's uncool mouche was dark, as was her upper lip hair. I wondered why a woman who was so well groomed didn't see fit to wax.

It might have been a tad disturbing, but I didn't hold this against her. *Au contraire.* My dirty goddess Baubo was a hairy bitch. She was depicted as a headless freak whose facial features were on her belly—her nipples were her eyes, her belly button was her nose, her vulva was her mouth. So the hair surrounding Baubo's 'mouth' was coarse 'n' curly pubic. At least Rhea's facial hair was downy.

Other than knowing Rhea was Greek, I knew nothing else about her roots. But I knew there was a tribe in ancient mythology, the Gorgades, whose women were hairy mongs. Maybe, like me, the ancient part of Rhea's brain was plump and full, and she had a strong link to the early stories and their characters. These bonds explained my foul mouth and, probably, her hairiness. Maybe they were also the reason Rhea and I had an instant rapport—we were like-(ancient)-minded.

I stopped staring and caught Hannah's look, which said, *It's not like I didn't warn you.* I remembered her obscure tip-off— '*thrrrrrilled*' and 'warm and fuzzy'. I threw a sarcastic look back at her that said, *Thanks for the heads up.*

Alex didn't appear to be embarrassed by his parents. I was impressed, but also a little concerned. Alex seemed too good to be true.

Hector intruded on my musings. 'Come! Let's go into the living woom.'

Okay, in his favour, unlike Elmer, he still had his L's.

The living 'woom' had exposed timber floorboards and a big, maroon, Persian rug in the centre. Two large, two-seater couches upholstered in taupe and white-striped linen faced each other on the rug and were separated by an oblong, glass-top coffee table. A long mahogany sideboard sat perpendicular to the couches and took up most of the wall facing the window. A tall mahogany grandfather clock stood next to the double doors that opened into the adjoining dining room.

Reuben pointed to it. 'My grandparents had one just like that,' he said to Rhea. 'It had an annoying Westminster chime.'

She smiled and nodded. 'I don't know what kind of chime this one has—it hasn't worked in years. Nor has the clock. It's really just a showpiece; it belonged to my grandmother. I haven't bothered to get it fixed. I think the chiming would drive me crazy.'

We filed past the sideboard. It was overcrowded with memory snapshots. About thirty framed pictures of various sizes competed for attention. Ralph scanned them as he walked past, slowed, and then stopped. Seemed one small picture partially hidden at the back like an afterthought had caught his eye. It was of a younger Hector with a big-busted, pudgy woman who was about the same height as him. They were standing in front of a restaurant, his arm was around her and both were smiling. She had curly black hair and a Mediterranean complexion. Her pretty face looked vaguely familiar. Ralph leaned forward, stared and pointed.

'Who's this with you?' he asked.

Hector hesitated, then said, 'That's my late wife.' He cleared his throat nervously. 'Alex's mother.'

That got our attention. All eyes were on Hector.

We'd just assumed Rhea was Alex's mother. After a moment's silence, I heard Hannah whisper to Alex, *'I thought I knew everything about you. Why didn't you tell me?'*

Before he could answer her, Hector explained, 'Alex was only two and a half when his mother died. We don't talk much about her. He doesn't weally have memowies of her. And Whea's been in our lives for so long, she's "Mum" to him.'

'That's why,' Alex said in a hushed tone.

Alex was the image of his mother. I assumed that was why there was an air of familiarity about her. I wanted to know what she died from, but Hector's comments didn't invite questions. I tried to listen in on Hannah and Alex's whispered conversation behind me, but got distracted by Ralph. 'That face ...' he said as he leaned in again and studied the picture. He turned to Hector. 'What was her name?'

'Lawissa.'

'Lawissa? Oh, La*r*issa.' Ralph examined the picture again. 'Not Larissa Pallas?'

'Yes! You knew her?'

'I did. I dated her for a few months.'

Ah, of course. I remembered Larissa, but I hadn't known her last name. She'd been a sylphlike version of this woman in the picture when she and Ralph were an item. Larissa was really into Ralph, but he broke up with her because she started making noise about getting married.

Hector slowly nodded. 'Intewesting. She told me about all her past boyfwiends, but she never mentioned you.'

Bitchy.

'Hmm, maybe because I was the one who ended it.'

Touché!

A little bit of tension there. Rhea tried to ease it. 'It is a small world, though, isn't it?'

'Yep, six degwees of sepawation,' Hector added with an edge of snarkiness.

'Well, technically, it's only three degrees of separation.'

Oh God. Please help! Ralph's gonna turn this into a pissing contest.

God heard. He passed the mantle on to Rhea, who gave one loud clap that jolted Hannah and Alex out of their little heart-to-heart and scared the crap out of everyone else. 'So. Who's for tea, who's for coffee?'

Rhea took our orders, refusing any offers of help. She asked us to please make ourselves comfortable and she disappeared into the kitchen. I sat in between Reuben and Ralph on the sofa facing the dining room. Hannah and Alex sat on the sofa opposite. Hector carried a chair in from the dining room and positioned himself at the end of the coffee table nearest Ralph. In his elevated position and with his chin jutting out, he favoured Ralph with a look that said, *My dick's bigger than yours.*

Uh-oh.

As Rhea came back into the lounge and placed a large plunger of coffee and a teapot on the coffee table, Ralph favoured me with a look that said, *Let the games begin.*

Uh-oh.

Rhea made several trips to the kitchen, returning with crockery, cutlery, serviettes, and trays of food. She pointed to each tray and told us the Greek and English names of the pastries and cakes: spanakopita (spinach and feta triangles), tiropitakia (little cheese pies), portokalopita (a Greek orange filo cake), pasta flora (Greek jam tart). There was also a platter of assorted sandwich quarters.

Rhea sat next to Hannah and handed each of us a plate. 'Please help yourselves. Don't be shy.'

Shit. I'm gonna be sick.

It wasn't like it seemed uninviting; it all looked appetising. But with the tension in the room growing thicker, it all took the shape of comfort food. The lounge room had turned into an amphitheatre. The two gladiators, Ralph and Hector, primed themselves for battle. Rhea felt it too.

The fierce, hairy Gorgades tribeswoman shot her husband a death glare. He cleared his throat and got fidgety. I elbowed Ralph, he who exuded confidence that he would be sacrificing

Hector to the gods. He remained focused on his plate, but there was no missing the little smile that played on his lips.

After a long, uncomfortable minute passed while the two men sharpened their tongues, I asked Hector, 'So, where does Alex get his height from?'

'Lawissa's dad was tall.' Hector was an open-mouth chewer. Like a camel. *Eww.* I wanted to vomit at the sight of the green and white slimy swill sloshing around in his mouth. 'Um—'

No-no-no. Please swallow before you say any more.

'—He was six foot thwee.' Some of the moosh sprayed out of Hector's mouth and landed on the spanakopita plate just as Ralph reached for one of the little triangles. He withdrew his hand, shuddered with revulsion and took a tiropitakia instead from the plate next to it.

There was another lapse in conversation. The only noise was the loud *tick-tick* of the grandpa clock.

Huh? How could that be? Rhea said the clock didn't work. And ... come to think of it, it was more a *click-click* than a *tick-tick.*

Jesus! It was coming from Hector. It wasn't enough that he ate with his mouth open; his jaw *click-clicked* as he chewed. I offered up a silent prayer of thanks that Ralph wasn't *nom nom nomming* today. Although, if he were, it would have been the only way he and Hector would be in sync. And then if Joe had been here—he used to suction his food: *ooophth-thp-thp-thp*— we could have had percussion, brass and wind.

Hector stopped clicking, made a short sharp *mm* noise, and lifted his finger to forestall conversation.

Swallow before you speak, for God's sake, man!

He didn't hear. I felt my food trying to come back up as he camel-spoke. 'Alex told me about your wespective pwofessions.

You're pwobably wondewing how I make a cwust?' He paused. It was like a drum roll.

Ralph shrugged. 'Not really.'

Shit. Hector threw him a dirty look. Ralph raised a taunting eyebrow at him. This was not going to end well. I felt my anxiety rising and shoved a sandwich quarter into my mouth to push it back down.

With a supercilious sniff, Hector said, 'I'm a top sales wep employed by a huge dwug company.'

That's it? You're not an undercover agent for ASIO? Or a nuclear physicist?

Ralph had just taken a bite of his tiropitakia. Without showcasing the contents of his mouth, he chewed and said, 'So ... what do you sell? Snake oil?'

Hector sat up straight. With chin up and a confident smile he said, 'No. That's not one of our pwoducts.'

You're kidding?

Ralph stopped chewing along with the rest of us and just stared at Hector. I caught Rhea looking at me with a teeny smirk on her face. I smirked back. She didn't seem in the least put out that Ralph was outdistancing her husband.

Your husband's a weenie, but you? I'm liking you even more.

Reuben, who'd been watching with amusement and hadn't said a word, stepped up to the plate. He steered the conversation in the direction it was meant to go: Hannah, Alex, baby.

We all agreed that with Reuben's German and Polish ancestry, my Egyptian one, and Hector and Lawissa's Gweco-Fwench one, Hannah and Alex's child would be blessed with a colourful heritage. Then we got down to the nitty-gritty—Alex's job offers; Hannah finishing her degree; helping them out financially; when they would move in together. And when

Hector brought up the issue of marriage, Hannah said, 'We're not getting married.' Polite, but firm.

Hector retreated. He looked like he'd just been castrated. He shifted in his chair, like a dog trying to find a more comfortable position after having its balls lopped off. Steering clear of my plucky daughter, Hector's beady eyes fixed on Ralph again. And like a desexed dog with a bone, this man persisted in punching above his weight. But just as he opened his mouth to say something, a small, souped-up red Honda zoomed into the driveway and screeched to a halt. A young man climbed out.

'Ah, Alex's little bwother.' Hector smiled with pride. 'Only eleven months diffwence between them, you know.'

Oh, I feel your pain, little brother.

'Unplanned, but definitely a welcome addition.'

In that case, maybe not.

Alex's 'little bwother' came in and stopped at the entrance to the lounge room.

'Hello, Son,' Hector said.

I turned to face 'Son', who hung back a bit. Unlike his car, he appeared to be shy.

He looked like Alex, had the same facial contours and the same brown eyes. But he had Hector's colouring—fair skin and ginger hair—and Hector's small but paunchless physical presence.

His father motioned him forward. 'Evewyone, this is Pawis.'

What? No way! So many names to choose from even when your alphabet only has twenty-five letters in it, and you settle on a name with the missing consonant?

Paris was as polite as Alex. He shook our hands as Hector introduced him to each of us—'Hannah, Wuth, Weuben, and Walph'. It evoked the same shivery sensations as when my third-year high school maths teacher deliberately raked his fingernails across the blackboard. Paris sat at the end of the sofa, squashed in between its arm and his big bwother.

I said to Hector, 'I assume Paris is named after your City of Light?'

'Yes, but also after the chawacter fwom the Twojan War. Lawissa was fwom Gweece so she had a fondness for the Gweek way.'

Shiiiiiit!

'With my backgwound, I have a fondness for the Fwench way.'

More shiiiiiit!

Reuben's eyes popped out; Hannah's mouth dropped open and she giggled; Casper, Ralph and I laughed; Rhea covered her face with one hand; Paris whispered, *'Christ'*; Alex looked down at his lap, blew out an audible breath and shook his head. (Ha, he was embarrassed! This made me feel better. I'm wary of people who are overly nice.) Hector looked puzzled by our reactions.

Really? How can you not *know the 'Greek way' is a euphemism for anal sex and the 'French way' is a euphemism for cunnilingus or fellatio?*

Just then, a kitten slinked into the room. It was ginger, the same colouring as Hector and Paris. It rubbed up against my legs.

Piss off!

'Ooh, she likes you,' Hector said.

Who cares? I hate fucking cats. I stroked the beast to be polite. *Ecch.* 'What's her name?' *Like I give a shit.*

'Clitemnestwa. After the wife of Agamemnon. He was the commanda of the Gweeks in the Twojan War.'

'Mm-hmm, I studied Greek mythology at school. And it's actually pronounced Cl-*eye*-temnestra.'

'No it's not! Lawissa chwistened our vewy first cat Clitemnestwa. And with her stwong Gweek hewitage, she would have known.'

No point arguing with this frickin' man-child. He came across as a know-all. If Joe were alive, he and Hector would have locked horns, for sure. Either way, it was a strange name to give to your cat.

Hector tore a piece off his spanakopita, bent down and chirped in a high-pitched tone. 'Come to daddy, Clit.'

Oh my God!

Rhea looked heavenwards then closed her eyes.

Ralph snorted. 'Really? A pussy called "Clit"?'

Hector got huffy. 'Yes.'

What the—? Does this idiot live in a vacuum?

'I suppose you'd call yours something common like "Kitty".'

Catty.

Ralph gave him a sardonic smile. 'I don't have one.' And he wasn't talking about a cat.

Reuben, Hannah, Casper and I were sniggering. It was a challenge to keep the lid on. Alex and Paris exchanged a look that said, *Like, Dude, like, not in company!* Hector didn't notice any of it. He was too busy stroking, feeding and kissing Clit.

It was the highlight of the afternoon. Still, I was worn out and couldn't take any more. I looked at the grandfather clock, which made it look like time had stood still. I snuck a look at my watch, which made it look like we'd only been here an hour and a quarter. Was it rude to leave so soon?

Dear God, please give me a good excuse to get out of here.

My prayer was heard—God spoke through Casper. 'Dad, can you drop me at Snowdome? Matt and Josh are going.'

Thank you, God. Bless you, son.

In this instance, I didn't care that Casper had lied. Then again ... it wasn't a complete bald-faced lie. His two friends, Matt and Josh, were holidaying in the UK with their families. God and Casper both knew there was a Snowdome in Adelaide, and that Matt and Josh had planned to visit the SnowDome—Santa's Winter Wonderland—in Staffordshire.

Reuben was up on his feet within seconds of Casper thinking on his. We all followed suit.

I said, 'Thank you for ha—'

Hector talked over the top of me. 'Snowdome?' He scrunched his forehead Cro-magnon-like.

'Yeah, you know, the indoor ski slope at Thebarton,' Casper said.

Hector tilted his head like a dog, still no sign of recognition on his face.

'It used to be called the Ice Arena,' said Reuben.

Mr know-fuck-all shrugged again. 'No, not familiar with that.'

For real? You've got two kids! What did you do for fun when they were little—take them to the library and the museum?

Ralph was standing behind Hector. He had a mischievous twinkle in his eyes, and a naughty schoolboy grin crossed his lips. He opened his mouth to say something. You can't keep a smart arse down.

'So—'

I cut him off at the pass. 'Thank you for having us.'

'Our pleasure,' Rhea said.

'No doubt we'll be seeing you lots once the baby awives,' Hector said.

Shit, I hope not.

We all said our goodbyes. Hannah and Alex were going to her friend's place, and Reuben was dropping Casper off at another friend's place (not Snowdome). Ralph complained to me when we were out of everyone's earshot. 'You spoilt my fun.'

I brushed him off—'There are other ways to entertain yourself'—then I moaned about feeling sick because I'd eaten too much. Ralph was used to this. He just shook his head. We got into the car and I let rip a humungous fart. Real classy.

Joe would have applauded me from Heaven, or Hell, depending where he was, but there was no reaction from Ralph. He was staring out the windscreen, pondering over something. He turned to face me. 'It's called wotacism.'

'Huh? A big, giant fart's called a wotacism?'

He scrunched his eyes. '"A big giant fart"? What are you talking about?'

I scrunched my eyes. 'What were *you* talking about?'

'Hector's speech impediment. It's called wotacism.'

'Wotacism?'

'Yes. Ar, aitch, owe, tee, ay, see, eye, ess, em.'

I digested this, then said, 'That spells rhotacism.'

'That's what I said.'

'No, you said, wo ...'

Oh, you! We exchanged wry smiles.

He started the car. 'Would've been useful if he'd had speech pathology intervention at five.'

'Mm.' I nodded. 'Would've done bugger-all for his dress sense, though—'

'Or his eating habits.'

This coming from you?

I left that one alone and got lost in thought until an uneasy one assailed me. 'Is it hereditary? Is his speech impediment hereditary?'

Ralph understood where I was going with this. 'I hope so! Evewyone needs someone they can welate to.'

'Yyye-ah. But I don't want my grandchild relating to Hector!' I shivered at the thought and then briefly reviewed the afternoon as a whole. 'And by the way, really? A psychologist inciting a war with someone who has a few screws loose?'

'Come *on*!' He gave a small derisive laugh. 'He gave me so much ammo.'

The two of us had fun as we brought up Hector's many flubs, then Ralph said, 'It wasn't a war; it was child's play. Anyway, I had it in the bag. He's just like his ancient namesake.'

'Huh?' I faced him. 'How so? Hector was a wealthy prince and the mightiest Trojan warrior.'

'I know. But don't forget ... after Achilles killed Hector, he tied him to his chariot and dragged his R's around the city?'

I laughed at Ralph's flash of wit, then we both withdrew into our own quiet reflections for a time.

We were stopped at a red light when I said, 'You know, it's kinda weird. In *The Iliad*, Paris was also known as Alexander. So, it's like Larissa named her second son the same as her first.'

Ralph turned to me with a half-smile on his face. 'I didn't date Larissa for her smarts. But ... knowing what she was like, and now that I've met Hector, it's pretty clear Alex didn't inherit his fine mind.' He rubbed his chin. 'Hmm ... here's another example of nature versus nurture.'

Oh, no, not again.

Before Ralph found out he was adopted, he had bored me senseless with his take on the nature-nurture debate when we were trying to figure out why he had a superior intellect, where his mother was no rocket scientist and his father and siblings were morons.

'Your environment can play a significant role in how smart you are—thank God mine didn't dumb me down.' He shook his head. 'And in this case, I'd say nurture's played a big part. Rhea's no dumb bunny.'

'Uh-huh. I got that, too. So, you reckon Alex gets his intelligence from her?'

'Mm. That ... and his five o'clock shadow.' He gave me a Mona Lisa smile. I cracked up. I was about to say more, but Ralph was in the throes of a stimulating discourse with himself.

'You know, this nature versus nurture debate, well, it goes back as far as ancient Greece. Plato was for nature, Aristotle favoured nurture—' Yada yada yada.

I lost focus. Ralph was still rabbiting on when we got to my place. The words melded together.

'—but a couple years ago, Judith Rich Harris wrote that parentalupbringingseemsto—'

God, make him stop, please!

'—looked outside the family and pointed at thepeergroup asanimportantshapeof—'

Seriously, God? What, you can't accommodate me more than twice in one day?

I swear I then heard God speak to me. He whispered, *'Work with me, here.'*

Okay. I turned to Ralph as I put my key in the door and talked over the top of him. 'What do you want to do for dinner tonight?'

He stopped talking. 'What? Dinner?' He was disoriented. Good. 'Uh, we've been eating all afternoon. And you said you felt sick. Anyway, it's too early and I'm not hungry,' he said and just picked up where he left off. 'As I was saying, it comes down to do genesmattermore,ordoesenvio—'

Helloooo. I just worked with you, Mr Almighty, and it was a bust.

God spoke again. *'Think inside the box.'*

Huh? Shouldn't that be ... Ohhh, gotcha. Thank You.

I closed the front door and turned to Ralph again, this time with tilted head and a come-hither look. 'You can have me for dinner,' I purred.

Bon appétit. We never made it to the bedroom. Already semi-turned on from his cerebral jerk-off, Ralph took me on the lounge room floor, and went back for second helpings. I ended up with carpet burns on my arse. It was so worth it, though, because he lost his train of thought.

But mine drifted to one of Sylvia's many superstitions about lost things: Losses come in threes.

CHAPTER TWENTY-ONE

A Fate Worse Than Death

The next couple of months flew by. Hannah's morning sickness abated and she sported a compact baby bump. Alex bought her a small diamond ring for her nineteenth birthday. Even though they had no plans to marry, she wore it on her left hand. He turned twenty-five, finished his studies, and accepted what he considered to be the best job offer. Not long after he started working, they moved into a little two-bedroom garden apartment in a boutique block not far from me. My firstborn flying the coop was my second big loss after Joe.

And Casper was rarely home. He'd graduated from learner driver status, and now that he had his car, he was out almost every night after he'd finished his homework. I saw more of Ralph, but he only ever slept at my place when Casper stayed at Reuben's.

Ralph and I had just finished dinner on a Tuesday night, and Casper had already gone out when Myron called. He and I hadn't crossed swords in the preceding months, but we hadn't crossed paths either.

'Mum's gone,' he said, by way of a greeting.

'Gone? What ... did she run away?' *Here's hoping.*

'What? No. She's dead.'

It took a while to sink in. Again, he'd delivered the news in the same way he told me Joe was dead. Life was a colourless monotone for Myron: *The price of apples has gone up. My wife's given birth to twins. Looks like it's going to rain today. Joe's dead. That's a nice suit. Sylvia's dead.*

Apparently, two-dimensional Myron had dropped in to see Sylvia and found her lying on the bed in the martyr position. She'd either had a stroke or a heart attack.

The news of her death released a tsunami of emotion in me, with guilt at the forefront. I'd just spoken to my mother the day before. The last thing she said to me was, '*Oeuf,* you're going to be the death of me! *Pest!*'

I was hysterical when I hung up from my brother, crying, screaming and ranting that it was my fault, that I had killed her. Ralph couldn't pacify me. Not one of his psycho-tools worked. But six words framed in Myron-speak did it: 'You don't have that much power.' It was what I needed to hear.

There were no moments of levity at the funeral the next day, or at the minyan like there had been when Joe died. And the weeks after were difficult for me. Mostly because, where I'd made peace with Joe to some extent when he called to give me his blessing about my relationship with Ralph, Sylvia had left me with a whole lot of unfinished business. I'd moved out of Elisabeth Kübler-Ross's theoretical first stage of grief—denial—but I got bogged down in the second stage—anger. I was overcome with feelings of resentment and hatred towards my mother and I didn't know what to do about it.

I bemoaned my lot to Ralph one night when he dropped in after work.

'All these times she said I'd be sorry when she died ... well, she was right! But only because I never told her what I thought about the way she treated me.'

'Then why don't you write her a letter?' he suggested.

'I'm scared she'll write back!' I laughed, then I shed more hot, angry tears. 'What good would it do, anyway? She's not here. It wouldn't resolve things between us.'

'No. But it'd resolve things within you. All those unspoken words from having bitten your tongue wouldn't remain locked inside you.'

'I guess. But still ... Why didn't I tell her how I felt when she was alive—how she made me feel unloved and unlovable?' I released an anguished wail.

Ralph held me as I wept bitterly. When I calmed a little, he said, 'Do you honestly believe she would have been receptive?'

'No,' I answered in a small voice. 'But ... I'm *frustrated*. I wanna hit back at her!'

'I know. The best vengeance, though, is making your life work. Letting yourself have love and happiness and a good relationship with your own daughter—all the things she didn't allow herself to have. For that, you have to unleash your pent-up pain. If you don't, it'll eat away at you. Then you'll be doing to yourself what she's done. You'll be hurting you.'

Ralph was right, so I started writing.

After I'd filled ten pages of an airmail pad with vitriol, I progressed to a spiral bound A4 notebook. What had started off as a letter became a journal. My rancour at my mother for having made me feel like an intrusion was like a festering sore that wouldn't stop weeping. It seemed to have no end to it, and that in itself pissed me off.

'I'm going backwards,' I said to Ralph.

'No. You're going deeper.'

I got what he meant when the nature of my journaling changed.

I started reading between the lines of fury and hate, and my words now conveyed feelings of terror, hopelessness, torment and heartbreak. My pain was primal, my thoughts, psychotic. Scary stuff! I was in no-man's-land. No-*modern*-man's-land, anyway. I was in the bowels of that primitive, mythical space of the psyche, I was flailing in shit, and my obscene goddess was nowhere in sight.

I called Ralph one night after Casper had gone out. 'I want the fairy taaaaale!' I cried. 'Why couldn't I have been satisfied with that in the first place?'

His tone when he answered was gentle but firm. 'Because at some level, you knew you were at risk of becoming the wicked witch.'

Huh? 'What?'

'Think about it,' he said. And then he ended the call.

'What! Are you kidding me?' I screamed at the dead air.

I didn't want to bloody think about it. I was fuming. My prince had deserted me, and so had Baubo—I couldn't find one iota of humour in any of this. I couldn't think about it; I couldn't write about it. I cried and screamed and spouted obscenities at Ralph and at the ugly goddess in their absence, which showed me Baubo hadn't deserted me. But I was mad about the way she presented. 'Oh, so this is how you come to me? Really? Through my trash talk? *It's not helpiiiiing!'*

I felt desperate. With reluctance, I stood in front of the mirror (I remembered Ralph telling me it helped him when he went through his dark time). I was used to its bitchiness, but looking at it now was so much worse. I saw no one. Or the nobody that, at some level, I still believed I was. And with no one there to save me, I fell. Just like Ralph had. I lay on the floor in a foetal position and sobbed to the point of exhaustion and nothingness. I stayed on the floor. And then, out of nowhere, I heard what was implicit in Ralph's answer—'Because at some level, you knew you were at risk of becoming the wicked witch'— *Just like Sylvia had.* And I got it.

I got that sometimes I needed the fairy tale. Sometimes, I wanted to be shallow and off with the fairies. Ralph knew this about me. When I felt steamrolled by reality, he backed my occasional escape to la-la land, closet romance-novel reader that he once was. But now, I recognised the danger of letting that trace of a fairy-tale imprint entangle me and turn itself into a lifestyle; of how it could eventually cement a caricaturised persona. Just like Sylvia had become the bitchy witch (and toady Myron had become the frog prince). No real depth. Sylvia hadn't wanted to look into hers to see her pain. And because she'd got stuck in her anger and clung to it, it had solidified over the years. So, she'd gone from having anger to *being* **ANGER**. It made it hard to see the whole person, made it hard to love her, then or now.

I got up off the floor and again braved the mirror.

It was different this time, though. Like I'd stepped through the looking glass and got to the bottom of my lifelong, shitty relationship with it. I understood that whenever I faced it, the superficial characters in the upper layers of my psyche became animated and gave me an earful:

The wicked witch: *'You're nothing but trouble—a bitch, a pest! You're not good enough. And you have cellulite!'*

The faint-hearted damsel: *'Help me. Someone please, please save me from the evil one that makes me feel bad about myself.'*

The inflated hero: *'SHE is the bitch! You're a loaded pistol, baby. You're the best, better than everyone else. I'm coming. Soon. And if I can't make it, I have proxies out there. You know, diet pills and exercise regimens and plastic surgery—all things*

*to make you so beautiful, she can't find fault. And if she still
does, you can huff and puff and blow her down!'*

Well, I had huffed and puffed—I'd hit back at my mother in
so many indirect ways when she was alive. But it had yielded
little of value. The truth was, anger frightened me. I'd bitten my
tongue too often because I'd seen the damage Sylvia did by
wielding her sharp one. But all that biting meant anger had
become angrier, and all that huffing and puffing meant it
struggled to breathe. And so, it'd started mutating into a monster
called RAGE.

Letting it vent on the floor in the privacy of my room was
safe. For me and for everyone around me. And as this emotion
started to soften and return to its natural state, I understood it
was far from the beast that had been burning up my journals.
But it was no wussy pussy, either. Real, unadulterated anger
wasn't like the picture-perfect fairy-tale character: The
cardboard cut-out Prince Charming—whose name was probably
Myron—brandishing a sword as a substitute (phallic) symbol of
power. No. Real, unadulterated anger was akin to the ancient
warrior, whose sword was no trifling symbol. It was an emblem
of his 'cut-the-crap!' attitude.

Images of recent times flashed before me. Moments when
I'd stood up to others—not aggressively or passive-
aggressively—and was given respect in return. I needed to make
that my default setting.

I called Ralph. I called him a whole lot of names for letting
me fall, then I thanked him for it. And I recounted the experience
and my insights. When he responded with, 'I knew you had the
hero in you,' he wasn't talking dirty even though I saw it that
way. Yep. I took comfort in knowing my beloved badarse Baubo
would never leave me high and dry.

Things started to shift after that. I felt freer and I was
breathing easier. I also started including the deep mythical

perspective in my articles. But where I used to get lots of emails praising my stories, the feedback was dwindling. I met with Maxi and expressed my reservations. She encouraged me.

'Just keep going. People are sceptical when you throw something new at them. Some of us get real bent out of shape.' We shared a knowing smile.

'Well, you came round, but not everyone's like you,' I told her.

'No. But when the old way of dealing with stuff stops working, and then starts to work against you ... let's just say people become a little more prepared to consider something different.'

She was right. I kept at it, and readers started coming round after one article: 'Going Down. Are You Doing It Regularly?' They might have been disappointed that it wasn't about sex, but the title hooked them, and the number of emails increased— people were cautiously curious.

As the days and weeks passed, I could see changes happening in my life. And Ralph was about to undergo a sea change.

CHAPTER TWENTY-TWO

Roots

A couple of weeks after Ralph had lodged his application with AFIS, he received a letter advising him that a veto hadn't been placed by his biological mother, but that it could be at any time during the search process. He hadn't heard any more from them since then, which he took as good news (unless she hadn't placed a veto because she was dead).

He called me on a Tuesday night after work to tell me there was a letter from AFIS in his letterbox.

'Ooh! What's it say?'

'I don't know.'

'Why? Is it still in the letterbox?'

'No. I just haven't opened it,' he said, his voice uneven. 'I'm scared. I'm scared they've found her and I'm scared they haven't found her.'

'Okay. How 'bout I come over?'

Fifteen minutes later, we were sitting in his lounge room looking at the envelope. Five minutes after that we were still sitting in his lounge room looking at the envelope.

'Ralph!'

'Okay. Okay.' Repetition.

He delicately opened the envelope. Ralph delicately opened presents, too. I ripped at wrappings. And I wanted to rip the letter out of his hands. Instead, I took a couple of deep breaths.

He read the letter to himself slowly. He looked at me in astonishment. 'Turns out she also lodged an application a few weeks ago to find me.'

'Woohoo!' I jumped on him.

He jumped me.

And afterwards, we shared pillow talk.

He smiled at me. 'The information package is coming.'

I sputtered a laugh. 'I thought the "information package" just came.'

'Huh? Oh, no, no. The letter said an information package about my mother was almost complete and I'd get it soon.'

Ooookay. 'Awesome.' Frickin' awesome. I'd worked hard to expunge Sylvia from between the sheets, and now ... now his mother, whom he hadn't even met, was in bed with us.

I let it go, didn't say anything. I didn't want to dampen his enthusiasm, which swelled mid-morning two weeks later when the information package came. Ralph called me after making contact with his biological mother. 'I just spoke to her. Put the kettle on, I'm on my way over.'

He had the day off from work. As I heard his car come to a stop in the drive, I poured our teas. Ralph, who now had a key to my place, charged in with the ebullience of a child. I was happy for him, but I was a little concerned. I had a feeling he was looking for someone to replace Norma.

We sat at the dining room table. I observed him as he adjusted the angle of the teacup's handle in relation to the edge of the table. Watching Ralph enact his strange rituals could be entertaining.

Hmm. I should get a round table. Throw him off his game; add to my viewing pleasure.

When he was satisfied the handle was parallel to the table edge, he looked up at me with a smile.

'We've arranged to meet this weekend.'

'Yay! Does she sound nice?'

'She does.'

'What's her name?'

He cleared his throat nervously, picked up his spoon and stirred his tea loudly, almost drowning out his words. 'Beth Johnson. We talked for half—'

'Wai-wai-wait. Beth ... *Johnson*?'

Ralph didn't answer. He tried to suppress a smile as he looked down into his milky tea. He knew there would be no stopping me, so he fed the beast. '—and, apparently, she named me Richard.'

Oh God. It was getting better and better! *Bet you no longer admire my impressive hippocampus? Hhhha.* A torrent of memories came back—Ralph's relentless wisecracking from years earlier.

Seven-and-a-half-inch Glen Jones might have been my official first love when I was nineteen, but a couple of years before I met him, I'd fallen in love with a stranger. I loved the stranger from a distance. I didn't know his name, but I just knew he was 'The One'.

Through means of deception—agreeing to date a loser only because he knew the stranger—I found out The One was called Phelan (pronounced *feelin'*) Johnson. Three months later, the gods conspired and brought Phelan and me together. He asked me out.

Although I'd had my heart set on this man for thirteen and a half months, I didn't tell him I loved him when he picked me up for the date. Sometimes a girl needs to hold her cards close to her chest. And just as well. The love died that night. Phelan must have eaten paint chips as a kid. Being on a date with him was as stimulating as watching that paint dry.

But many got a rise out of his name. Not least Ralph, who did not let up for those three months once he'd found out Phelan's name.

'Phelan Johnson,' Ralph said, 'is a synonym for *masturbatin'*.'

I'd waited a long time to settle an old score.

'Sooooo. Richard Johnson, hmm?'

Ralph looked at me with a boyish grin and braced himself.

'Shortened to Rich Johnson—wealthy dick? Or Dick Johnson. Isn't that what you call a tautology? Is it a good thing she called you Richard, then? You could have been Ken Johnson—clever dick. Or maybe Frank Johnson—honest dick. How about Robin Johnson—plunderin' dick? Or Terry Johnson—towelling dick?'

It was rare that I could beat the master of glib at his own game and I was loving it! He said nothing. Like a good sport, he took the payback on the chin. He even seemed to take pleasure in my enjoyment. I mean, like, real pleasure—I got a rise out of him, I mean like, a real rise—and we celebrated my win in the lounge. He pulled me down onto the floor with him. No, let's do it on the sofa, I said. But it's more organic on the floor, he said. I don't give a flying fuck if it's more orgasmic, I said. I reminded him the carpet was a Berber, not a shag pile.

Four days later, Ralph dropped in on his way to meet Beth Johnson.

'Where's Casper?' He looked around as he asked.

'He's at Christies Beach with Matt and Josh for the weekend.'

'Good. I need something to take the edge off,' he said, a suggestive grin plastered on his face.

'I have Rescue Remedy,' I answered, a teasing grin plastered on mine.

Rescue Remedy would do nothing for his dilated pupils, though. Ralph's 'something' was a panacea for everything. The man was a sex god. Who was I to deny him?

He left with a smile on his face.

He returned three hours later with a smile on his face.

Beth Johnson had burst into tears when she saw Ralph. Seemed he was a dead ringer for his father, David, who Beth hadn't seen since she fell pregnant at sixteen. David Mitchell was two years older than Beth and they'd been deeply in love. She had kept an old picture of him. Ralph said it was like looking at a younger version of himself.

'I asked her if he was her Twin Flame,' he said. 'She smiled and said yes.'

'She also knows about Twin Flames?'

'Sure does.' Ralph beamed. 'She's Emeritus Professor in Philosophy at Adelaide University.'

Wow. Totally phat. First Alex, now Beth. Ralph was rediscovering members of a lost tribe.

'They wanted to get married,' he continued, 'but she was from a wealthy family and he was from the wrong side of the tracks—he wasn't good enough for her parents.' I knew what that felt like. 'They drove him away and forbade her from having any contact with him.'

Beth had told Ralph his was a forced adoption. She'd been sent away to a place in country South Australia early in her pregnancy because of the stigma attached to a baby being born out of wedlock. And there wasn't financial support for single mothers back then. Her parents had threatened to disown her. With no means of support, emotionally or financially, she felt she had no choice. She was inconsolable when they took him away, but they said the baby would have the opportunity for a better life. Still, not a day had gone by when she didn't think about her son. Or David.

Beth needed Ralph to know he was wanted. Other than that, she didn't say anything more about her life after him. She was very interested in his, though.

'Has it been a good one?' she'd asked him. He told her he had a loving mother (it was too soon to tell her he was barely talking to his loving mother), that he'd made good money as a model, and that he'd found his calling later in life as a psychologist. 'Beth seemed perceptive,' he said. He'd felt her looking right through him and picking up on what he didn't say (but it was too soon for her to ask). She didn't hide her sadness over what she'd lost. And she didn't judge his relationship with me. She was elated.

'She said, "Sounds like Ruth is your Twin Flame. Don't let her go, no matter what." I told her I had no intention of letting you go.' Ralph pulled me close to him and kissed me. 'I need to celebrate.' Things were dilated again.

Things were looking up for Ralph. After meeting his mother, he was floaty most of the time, like he'd been sniffing the glue that binds. He got together with Beth once a fortnight. He learned she'd married at thirty-one. Edward Spencer was a reputable lawyer—ideal husband material, so said her parents— and they had two children, Nicholas and Amelia. Beth had told Ralph that Edward was a good man, but he wasn't David. She ended the marriage when Amelia moved out of home at twenty, and reverted to her maiden name. She was tired of doing what was expected of her.

Nicholas and Amelia had partners, but neither had children as yet. And they weren't ready to meet their long-lost half-brother. They were shocked to learn they had one. And they were angry. Beth's parents had pressured her into keep that part of her life secret and the longer she left it, the harder it got to reveal it. And when she started looking for Ralph, she didn't see the point in saying anything if she couldn't find him or if he didn't want to meet her. Ralph wasn't quite ready to meet them, anyway. It would happen when the time was right. And in time, he wanted to introduce me to Beth.

'No rush,' I said. He and his mother had a lot to catch up on.

Hannah sensed the change in Ralph. There was also a change in her. Even though she was getting big and uncomfortable, she was schnockered on hormones and calmer than I'd ever seen her.

It was the calm before the storm.

CHAPTER TWENTY-THREE

Beware of Geeks Baring Gifts

On a Sunday, late afternoon–early evening, Ralph and I had just finished watching a romantic chick flick on TV. He stared at the rolling credits, looking floatier than ever. I told him he needed to ground out.

'How do you propose I do that?'

'Eat. Let's go out for dinner.'

An hour later, he was tucking into a super-rare rib eye and I was enjoying my crispy-skinned chicken. I was sure Ralph ordered his steak *bleu* because he knew there was no way I'd ask to taste something that was still mooing. And I ordered chicken because I knew there was no way he'd ask to taste poultry. (When Ralph had turned seven, his mother served up his beloved pet duck, plucked, roasted, quartered, and à l'orange as a special birthday treat for dinner that night. He'd sworn off fowl ever since.)

Ralph and I were happy to swap spit, but never our food.

The meal was so good, we ate in silence. We were almost done when my mobile phone came alive. Vibrating against the edge of my plate, it struck a jarring note when I noticed Alex's name flashed on the display. Shit.

I stopped chewing. 'It's Alex. Something must be wrong.'

Ralph took another mouthful. 'Not necessarily.'

'Yes, it is. I can feel it.' I was intuitive. I knew these things. In my skittish state, I stared abstractedly at the keypad.

'The call key. Press the call key. The green one.' Ralph was pragmatic. He knew other things.

Right! 'Alex! Issomethingwrongwhat'swrong?'

'No, it's meeeee; I'm in laaaaabour! It fucking hurts! You didn't tell me it was gonna be this bad! WHY DIDN'T YOU TELL MEEEEEE!'

I started panting. 'How far apart are your contractions?'

'OWWWWWWWWWWW. Three OWWWWWW Three min-min-minutes!'

I heard Alex in the background. 'Breathe, Hanny. Breathe.'

'SHUT THE FUCK UP UNLESS *YOU* WANNA DO THIS!'

Oh boy. 'Hannah, sweetie, put Alex on the phone.'

'HERE! OWWWWW!'

'H-hello.' Alex's voice was shaky.

'Alex, better get her to the hospital.'

'We are at the hospital. *I don't know what to do for her,'* he whispered.

'Not much you can do. Ask for nitrous oxide. For her. And anything she says to you, don't take it personally.'

I hung up. Hannah was just under three weeks away from her due date. Feeling flustered, I grabbed my bag, threw my phone into it and looked up at Ralph. 'We gotta go. Let's get the bill.'

He made a palm down 'calm down' gesture with his hands. 'I don't think we need to rush. It'll probably be a while.'

I felt my face flush. 'Oh really? Like *you* would know?'

Ralph winced at my harsh tone, but he saw through my bluster. He took my shaking hand in his. 'You're right. I don't know. But Hannah's in labour. You're not.'

He had a point. Sometimes I felt my relationship with Hannah was a little too enmeshed. I needed to cut the cord. I took a deep, steadying breath and gave him an apologetic look.

Ralph respected my concern, though. He paid the bill and we left for the hospital.

I called Reuben. The three of us arrived at the same time and were ushered into a small, antiseptic-scented waiting room down the hall from Hannah's birthing suite. I asked the nurse how Hannah was doing. Five centimetres dilated, she said. I asked her to let Hannah know her parents were here. She told us to make ourselves comfortable.

There were twelve tub chairs in the waiting room. Four chairs were lined up against each of three walls. Connected by two low beige polyurethane corner tables, they formed a U-shape facing the entrance, with its wide opening glass door and half-glass walls. The chairs were upholstered in faux leather, café au lait colour. The thick, cushiony seats were designed for long waits. The waiting room floor was beige speckled vinyl sheeting, and the walls were a light beige colour. A few indifferent, neutral prints lined each wall. The overall ambience of the waiting room was sedate. Why? Would there have been an uprising if the walls were painted in the popular hospital blue? Or if the prints held splashes of vibrant colour?

The three of us went directly to the chairs against the left wall and sat next to each other. We leaned back like airline passengers making ourselves comfortable for a long-haul flight. Reuben rubbed his eyes with the heel of his hands and Ralph ran his fingers over his undetectable stubble.

Ha! We were the proverbial three wise monkeys: see no evil-Reuben, who'd never wanted to see what was happening in our marriage (or not happening); speak no evil-Ralph, who'd never had his mouth washed out with soap like I had, because he never swore (except for that one time when I was in hospital); and hear no evil-me, who'd tried (often in vain) to tune out Sylvia's kvetching while she was alive, but was hell-bent on shutting her up now that she wasn't.

Ralph got up and straightened one of the prints on the opposite wall. He surveyed the prints on the other two walls as if it were a normal thing to do. He hadn't whipped out a spirit level, so that was a good sign. He nodded in satisfaction when he determined no others were askew, and sat back down.

I called Casper. It went to voicemail. I left him a message about Hannah, and said I might be home very late. Half an hour passed and my initial excitement waned. It was replaced by beige feelings.

What crashing bore decided on this décor? I wondered. Must have been one of Myron's cohorts.

I'd briefly worked as an interior decorator when the kids were little, so I knew about colour. I would have chosen a soft, sunny yellow. Gender neutral, but with a bit of zing. Was it unrealistic to expect some life in a hospital wing that welcomes new life?

Ralph stirred me out of my broody state when he whispered, *'Ooh, goody. Fun time.'* He was staring at the entrance.

'Shit,' Reuben and I muttered at the same time.

Rhea was on the other side of the half-glass wall and just rounding the corner into the waiting room. The bastardised version of Elvis the Pelvis trailed behind her. Looking like a rear fog light, he was ablaze with colour in harlequin trousers that had a red, green, yellow and blue diamond print, and a polo shirt in high-vis lime. Against the waiting room backdrop, he stood out like You-Ain't-Nothing-but-a-Hound-Dog's balls. And he was about as attractive. God was mocking me.

We hadn't seen Rhea and Hector since that Sunday afternoon at their place. I knew I should reciprocate. I'd experienced pangs of guilt because I hadn't. Ralph stipulated that while I could grumble about my guilt all I liked, I mustn't act on it. No way. And if I folded, he wanted to be invited at the same time, just for the sport.

Reuben and Ralph stood as Rhea greeted us all with warmth.

Hector, who was hugging a large thermos against his chest, greeted us with cool—'Hell*ooooo* peoples. Whassup?'

Other than your head up your arse?

Spoken in the parlance of a game-show host, it was fair to say he didn't expect or desire an answer.

As they sat down in the chairs opposite us, Hector tapped the thermos and smiled. 'Something to help us thwough the labour.'

To help 'us'?

With a fiendish smile splitting his face, he leaned forward and lowered his voice. *'Shwoom tea.'*

What! You wanna go psychedelic tripping in the labour ward? Are you fucking kidding?

Rhea rolled her eyes. 'He's kidding. It's just chamomile tea.'

Sure it is. That's what he tells you. And what the hell kinda drug company does he rep for?

Hector unscrewed the lid of the thermos and filled the serving cup that came with it. A little of the dodgy-looking, yellowish liquid sploshed onto the floor as he held it out. 'Anyone?'

I shot him a sour look. 'I'll pass, thanks.'

Rhea drew back. Reuben declined. Ralph didn't bother to answer, but I could hear the cogs in his brain turning. I sensed them come to rest, and turned to look at him. His faint crow's feet were pronounced as he peered at Hector through narrowed slits. He sat forward and rested his forearms on his thighs, clasped his hands and then ... there was that final move in the dance of a stealth predator preparing to ambush his quarry—the subtle curling of the corner of his mouth. Oh God, it was like foreplay; the anticipation was turning me on! Just as Hector brought the cup to his lips, Ralph pounced.

'You know ... a recent study has found that men who imbibe shroom tea can end up with severely shrunken testicles.' Ralph raised an eyebrow at him. 'So ... guess you've got nothing to lose, hey?'

Reuben tried to stifle a laugh. I covered my mouth and lowered my head, but not before noticing the small smile on Rhea's lips.

Hector lowered the cup and smiled broadly. 'Guess not.'

Jesus! The idiot had taken it as a dare, not as the veiled insult that it was. He raised his cup and sipped. *'Aaaah. Magic.'* He winked, already on his way to wasted.

I suspected it was going to be a long night, but by God, it would be a stimulating one!

Ralph leaned back, stretched out his legs, rested his head against the wall, folded his arms and closed his eyes. Reuben rummaged through the stack of magazines piled neatly on the corner table next to him. Over the next hour, he flicked unfocused through one after another; Ralph remained in his semi-supine position; Rhea and I talked about baby stuff; and Hector donned his sunglasses to 'avoid the papawazzi' and to shield his eyes against the 'stwobe lighting'. Then he worked up a sweat ducking and swatting a swarm of imaginary bugs. When he'd finally triumphed, he tried baiting Ralph.

Ralph's eyes remained closed as he squashed Hector— annoying pest that he was—with smart rejoinders. Hector grew sullen.

Have some more shroom, dipshit. Or 'chamomile'. Whatever.

Rhea stood up and stretched. 'I'm getting a coffee. Would any of you like one?'

We all said no thanks. After she left, Reuben and I reminisced about my eight-hour labour with Hannah. Hector weighed into the conversation. 'Alex slipped out in no time.' He smirked. 'And I'd slipped in in no time.'

Huh?

Seeing the confusion on our faces, he leaned forward and looked towards the door to make sure Rhea wasn't about to walk back in. He whispered, *'Lawissa found me iwwesistible. She put out on our vewy first date. I'm a weal stud; got her pwegnant wight off the bat.'*

Ecch. I gawped at this awful little man as he snickered.

Ralph's eyes were now open in an angry squint. 'I don't think you should say anymore.' His warning tone got Hector all excited.

'Ooh!' He rubbed his hands together. 'I think someone's jealous.'

'No. "Someone" just doesn't have much respect for kiss-and-tell. And you're talking about your late wife!'

Ralph stared Hector down. Hector's face crimsoned.

Rhea came back in with her coffee. She sensed the tension. 'Have you heard something? Is something wrong?' She looked worried.

Hector looked worried.

'Uh, we were just talking about, um ... uh ...' I drawled, delighting in watching big globs of sweat beading on Hector's upper lip. *God, I am such a bitch.* '... Um, we were talking about ... about ... uh, uh ...'

Hector kept wetting his lips, his eyes darting back and forth between Rhea and me.

'Um, Reuben and I were talking about my labour with Hannah.'

'Yes, yes, that's wight! And I was just about to say Alex was a big baby. Seven pounds.'

'Seven pounds is not that big,' I countered.

'Yes it is. He was a pweemie. Six weeks.'

Oh dear God. I now worried that my tiny-framed daughter, who was almost full term, was in there struggling to push out a macro-baby like its father.

Another three hours with this creep crept along before we heard a whole lot of activity around Hannah's room. We moved into the passage, expectantly. About ten minutes later, a baby's cry pierced the air. It was the most beautiful sound. Any reservations I'd had about becoming a grandmother dissolved in that moment. My heart was so full of joy, I thought it would burst! The others appeared just as moved. I even felt magnanimity towards Hector. We hugged and laughed and cried ... until a heated argument cleaved the air.

We all fell silent as it grew louder. It lasted for a few minutes. Then, amidst the yelling, the door to Hannah's room burst open and Alex stormed out. The five of us stood there slack-jawed as he approached us, his nostrils flaring.

'It's a boy!' he roared. His eyes welled with angry tears and he stamped off towards the exit.

'What the hell was that?' Reuben said, as we watched Alex thrust the door open and disappear behind it. Rhea started to go after him; Hector didn't move. She turned back, grabbed him by the sleeve and dragged him along with her.

'Do you think something's happened to Hannah?' Reuben had paled.

Hannah? *Oh no. Maybe she died in childbirth. Oh God, NO! Please God, not that!*

Reuben and Ralph stood riveted to the spot. I bolted for the birthing suite. I reached the door and almost collided with a nurse coming out. Through the open door, I heard Hannah's soft sobs. *Phew*. Sort of. I tried pushing past the nurse, but she blocked me with her arm. 'Hold on. You can't go in—'

'That's my daughter in there.'

Seeing the distress on my face, she relented. 'Okay. Give me one second.' She dipped back inside, closing the door behind her. Twenty seconds later, she came out. 'Can you wait just a few minutes? Hannah's delivering the placenta.'

I nodded. With a sick feeling in my stomach, I asked, 'Is there something wrong with Hannah? With the baby?'

'Uh, n-no. No.' She patted my hand. 'Mother and baby are fine.' She opened her mouth to say more, but then seemed to think better of it.

Shit.

'Someone will come out and get you, shortly,' she said, and then took off down the hall.

I collapsed back against the wall, expelled a long, slow breath, tilted my head upwards and gave thanks. Then I looked in the direction of Reuben and Ralph. Like a pair of Madame Tussauds wax figures, neither had moved a muscle. I gave them the thumbs up, then mouthed and indicated with my fingers that I'd be going in in a couple of minutes. They both melted and gave me a return thumbs up.

Mother and baby were fine, but clearly, something was wrong. What did 'fine' mean, anyway? Weren't there varying degrees of fine? Didn't it come down to perception? It was like a waiter at a restaurant telling me, *Oh, it's not spicy*, when I inquired about a dish. So, I'd order it, eat it and feel like my oesophagus had been cauterised. Not spicy for him, maybe. Perception.

'Fine' probably meant the baby's heart and respiratory rates were perfect. 'Fine' probably meant his muscle tone, reflexes and colour were all good. But maybe he had webbed toes. Like a duck. Would the baby not having perfect toes like his parents be grounds for Alex to desert Hannah, to leave her by herself? *Nada*. He would still be *fine*, you chicken-shit!

Mercifully, a nurse popped her head around the door. 'Hannah's mum?'

I nodded, she motioned for me to come in and handed me a gown to put on.

Several nurses were milling around in the room going about their business. Other than Hannah's crying, there were the expected sounds—the clanging of instruments in stainless steel bowls, the beeping of the baby's monitor, the buzzing of the overhead lights—but the staff chatted in whispered tones.

I went straight to Hannah's side, held her hand and stroked her head. 'Hannah?'

She spoke brokenly between sobs. 'I di-di-didn't ch-ch-cheat on Alex, M-m-mum, I swear. I *swear*, Mummy!'

'What? *What?* Why would he think that?' *And why the hell bring it up now!*

A sob constricted her throat, cutting off the words, so she pointed to the baby bassinet.

The nurse standing in front of it moved away just as I turned to look.

Oh dear God ...

My grandson was black.

CHAPTER TWENTY-FOUR

The Potz Calling
the Kettle Black

Not black black. But he didn't look Caucasian either. Much darker than Hannah and Alex's olive complexion, he was the same café au lait colour as the waiting room chairs. I stood looking down into the bassinet. I was already in love with this little boy. With his thatch of wispy, black hair and blue eyes, he was beautiful. I was baffled by his skin tone, but he could have been purple and it wouldn't have mattered.

Hannah was also stumped, but it wasn't an issue for her. Alex's accusation was.

Her labour was awful, she said. She'd managed with the gas but then begged for an epidural. It was too late, they'd said. Fortunately, she didn't have to have an episiotomy. Unfortunately, Alex railed at her just after the midwife put the baby in her arms. Then he took off, leaving her holding the baby—in more ways than one. She was no longer overwrought, but she was furious at him for doubting her. I was also incensed. I left to go and find him, but didn't have to look far. He was standing in the passage surrounded by his parents and Reuben and Ralph, all with stunned expressions on their faces.

I strode up to Alex.

'My daughter is not a cheater!'

'I know.' He looked at me with contrition.

'Then why the fuck are you out here!' Framed as a question, but issued as a command.

Hector moved forward. 'Now, hang on—'

I swivelled towards him, glaring and daring. He shut up.

Alex went back into the birthing suite. The five of us filed back into the waiting room, sat down in the same chairs we'd occupied earlier and got lost in our own thoughts.

Ralph spoke first. 'Well, we did say this baby would have a colourful heritage. Who knew it would be literal?' We all nodded. He added, 'Obviously, an ancestral throwback.' We all nodded again.

'Must be fwom my side.'

Yes, of course it must be.

'I have a Macedonian pwince in my ancestwy.'

'What?' Ralph said, his tone and expression registering disbelief. 'Hector was a fictional character.'

Hector—he who was too ridiculous to be real—had egg on his face, which was turning florid as he looked away. I almost felt sorry for him but couldn't help let slip a stifled giggle. A treacly silence ensued. It threatened to get even tackier as Hector's bearing turned ugly. His jaw clenched, the corners of his mouth dropped down in a grimace of derision just before he opened it.

'Actually, it pwobably comes fwom *your* side.' Hector pointed at me and scoffed, 'Knowing the kind of things going on in your family—'

'HECTOR!' Rhea was outraged.

Ralph surged to his feet, took two giant strides and stood over Hector with a menacing look. He leaned forward, rested his hands on the arms of the little man's chair and spoke in a menacing tone: 'You watch your mouth. Or you're gonna be seeing a lot more stars, and not just from that "shwoom" tea you're drinking.'

Ralph loved playing with words, but they were also his weapon of choice. He never resorted to physical violence, except for one time when he snapped after being Albie's punching bag for twenty-five years. Ralph had slammed his father against the wall and promised to hurt him badly if he ever raised his hand to him again, and to kill him if he dared harm Norma.

He straightened up and directed his gaze at Rhea. 'I suggest you get your husband a cup of coffee. A strong one.'

Rhea nodded, her face a dark red mask of embarrassment and anger. *'I'm sorry,'* she mouthed as she came out of her chair. She was back a few minutes later, handed Hector his coffee, then sat next to me.

Hector cut a lonely, pathetic figure sitting by himself. I didn't care. The guilt I'd felt from not having invited them to my place was gone.

Rhea took my hand and gently squeezed it.

So, maybe I still have some guilt. But not nearly as much.

Nobody said another word. I sat there wrestling with conflicted feelings. I was overjoyed at the birth of my grandson and relieved that Hannah was okay, and though I was affronted by Hector's accusation, I was also upset that he knew about what went on in our family. Had Hannah complained to Alex in those months before she and I had made peace? Probably. And no doubt, he was the one who told his family. *Big mouth.* I was making assumptions, getting myself worked up and preparing to pounce. But now was not the time or the place.

Another thirty-three minutes and twenty-two seconds stretched out like medieval rack torture before a sunbeamy Alex rounded the corner.

Well, hello Mr Blabbermouth! Shh, shh. Be pleasant.

'Hannah and the baby have been moved to a private room,' said Loose Lips.

On the way there, Alex—*that's it. Alex. Nix the huffing and puffing. His name is Alex*—told us the baby's complexion must be a reversion to an earlier ancestral characteristic. We said we'd come to the same conclusion.

We arrived at a juncture. A blue sign suspended from the ceiling indicated the Maternity Ward was on the left, Gynaecology was on the right and Psychiatry was straight ahead. I turned around and glowered at Hector.

Go straight, arsehole.

He and I were not in concert, so he didn't 'hear' my projection. He followed Alex and the rest of us through the double doors on the left that opened into the Maternity Ward's long hallway. Background music filled it—an orchestra of crying newborns tuning up.

'Here we are,' Alex said, as he stopped halfway down the hall and pushed open a wide door on the left of it.

Hannah's room was as nondescript as the waiting room. But the radiance of her smile zhooshed it up. It was a welcome relief from her despairing demeanour of an hour earlier. With her little boy nestled in her arms, the mother and child image was a Kodak moment.

Alex sat on the bed next to her and drew her close to him, completing the picture. Their eyes met and they kissed.

Just as well, buddy. It helped me get off the warpath.

They gazed in awe at their beautiful son as we crowded around them *oohing* and *aahing* over our grandson. Hannah said, 'Say hello to Luca.'

'Ooh, *Luca.* I love the name!'

Rhea, Reuben and Ralph smiled and *mmmed* and nodded their approval. Hector bristled. He cleared his throat. 'I thought you were going to give the baby a Gweek name.'

Hannah threw him a wintry look and said in a wintry tone, 'He has got a Greek name. It's in his surname. Gold-*Agathe.*'

Hector responded with a timid nod.

Alex *ahemmed.* He spoke to Reuben and me. 'Um, I'm going to look into my family tree on both sides. *Ahem.* Would you mind looking into yours?' His gaze faltered and fell. Alex knew he would have to redeem himself in our eyes.

Reuben said he'd ask his parents, Greta and Rudy. I said I'd ask Aunt Norma and Uncle Isaac. They might also know something about Joe's side. He'd never talked much about his family. All I knew was that his mother died just before I was born and that he rarely saw his father, who had left when Joe was four, and died eleven years later. An only child, Joe was brought up by an exacting, smothering, single mother (according to Sylvia-the-stone-thrower who lived in a glass house).

Hannah yawned. The labour had exhausted her, but the emotional turmoil that followed had also taken its toll. We said our goodbyes and Ralph dropped me home. I was wiped out and wanted to fall into bed, but Casper, in a half-asleep state, yanked the front door open as I was putting my key into it.

We had a grunt-like conversation string:

'So?'

'A boy. Name's Luca.'

'Sweeeeet!' Occasionally Casper sounded like the teenager that he was. 'Wuzz he look li—?'

'Gorgeous. Blue eyes, lotsa hair. Dark.'

'Sweeeeet! Can't wait to see 'im.'

And I can't wait to see you when you see 'im. 'I'm going to the hospital at ten after I make some calls.'

'I'll go a bit earli—'

Shit. 'No! You can come with me. Visiting hours don't start till ten.' (He was on school holidays.)

'I can drive mysel—'

'Parking's a bitch.'

'Mmkay. Goin' back to bed now.'

Casper's reaction the next morning following his knee-jerk, slack-mouthed gasp was not so sweeeeet. 'Bullshit!'

Hannah took it in her stride. She laughed at him. She and Casper rarely fought. I was lucky to have kids who liked each other.

'You do know there've been stories about babies being swapped in the nursery.'

'Uh-huh, I know. But I saw what I pushed out,' she said to Casper. Then she turned to me. 'I can't believe you didn't tell him.'

'Yeah.' Casper cast me a disapproving look. 'Not cool, Gran'ma.'

'What? I told you he was dark.' I smiled and shrugged.

'"Dark" is a bog-standard description. As opposed to fair, *I'm* dark.'

I looked towards the door to make sure Alex wasn't about to come back into the room. He'd gone to the pharmacy to get a few items for Hannah. I whispered, *'D'you remember when I first met Hector, when you and your sister withheld vital information?'*

The two of them laughed. 'This means war,' he said, his eyes dancing with mischief. But he forgot all about it when Hannah put Luca in his arms. Moved beyond words, Casper was enamoured of his nephew.

He was a daily visitor while Hannah was in hospital. He was one of many. Her room was filled with floral arrangements, and often overflowed with people. Everyone who visited was taken with Luca ... after their initial reaction. Some *Holy crapped*, some *Jesus Christed*, Reuben's parents *Mein Gotted*. And when Uncle Isaac *Oy veyed*, I picked his brain. He racked it.

Aha, yes! A vague recollection that somewhere way, way back in our ancestry, there was an Ethiopian—a plausible explanation that outdid a mythical 'Macedonian pwince'. Luca was most likely a faint echo of this relative.

I couldn't wait for day five when Hannah was due to take our little prince home. I dreaded day eight.

CHAPTER TWENTY-FIVE

Skin Crawl

Luca's bris—his ritual circumcision—was scheduled for when he was eight days old, as is the custom in the Jewish religion. Hannah didn't have a religious upbringing, but we still observed the most basic practices. A bris was one of them. 'Alex is happy to respect that,' she said, 'especially seeing as he's also circumcised.'

Didn't really need to know this.

I offered to hold the ceremony at my place.

Hannah and Alex were there at six-thirty on the Monday morning, an hour and a half before the appointed time. I was out the front door as soon as I heard their car pull up, and Casper was right behind me. Luca was awake and protesting. Hannah had been instructed not to feed him within one hour of the bris, but she wanted to feed him as close to it as possible so he'd be milk-drunk during the procedure. She took Luca out of his capsule and handed him to her brother.

Casper cooed at his newborn nephew as he rocked him. Then he looked at me and got all solemn. 'You know, it's a damn shame Nanna's not around to see her great-grandson.'

Imagine. I just nodded. Solemnly. Casper was being thoughtful. Or not.

'Black was her favourite colour.'

We all laughed.

'Shit,' Casper whispered and stopped rocking.

'What's wrong?' Hannah, who'd been digging around in her tote bag for a dummy, hurried over to Casper.

'The gap in Deep Throat's venetians just widened.'

We all looked across the road.

'Jesus. Why is she awake?' I said this to myself. Didn't an alcoholic stupor make you sleepy? Portnoy had been trashed the night before. At eleven o'clock I'd seen her tottering around the brotherhood of inanimate, grizzled uglies, thwacking them. Little bastards hadn't been doing their job. Armed or not, they hadn't repelled the neighbours, who were becoming increasingly irate about the dreck in her front yard.

Luca turned up the volume. Casper tried to soothe him, *'Shh. Shh.* The world is full of sociopaths, little man. Best to prime you early, but it's quite enough for one day.' As he took Luca inside, he said over his shoulder, 'Give it about half an hour before some kind of dark story spreads all through the community like crotch rot.'

I laughed at his prediction, but it had me worried. Still, it was a good sign that our phone wasn't ringing off the hook an hour later when Reuben arrived. He'd picked up the food from the caterers—a couple of kosher cakes and trays of kosher open bagels, some topped with cream cheese and lox, some with egg mix, others with tuna salad. Maxi and Vette, who'd driven up at the same time, helped me set out the food on the sideboard. As well as the bagels and cakes, I had a couple of platters of cut up fruit, and drinks—orange juice, mineral water and kosher wine. The hot water urn stood gurgling on and off at the end of the sideboard next to the teabags, coffee, sugar, milk, Styrofoam cups, plastic wine glasses, plates and cutlery, and serviettes.

Fifteen minutes later, people started trickling in (I'd left the front door open, it was easier) and the lounge room was filling up.

Hannah wanted the ceremony low-key. Suited me, I wasn't into fuss—just the immediate family and some good friends. We needed a minimum of ten men for a minyan. Myron wasn't one of them. He couldn't make it, he had 'commitments'. I didn't believe it, didn't much care. I'd invited him out of obligation in the same way I'd informed him of Luca's birth. But neither he nor Tammy had visited Hannah in hospital.

We knew we'd have enough men without him, and a few extras: Alex, Reuben, Casper, Ralph, Rudy, Joel, Ari, Uncle Isaac, Hector, Paris, Otus (one of Rhea's brothers. The other one was away on business), Alex's two closest friends, Phoenix and Hunter were coming, as well as Henry the First. He and Vette were now a solid item. Henry had changed, Vette didn't need to have sex with herself anymore and both their complexions were glowing. Albie wasn't invited. Ralph didn't want him here and told Norma as much. It wasn't his call, but I didn't want him here either.

The mohel, the doctor who'd be performing the circumcision, was setting up in the dining room. His instruments, ointments, gauze and whatnot were laid out on a sterile cloth on the dining room table. He seemed satisfied that everything was in place.

As I gave the sideboard another once-over to make sure everything was in place, someone tapped me on the shoulder. It was Rhea. We kissed and she introduced me to the man standing next to her, her brother, Otus. I exchanged some pleasantries with them, but I was sidetracked when I noticed the nattering in the room had all but died down, and one by one, heads were turning in the direction of the front door.

Jeeeeesus!

About to make a grand entrance, Hector was framed in the doorway, looking like a Salvador Dali painting—one the artist himself would have thrown on the scrap heap because it was too off the wall even for him.

Hector wore a retro seventies, low-cut, groovy dancer disco jumpsuit in a crocodile skin pattern. The three large buttons above the zip that kept it closed were under so much pressure, they threatened to pop and fly across the room like champagne corks. The black satin shirt under the jumpsuit was half undone, revealing a thick gold medallion suspended from a chain and resting on a nest of ginger chest hair. And to round off the look, his pants were tucked into python skin cowboy boots.

I looked at Rhea, mystified and mortified. She gave me a resigned smile. This was the poor woman's norm.

Maxi caught my eye from across the room. *'What the fuck?'* she mouthed.

And you've yet to hear him speak. I shook my head.

Hector was heading in our direction. The crowd whispered, and parted like the Red Sea. I turned tail, pretending I'd forgotten something in the kitchen.

I sidled up to Ralph, who was leaning against the breakfast bar with ankles crossed, arms folded and a lazy smile. I whispered, *'Dear God, he looks like a dick!'*

'Amen to that.' He stared at Hector then whispered back, *'So ... how many crocs and snakes do you reckon had to be circumcised to outfit him?'*

I laughed out loud. Fear of Luca's impending procedure and Portnoy's Chinese whispers had made me feel a little twitchy. Ralph's quip appeased me.

The ceremony started fifteen minutes later. Jewish law and custom had the men at the centre of the action, time-travelling into the past to watch what had happened to their eight-day-old mini schlongs. They were gathered in the dining room while the women stood on the outskirts in the lounge. I introduced Rhea to Maxi, Vette, Greta, Leah, Hannah's two closest girlfriends, Grace and Cleo, and my aunts, Norma and Miri.

Hannah, who stood next to me, caught a glimpse of Hector and muttered under her breath, 'Oh my God. It's a bris, not a fancy dress party, you idiot.'

We were five minutes into the service when Joel rushed past us and joined the other men. Iris tapped me on the shoulder and whispered, *'Sorry we're late, hon.'* We kissed and hugged. *'Joel forgot—'* She was looking past me. She screwed up her face and gave me a disbelieving look. *'Bugger me dead! Who's the fuckwit with the Elvis do and the Stayin' Alive duds? And, really? Is it appropriate to wear the skin of anything—except maybe cowhide—at a bris?'* Iris and I had had several conversations on the run since Leah's engagement. We kept catching each other at a bad time, so I hadn't got around to telling her about Hector.

I mouthed, *Shhh.* Rhea, who was standing next to me, turned towards Iris, outstretched her hand and said in a good-natured whisper, *'Hi. I'm Rhea. And "the fuckwit" is my husband, Hector.'*

Iris the Amazon warrior took her hand and blanched. 'Uh ... uh ... sorr ...' She fixed Rhea with a catatonic-like stare. 'Sssorry.'

Oh boy. *Look away! Look away, Iris!*

Iris has chaetophobia—a fear of an excess amount of hair. For her, it's unwanted body hair on women. She never went on holidays without razors, an electric shaver, depilatory cream, a tub of wax, and tweezers. And she had her dyed flame-red super-short boy crop trimmed every three weeks. When I told her about Baubo, she'd said, 'Huh. Prob'ly why you end up in hairy situations so often. Epilate her, babycakes, or get another muse.'

Iris couldn't take her eyes off Rhea. *God, please make her turn away before she emerges from the trance and says something inappropriate.*

Luca's sudden, shrill cry distracted all of us. Hannah and I teared up. We put our arms around each other. Thankfully, Luca settled quickly. We'd chosen a merciful mohel, but I hated the thought of my grandbaby being hurt. I refused to buy the claim that the snip didn't.

With the service over, Hannah took Luca to pacify him with a feed, and the men made a beeline for the sideboard to pacify themselves with a feed.

I watched Hector stagger to a chair, collapse onto it, cross his legs and cross his arms over his legs. His already pale face was ghost-white.

I elbowed Ralph, who was standing next to me with a plate full of food, and I whispered, *'Check it out.'*

Ralph turned to look. 'Aha.' He smiled. 'That explains the source of his many problems.'

'Which is ...?'

He licked the cream cheese off his fingers and dropped his voice to a whisper. *'He has castration anxiety.'*

'Huh? I thought you'd already established he has no balls.'

'Yeah. But castration anxiety isn't just restricted to fear of losing your balls. It's a fear of having any part of your genitalia disfigured. I mean ... you could do without the two Brussels sprouts, but a man's not a man without the meat.' He shivered at the thought, took a bite out of his non-meat bagel and continued with his little tutorial. *'And thing is, once you've been emasculated, it keeps getting reinforced. If his mother was a*

ball-breaker, he'll keep being drawn to women who do the same thing to him.'

I looked back at Hector. The snake was sweating like a pig. Rhea stood in front of him, arms akimbo, lips pressed together into a thin line. She said something to him, he responded with a submissive nod. Then her eyes searched the room until they found me. She left Hector there and came over. She smiled an apology. 'We have to go. Hector's not feeling very well. He says it must be from something he ate before we left.' We shared a look that said, *What a crock.* An appropriate evaluation; we'd shared a moment.

Yep, you and I are destined to be friends.

As I watched them leave, his arm hooked around hers for support, I was starting to get that behind Rhea's politeness, the woman had balls—her own, and his. She looked back and winked at me before closing the door.

About ten minutes later, the doorbell rang.

Casper walked past me. 'I'll get it,' he said.

Two burly police officers stood on the other side.

CHAPTER TWENTY-SIX

Cut 'N' Paste

S hit. Whorebringers of doom, even worse than an early-morning or late-night phone call.

I rushed to the door. 'What's wrong? Has something happened?' The people I was close to were all present and accounted for, but I still felt panicky.

Conversation behind me was petering out and the room fell silent.

'Are you the home owner, Ma'am?' the blond cop asked.

'Yes, it's my place.'

'We've had a complaint about noise pollution.'

Ooh ... that bitch! Casper and I exchanged a knowing look. His prediction of crotch rot had come in the form of the fuzz. Clearly, the old boozer had thought outside the box, adding ammunition to her existing cache to further blacken my name. Or try to.

'Ma'am?'

'Mm?'

The dark-haired, younger one looked past me at everyone in the lounge watching us. 'I said it's a bit early for a party, isn't it?'

'Not when you're being circumcised.'

Oh, Casper.

'Pardon?'

'My nephew just lost his foreskin. It's a Jewish ritual circumcision that's cause for celebration.'

Both big uniformed beefies winced. I didn't know if this meant they were circumcised or not. Either way, it wasn't relevant. The source of the complaint was.

'You probably can't tell us who reported us, but we know, all right!' I scowled. 'Our neighbours are great. They knew about this, but even if I hadn't told them, they'd be fine with it. It's that drunken hag in the dung heap across the road.' I pointed in the direction of the dung heap. Both turned and glanced at it. Dark's face twisted into a pained smile. Light's remained impassive. 'She's on a permanent bender. I swear she's made it her life purpose to drag all of us down with her.'

Light sermonised, 'There's not much you can do about people like that.'

'*Hmph.* Easy to say when it doesn't affect you.'

He fixed me with a murderous look and assumed a patronising manner. 'Ma'am. A lot of the complaints amount to nothing, like this one. And there's only so much we can do. But we're doing our job—at the very least, we have to follow up on a complaint.'

A short, prickly silence ensued, then Casper said, 'Hmm ... Okay. How 'bout we lodge a counter-complaint? Visual pollution.' He turned towards Dark. 'You know, the presence of any unpleasant sight that can ruin the aesthetic appeal of an area?'

Dark nodded like he pretended to understand.

Casper added, 'She herself is visual pollution. Not much you can do when someone's ugly, right?' He directed this at Light. Then he said to Dark, 'But at least she doesn't come out during the day.'

'That ugly, huh?' Dark remarked.

Light shot Dark a dark look.

'You have no idea.' Nor did Casper. He had relied on my description. He continued, 'Here's the thing, though. I don't have a problem with art, but half a dozen of her garden gnomes are toting guns, and one's penis is exposed!'

Dark smiled again. Light remained poker-faced as he spoke to me. 'I'm afraid you'll have to take that up with your local council.'

Right. You've done your job ... at the very least. 'I did, and so have the neighbours. It got us nowhere.'

'Well, you can start a petition,' he said. 'Go to your ombudsman. Lobby your local MP—'

'Could you maybe say something to her?' *Scare the bag.*

'It's out of our hands, Ma'am.' Light was getting impatient.

I fixed him with a bold look and assumed a self-assured manner. 'Yes. I understand. But can you please go over there and check it out?'

Dark said, 'Yeah, we could do that.'

Light wasn't happy. He silenced the rookie with an angry stare, but agreed to go and look.

'Good.' Casper smiled at Light. 'Like you said, at the very least, you have to follow up on a complaint.'

He and Casper eyeballed one another until Light turned away.

As they were about to leave, Casper said, 'Wait up. Why don't you take my nephew's foreskin, cover the gnome's genitals with it? And in the interest of decency, leave a note for her to rub it every morning so it grows into a sheet.'

Dark laughed, our guests laughed. Even Light had trouble suppressing a smile.

Everyone fought for a front row view at the window after I closed the door. We watched the cops make their way across to Portnoy's. Light seemed to be giving Dark a mouthful. They stopped in front of her yard, surveyed it from the footpath. I saw the diamond shape in her blinds get bigger. And lighter. Her eye must have nearly popped out. Wouldn't be much of a stretch.

Like tennis match spectators, Light and Dark's heads moved from left to right. Dark must have spotted the flasher. He threw his head back and laughed. Dark's reaction would have made me laugh if Portnoy hadn't witnessed it. But Light was pissed off. I lip-read 'Shut up!'

I felt happier now, knowing a first step had been taken, making it clear to her that I'd had a gutful. I waited until after everyone left, about an hour later, to take the second step. I called the council.

The customer service officer did a search and located the data on the original complaints. He said the inspectors found there was nothing that posed a public health risk.

'Doesn't harbouring vermin constitute a health risk?' I asked.

'Do you have proof?'

I detected a little snigger when I told him I thought a rat lived in her letterbox. And when I provided the additional bit of data—the gnome displaying the additional bit—he guffawed.

Bad call. Bad, bad call, mate!

I was sick of having my views, grievances and ideas ridiculed or discounted. I was sick of *me* being ridiculed or discounted, treated like I didn't matter. Portnoy with her need to target someone. Cops that cop out. And these public servants with their punch-clock mentality—flurries of activity only when they were feeding the office rumour mill or having their smokos and lunch breaks, sitting on their fat arses in between and doing the bare minimum while watching the clock. Screw that!

'Oh, so you think this is funny?' I said to the hyena. 'You call this customer service? You think you're my only option? Well,' I said, 'think ombudsman, think local MP, think a picture and article in *The Advertiser* with the street name and suburb mentioned.' Then I argued like a lobbyist. 'The unmentioned council's indifference and lack of pride in the suburbs within its boundaries would be exposed, just like the gnome's penis. And the unmentioned council's promise to represent and promote the interests of ratepayers and residents, to protect the environment and improve local amenity would be exposed as a big fat lie!'

The hyena wasn't laughing anymore. He cleared his throat and said he'd get straight onto it. 'Give it a couple of weeks,' he said.

Hail the warrior princess!

It only took a couple of hours.

I was at my computer when a car pulled up across the road and two official-looking men—one with a clipboard—stepped out. They scanned the junkyard and shook their heads. I rushed to the window for a closer indirect piece of the action, just in time to see Portnoy's fingers further parting the aperture to accommodate her prying cyclopean eye. The man without the clipboard studied the yard and spoke to the clipboard man, who took notes. The unclipboarded man then turned and headed in the direction of my place. With stealthy steps I moved away from the window, counted to ten after the doorbell rang, then answered it, trying to appear nonchalant.

This man was tall, trim and well groomed. And unlike the short, fat, slobby, curmudgeonly inspector, he was polite and respectful. He introduced himself as the Environmental Health Team Officer, and said the complaints were justified. I asked if he'd seen the nude gnome.

'Gnomes-*ss*, you mean. There are four of them.' *Oh dear God.* The flasher had reproduced since I'd last looked. 'Two male, two female,' he added.

Well, that's just bloody great. If they procreate, we're gonna end up with a nudist colony in the 'burbs. Do the females have a fig leaf over their vaginas, at least? Does the second male gnome look like the fat, retired inspector?

The man cut into my thoughts. He said there were signs of life in the squalor. He saw rub marks and an accumulation of rat droppings. I had a case. He would submit a report, but, bureaucracy being what it was, and depending on Portnoy's level of cooperation, he told me it might take a while for something to be done.

No matter. I felt vindicated. A process was being put into action.

A week later, Casper, Ralph and I had just cleared up after a late dinner when a blood-curdling scream rent the air.

CHAPTER TWENTY-SEVEN

Rats in the Belfry

We stopped talking, looked at each other, and then made for the front door.

The noise was coming from across the road. Portnoy's keening, shadowy form in the middle of her front yard was semi-illuminated by the streetlight. Her head thrown back, she was yowling and screeching, 'Where are their knobs? Where are my boys' knobs? You're gunna paaaaay!'

It didn't take us long to figure out that Flasher Gnomes had been John-Wayne-Bobbitted. But where Bobbitt's penis had been found and reattached, I held out no hope for Portnoy's boys' 'boys'.

'Bitchin'!' Casper punched the air. Ralph and I air punched. *Phoo, phoo, phoo.*

'You're gunna paaaaay. You're gunna diiiie!' she rasped.

'Bloody hell!' said a voice to our right. It was my neighbour, Zac. 'That hag's seriously not playing with a full deck. Grog musta fried her brains. Kinda tragic, hey?'

'Yep,' I said.

'Pretty satisfying, though, innit?' He favoured us with a wicked smile.

'You betcha.' We sniggered.

'Any idea who did it?' said Cilla, the neighbour on the other side.

We all said no.

'When we find out, how 'bout we reward him? Or her?' said her husband, Phil.

We agreed it was the right thing to do and went back inside our respective homes, leaving coyote ugly to howl at the moon.

Ralph closed the door and said, 'Looks like someone's castration anxiety's been realised.'

'Huh? She's a woman.'

'Ya think?' Casper said.

Ralph said, 'Let's assume she is. The female equivalent of castration anxiety is penis envy. She's just lost the only two she's probably ever had.'

I laughed at him, but then quickly sobered when I realised that Portnoy was pointing the finger at me, even though the identity of whoever was 'gunna paaaaay' and 'gunna diiiie' was a mystery. I confessed that her threats terrified me.

'Don't worry. She'll just hit back with gossip,' Casper said. 'You know, sticks and stones. But people'll stop listening. You know, the boy who cried wolf.'

I scrunched up my face. 'You realise you just sounded like your late grandmother.'

Casper gasped. 'You t-hhake that back, *pth pth pth*!' He and Ralph did one of those up high, down low, too slow man-things. Then Ralph got serious.

He said to Casper, 'Idioms, proverbs—whatever—they don't apply so much to sociopaths and psychopaths. This lot can be unpredictable.' He said to me, 'D'you want me to stay here for a few nights?'

'No. I'll be okay.'

False bravado. I wasn't okay. For the next three nights I tossed and turned, my gut knotting every time I heard a noise.

On Friday morning, Casper opened the front door to bring in the paper. *'Eeeoow!'* He recoiled.

'What is it?'

He bent down, then stood up with the rolled newspaper in his left hand, and a dead rat dangling by the tail between his right thumb and forefinger. 'Looks like Portnoy's given birth on our porch.'

I felt sick.

He threw the newspaper to me, went outside, crossed the road and slung Portnoy's lifeless progeny into her front yard. He flipped her the bird, then came back in and scrubbed and disinfected his hands.

The two of us ate our breakfast in silence until Casper said, 'Mum, do you want me to sleep in the lounge tonight, you know, just in case she comes back?'

'No, no.' I tried to sound confident even though I didn't feel it. A mother was supposed to protect her children, not the other way around. But how could I protect Casper if I couldn't even protect myself?

Nothing happened that night or on Saturday or Sunday. Ralph had insisted on staying over. I slept well those three nights, and I left the front porch light on through the whole of Monday and Tuesday nights.

'D'you really wanna live like this?' Casper asked, when he turned the light off and brought in the paper on Wednesday morning.

He was right. Bugger that—Wednesday night, no light on.

Sleep took a long time to come and when it did, it was fitful. I dreamt of the pitter-patter sounds of rats scampering around my bedroom. The next morning, Casper found another satanic offering on the porch. 'Jesus! What, does she breed them?'

Maybe I'd been right two years earlier when I'd imagined her letterbox was a rat dwelling. I felt agitated for most of the day, but I refused to leave the outside light on. I wasn't going to be bullied by this woman. Still, I couldn't sleep.

Around one o'clock, I thought a cup of hot milk might help settle my nerves. I was about to switch on the kitchen light when I heard a scraping noise near the front door and a faint but familiar gravelly voice. Fear gave way to anger. I stalked across the lounge, and ripped open the door as I flicked the porch light switch. Portnoy gasped and shielded her eyes. A dead rat lay at her feet. She tried to flee.

'You stop right there!'

She half-turned towards me and froze like an apprehended fugitive staring down the barrel of a gun. I glowered at her, willing myself not to look away. The fact that her mega-eye was out of sight made it easier. Her other one was darting all over the place.

I spoke in a direct and forceful manner. 'I don't know what your problem is'—*apart from the fact that you're so fucking ugly*—'and I don't care.' I stressed these words. 'I have no idea who dismembered your stupid gnomes, but it wasn't me. And you're not gonna scapegoat me again. Dumping dead rats on my doorstep ... despicable behaviour! Now, you pick this *thing* up and get it and yourself off my property.' I made an angry jabbing motion with my finger. 'And if you so much as put a toe over the boundary line, I'll sue you for trespassing!'

She looked down and shuffled her feet as she muttered, 'Got no proof.'

'Yes, we have.' Casper's voice coming from behind me startled us both. An involuntary *'Oof'* escaping his lips, he shuddered as he caught an eyeful of Portnoy—a full-frontal view of her face. He shook off the feeling and tapped the video camera. 'Got it all right here.'

Bitchin'! Casper—always quick on the trigger. I gave him a thumbs up and turned back to her. 'In fact, now that we do have proof, if you're thinking of targeting me again by spreading vicious rumours, I'll take that video to the police. And I won't think twice about giving the neighbours a copy if you dump rats at their doors!'

Cowed by my dour tone and my warning, she edged back towards the doorstep, picked up the rat by its tail and left with her tail between her legs.

'And put your obscene gnomes in ya back yard where nobody else has to look at 'em!' I yelled, as she scuttled across the road like one of her rats.

Xena blinded the Cyclops. Ooh, yeah!

I closed the door, switched off the outside light and turned to Casper. 'Well done, Son.'

He moved his head in an almost imperceptible nod. He was crouched down in front of the television unit rifling through the drawer that housed the DVDs. I watched him as he fished out *A Nightmare on Elm Street*, slotted the disc into the drive, dropped onto the sofa and aimed the remote at the TV.

'You're kidding? You're gonna watch a horror movie?'

He pressed pause and turned to me. He was in a stupor. 'I've just starred in one.'

I smiled. 'We both have—'

'Yeah, but at least you knew what to expect.' He shivered violently, his face contorted like he'd chewed and swallowed a garden slug. 'And honestly, I thought you were exaggerating when you described her.'

'Clearly, not. But, uh, how is watching a horror movie supposed to help you?'

He sighed. 'Well ... it's not gonna erase the memory. But I need to superimpose a horrible fictional image over the real one that's emblazoned on my *normal*-sized eyeballs!' Casper liked watching the occasional scary movie. When I'd tried protesting, he told me the genre tapped into the dark side of his mythical consciousness and paid homage to his fears. I was in no position to argue with that. Casper assured me he felt loved and wouldn't become Freddy Krueger. With his powers of persuasion, I worried that he'd become a lawyer or a politician instead.

'Okay. Just don't stay up too late.'

As I headed for my room, he called out, 'Mum?'

I turned around.

'What if she comes back?'

'She won't.'

And I was right to feel confident. No more rumours, no more rodents. It wasn't the threat that kept her away from my property and my life, though. I knew that constructing a ten-foot, brick boundary wall with barbed wire on top wouldn't have done it either. It was setting a personal boundary that did it.

And the council did their bit. Three weeks later, contractors were in Portnoy's front yard cleaning up. I learned they couldn't take away her gnomes because the little shits didn't breach the *Public Health Act*, but she removed them anyway. I doubted it was out of respect for the neighbours. It was probably because she feared for their safety.

I also doubted her front yard would remain barren. Hoarders have mental disorders; the environmental officer had said so. *You don't say.* Cleaning up the mess would only scratch the surface. If she didn't clean up her issues, it was only a matter of time before we'd hear the sounds of rats scratching the surface again.

For now, though, the reformed warrior princess had fought evil and won! Life was on an even keel again. I savoured it while it lasted. A wise choice, because it wouldn't last for long.

PART THREE

WAKING OVER THE COALS

CHAPTER TWENTY-EIGHT

Persona Non Gwata

Ralph was enjoying getting to know his mother. He'd stepped up his fortnightly visits to once a week. I was yet to meet Beth, but it was just a matter of time, Ralph said. It didn't bother me. I was enjoying getting to know my grandson.

A contented baba with a chilled mama, Luca grew more beautiful every time I saw him, which was often—Hannah either came over with him or I'd go to her place. In the early days, I'd text before leaving home:

Is it safe?

Hannah was happy for me to drop in, whenever. She wasn't happy for Hector to drop in, ever. He'd taken to swinging by on his 'twavels'. After the third time, she told him there would be no more of this unannounced popping-in rubbish. As a grandfather, he had visitation rights. As a pain in the arse, his rights had restrictions. He was to call first. Hannah told me I didn't need to text anymore because she had an arsenal of excuses to keep him away (unless Alex was home, in which case she'd text: Unsafe). She didn't want to see Hector, and I was in no rush to see him again. I didn't have to until Luca was six months old.

Hannah invited us all over for afternoon tea for Alex's birthday. Casper couldn't come. He and his mates would be at Christies Beach again that weekend. And Ralph had to attend a mental health conference. His disappointment was threefold: 1) He'd be missing out on seeing and playing with Luca. A mutual adoration had sprung up between the two of them. 2) He'd be missing out on seeing and playing with Hector. 3) Mental health conferences were insane, he said.

Reuben was already there when I arrived and Luca was having his afternoon nap. I stole into his room to have a look. I wanted to pinch those angelic little cheeks.

'Can I wake him?'

'No!'

Not-so-chilled Mama tried to drag me out of the nursery, but the doorbell rang.

A minute later, Rhea, Hector and Paris tiptoed into the room behind Hannah, who was rolling her eyes.

Holy crap!

Hector was sporting a long-sleeve, men's stripper tuxedo T-shirt and low-rise jeans. With the T-shirt's photorealistic design displaying an image of an open black dinner jacket exposing an impressive naked six-pack, and a half-undone fly revealing a taut, bare belly, it would make any woman look twice. But with an inch of Hector's pasty flab screaming peekaboo between the hem of the shirt and the waistband of the jeans, it would make any woman look away. Pity Ralph wasn't here.

Rhea and I hugged, Paris kissed me on the cheek, Hector and I nodded at each other with cool civility. Mine carried a *go-fuck-*

yourself subtext. He blanched. I was kind of thrilled because I'd been honing my telepathic skills ever since learning about them at a woo-woo night I'd attended twenty-seven years earlier. Hector and I were no more attuned now than we were that night at the hospital when he didn't 'hear' me, but now that he did, I took it to mean my ability to transmit had improved. Still, I reined myself in because I knew that projecting bad shit could backfire.

Hector peered into the cot, regarding Luca like he was some sort of curio. *'His skin's faded a bit,'* he whispered.

'Must be from the daily baths,' Hannah replied.

'Mm. Mm. Wegular washing will do that.'

Stupid.

Hannah rolled her eyes again. No point saying anything. Nobody did. Except Luca. He woke up, saw Hector eyeballing him, dropped his bottom lip and squealed.

Don't blame you, Booboo. You can't fool kids and dogs.

Hannah picked up Luca and made *'shh shh'* noises. She took him into the lounge, draped a sarong over her shoulder and fed him. Twenty minutes later, she handed him to me—Heaven— and went off to organise the birthday cake. We sang 'Happy Birthday' and Hannah served up cake, coffee, and an announcement.

'Alex and I want to get married in three months.'

We were all dumbfounded. Even Luca stopped his little *meow-meow* noises.

'Oh. I thought you didn't want to get married,' I said.

'Well, I've changed my mind.'

'Okay. But ... what's the hurry?'

'Really? *You* wanted us to get married during my pregnancy!'

'Uh, what I meant was three months isn't much time to organise a wedding.'

'We don't want a big deal, just something intimate.' She looked at Reuben. 'Maybe we could have it in Auntie Iris's backyard?'

Reuben slowly nodded. 'Good idea. I'll ask—'

'Well, I'd like to pwopose that Whea and I host it in our backya—'

'No, no, no. Parents of the bride and groom shouldn't be hosting the wedding.'

Nice save, Reuben! He would have asked to have Clit as the ring-bearer.

Reuben was already dialling Iris's number. 'My sister had her daughter's engagement in her backyard, and it was lovely.'

Iris was a high-octane chick. Not much left her frazzled and, apart from excess female body hair, not much bothered her. She was more than happy to have the wedding at her place and be involved in the planning. It was a good start.

Step two. 'Mum, maybe you can ask Maxi to pull some strings with caterers and stuff?'

'Sure. Good thinking.' Maxi had a lot of connections through her line of work.

'Can you call her? Please?'

'Sure.'

'Hello, like ... *now*?'

Oh, yes. The instant gratification of Gen Y? I gave her a curious look.

She responded with a wide-eyed one. 'It makes sense to get the ball rolling now, you know, while everyone's here.'

Ahh. The pragmatism of Gen Y. 'Now' as opposed to having to get together again with Hector.

I called Maxi. She was tickled pink and started tossing around ideas about catering, seating, photography, videography, floral arrangements, and music.

'Uh, I don't want to dampen your enthusiasm, Max, but they want something very small.'

'No worries. But small or large, you still have to consider all these things.'

I told her I'd call her when I got home. She said she'd let Vette know the good news.

Ten minutes later, Vette called, also tickled pink. She asked if she could be involved in the planning and said, 'I'd love to organise Hannah's dress if she'll let me.'

Hannah was chuffed. Both Maxi and Vette were her godmothers. They would do anything for her, and I knew they'd pull out all stops to make her day special.

For the rest of the afternoon we discussed the logistics and agreed on a date. As we all got up to leave, Hector said, 'We should have a blue and white theme. Like the Gweek flag.'

Hannah started to protest. 'That's our de—'

'And the Iswaeli flag.'

Surprise.

Silence.

More silence.

'*Ahem*. That's a great idea, Dad.'

Hector raised his chin. 'Thank you.' *Smug.* 'And I'm alweady thinking about my speech.'

Your speech? Sweet mother of Jesus!

Nobody commented, but Hannah looked like her puppy had just died (even though she didn't have one). The scourge of foresight. We said our goodbyes, I hugged her and whispered, *'I'll see what I can do.'*

Ralph called around five-thirty to say he was on his way. He'd stayed for the wrap-up, but didn't feel the need to hang around for the drinks reception.

He picked up some burgers and chips on the way over, and asked me all about my afternoon while we sat at the breakfast bar and ate. He was happy for Hannah and Alex, but mostly, he wanted to hear about Hector. The expression on his face as I talked was one of perverse glee.

I swallowed a mouthful of food and looked at him through narrowed eyes. 'Do you get this excited when you hear your loony clients' stories?'

'Of course not.' He took a big bite out of his burger. 'It's not the same. I can't toy with them. I'd be out of a job.' He chewed and swallowed. 'But if I'd been a keynote speaker at the conference today, I would have taken Hector along for show-and-tell.'

I laughed at him, took a swig of water and said, 'So. Did you learn anything there about how to gag the mentally insane?'

'Nup. And I'm not much wiser than I was when you faced that predicament.'

I thought back to the time my mother was planning my wedding:

I had almost no input. Sylvia was at the helm. But when Joe asked if Albie could propose the toast to the parents of the bride, Sylvia agreed. She could foresee a problem, though, and suggested Albie record his toast and then mime it. *Dumb.* The recorded toast might be stutterless, but his lip-sync would be a total f-f-f-fuck-up. His mouth would be moving long after the speech was over.

Now, all these years later, even my mind was speechless at the memory of Sylvia's stupid, short-sighted solution. I couldn't stop Albie from speaking, and I'd suffered from the scourge of foresight, just like Hannah was suffering now. But I'd spoken up back then and no-way-Joséd my mother's idea. I told her Albie could propose the toast only if he said, 'Here's to Sylvia and Joe, the parents of the bride'. Not a word more. I should have said not a syllable more. He got in an extra ten with 'p-p-p-p-p-parents' and 'b-b-b-b-b-bride'.

Ralph cut in to my reflections. 'Look, you know you can't stop him from speaking at his own son's wedding, but why don't you offer to polish his speech for him, you know, in your capacity as a writer? Then replace all the words with 'r' in them with r-less synonyms.'

'Oh, yeah? What's a synonym for Rhea? And Paris?' I gave him a wry smile. 'It's an interesting idea, but we both know he has to have the last word.'

'Tries to.' Ralph smirked.

'Okay, so maybe he doesn't succeed with you, but ...' I shrugged.

'Well, then, you just gotta do what you did with Albie at your wedding. Make sure he keeps it brief. I remember that worked out okay.'

I scoffed at him. 'You *remember*? You weren't even there!' Mr keep-it-brief had lost his briefs. He'd gone missing during his father's speech. Myron found him bare-arsed in the back of Albie's car, boffing Maxi (an act of nostalgia, he'd said).

He smiled at the memory.

I called Hannah. 'We'll give him a time limit. I'll speak to him and tell hi—'

'Uh-uh,' Ralph cut in in the background. 'You speak to Rhea.' Good point.

Hannah was a little mollified, but she still worried that Hector would turn her wedding into a three-ring circus. As it happened, she wasn't far off the mark.

CHAPTER TWENTY-NINE

Her Small,
Slim Grewish Wedding

I called Rhea the next morning. We chatted for a bit about the upcoming wedding, then I said, 'Hannah wants the speeches kept short. Would you mind overseeing Hector's?' *Would you mind bridling his bazoo?*

She agreed—'Absolutely'—and she asked if she could please be included in the planning.

I agreed—'Absolutely'—and I didn't regret it.

Rhea was easy to be around and she worked well with Maxi, Vette, Iris and me. We got together once a week, and although Iris couldn't entirely overlook Rhea's wanted unwanted hair, she stopped her blatant staring and resisted the urge to say something. Hannah joined us occasionally, but mostly, she trusted us to choreograph the whole affair.

We presented her with a few invitation options. She chose the simple, modern design printed on off-white cardstock, layered on rustic kraft cardstock and wrapped with twine. It was the perfect choice—her wedding was going to have a rustic flavour.

We rotated venues, which meant Maxi, Vette and Iris got to officially meet Hector the first time we convened at Rhea's house. The minute Maxi and Iris were introduced to him, he looked like he'd been neutered. Again. With their alpha female auras, they had him (by the knackers) at 'Hello'.

We five girls collaborated effectively in the limited time we had: the invitations went out; the rsvp's came in; the time flew ...

... and just like that, the big day arrived.

Maxi, Vette and I were at Iris's place very early on the day to attend to last minute things. Hannah arrived with Luca not long after. She'd packed two bottles of expressed milk, Tupperware containers of pear and cinnamon porridge for breakfast, puréed meat 'n' veggies for lunch and puréed tuna 'n' veggies for dinner. Joel took the portacot out of her boot and set up in the spare room. Leah, who was Hannah's only bridesmaid, was there ten minutes later (no longer living at home, she had moved in with Ari a couple of months earlier). The hairdressers and make-up artist also turned up around the same time.

It was spring and a beautiful day was predicted. A pagoda marquee, open on two sides, had been set up for the reception. Looking out onto Iris and Joel's backyard, it was on the far right and took up almost one half of it. Two men and the florist were on the opposite side of the yard and had just finished constructing a chuppah—the canopy under which a Jewish marriage ceremony is performed. The four wooden poles that held up the corners of a large white square silk cloth were festooned with branches and blue, purple, white and violet gerberas. It gave the chuppah a countrified vibe.

Two other men were putting out white folding chairs in two lots of eight rows to accommodate the ninety-odd guests—thirty from Rhea and Hector's side, thirty from ours and thirty plus of Hannah and Alex's friends.

'It's way too many people, I don't want all these people!' Hannah had whined.

'Fine. Some divvied pruning, then? Some of our friends go, but so do some of yours,' I flung back.

No response. End of discussion.

The seating was being organised in a Chevron configuration—a V formation along a central aisle—so that the guests would be looking in between the heads of those in the row in front of them. Everyone would get a decent view of the ceremony.

Inside, we rhapsodised over Hannah's gown after Vette removed it from its garment bag. She had sourced an exquisite ivory, Grecian-goddess empire dress. In an elegant corded lace, the bodice had a low V-neck bust with a delicate scallop, and a wide under-bust panel that peaked upwards in the centre. With its small cap sleeves and an open back, the dress softly cascaded to floor length.

Hannah fed Luca just before getting dressed, then handed him to Lila. A capable woman in her sixties, Lila occasionally babysat Luca. He loved her, she loved him, so Hannah hired her for the day.

Both Reuben and I cried when, at ten-fifteen, our gorgeous girl emerged coiffed and dressed. Iris cried, Maxi cried, Vette cried.

Hannah wore her hair in a half-up, half-down style. She didn't want a veil. Instead, she'd chosen a simple floral crown of baby's breath.

Leah looked beautiful in a light sapphire-blue chiffon dress. It had a criss-cross pleated bodice with a sweetheart neckline, wide ruched straps and a skirt that flared slightly from the waist and ended in a midi-length handkerchief hem. Both Hannah and Leah would carry simple bouquets of baby's breath.

I wore a lacy knee-length, lavender-blue sheath dress with a strapless white lining. The dress had cap sleeves, a scoop neckline and V-back.

Casper, a snappy dresser, had been charged with selecting Reuben's garb (he has colour and pattern coordination problems). Our son had done a fine job. He'd selected a blue-grey, lightweight suit with a white shirt for his father, and for himself, greige cotton trousers and a preppy-look, trim-fit cotton-and-linen blend shirt in a light lavender-blue with a fine, horizontal chambray stripe.

The ceremony was scheduled for midday, allowing us ample time for photos. Hannah, Reuben, Leah and I struck a variety of individual and group poses in the lounge room under the photographer's direction. Vette was his self-appointed assistant. Maxi was nowhere to be seen, but also everywhere at the same time. She was busy liaising with the caterers that had taken over Iris's kitchen, and the marriage celebrant and musicians—a female vocalist and a male guitarist/vocalist hired for some intimate, laid-back music during the reception. Maxi had used them before at staff parties and raved about them. Iris zipped back and forth between the garden and the lounge. Maxi came back inside half an hour into the shoot to tell us Ralph and Casper had arrived, and Iris poked her head around the door about ten minutes later.

'Your groom's coming up the drive now, honey.'

Hannah beamed.

'Rhea, Paris and the dick are with him.'

Hannah groaned. 'Jesus, Auntie Iris! He's gonna be my father-in-law.'

'Oh, I'm sorry, sweetie. I didn't mean to offend.'

'No. I meant, *he is going to be my FATHER-IN-LAW!*' The grim reality was setting in.

'Uh-huh. I hear ya. So then, would it make things worse or better if I told ya you gotta check him out before the ceremony?'

With that, Hannah asked the photographer to sit tight, and we rushed into the family room overlooking the backyard. Making like Olive Portnoy, we splayed the venetian slats with our fingers.

Alex, Rhea and Paris had rounded the corner and were moving into the middle of the garden. Hannah *OhmyGodded* when she saw Alex. He looked devastatingly handsome in an ivory linen suit and pale blue open-neck shirt. Paris looked dapper in a pale blue linen suit and white shirt. And Rhea, who was facing towards the window, was understated elegance. She wore a stylish, slim-fitting, indigo dress that sat just below the knee. It had a boat neck, cold-shoulder cut-outs and short flutter sleeves. She looked très chic. But, oh ...

Très shit!

Hector materialised. He wore a dark blue jacket, white trousers with thick vertical cobalt-blue stripes, a white shirt with a blue grid pattern and a blue and white-striped bow tie. Hector wasn't just flying the flag for Greece. He *was* the fucking flag! And with his red bouff and a newly sprouted moustache (which didn't quite rival Rhea's), he looked like George Costanza's father from *Seinfeld*. It seemed he was trying to upstage Hannah and Alex.

Just try it, buddy, and I'll shove a flagpole up your arse to complete the picture.

'Christ,' Reuben muttered under his breath.

Hannah had gone pale. 'Can it possibly get any worse?'

'Yeah ...' I said, staring at this tragic caricature of a man. 'There's still his speech.'

An audible gasp escaped her lips, but then she started laughing. We all did. Hector was going to be our freebie entertainment. No point fighting it.

I took one last look and nearly fell backwards. Ralph was standing with his face up against the window. He'd spread his left eye open with his left thumb and forefinger, and pointed at me with his right forefinger. I stuck my right middle finger up in between the open slat. He laughed at me and turned away. I snuck another peek at him. My God, he was one bangin', hotsy-totsy fashion plate! In light grey Chinos and a navy-blue shirt with epaulets, he looked like a man in uniform.

Quelle sex appeal! And who doesn't wanna fu—

'Mum! Come on. We have to finish the shoot.'

We made good time. Half an hour before noon, the photographer and videographer went outside to take snaps and reels of the groom and his family. And Iris, Maxi and Vette went off to get changed.

The guests were milling and mixing behind the arranged seating. Joel, Ralph and Henry were handing out light-blue suede kippot to the men—Jewish custom requires that men have their heads covered—and at ten minutes before twelve, they asked everyone to please be seated.

Casper was in charge of the CD boom box. At ten minutes past noon, we signalled to him to start the music. For their wedding march, Hannah and Alex had chosen Bond's 'Lullaby'—an upbeat version of the classical 'Peaceful Pachelbel'.

Leah made her way down the aisle, and a few beats later, Reuben and I walked Hannah towards the chuppah. We were both emotional. Alex burst into tears when he saw his bride, Rhea teared up, Paris (Alex's only groomsman) was clearly moved, and Hector was seized by a violent coughing fit.

Nice timing, dipshit! He must have swallowed a fucking fur ball building up on his jacket, tufts deposited there willy-nilly by his stinking cat ... Clit! *Where's a flagpole when you need one?*

Hannah had to circle Alex seven times—a custom representing seven wedding blessings, seven days of creation, and demonstrating that the groom is the centre of her world. By the fourth lap, she was stepping in time to Hector's rhythmic croak. Rhea handed him a lozenge.

Yeah, suck on that! He did. He shut up. We could now focus on the service, which the marriage celebrant had fashioned into a stirring, reverential blend of two traditions reflecting Hannah and Alex's ethnic backgrounds and religions.

From Alex's side, there was the 'stefana' ceremony. Paris placed flowered crowns on Hannah and Alex's heads. These two crowns were connected by a single white ribbon to represent the couple's union. The bride and groom were then led around in three circles that symbolised their past, present and future. (I couldn't watch. All this bloody circling was making me dizzy.) Both Hannah and Alex sipped wine from a common cup during the ceremony—a Jewish and Greek custom. And as the ceremony came to an end, the celebrant placed a glass wrapped in a white cloth napkin on the ground in front of Alex. He stomped hard on it and it shattered—the breaking of the glass symbolising the destruction of the Temple in Jerusalem, the glass reminding us of sadness even during the most joyous of occasions.

'*Mazel Tov!*' yelled half the guests (a Hebrew/Yiddish expression of congratulations). Everyone applauded as the newlyweds kissed.

There were kisses all round under the chuppah, which started to get crowded as guests converged. *Mwah, mwah, mwah.* But ... oh. *Shit, shit, shit.* Hector clapped eyes on me, and with a big grin on his face, he started zigzagging through the minithrong towards me. Why? I was happy with our distant, faux cordial salutations.

This canopy was open on all four bloody sides, but I was cornered. Ralph approached at the same time as Hector, who'd pushed through and planted one hand on each of my shoulders, and one sloppy, foul-breathed kiss on each of my cheeks.

Ecch.

'*Mu*zzle *off*!' he said to me.

Ralph turned away and muttered, 'Do us all a favour and put it back on.'

I wanted to laugh, but not just because of what Ralph had said. Notwithstanding Hector's buggered-up pronunciation, his raspy timbre had both a soprano and baritone range. Hector had laryngitis.

Woohoo! 'Thank you. And, uh, *sin-ga-ree-TEE-ria* to you also,' I said in my best Greek. 'But it sounds like you're not going to be able to make a speech.' *Boohoo.* 'Maybe Rhea can do it for you?'

'Oh, *no*. I won't let this stop me!'

Words failed me … *May the same condition be bestowed on you.*

He reached into his jacket inside pocket, pulled out a blue and white hanky—*really?*—and hawked a loogie into it.

Seriously? Then again … here's hoping the videographer captured the moment.

The missing 'r's' in Hector's speech were going to be the least of our worries.

'Gotta go circulate,' I told him. I dry-retched as I 'excused-me' through the crowd and out of the chuppah. I tried to feel grateful that Hector had used a snot rag … unlike my late father. God's green earth had been Joe's receptacle. He would have fired a phlegm wad onto the grass—*pt-thoo!*

I moved through the well-wishing crowd as the photographer shepherded the bridal party to the patio for pictures, and Joel, Ralph and Henry removed the chairs, scattering some around the perimeter of the garden. I spotted Maxi standing next to the marquee, talking to the caterer. She was wearing an emerald green, figure-skimming dress that fell just below the knee, had a low square neckline and wide straps. With her long chestnut hair, piercing blue eyes and red pout, she looked a knockout.

The caterer left just as I approached.

She smiled at me. 'I told him to start circulating appetisers and drinks once the seating's all cleared.'

'Thanks so much, Maxi.' I gave her a hug. 'You've done a brilliant job.' Maxi was well connected. She had called in some favours and also got a lot of things at cost.

'*We've* done a brilliant job.'

I nodded and looked past her into the marquee. Twelve round tables of eight were set with white tablecloths and mid-blue napkins. The centrepieces were small, hessian-covered and twine-tied glass vases filled with twigs and the same colour gerberas as on the chuppah. The guests would be sitting on dark walnut, white-cushioned Tiffany chairs, each with a natural jute chair bow on the back.

The waiters flitted between the tables placing bottles of drink—ouzo for the Greek guests and soda water for the Jewish guests—and baskets of poppy seed bread rolls.

'Poppy seeds? Didn't you say we should get plain?' I asked.

'Uh-huh. But then I thought it might be fun seeing photos of people with the seeds stuck between their teeth.'

I laughed at her. 'You didn't think Hector would be enough entertainment?'

Maxi didn't answer. She wasn't looking at me.

'Maxi?'

Still no answer. Still staring fixedly at something. I followed the direction of her gaze.

Oh, my. He was a Greek god, no less. Dressed casual-chic in milk chocolate-brown trousers and a black shirt, he stood next to and looked like a male version of Rhea, who was also a male version of herself. But this guy was just more so. Where Rhea could go either way, the tall, dark, lean, broad-shouldered, beautiful specimen of a man with her was pure masculinity. Rhea was talking to him, but he wasn't looking at her. He was staring back at Maxi. Rhea followed the direction of his gaze. She smiled when she saw us, linked her arm in the god's and brought him over to us.

'Ruthie, I'd like you to meet my twin brother, Nestor.'

Ruthie. Until now, Rhea had called me Ruth. It seemed our relationship had advanced to a more intimate level.

Nestor shook my hand and said, *'Mazel Tov.'*

'Thank you. And same to you, for your nephew. *Sin-ga-ree-TEE-ria.'*

'Efharisto.' He smiled and nodded politely, but then turned towards Maxi.

'And this is Maxi,' Rhea said.

Nestor extended his hand. 'Hello.' His voice took on a deeper, husky quality.

She extended her hand. 'Hello.' Her voice took on a deeper, husky quality.

They shook hands. Neither was in a hurry to let go. They locked eyes. Neither was in a hurry to turn away. And what passed between them ... well, I swear it was a *Jerry Maguire* 'you-complete-me' moment.

Rhea and I looked on in fascination. She turned to me with a closed-mouth smile and raised eyebrows. I mirrored her, and then looked from her to Nestor in fascination. Obviously, they were fraternal twins because they weren't the same sex, but they could have passed for identical. Only, Nestor was clean-shaven—no mouche, no moe.

Can I say something to Rhea about this now that she's calling me Ruthie? Am I betraying the sisterhood if I don't say something? Then again, could it be that the sisterhood has grown whiskers? Radical feminism sure generated a lot of cattiness—

'*You look absolutely gorgeous.*' Ralph's whisper cut off my thoughts. He'd come up behind me and wrapped his arms around my midriff.

I put my hands on top of his and leaned my head back against his shoulder. '*Thank you. You look pretty hot, yourself.*'

He squeezed me tighter, bent his head and kissed my cheek. Ralph was so happy that I'd initiated public displays of intimacy in the last month. And I enjoyed them. They felt good. But now, watching this public-private display of intimacy building between two people who had been strangers not five minutes ago felt delicious.

Maxi and Nestor had inched closer to each other. They were generating so much heat, you could hold a sausage sizzle in the space between them. Although ... Nestor probably already had one going on in his trousers. It was hard to resist looking down, but I remained strong.

He put his hand on Maxi's arm as he leaned in and said something to her. She threw her head back as she laughed at it, while his eyes scanned her body.

Her nipples got erect.

My nipples got erect.

Ralph *mmmed* softly.

Rhea sighed LOUDLY.

And that was the end of that.

I thought back to one of our wedding planning sessions at Iris's place.

All of us—Maxi, Vette, Iris, Rhea and I—were exhausted and frustrated after a whole lot of little things went wrong that day. Maxi sank back into the cushions of the sofa and closed her eyes. 'Oh God, I so need to get laid,' she said. Hear, hear. The consummate solution. (Her date with the media mogul and with a succession of men after him had amounted to nothing.) We all nodded in agreement. Not Rhea. Rhea did not nod in agreement—well, *duh!* But she did tell us her recently divorced 'hunky cousin Stavros' had said the same thing to her only the day before. She showed Maxi a picture of 'Stavi'. Maxi feigned an orgasm then looked at Rhea. 'Please seat him next to me at the wedding.'

That was three weeks ago. Rhea must have also been reflecting on this. She now whispered, *'I think I need to make a minor seating adjustment.'*

I nodded. *'Yeah, I think so.'*

She headed into the marquee to swap a couple of place cards and make a couple of changes to the seating list. She winked at me as she came out again. Stavi was going to be sitting with familia. Stavi was not going to get laid tonight.

I stood there with Ralph and Rhea, each of us sneaking peeks at Maxi and Nestor. Rhea introduced us to some of her friends who approached us. I introduced her to some of my friends who approached us. The photographer wrapped up the shoot and Hannah and Alex mingled with their friends. Mr Agathe had his right arm around the new Mrs Agathe. His left shoulder was doing its usual little cha-cha. I'd become accustomed to Alex's joggles, just like I rarely noticed his *ahems*. I smiled at the look of sheer joy on both Hannah and Alex's faces. Rhea sighed longingly and gazed off into a distant past, but then the ugly, wheezy present sidled up to her and made like Ralph. He wrapped his arms around her midriff. She squirmed.

Only a squirm? You're a better woman than me. I would have turned around and kneed him in the groin.

As the four of us stood there silently watching the newlyweds, Alex's arm suddenly shot up and out.

'Ooh. What was *that*?' I asked.

Rhea started to answer but Hector cut her off. 'what was what?'

'Alex's arm.'

'It's nothing.' Hector was curt.

'Uh, it's not nothing. Look. He's doing it again.'

Ralph was quietly observing; Hector was on edge.

'Well, if you must know, he has a mild kind of Touwette Syndwome. It's weally no big deal!'

The hell it's weally no big deal!

'Oh, look at the time!' Rhea said.

Nice diversion.

'It's been forty minutes since the waiters started serving the appetisers, Ruthie.'

I absently looked at my watch. I didn't care how uncomfortable they felt talking about Alex's disorder. I needed to know more. I had a grandson who might one day be jerking, blinking, grunting and yelling profanities! Action had to be taken.

'Shouldn't we be moving everyone into the marquee?' Rhea added.

Good point. The other action would have to keep.

I turned to Maxi. She and Nestor were still engaged in their flirty tête-à-tête and impervious to the time and their surrounds. Maxi would have normally been on top of this, but I imagined she was imagining Nestor on top of her.

'Leave it with me,' I told Rhea.

I found Iris and deputised her. Within ten minutes, she had mustered the guests into the marquee, and five minutes later, all were in their designated seats. Ralph and I sat with Iris and Joel, Vette and Henry, and Maxi and Nestor.

Casper was emcee. Ever since he was little, his favourite toy was words—he was one of the few people who could outwit Ralph. Casper's talent for wordplay had me beating a familiar and well-trodden path to the headmaster's office. I was in a permanent state of cringe throughout much of his primary school life, but I kept telling myself his gumption would serve him well one day. Today, it showed. His five-minute welcome speech had everyone roaring with laughter.

An entrée of seared salmon with Israeli couscous was then served while the musical duo did their thing. Hector provided backings with his hackings—*arf arf arf.* It was like being at Sea World.

'Oh my God, someone shove a piece of fish in his mouth or I'm gonna fucking kill him!' I stage-whispered through gritted teeth as I stabbed at the salmon.

I glanced up from my plate with a piece of fish harpooned and suspended on my fork. Maxi was staring at me.

Wha—?
Nestor was also staring at me.

Oh shhhhhhit. Brother-in-law.

With a barely-suppressed smile on his lips, Nestor raised a questioning brow. 'Do you need an accomplice?'

Yowza! This hot man was cool. Ralph, Iris, Joel, Vette and Henry laughed. Maxi eyed him adoringly. I *phewed*, and fell a little bit in love with him.

Five minutes later, Ralph whispered, *'You're staring.'*

I couldn't help it. Maxi and Nestor's social intercourse made it hard to turn away from. They were lost in conversation, lost each other's eyes and oblivious to their surroundings. Only the clearing and replacement of plates served as disruptions.

The waiters brought around the main meal: pecan-crusted chicken breast with herbed rice pilaf and roasted vegetables. Or, broccoli, white bean and ricotta 'meatballs' with herbed tahini yoghurt for the vegetarians. Large bowls of Greek salad joined the breadbaskets in the centre of the table. Everything looked beautiful; everything was falling into place beautifully.

We girls had all been committed to organising a marriage of the two cultures from start to finish and down to the minutest detail, but we vetoed ameletita (breaded lamb testicles) and the plate-smashing tradition. Hector had accepted our ban on the crumbed nuts, but he'd been upset about the plate-smashing.

> *'You have the glass bweaking custom. Why can't we have our plate bweaking custom?' He made a little moue with his lips.*

> *Oh, puh-leeze! Archimalakas! (Chief of arseholes!) Rhea had taught us some awesome Greek expressions.*

I smiled to myself at the memory of our get-togethers. I stopped smiling when I saw *Archimalakas* heading towards our table.

He stood behind Nestor, rested his hands on his brother-in-law's shoulders and kneaded them. '^{How} is it _{going,} my main man?'

Right. Like he's ya bruddah, ya wingman, ya homeboy? As if.

Nestor squinched up his eyes as if he'd just swallowed an ameletita. 'Very well, thank you.'

Man! This main man was mannerly. I imagined I'd receive a thankyou note from him in the next few days because I'd passed him the salt earlier.

'You've ^{done} a twuly _{tewiffic} job, ladies.'

'Thank you,' I answered for all of us. I was also mannerly. *Now piss off. Please.*

Arf arf. Arf arf. 'Whea ˢᵃⁱᵈ I should ₐₛₖ you when the ˢᵖᵉᵉᶜʰᵉˢ would begin.'

Rhea knew we'd arranged to have the speeches after the main course. She probably also wanted him to piss off.

'Soon,' I said.

'Excellent!' *Arf, arf.* He clapped his hands. A ball balanced on his nose was the only thing missing. 'I'm looking vewy ᶠᵒʳʷᵃʳᵈ to ᵐᵃᵏⁱⁿᵍ mine.'

No response except from my palms. They broke out in a sweat.

'Soon' came sooner than I thought. The waiters had finished clearing the tables and Casper was at the microphone asking for everyone's attention. He introduced the father of the bride. I reached for a tissue as Reuben spoke lovingly about our beloved daughter and praised me for my fine job of mothering. Alex was up next. I dabbed at my eyes as he spoke emotionally about having found the love of his life. And then it was Hector's turn. He should have spoken before Alex, but the attention seeker wanted to have the last word, like we'd expected.

'Showtime!' Ralph whispered.

Hector had the floor. He smiled broadly. 'My ʷⁱᶠᵉ Whea and I ʷᵒᵘˡᵈ like to ʷᵉˡᶜᵒᵐᵉ evwyone!'

An unnatural kind of hush descended. I heard our friend at the next table whisper, *'Holy cwap! Elmer J. Fudd is WEAL!'*

The faintest smile crossed Nestor's lips. Yep, mannerly.

Hector pwaised ʰⁱˢ son, *arf, arf,* said ʰᵒʷ pwoud he, *arf arf,* Whea ₐₙₐ Pawis ᶠᵉˡᵗ. *Arf arf.* Hector waxed lywical. He waxed on and on. He just didn't know when to wax off. I should have invited Mr Miyagi.

Ten minutes later, I saw Hannah looking at me, telepathically projecting, *'Mummy, DO something!'*

I turned towards Hector and telepathically projected, *'Shutthefuckup!'*

The thought was loud and clear, but Hector didn't hear. He was riding his own waveband and blissfully unaware of anybody else's. I saw Rhea projecting the same thing, only she was using hand gestures: blah-blah sock puppet, zip the lips, stop sign, throat slit—his or her own? Who knew? Hector didn't see. He didn't even notice that Casper had disconnected the mic from the amp. But he noticed the increasing chatter amongst the guests drowning him out. With his hoarse voice, the schlub couldn't compete, so he shutthefuckup. Casper then directed everyone to the dessert buffet at the back of the marquee.

Again, the two traditions were honoured. Bougatses (delicious, custard-filled pastries) and Greek baklava sat alongside traditional Jewish cheese blintzes. There were trays of fresh fruit and lots of minis: mini pavlovas, tiramisus, chocolate cases with mousse, cannolis, and strawberry soufflés. The wedding cake was a breathtaking sculpture of profiteroles— cream 'poofs' had been Hannah's favourite dessert since she was a little girl. It all added up to nirvana on a dressed trestle table.

I loaded up my plate with a sample of each—they were mini—and sat at the table savouring the treats.

Ralph leaned towards me and whispered, *'Watching you eat is such a turn-on.'*

I looked at him. His eyes widened and he laughed at me. *'Even more so if I batted for the other team!'* Both my cheeks were puffed out with food, and a cannoli was sticking out of my mouth. I took the cannoli out, chewed and swallowed the rest, and whispered back, *'Do you actually* hear *yourself when you eat?'*

Guess not. He looked puzzled. I put the cannoli back in.

Waiters came around and placed cups and saucers on the tables. Other waiters followed with pots of freshly brewed coffee and tea.

The reception started winding down around five o'clock. The guests thanked us for a wonderful afternoon. By six-thirty, everything was cleared away, tables were folded and chairs were stacked for pick-up the next day. The newlyweds left with Luca in tow and, thanks to Casper and Paris, much of their car mummified with toilet paper. Iris, Maxi, Vette, Rhea and I group-hugged. Then Maxi and Nestor floated away on a nine-cloud, and Ralph and I were on our way home.

It was only then I remembered Myron, Tammy and their sons' absence. They were overseas. Myron and I had had little contact since Sylvia passed away, but as with Luca's bris, I'd invited him to the wedding out of obligation. I thought back to my conversation with him when I called, annoyed at having received his inability to attend because he'd be away.

'We booked the holiday six months ago, what do you want me to do, Ruth?'

'Postpone!'

'We'll lose money!'

'I didn't say cancel. I said postpone. Hannah's wedding is a one-off. The Hawaiian Islands will still be there a week later.' An inconvenient truth.

We hadn't spoken since. I was about to say something to Ralph but he looked distracted.

'What's up? You looked bothered.'

'Mm. I am.'

'Bothered about ...?'

'I don't know. I can't put my finger on it.'

'Well ... like you always tell me, it'll come to you when the time's right.'

It would take another several weeks before the time was right. And right or wrong, it would up-end Ralph's world ... and it promised to up-end everyone else's.

CHAPTER THIRTY

Pyjama (Third) Parties

The doorbell rang at two o'clock the following afternoon. I was surprised to see Rhea standing there. She was surprised to see I was still in my jammies. I looked down at my pink loose tee and leggings with their pig and *oink* print, and shrugged.

'Lucky you! If I'd known, I would have worn mine.' She smiled.

You cool chick, you! I smiled back. 'Come in. I'll make us a coffee.' I was beginning to feel as comfortable with Rhea as I felt in my pyjamas.

'Have you heard from Nestor?' I asked, as she followed me into the kitchen.

'No. I've called a couple of times and left messages. You heard from Maxi?'

'Nup. I rang her office. They said she called this morning and told them she was "laid up" today.' We both laughed. 'I texted her about five minutes ago.'

Just as I said this, Maxi replied to my SMS.

On "bathroom break"

> OMG I'm in love!
>
> Never felt like this ♥ ♥ ♥

I beamed and showed it to Rhea, who let out an exhilarated sigh. Then *her* phone pinged. A radiant smile lit up her face as she read the message. 'Have a look. From Nestor.'

> Sorry didn't take calls.
>
> With Maxi.
>
> First time alone for 5.
>
> Love at first sight.
>
> So happy happy HAPPY!

We squealed like a couple of schoolgirls and hugged each other. Rhea then replied to Nestor, and I replied to Maxi. We said the same thing.

> Thrilled to hear! xx

Except I added:

> Details please ... later!

I hoped Rhea hadn't added the same thing in her brother's text. That would be creepy.

I got the dripolator going, and filled a plate with several assorted minis left over from the wedding—we'd all taken some home.

'They make a beautiful couple, don't they?' Rhea said.

'You bet!' But no sooner had I answered than my excitement took a dive. 'Mm ...'

'What?' Rhea asked.

I sucked air through my teeth. 'They only met twenty-four hours ago. Aren't you a bit wary of instant intimacy?'

'Ordinarily I would be, but I know my brother.'

'Yeah, well, being twins and—'

'No. It goes beyond that.' Her expression became sombre. 'I really like Maxi but I set her up with Stavros instead of Nestor because she said she needed to get laid. I didn't think she wanted anything more. And I wouldn't do that to Nestor.'

I couldn't mask my surprise.

'Yes, I know that sounds strange. I mean, what man wouldn't want to hop into bed with a gorgeous woman, right?' She gave me a wan smile. 'But Nestor's been through a lot, and I couldn't bear to see him hurt again.' She hesitated, her eyes revealing a pain so raw it was almost tangible. Her voice cracked as she continued. 'He'd been happily married for five years when his wife was killed in a car accident. She was eight months pregnant.'

I gasped.

'The baby—it was a boy—didn't survive. Nestor was shattered.'

I touched her arm. 'I'm so sorry. How terrible for him ... for all of you.'

'It was. Athena was a lovely person. She'd had trouble conceiving, and they were thrilled when she did ...' Rhea's eyes misted over. 'It was hard watching Nestor. He could barely get out of bed for a year. Then he just threw himself into his work. He started dating a little, but it took him five years to be open to the idea of it. And even then, he didn't really take the initiative. It was mostly arranged dates. He didn't want serious but he didn't want casual either. As you can imagine, that's kind of limiting.'

I nodded.

'You know, he used to be such a playboy before Athena, but it's not his style anymore. I'm not sure it ever was. My brother was a very caring and sensitive child. Not your average male.'

'Mm. Sounds a bit like Ralph—'

'Yeah. I get that about him.'

'He also used to be a playboy.'

'I can't say I'm surprised; he's gorgeous-looking. And very quick-witted.' Her smile seemed to say, *At Hector's expense.* But it carried no condemnation. She continued. 'I think men like Nestor and Ralph ... I think womanising goes against their grain, and it has more to do with craving connection and belonging.'

'Mm-hmm. I agree. And it might make you feel better to know that Maxi wants that too. This "I-wanna-get-laid" attitude, well, it's hot air. She's ready for love.'

Rhea breathed easier. 'Thank you for that. Anyway, on a brighter note ... the wedding!'

'Yes!' I poured our coffees. We took them and the plate of petits fours into the lounge and action replayed the day: the ceremony, Hannah's dress, our dresses, the food, flowers, music, speeches. She apologised for Hector's speech and Hector's attire. She apologised for Hector. Rhea opened up.

'I know what people think of him. Hell ... half the time *I* think it! But believe it or not, he didn't used to be like that.'

Really? Archimalakas wasn't always the chief of arseholes? Maybe just a lowly tribe member, then?

Rhea seemed wistful.

I took a risk. I asked her, 'Are you happy?'

She didn't answer.

'Tell me to mind my own business, it's a very personal ques—'

'No. I don't mind answering. I guess ... I'm not *un*happy.' She gave a half-smile of resignation. 'And you're probably wondering why I stay, yeah?'

Caught out. I felt my face flush a little.

'The thing is, I'm from a traditional Greek background and family's very important. Hector used to be quite charming, believe it or not.'

Not.

'And I fell in love with his sons.' She studied me for a moment as if to convince herself that it was safe to reveal more. She decided it was. 'But I admit, I wanted to leave when they were in their early teens. I couldn't do it to them, though. It was bad enough they'd lost their mother.'

'They're grown men now.'

'I know. But Hector gives me my space. We're like a pair of flatmates.'

Hmm. So ... not the Gweek way, not the Fwench way, not even a twaditional woute.

I shook Baubo off—now was not the time to let her mess with me. I felt sad for Rhea. I knew about life in the comfort zone. But Reuben had been nothing like Hector. I wondered why someone like Rhea would settle for someone like Hector in the first place. Again, she seemed to pick up on my thoughts.

'When I was eighteen, I was in love with a man my parents didn't approve of. He was ten years older than me, he wasn't Greek, and he wasn't good enough for their daughter. Well, I got pregnant. They threatened Russell and drove him away. They tried to convince me it was puppy love and that I'd get over him. But the worst thing was, they insisted I have an abortion.' Rhea's face tensed as she relived the memory. 'It did some damage and I couldn't have children. And that was devastating because I love kids. I'd dreamt of having a big family. Anyway, I didn't speak to them for a long time after that; I couldn't bring myself to. But I missed that sense of family. Then Hector came along and ...' she shrugged. 'Well, he offered a ready-made one.'

It sounded similar to Beth's story. Worse. At least Beth had other children and she was reunited with Ralph. I asked Rhea what happened to Russell.

'I don't know. I try not to think of him. But ... that "if only" feeling never completely goes.' Her eyes grew moist with tears.

She quickly wiped them away as Casper barrelled in through the front door.

He was surprised to see Rhea. Without stopping, he said a polite hello-how-are-you? to her, asked me why I was still in my pyjamas, didn't wait for an answer to either question, and disappeared into his bedroom. He whirlwinded out a few minutes later toting a plastic bag with one leg of his pyjama pants hanging out of it, told me he was going to Matt's to study and would spend the night there. He said goodbye to Rhea and me, and slammed the front door shut.

We stared after him. Rhea looked back at me and said, 'Oh, I like your son!'

'Me too!'

We both laughed. But Rhea's melancholy returned, showing itself in her sombre expression. She gave me a forced smile as if trying to shake off the leaden emotions. I sensed she had more that needed to be said, so I drew her out.

'If you weren't speaking to your family, how come you didn't try to find Russell, you know, turn the "if only" into "what if?" … or did you?'

'No, I didn't. My parents kept trying to make peace—they felt really bad—but I kept rebuffing them. I didn't think I'd ever forgive them. And that was hard for me because before all of this, I had a *good* relationship with them. But, to answer your question—why didn't I try to find Russell? I was scared. I kept hoping I'd get to that point where I wanted to reconcile with my parents and I felt like I had to make a choice. I'd already rocked the boat. If I'd gone looking for him, I probably would have capsized it!'

'Hmm. I know what it's like to capsize boats. My relationship with Ralph is just the latest one.'

Rhea looked at me blankly.

It turned out, despite Hector's jibe in the hospital waiting room about what went on in my family, he was just blowing smoke. Alex hadn't said anything to them. I told her the story.

With an indignant shake of her head, Rhea said, 'It's such a betrayal, isn't it, when the people you most expect support from turn on you? But good on you for holding your ground. I really admire you.'

'Thank you.'

'I mean it. You are one spirited woman! I can't imagine you'd ever sell your soul.'

'Oh, I did.' I gave her a wry smile. 'And for a long time—too damn long,' I muttered. 'I was hostage to other people's wants. Well ... no. Let's put it this way. I held myself hostage to them.' I told her about how Sylvia had pressured me to end it with Glen Jones, and about the lost years that followed.

Rhea and I talked non-stop for three hours. And laughed. We got high on caffeine and sugar, and swapped many stories. We found we shared many views. Rhea and I bonded.

Half an hour after she left, I was still wondering about *my* 'if-onlys' and 'what-ifs' when Ralph turned up.

'Ooh. You're in your jimjams early.' He raked his eyes over me.

'I'm in my jimjams late. I've been in them all day.'

'Mmm. Wanna go to bed?' He gave me one of his crooked, closed-mouth, flirtatious smiles.

Ralph was hard to resist in tight jeans that hugged his firm buns, and a fitted polo shirt that showcased his toned torso and biceps. He pulled me towards him and kissed me. I finally got out of my pyjamas that day.

I lay in his arms after and told him about my afternoon with Rhea. It didn't feel like I was breaching her confidence. Ralph was discreet. And I knew he'd see it through a psychological filter.

'She's such a lovely person, but she's not all that happy. I wish I could help her,' I said.

'You have. You've planted a seed. Now it's up to her.'

We snuggled in a comfortable silence for some time before Ralph pulled away. He gazed at me, wordless.

'What?'

He slid his arm under the pillow and gave me a nervous little smile. He closed his eyes, drew a measured breath through his nose, released it through pursed lips and opened his eyes. 'Will you marry me?'

I stared at him, mute.

He stared back. 'It wasn't a rhetorical question.'

'Uh ... why?'

'That one is a rhetorical question.'

'I-I don't know what to say.'

'"Yes" would be good.' His voice was soft, his tone uncertain.

I rolled onto my back. I suddenly felt dog-tired, weighted down by two and a half years of big shifts and big adjustments. I wanted to be Sleeping Beauty, but only because I envied her hundred years of shut-eye. I let out a long, weary sigh and turned to face Ralph. 'I've been married, Ralph. I don't wanna get married again.'

He appeared crestfallen. 'I thought I was the love of your life.'

'You are! But I don't need a piece of paper to prove that.'

He rolled onto his back, stacked his hands under the pillow and lay staring at the ceiling. 'You know that one of my biggest regrets is that I never married and had children.'

'Yeah, but the opportunity was there. A couple of ti—'

'I know, I know. It was my choice. But I didn't wanna settle. I wanted "The One", my Twin Flame.' He turned on his side again. 'You know you're it.' He smiled and added, 'And I wanna ride off into the sunset with you.'

I looked at him in surprise. 'Really? You want happily-ever-after?'

He grimaced. 'N-no, that's not what I meant. You know me better than that! I wanna spend the rest of my life with you. Is that asking too much?'

The tinge of vexation in his voice tripped guilt, which tripped the all too familiar gut clench. It was hard to ignore. Memories of that night just before I had the accident came flooding back. I started to feel like I was drowning. I wanted to run away from him. I rolled onto my back again. *Oh God, Oh God. Ah-ha-ah-ha-ah-ha.*

Ralph cupped his hand over my mouth.

My breathing slowed but it remained shallow. I felt stricken and started to cry. Ralph's face hovered above mine. It seemed he'd read my fears and was reliving some of his own. He looked stricken.

He lay back down, pulled me close to him and whispered into my hair. '*Ruthie.* I'm sorry. I won't push you if it's not what you want. It's just, it's ... for me it's about having a sacred covenant with you. At this point in my life, that means a lot to me. And you're the only woman I've ever wanted that with. I guess what you said about Rhea—about the "if-onlys" and the "what-ifs"—well, it made me think. What if I hadn't told you how I felt a couple of years ago ...?' His voice trailed off as if he were contemplating the import of that particular what-if?

I looked up at him. I'd calmed enough to find my words. 'But you did.'

'I know. I guess I just don't wanna get to the end of my life wondering "if only".'

I asked him if that was what had been playing on his mind after the wedding. No, it wasn't. He still had no clarity on that score. But his fear of 'if only' was quelled. He realised it wasn't so much about looking back in hindsight and regretting that we didn't get married, it was about regretting that he didn't ask.

He felt better.
I didn't.

CHAPTER THIRTY-ONE

What If? Whatev.
What the Fuck!

For the next week, I what-iffed and if-onlyed myself into a frenzy. What if this, what if that? What if I hadn't listened to Sylvia? If only I hadn't broken up with Glen. What-iffing and if-onlying were doing my head in. They sowed seeds of doubt that sprouted like a noxious weed infestation. I was fertilising the shit with shit! But then I remembered what Ralph had said to me when we first stepped things up—when I said it was pissing people off, and that it—he and I—wouldn't work. He'd reminded me what happened the last time I let other people's opinions influence me. I thought about my exchange with Rhea and realised I wasn't prepared to sell my soul again. I loved Ralph, but I reminded myself that his desire to get married was his desire, not mine. I felt better. And I'd reached a good place when Maxi called and told me all about Nestor.

'I thought this "Twin Flame" thing was a load of crap,' she said. 'But Nestor ... Oh my God! We both went back to work today and I miss him so badly. I can't think straight. He can't either. We've spoken five times today. And it's only eleven o'clock! Oh God, Ruthie, I am *so* in love!'

I squealed. 'Max, I can't tell you how happy I am for you!'

She and I talked for about half an hour. She wanted to know what the wedding reception was like.

'Sorry. I wasn't really all there, if you know what I mean.'

I did. And she still wasn't really all there. She was lost in the dreamy state of the lovestruck. I had to repeat myself several times, but I didn't mind. Maxi had waited a long time for this kind of love. It seemed she'd opened the door to it when Ralph and I got together. Now, listening to her get all gooey about this man reminded me of when we were teenagers and would gush about a crush. Only, this time, it was the real McCoy. And when she said, 'You know ... Nestor means "one who comes home",' I instinctively knew she had met the man who felt like home to her. I wondered if she was drawing hearts and flowers on a notepad as we spoke.

I said, 'Well, from what Rhea tells me about him, it's the right name for him. Sensitive, soft—'

'Soft? Honey, he is hard all the time! And he comes home, in the back of the car, at my place ...'

Oh. Seemed I needed to home in on my instincts and hone them.

I had no contact with Maxi for the rest of the week or the week after that. She was incommunicado. Mostly, she was inthesacko. Vette, Iris, Rhea and I knew to leave her alone. But the four of us decided we five needed a regular, monthly girls' night out seeing as we had such a great time together planning Hannah's wedding. I felt increasingly closer to my 'sisters'. Yet, at the same time, I felt increasingly distant from my own brother. I received a text from Myron on the Sunday morning just as Ralph walked in the door.

Back from trip.

Was pleasant.

I was gobsmacked, and not just because he'd described a holiday in paradise as merely 'pleasant', but because he didn't even ask about the wedding. I showed Ralph. His expression mirrored my thought: *Really?*

Another text came through—an afterthought.

Hope wedding was okay.

REALLY? I gritted my teeth and released a low, enraged growl. Ralph let me have my rant about the self-centred, cold-hearted tosser that my brother was. When I was done, he suggested we go down to the beach. He knew that being near the ocean always took the edge off for me. And he knew Glenelg was my favourite beach.

A twenty-minute walk along the esplanade helped me unwind. Then with our arms around each other, we strolled down Jetty Road looking in shop windows. We were at the quieter northern end of the street, in front of a high-end women's swimwear boutique, when Ralph turned towards me, grabbed my face and kissed me passionately. He looked into my eyes. 'I love you so much.'

'I love you, too.'

We hugged. But then Ralph started having trouble breathing. I pulled back, thinking he might be having a heart attack. What if he dies? *No, no, please, NO!* He wasn't sweating or clutching his chest or his arm like I'd seen in movies.

'Are you okay?' I asked in a panicked state.

'Yeah, sort of,' he panted. He nodded in the direction of something behind me.

I turned to see an old, homeless person sitting on a bench seat in front of the next shop down. His clothes were dirty and frayed, he had long, bedraggled, matted hair, a bushy, untamed salt 'n' pepper beard, and he was super-fat. I turned away and started to hyperventilate a little: My cacomorphobia was no longer all-consuming, but being within spitting distance of an obese person stoked the embers. I looked back at him and noticed the hobo was an amputee, left leg missing from the knee down. I got why Ralph was so agitated.

> After his well-endowment fell out of his shorts when we were fifteen, he not only developed OCPD, but also apotemnophobia (fear of amputees), probably as a form of PTSD (post-traumatic stress disorder)—a delayed result of Norma dishing up Daffy for his seventh birthday dinner. Since then, whenever Ralph saw an amputee—a real one; not a gnome—he suffered a kind of psychic phantom sympathy pain from the person's missing 'drumstick'.

My phobia was swept aside as I now focused on Ralph. Facing away from the unsightly sight, he was running his fingers wildly through his hair. He bent down and rested his hands on his knees as he tried to catch his breath.

I was about to slap my hand over his mouth, but he shooed me away. Where this worked for me, it didn't do anything for him. He'd once told me I needed to let him ride out these episodes without doing or saying anything. So, I watched in silence, willing him on: *breathe slooooooowly.*

He stood up and steadied himself, pressing his forehead against the window of the boutique. With his hands in his pockets, he jackhammered his leg. I assumed his eyes were closed and he wasn't aware of the four people inside the shop— two shop assistants and two customers—who were staring at him with mouths agape. But as if he'd heard my thoughts, he inhaled deeply, then exhaled.

Patches of condensation formed on the window as he blew out. One of the wide-eyed assistants took a few steps towards the store entrance and yelled at Ralph.

'Sir!'

Ralph jumped back in shock.

'You get away from there *now* or I'll call the police!'

Ralph put his hands up. 'Sorry, sorry!'

Suddenly, the derelict behind me burst out laughing. 'She musta thought you were whackin' off to the store dummy, mate! Don't blame ya. She's a nice piece of arse even if she is plastic,' he cackled.

I turned and glanced at the old man in disgust. He stopped laughing and stared at me. He leaned forward and narrowed his eyes in concentration.

Ecch. I looked away.

'Ruth? Ruth Roth?'

I looked back. *Oh dear God.* This person *knew* me? Maybe he'd known Joe. They would have been around the same age.

'It's me, Glen. Glen Jones.'

Oh fffuck!

Seven-and-half-inch Glen Jones! My age, plus two years. First love, first screw. Pity you can't *un*screw someone. Even so, Glen looked like he'd come unhinged.

Me and my bloody what-ifs and if-onlys! If only I could've left well enough alone!

Glen used to be drop-dead gorgeous and was quite the catch amongst 'his own', as Sylvia had called them—working class, high school dropouts; non-Jewish tradies. But I'd caught him. I was hopping mad when Sylvia made me throw him back. Now, it looked like she'd had a better handle on the future than I did. She'd saved me from disaster. This distorted version of the man I once loved, or thought I loved, smiled at me. *Geez Louise!* Talk about bad juju—he was also missing his four front teeth.

He cocked his head to the left and looked past me at Ralph, looked back at me, then did a double-take.

'Ralph?' he squawked. *'Fuuuckin' hell!'*

Glen Jones started to laugh again. He amped it up—he hee-hawed and convulsed. 'Oh ... toooooo funny ... just too ... funneeee!' he screeched. 'I don't believe it. I do *not* believe it.' His laughter petered out and he sneered. 'And to think yer old lady made ya dump me, and yet, she seems okay with you rootin' yer cousin! I 'ssume that's what yer doin', 'cause baby, that kiss was an "I've-gotten-way-waaaay-past-first-base kissy-face".'

I cringed, rooted to the spot.

Glen got serious. 'How is yer mum, by the way?'

I shook off the revulsion and stared at him, befuddled by the sudden digression. I answered without emotion. 'Dead.'

'Oh, well ... guess she can't hassle ya no more, hey?'

Don't kid yourself.

'An' I guess ya can go out with whoever ya want now.' He looked from me to Ralph with a smirk on his face.

'We're not cousins,' I blurted out. I was annoyed with myself the minute I said it. Why was I justifying myself to him?

'Yeah, yeah. Whatev, sweet'eart. You keep tellin' yerself that.'

Ralph grabbed my hand. 'Let's go.'

We started to turn away, but Glen wanted to know more. Sort of. 'Hey, how's yer mum?'

What? 'Still dead.' *Idiot.*

'Oh, sorry to hear.'

We turned away again, but Glen, it seemed, craved social contact. 'Ya know, I remember back then, when you were the spunkiest piece of arse on two legs!'

Yeah, and I remember back then, when you weren't the chunkiest fatarse on one!

'Don't get me wrong. Y'v aged real well. Still slim, still sexy. But, hey ... them were the days, huh?' Glen's eyes glazed over with remembrance and he sighed mawkishly.

His past, especially the chapter that included me, was not a place I wanted to revisit, but I couldn't resist asking, 'What happened to you?' I looked down at his half-leg.

'This little bewdy?' He looked down as he said it. 'Got conscripted. Vietnam. I 'n' me met a mine.' He laughed at his own joke. 'But at least I've still got me middle leg.' He winked at me; I shuddered. 'All eight 'n' a half inches.'

SEVEN 'n' a half, dipstick! Long in the tooth (if you had 'em), short 'n' shrivelled elsewhere.

Glen kept yackety-yacking, swelling with pride. 'Yip. Eight 'n' a half inches. S'bout the same length as what's left of me left leg.' He chortled and slapped what was left of his left leg.

Being informed and typically male, Ralph couldn't leave that one alone. 'Highly unlikely,' he said as he dared to look at Glen. 'An adult femur is longer than eight and half inches. Unless of course ... you're a hobbit.'

Being uninformed, Glen said, 'What? Wassa fema? Wassa hobbit?'

Ralph lowered his head and shook it. He knew when to cut his losses. He glanced at his watch and said to me, 'Don't we have to be somewhere?' He raised his brow at me. 'Anywhere?'

I nodded. 'Yep,' I said with firmness of purpose. 'Nice chatti—'

'Off fer a bonk, then?' Glen flashed us a lecherous, gap-tooth smile, then once again, lapsed into sloppy sentimentality. 'Startin' to forget what that was like. S'been a long time since I 'ad a root, ya know.'

Geez. Can't imagine why.

'Been datin' Missus Palmer an' 'er five ugly daughters for a while now.' He held up his right hand, wiggled his fingers and let out a phlegmy laugh.

Ecch. Get used to your ménage à moi, buddy.

He leered at me. 'Now, if *you* wanna do me again! You were a bit of a tiger in the sack as I rec—'

Eeeewwww! I think I'm gonna be si—

'I know someone who might be able to accommodate you,' Ralph cut in.

I looked at him. My hero. But ... *are you kidding? What the hell are you doing?*

Glen narrowed his eyes suspiciously. 'She anything like Ruth, here?'

'Close. Ruth's neighbour, Olive. A real looker. I think she'd have an eye for you.'

I stifled a laugh.

''Er name's Olive? Like Popeye's squeeze, Olive Oyl?'

Like an olive eternally submerged in a dirty martini.

Ralph talked over the top of my thoughts. 'Uh-huh.' His lips curled into a smile. 'This Olive's a Popeyed gal all right.'

'Mmm.' Glen stroked his beard thoughtfully. 'Is she skinny like Olive Oyl? I like 'em skinny. The skinny ones give me a fat!' He grabbed at his crotch and guffawed.

Ecch.

'Oh, you want "the skinny", then Olive's your girl.'

'Ooh, yum! Give 'er one of me addresses, then.' He tapped the seat. 'This bench seat 'ere on Jetty Road'll do.'

I laughed; Glen didn't. Oh. *Well then, probably gonna need a bigger real estate portfolio. Her patootie is the same size as yours.*

'Okay, we *really* must run,' I said to him of no fixed abode and grabbed Ralph's hand.

'Oh, uh, okey-dokey, love.'

As we turned and walked off Glen called after us, 'Oh, and give me best to yer mum.'

I didn't look back, just lifted my hand in acknowledgement.

'Nice move,' I said to Ralph when we were some distance away. 'A little cruel, maybe?'

'Mm, it probably would have been if he didn't have a short-term memory deficit.'

I sighed. 'Pity he doesn't have a long-term memory deficit. It's all that's left in common between us.' I cringed at the thought of having anything in common with him. And that I'd once had sex with him. I cringed at the thought that he was the one who had popped my cherry.

Ralph and I walked back towards the car in silence. 'Wait a second.' He stopped and put his hand out to stop me. 'He *does* have a long-term memory deficit. He couldn't have been in Vietnam. Your relationship with him ended around the same time the troops came back from there.'

I breathed relief. 'Thank God!' The common bond had frayed. We continued walking. 'I wonder how he did lose his leg,' I said.

'Probably chewed it off,' Ralph muttered. Then after a pause he said, 'You know ... I'm kind of glad we ran into him. I think it's cured me of my phobia.'

'Mm.' I nodded. My mind was elsewhere.

'You okay?' His brow furrowed with concern.

'Uh, yeah. No.' The interaction with Glen had left me feeling a little dirtied. 'Can we go sit on the beach for a bit?'

We headed towards the grassed area at the less crowded eastern end, and sat down. I took off my shoes and lay on my back, inhaling the cleansing sea air and soaking up the sun. Ralph didn't press me to talk. He knew I would if I felt the need.

After ten minutes, I slipped my shoes back on and said, 'Let's go get something to eat.'

We stood up and ambled back towards the main drag. I felt warmed, calmer and stronger. And clearer. The sun did that to me. But then ... so did Ralph.

Ralph was like the sun. He did all those things to me. And more. He was hot and he got me hot. Sure, he could burn me up sometimes. But overall ... I asked myself, what if I'd listened to Sylvia this time? I wouldn't have been blessed with the full range of emotions and experiences that come with the kind of intimacy I shared with Ralph. He was my sun. Ralph was the prince who'd awakened me and helped me feel things that had been dormant.

I stopped walking. 'Yes!' I said.

He stopped walking and gave me a bemused look. 'Yes ... what?'

'Yes, I will marry you.'

Ralph's jaw dropped, at first. Then his face lit up as he picked me up, twirled me around and *woo-hooed*. He gently lowered me to the ground and took my face in his hands. Tears filled his eyes and he kissed me with an ardour that almost left me breathless.

I drew a deep breath, and with just as much ardour, I said, 'But I don't want to take your name.'

He laughed. 'That's okay. I don't really want it either.'

CHAPTER THIRTY-TWO

Not So Black and White

R alph didn't want it because he bore the surname of a man he detested. I might have been willing to take his name if it were Johnson, because I was invested in the belief that size matters.

Yessiree, Bob! Size matters. Sylvia had taught me that. In a general sense, at least.

As a five-year-old, I felt aggrieved because my given name had only one syllable, and I wasn't given a middle name. What rankled even more was that Sylvia was into quantity over quality, as in, your worth was supposedly directly proportional to the number of friends you had, phone calls you got, dollars someone spent on you. Lots of friends, phone calls and expensive gifts meant you were A-OK. So, the fact that she and Joe gave Myron Stephen Lawrence Roth a two-syllable first name and two two-syllable middle names meant that he was worthy. Logically then, I was unworthy. And as if to confirm it, I married a monosyllabic Gold. This distorted reasoning no longer controlled me, but I still saw no point going from Gold to Brill.

I would have bet my boots that quantity wouldn't have surpassed quality if I'd given Sylvia the details concerning her missing bloody tape measure!

Anyway, Ralph and I grabbed a quick bite and rushed home. We wanted to share our news with the important people in our lives, not café patrons. And it was well received, quantitatively and qualitatively. Even Hannah and Casper were happy for us. So was Reuben (he'd been on a couple of dates with Ida, a very nice friend of Rhea's who he'd met at the wedding). I didn't tell Myron. He could go fuck himself. Ralph called Beth. Their relationship was evolving into something special. She said the news made her day. I was a little perturbed that Ralph left it to me to let Norma know. I could tell it saddened her even though she was happy for us.

Iris graciously offered to host our wedding at her place. We graciously declined. With Leah's engagement, Hannah's wedding, and plans to have Leah's wedding there—although it was six months away—well, even Amazonian chicks get tired. But she insisted on being involved in the preparations with Vette and with Maxi, who'd come up for air to call me back not long after I left her a message.

Rhea also asked to be included. 'I'd love it if you'd let me be part of the planning.'

'With pleasure!' *I'd love it if you left your husband home on the day.*

IB: *'You are SUCH a bitch!'*

HRA: *'No. I'm not. I only thought it, I didn't say it out loud.'*

What I did say out loud was that Ralph and I wanted something twice as intimate as Hannah's wedding, with half the number of guests, and that I expected it would be relatively fuss-free because we already had a tried and trusted package from Hannah's. Rhea agreed. All that was left was to find a venue.

'Problem solved!' Ralph sounded excited when he called from work the next morning. Dawn Hyde, a colleague of Ralph's who had a soft spot for him, had offered her garden. She and her husband, Harmon, lived in Bridgewater, a town in the Adelaide Hills about forty-five minutes' drive from my place. Ralph and I went there at one o'clock on the Saturday to have a look-see.

Their home was on a huge property at the end of a no-through road. It was airy, light and spacious, and had a contingency-plan-sized family room. A large glass sliding door at the rear opened onto an enormous pergola-covered deck. It was indoor-outdoor living at its best. And three little steps off the deck led down to a manicured expanse of lawn that extended into bushland. It was a tranquil setting. The neighbouring houses were a good distance away. A post and rail fence separated Dawn's yard from the one on the right, with an enormous stretch of lawn between the fence and the neighbour's homestead. And dense shrubbery separated and screened her yard from the one on the left. It was perfect. We discussed some possible options where the ceremony could be held, and settled on the area next to the shrubbery. We talked about the date. Ralph suggested we get married on a Tuesday. I was thrilled.

When Reuben and I got engaged, I told Sylvia I didn't want to get married on a Sunday. I told her I wanted to get married on a Tuesday. I'd done some research and informed her Tuesday was an especially auspicious day for a wedding, because in the account in Genesis 1:10,12 concerning this third day of creation, the phrase 'God saw that it was good' appeared twice, meaning Tuesday was a doubly good day to get married. Sylvia didn't buy it—quantity did not win out over quality. The fact that she worshipped clichés meant she also worshipped common practices. She insisted on tradition. My wedding would be on a Sunday. So I tried telling her I had Dimanchophobia.

This strung out woman, who hung glass eyeballs on cupboard doors, *oeuf-pested* me and ridiculed my fears.

Ralph knew how I felt about Sundays. And I thought he warmed to the idea of a Tuesday because of the words 'twice' and 'doubly'. But he was very specific about the date—a Tuesday four months away. Why that date? He smiled at me. It clicked. It would be the three-year anniversary of that night he'd shown his hand.

We knew the people we wanted at our wedding would accept that they'd have to take a day off work. The people we wanted at our wedding would rejoice at having an excuse to take a day off work.

We thanked Dawn and Harmon, and left. On the way home, I commented to Ralph that everything just seemed to be falling into place.

'It's because you and I are meant to be.'

He was right. No struggle.

It was a bit of a struggle, though, to get Maxi to join Vette, Iris, Rhea and me on Tuesday night at six-thirty to start planning the event.

She barrelled in at seven o'clock, kissed and hugged each of us and looked at her watch. 'Let's make this quick. It's *way* past my bedtime!'

'You look very happy,' said Rhea.

'So does your brother.' Maxi smiled and held up her mobile. Her wallpaper was Nestor's face with a beatific smile.

We got stuck into the planning and made good progress. An hour and a half later, I pushed Maxi out the door and said, 'Go come.'

The five of us exchanged many positive calls, texts and emails over the next couple of days. Yep, things were falling into place. And Hannah called Friday morning to tell me she had the proofs from her wedding. I said I'd drop around the next day while Ralph was at Beth's.

Ralph called from work just after I hung up from Hannah. He told me he was knocking off work at three and that I should pack an overnight bag with a nice dress, no jammies necessary. He'd pick me up at four and we'd be spending the night at the Hyatt Regency.

'*Ooh.* But, why?'

'I want to celebrate our engagement under the stars. Five of them.'

I loved that he understood my idea of camping out.

Ralph had booked a room with a sweeping view of the river. We checked in, went for a walk through the city, then got ready for dinner. We'd just finished a sumptuous meal of pistachio-crusted snapper with truffle mash and wilted spinach, followed by dessert—mocha soufflé with tiramisu ice cream for me, and banana tarte tatin with cinnamon ice cream for him—when he got up, came around to my side of the table and, on bended knee, formally asked me to marry him. He opened a ring box and presented me with two carats of gorgeous compressed carbon— a brilliant-cut diamond supported by four claws and sitting on a narrow, D-shape white gold band. Awestruck, I clapped my hand over my mouth. The diners around us clapped their hands.

The rest of the night was a lovefest. The man was inexhaustible! In between shtups, we discussed where to go for our honeymoon. He wanted to take me on a month-long round-the-world trip, but I was a homebody. We agreed on a week at the Sheraton in Fiji.

He took me home late the following morning and went off to take care of a few bits and bobs before he went to Beth's. He was going to meet me back at my place around four.

I couldn't stop staring at my beautiful ring. I felt happy. In my mind, I was dancing around the room. But only in my mind.

I was too rooted to do anything, so I made myself a sandwich and a cup of tea, and crashed on the couch until it was time to go to Hannah's. Ralph called an hour after he'd dropped me off.

'Didn't I see you, like, an hour ago?' I said.

'I know, but I just spoke to Beth. I couldn't wait to tell her about your reaction. She wasn't surprised. She thinks it's one of the most beautiful rings she's seen.'

Hmm. 'When did she see it?'

'I took it there last Saturday.'

'Oh. Has Norma seen it?'

'No. Course not.'

That felt wrong. But I left it alone. I was a little worried that Ralph was idealising Beth. I recognised this because it was something I tended to do when a motherly figure threw me a bone.

'Anyway, Beth's dying to meet you and it's about time! So, I'll organise for the three of us to go out for dinner, maybe some time next week?'

'Sure.'

I was left with an uneasy feeling after we hung up. It persisted until I got to Hannah's at two and was greeted with a big smile from Luca. He sat on my lap and looked at my nose, while I looked at the proofs and picked out the pics I wanted for myself, and Hannah looked at my bling-bling. We chatted about the wedding plans, she OMG'd every time the light caught the diamond, and I left her place just before four. When I got home, I found Ralph sitting in the lounge in a dazed state. He was as white as a sheet.

I rushed over and sat next to him. 'What's wrong?'

He looked at me and opened his mouth, but nothing came out.

'Ralph!'

He took a deep breath and blew out. 'I know what's been bugging me since the wedding.' His tone was flat, not like you'd expect from someone who'd just had an epiphany. It didn't sound good. I waited for him to expand on it.

'Alex's Tourette Syndrome—'

'Yeah, it bugs me too. But it's not a dangerous thi—'

'No. I know it's not. And I'm not bothered that he has it.' He paaaauuuuuuuuuuuussssed.

I tried to be patient, but I was too tired for 'I'll-play-along'. And knowing Ralph couldn't be hurried didn't help.

Hoo aah hoo aah. Let's breathe through the impatience. Hoo aah hoo aah. Let's investigate how impatience feels in my mind and body. Hoo aah hoo aah. Let's transform impatience into patience. Hoo haa hoo haa. Let's remind myself that Ralph's idea of getting to the point is to map out the whole fucking course that gets you to the point, toilet stops included! And let that be okay. Hoo aah hoo aah.

'But here's the thing,' he continued. 'Tourette's is considered a neurological disorder, but there are also theories about it being genetic or environmental ...' He stared off into space.

Hoo aah hoo aah. Hoo aah hoo aah.

He shook himself back into the present. 'So ... my OCPD is a personality disorder, right?'

If you say so. 'I guess.'

'But you can't rule out the possibility of a connection between OCPD and Tourette's.'

I stopped my in-breath-out-breath drill and gawked at him. 'Seriously? That's what this is about? You're trying to find more things in common with Alex?'

'No. Of course not!'

'So, what's your point?'

'My point is I don't think our commonalities are a coincidence.' Ralph looked at me like I was an idiot, like I should get what he was on about.

I tried to sound intelligent. 'Yes, I know you don't believe in coincidence. I know we attract people for a purpose, that—'

'It's more than that!'

Really? You're getting impatient with me? Hoo aah hoo aah. Hoo aah hoo aah.

'Do you remember when Hannah was in labour and you, Reuben and Hector were talking about her birth and Alex's birth?'

'Uh, yeah. What about them?' Dear God, the man was all over the place! *Hoo aah hoo aah.*

'Hector said Alex was premature, but he was large for a preemie. He said Larissa got pregnant straight away.'

'Yyyeah. And?'

'What if he wasn't a preemie? What if he was full term?'

'Jeeesus, Ralph! *Get to the point!*'

'Well ... I've been working back from Alex's birthday. I broke up with Larissa about nine months before he was born.'

It didn't sink in immediately. I wasn't good at maths. But then ...

'Nooooo! You don't think—'

Ralph nodded.

I scrunched up my face. 'Mm. You don't think that's a bit of wishful thinking? I mean, Alex is—'

'Ruthie—'

'—eccentric, like you, but it's not like he resembles you—'

'Ruth!'

Ralph looked shaken. I stopped talking.

'Beth opened up about my father today. She told me his grandmother was Aboriginal.'

It took me a moment to absorb the implications of what he'd said. My mouth dropped open. 'Oh my God ... Luca!'

Ralph nodded again. *'Yes. The throwback,'* he whispered.

CHAPTER THIRTY-THREE

Rules of Engagement

I stared at Ralph in stunned silence, then shook my head. 'You know, there needs to be a book about our life. These things only happen in novels. Or in movies. It's like a soap opera.'

'Mm,' Ralph said. He was miles away, though.

Another spell of bewildered silence elapsed. Between us, anyway. The brouhaha between my ears was deafening. So many thoughts were competing for the upper hand. But this little sucker won out and spilled out of my mouth: 'Oh my God! So it could be that Hannah's with *her* cousin too!'

My words cut through Ralph's benumbed senses. He looked at me with undisguised belief, then his eyes flashed with anger. *'Really?'*

Oh, what was I thinking? Lacking sense and sensitivity. I took his hand. 'I'm sorry.'

Again, neither of us spoke. His countenance told its own story, one that alternated between joy and pain. Both lost in our thoughts, my mind drifted fifteen years into a hypothetical future. Three generations of males—Ralph, Alex and Luca at a restaurant having lunch. Ralph touching everything twice and *nom nom nomming*, Alex shoulder-twitching, throwing his arm up and *ahemming*, Luca punching himself in the face and yelling *Motherfucker!*

'Ruthie!'

'Huh? What?'

'I said this is a delicate situation. How do we find out?'

'*Duh*, DNA testing.' *Real delicate.*

'I *know* that. But I can't very well ask Alex to swab the inside of his cheek with a cotton bud, now can I?' Ralph was getting impatient with me again. And he wasn't looking for an answer. He probably wouldn't have heard it, anyway—he'd slumped back into a glassy-eyed state. But something occurred to me.

'You didn't say anything to Beth, did you?' *God, I hope not.*

'What?'

'I asked if you said something to Beth about your hunch.'

'Uh, no—'

'Good. Don't. And I don't think we should do anything about it till after the wedding.'

Ralph nodded absently.

For the next week, Ralph disappeared into a world of his own. And he remained there for two weeks after that. He had trouble concentrating. I didn't see much of him. He was either 'busy' or 'tired', and we were having a dry spell. When he did drop by, he mostly talked to Casper. Ralph was a little fragile and a lot snappy. I was tolerant of his constant pissy mood. I understood there was plenty to process and he was dealing with a bittersweet revelation—there was a very good chance he had a son, and he'd been deprived of a relationship with him.

He kept up his regular visits to Beth, but didn't offer to take me. And the promise of a dinner, when I would finally meet her, remained unfulfilled. I thought it best not to push it. I had to get together with the girls more often, anyway. Things had stopped falling into place and we needed to brainstorm.

On the third Saturday after Ralph found out he might be a father (and grandfather), I sat in the kitchen feeling despondent. It was four o'clock and the girls had just left. We were all frustrated. Our think tank seemed to be tanking. The doorbell interrupted my gloom. It was Ralph.

'Oh, hi. Why didn't you use your key?'

'I left it at home. Casper around?'

'Uh, no. He's away for the weekend.'

'Oh.' He looked behind me and saw nobody.

Proof positive?

'His car's out the front, so I assumed—'

'He's gone to Christies Beach again. Matt picked him up.'

'Okay.' He held up a *Shrek* DVD. 'Could you give this back to him, please? Tell him I thought it was great.'

I felt sick. Ralph loved sharing the movie experience with me. When I didn't take the DVD from him, he reached around the corner and tossed it on to the console table.

'Aren't you coming in?'

'No, I'm off to see Beth.'

'Oh. That's a late visit.' Ralph usually went to her place at two. 'You could have brought it back after seeing her.'

'I won't be coming back. She's taking me to dinner tonight.'

'Oh.' *Speak up, speak up!* 'I, uh, thought you wanted me to meet her and she wanted to meet me. So, um, how come that hasn't happened?'

Ralph stared at me, his expression darkening. 'Because Beth's helping me cope with this possible paternity issue. The time's not right yet. I'll know when it is.' His frosty tone brooked no argument; his remark was a slap in the face.

I reflexively took a small step away from him. Without another word, he turned and walked back to his car.

My shoulders slumped. I was steeped in shame. What had I said? I didn't think I'd been critical. Had I sounded whiney? Was I being demanding ...?

Wait a second!

I tore out after him. He'd just got into his car and lowered the driver's side window. I leaned in.

'You're discussing this thing with *her*? After we agreed you wouldn't say anything!'

'No. *You* decided I shouldn't say anything. But she's my mother. And she has a vested interest. She might well be a grandmother. *And* a great-grandmother.'

What? 'She might have given birth to you, Ralph, but she's a stranger! And you're talking to her instead of me!' I tapped my chest to emphasise my point.

That upset him. 'I don't believe this. You're actually *jealous* of her?'

Damn right I am! 'No, I am not jealous of her! But *I'm* supposed to be your confidante.'

'*Supposed* to be, yeah. And here I was with all these feelings and needing to talk to someone, but you said you didn't want to talk about it till after the wedding!'

'Bullshit! I said we shouldn't *do* anything about it until after the wedding.'

He looked away; gave an apathetic shrug.

Whoa! It was like a red rag to a bull. I struggled to keep my voice steady. 'I know this whole thing is difficult for you and of course, you need to talk about it. But you weren't saying anything, so I assumed you just wanted space. I was giving it to you! Obviously, there was a misunderstanding, but you ran to her instead of being honest with me. And you've been seeing her for, what, over a year now? I can't believe I still haven't met her!' I didn't realise this bothered me until now. 'It's like I don't exist. And over the last couple of weeks, that's how you've been treating me, or you've dumped your frustrations on me.' I glared at him. 'If this is what I have to look forward to, I don't want to marry you!'

I took off the ring, dropped it in his lap and stormed back inside the house. I slammed the front door, leaned against it and let myself slide down until I was sitting on the floor.

A two-carat diamond ring—for God's sake! You keep that sort of thing. Stupid, stupid, stupid!

I heard Ralph's car start, heard him reverse out of the driveway. But he didn't burn rubber as he took off. There was that cold indifference again, like on the awful night of the accident.

He doesn't want you anymore. I told you it wouldn't work. I told you no one would put up with you!

Sylvia was back from the dead and I was drowning in her insults. My inner human rights advocate didn't stand a chance.

You're difficult. You're going to get fat like Zelda (this default bit of terrorism permanently and irrelevantly attached itself to every situation under attack). *He's not even upset. He's driving while he's upset* (contradiction was also a default one—screwed either way). *He's going to have an accident and get killed and it'll be your fault! Everything is your fault! You're a horrible person. And so materialistic!*

I put my hands over my ears and sobbed. I sobbed out feelings of powerlessness and helplessness. Even worse, I was overcome with a paralysing sense of hopelessness. I wanted to die. And not because Ralph and I might be over, but because I thought that this searing self-loathing would define me for the rest of my life—because *I* would dump on me till the end of it. I wept until there was nothing, and I sat there, exhausted, staring at the nothing. But then ... then, there was *something*.

It emerged from the void. A little glimmer of hope. It wasn't the fairy-tale kind of hope where someone—Ralph—would save me from the darkness inside me. It was realistic hope that showed me I'd been Sylvia's pack mule, burdened with all her disowned despair. Perverse as it was, I'd unconsciously taken on the mantle because it was how I mattered as a child. I better understood the extent of a child's need to matter to her parents, and that mattering in this distorted way was preferable to not mattering at all. But I also understood that to strip off the mantle, I had to feel and release the frozen hopelessness that kept it in place. I'd just done that. Or, started to. I also got what Portnoy mirrored. Her physical distortion symbolised her tendency to distort the truth. It reflected my tendency to distort the truth about myself—the lies I told me about me. I knew there was a long way to go and that a lot of work lay ahead, but I felt lighter.

As I stood up, the doorbell rang. I didn't expect it. I jumped at the sound. An insistent knocking followed.

'Ruthie, please let me in.' Ralph's voice was muffled against the door. 'Please. I'm sorry. Please open the door. I've been a bastard. I'm so sorry.'

Is 'bastard' a swear word? Baubo. A strange source of comfort—always there to show me the comedy in the tragedy.

I opened the door a crack. Ralph and I looked at each other, both with red, swollen eyes. He pushed the door open and pulled me towards him, holding me tightly and whispering over and over, *'I'm so sorry. I love you so much. Please forgive me.'*

He kissed me. I returned his kiss, tentatively at first, a hint of mistrust trying to undermine my body's natural response to him. But I crumbled, and melted against him as our kisses became more fervent and more urgent.

He kicked the door closed with his foot and we sent the papier mâché vase on the console table flying as we frantically grabbed at and ripped off each other's clothes. With a pulsing, sexual longing, we stumbled towards the bedroom. A trail of his 'n' hers lined the passage, and Ralph stripped off the last vestige of clothing—his jeans and jocks—dumping them next to the bed. We collapsed onto it, panting, naked and ravishing each other.

Afterwards, with our heartbeats slowly returning to their normal rhythms, we lay entwined in each other's arms for a while. He whispered sweet nothings, but I heard sweet FA. I was lost in thought.

He disentangled himself from me and leaned over the side of the bed reaching for something. I rolled onto my back.

'Ruthie?'

'Mm?' I faced him.

'Will you marry me?' He held the engagement ring up, his eyes filled with expectancy.

I looked at it and then back at him. 'I don't know.'

Ralph's face crumpled.

CHAPTER THIRTY-FOUR

Out, Damned Spot!

'You need to make peace with Norma, Ralph.'

He turned onto his back and stared at the ceiling. 'I know. But I'm angry with her. And we're not talking about a minor transgression, here. It's a huge thing.'

'I agree. But what Beth did is a huge thing ... and you've forgiven *her*.'

He spun his head around and looked at me. 'She didn't have much of a choice. Norma betrayed me and she knew what she was doing!'

'I'm not defending what she di—'

'Yeah, well, it sounds to me like you are.'

A sinking feeling started to engulf me. I could change myself, but I couldn't change him. A long, weighty silence ensued.

Ralph let out a ragged breath. 'Ruthie. Come on. I don't wanna fight with you.'

He reached for me as I wiped away the tears that had started pooling in my eyes, but I resisted him. 'I don't want to fight either. But here's the thing. You've held onto your anger at Norma for almost three years. And I'm not prepared to bear the brunt of that anger every time I do or say something that in any way reminds you of her betrayal. I was married to someone who made everything my fault. I'm not going back there.'

He nodded, his eyes downcast.

'Look. I know you can't turn it around in your mind just like that, but you won't get even close to it if you don't at least open up the lines of communication with her. When Sylvia died, you told me I needed to get my feelings out or they'd eat away at me. You need to take your own advice.'

He sighed. 'You're right. And I'm sorry I didn't communicate with you.' He reached for me again and pulled me towards him. This time I didn't resist.

After a few minutes he said, 'You haven't answered my question.'

'What question?'

He held up the ring again.

I remembered when Reuben had asked me that question years earlier and I'd said yes. I was ready to settle down. I was ready to settle. I'd loved Reuben, but not like I loved Ralph—I was in love with him and wanted to be with him, but I needed a commitment from him. I needed him to show me rather than tell me. I was firm, but gentle when I responded.

'Yeah. I have.'

The pitiful expression on his face tugged at my heartstrings. I wanted to give him what he wanted, but if I didn't respect me, then I couldn't expect him to. I told him I needed a little space, some time to be by myself. I said that he had a lot to deal with and it might also be good for him. He didn't argue.

We didn't see each other or even speak for the next week. I spent a lot of time thinking and probably too much time navel-gazing, but it was what I needed.

And on the Friday morning, I had a surprise visit from Norma. In the past, she and I had the occasional phone conversation, but this was the first time she'd come over.

'I know you said something to Ralph. He's been ringing me every day this week and shouting at me.'

My breath caught. I knew she wouldn't hurl abuse at me because that wasn't Norma's way, but I feared I'd really upset her. She surprised me.

'*Merci beaucoup, chérie.* It makes me very happy he's yelling instead of treating me like a stranger.' She placed her hand over her heart. 'I feel more hope in here.' We exchanged smiles: hers, one of gratitude, mine, one of relief. 'You know, your mum would have been proud of you.'

I stopped smiling. 'No, she wouldn't have.'

'Yes, she would. She loved you very much.'

I shook my head; I couldn't speak, couldn't stop the tears. Norma drew me to her and hugged me. She stroked my head as I cried. And cried, and cried.

'She was hard, yes. But she loved you and she was very proud of you, even if she didn't say it or show you.'

'It's not just that she didn't sh-sh-show me; she showed me the opposite,' I sobbed.

Norma held me for a very long time, until the tears stopped. For another hour, we sat in the kitchen and talked about a lot of things. Important things. It felt cathartic to be able to tell my aunt how I felt about her sister without feeling judged. She shared things about my mother and about my parents' marriage that I didn't know; things that helped me better understand Sylvia. We talked about Ralph, the adoption, his budding relationship with Beth, Norma's feelings about that and about the pain of her estrangement from Ralph. I was careful not to mention his suspicions about Alex. But Norma and I bonded. I got that she couldn't replace my mother, but she'd given me the nurturance

I craved and needed. When she left, I knew that everything would be all right. And I also knew that, like Ralph, I needed to make my peace with Sylvia, inasmuch as I could with her no longer being around—physically, anyway.

I sat for an hour thinking about everything Norma and I had discussed, and about nothing at all. Then something came to me.

I realised the popular fairy-tale undertone of love as all hearts and valentines had escaped containment in my psyche, and overshadowed love's true meaning. And maybe I'd been drawn to Reuben because he avoided confrontation. It was deliverance from the hostile environment I'd grown up in. But neither all-out war nor peace-at-any-price constituted *real* love. I recalled what Mr Kosta had said about Eros. He'd told us this ancient love god—whose Roman name is Cupid—shot both gold and lead-tipped arrows. The gold ones instilled love and desire; the lead ones instilled a hatred of passion and desire. Love wounds *and* heals. Cupid was not just about Hallmark moments. This arch archer could shoot you in the arse with no compunction! Sacred love.

I called Ralph, asked if he wanted to go out for dinner. Of course he did. We decided on Stella's at Henley Beach. I said we should meet there. He had late sessions scheduled so he said he'd come straight from work.

He looked lighter when he walked into the restaurant at six o'clock. And he turned heads. Ralph looked yummy in his black dress slacks, white oxford shirt and tan sports jacket. Good thing I'd chosen a public place to meet (it meant I couldn't give in to the desires of my doodah).

He bent down and kissed me on the lips and looked into my eyes for several seconds. He hesitated before sitting opposite me. 'You're not going to ask me to make peace with Albie, are you?'

I laughed and shook my head. 'No.'

'Good.'

A waiter approached. Did we want to order drinks? Yes. Neither of us liked alcohol, so it was sparkling mineral water for both of us.

Ralph sat back and gave me an appreciative smile. *Ooh. Mmm, mmm.* It felt like we were ... courting again. But then he leaned forward, rested his forearms on the table and became serious. 'I know that you know I started speaking to Norma—'

'Speaking?'

'Okay. Yelling.' He smiled, half-turning, half-tilting his head in concession. 'And I need you to know that I haven't told Beth about you and me—about our fight—and I don't intend to.'

I nodded, relieved.

He went on. 'In fact, I haven't spoken to her at all this week. But I've had the feeling you're mad at her.' He held up both hands before I could respond. 'I understand. And I can't say I blame you. For what it's worth, though, she's also been at me to mend fences with Norma. She hasn't been trying to replace her, even if I have, and I'm ashamed to say that. And, yeah, I should have introduced you to her a long time ago. I've idealised her and I think I was afraid you'd see right through it and shoot holes in it. And, well, humanise her ... which you did, anyway. But I'm glad you did because I needed that.' He gave me an embarrassed smile. 'I guess you were right when you asked if I wanted happily-ever-after.'

Ralph was also ashamed to say that his anger at me was misdirected. It had been at himself. He'd been overwhelmed by the sudden onslaught of emotions from his discovery, and he was hard on himself because helping others cope with this sort of thing was what he did for a living. But he didn't own up to his feelings of inadequacy because he feared I'd see him as a failure.

'What?' This one came as a surprise. 'Firstly, you've never hidden your insecurities from me. And second, you've worked hard to get to where you're at. I've never considered you a failure, you know that.'

'Except after your accident. What you called me.' It wasn't said as an accusation. He gave me a defenceless shrug. I gave him a confused one. He reminded me: '"Mr big-shot psychologist".'

Oh. I closed my eyes remembering that and all the other shitty things I'd said. I opened them and looked at him with remorse. 'That was in the heat of the moment—'

'I know. And you apologised. But ...'—he frowned as he gathered his thoughts—'finding my mother, and knowing that she did want me, even though she was backed into a corner and had to give me up ... well, as you know, it put me on a high. And now, finding out that I might have a son—*and* a grandson—it's been a lot to absorb, lots of high highs. But some incredible dark lows when I've thought about what was there that I've missed out on. Talk about an emotional seesaw.' A shadow of sadness crossed his face. 'And maybe I've been an overachiever to stop me from feeling like I've failed in my personal life.'

Again, I was surprised. 'How have you failed? You had no control over what Beth did, or over Larissa's choice.'

'Yes, but I don't have what most men my age have. I don't have a family. What have I got?' His expression was wistful.

'Me,' I said softly. 'You've got me.'

He looked at me with sad, puppy-dog eyes. 'Have I?'

'Uh-huh.' I reached across the table, took his hand and asked, 'Will you marry me?'

Ralph's eyes brimmed with tears. *Yes,'* he whispered. He dug his free hand into the inside pocket of his jacket, pulled out the ring and slipped it on my finger. He told me he'd ducked home on the way to Stella's to grab the ring in the hope that I'd want to wear it again.

We had our dinner and talked about what the week had been like for both of us, and agreed to leave the paternity issue alone until after our honeymoon. We went to his place to celebrate our re-engagement. Four times. In the morning, I told him that once we were married he had to let me sleep, and that he could celebrate by himself. Singlehandedly. He said he didn't feel right about putting a notch on the bedpost if he did it with himself.

And then he rang Beth.

CHAPTER THIRTY-FIVE

The Apple Doesn't Fall Far from the Pruned Tree

Beth Johnson's house was on a quiet, leafy street in Unley, an upmarket suburb about twenty minutes from my place. The word 'neat' came to mind as we walked to the front door. The single frontage house was attached to a double garage. The gated driveway of clay pavers leading to the garage had no stray weeds poking between them, and the lawn in front of the house looked like it had been hand-trimmed with a pair of scissors, then ironed.

The path leading to the front door was paved in irregular oatmeal and cream-coloured flagstone. The irregularity was at odds with its surrounds, which included the tidy box hedges that flanked the path, and looked like two rows of guards standing tall and without a whisker out of place. The overall neatness made me feel nervous (although this didn't make much sense considering I was engaged to an obsessive-compulsive).

When Ralph had called Beth the morning before, he told her it was high time she and I met. And he wanted it to happen this weekend. So, we were here for Sunday lunch.

Beth opened the door just as we stepped onto the heritage-tiled verandah. She was an attractive, youthful-looking woman. Tall and slim, she had friendly blue-green eyes. She and Ralph shared the same face shape and chin dimple. And she was ... neat. Her grey hair looked like her front lawn—trimmed short and ironed. She wore a long, floaty, lilac silk shirt, and black jeans that—*dear God*—had a crease pressed into each leg.

She kissed and hugged Ralph with unbridled affection. As he then introduced us, Beth took my extended hand in both of hers and shook it with warmth.

'I'm so happy to finally meet you, Ruthie!'

Ruthie.

'Same here,' I said, and I handed her the bouquet of pink roses we'd picked up on the way. 'For you.'

'Ooh. Thank you!' Beth inhaled the sweet scent with eyes closed and a dreamy sigh. The sincerity in this woman's voice and demeanour dissolved any reservations I might have had. Beth was appreciative and gracious—I was glad she didn't say 'You shouldn't have'. I hate that. It seems unappreciative and implies the receiver doesn't deserve it.

Beth smiled at me. It was a smile that lit up her whole face. Ralph has a smile like that. He has a killer smile. His eyes crinkle up small, his face lights up and he can charm the pants off you.

Your son charms the pants off me with his smile. Your son charms the pants off me without his smile. And often. I gave her *my* killer smile.

Ralph gave me a killer look that said, *I can tell your mind's in the gutter. How about we leave it out there and not bring it inside?*

'Well, let's not stand out here!' Beth drew us both into the hallway.

She chatted away as we followed her through the house. I looked around and took in everything. The décor was modern: beige carpeting in the three bedrooms, parquetry flooring in the hallway and living area. Fresh, simple, geometric prints adorned the walls, which were white, just like the ceilings and furniture. But the ambience was not sterile. It was clean and sleek. Like Beth. And nothing was out of place.

Neat.

Does Beth have OCPD?

She took us to the back of the house, which was open plan living with an all-white, minimalist, U-shaped kitchen and a large family room on the other side of the breakfast bar. The room had white-framed, floor-to-ceiling walls of windows on either side. The floor-to-ceiling back sliding doors opened onto a spacious courtyard. Paved with the same flagstone as the front path, it was bordered by Australian natives.

Hmm. Odd. Natives attract lots of birds, and lots of birds drop lots of dookies.

The ground was wet. Looked like Beth had recently hosed away the turds, but how many times a day could you do that?

'You have a lovely home,' I said to her.

'Thank you.' She smiled at me and squeezed my hand. 'So, are you hungry?'

Ha! Do kookaburras use your courtyard as a shithouse?

'Ruthie? Beth asked if you're hungry.'

'Huh? Oh. Sorry, I thought it was a rhetorical question. I'm never not hungry.' I smiled.

Beth laughed. It was a rich, earthy sound. 'Well, let's have lunch, then! We'd eat outside, but we'd probably get rained on.'

'Uh, it's a clear day,' Ralph said.

'Oh, not precipitation, darling. Bird shit.'

Oh my God ... you swear! We all laughed. *I've fallen a little bit in love with you, Beth Johnson.*

We offered to help her bring the food to the family room table, but she insisted, 'No. Sit, sit. I can manage.'

I understood why. In one hand she carried a plate with a few cold cuts, a few slices of cheddar cheese, some garnishes— tomato, cucumber, avocado. In the other, she held a small basket with half a dozen dinner rolls. Beth placed both in the centre of the table and sat down.

What? That's it? No lox, no bagels, no cream cheese? And where's the cake? Clearly, Beth wasn't Jewish. How were Ralph and I going to cope with this famine? I should have brought cake instead of bloody flowers.

I had to eat like one of those birds raining shit out there in her courtyard, but at least we talked up a storm. I enjoyed watching Beth and Ralph interact. Their mutual admiration, combined with similar facial expressions and mannerisms, made it clear their blood ties were unmistakable. The comfort we felt around this woman was also clear—Ralph didn't *nom nom* and I didn't feel the need to stuff down feelings with food (not that there was the option to). Three hours flew by. We talked about everything: things that happened when Ralph and I were growing up, my children, Ralph's half-siblings, Ralph's paternity predicament. Beth was interested, and interesting. And when we talked about Ralph's father, she said to me, 'I want to show you a picture of him.'

As she disappeared into her bedroom, Ralph turned to me and whispered, *'So, what do you think?'*

'She's lovely. But I'm staaarving.'

'Mm. Me too.'

'Well, say *something, she's your mother!'*

Beth came back with a little black and white photo and handed it to me.

I gasped. 'Oh my God, it's Ralph!' I looked up at him. 'This is you at eighteen.'

He smiled and nodded.

'How about I get us some more coffee?' Beth said.

'I'm in,' Ralph said. 'And Beth, maybe some biscuits? Ruthie's still hungry.'

'Oh, darling, of course!'

I shot Ralph a fuck-you look; he gave me a killer smile.

'I hope you like Iced VoVos and Savoiardi Sponge Fingers,' Beth said as she placed them on a plate.

God no. I think they're fucking horrible, but who the hell cares? Bring 'em on!

She came back with the refilled coffee pot and the bickies. She released a nostalgic sigh as she sat down again. 'David was a beautiful man. Not just in looks, but as a person. He was sensitive and intelligent and caring ... You're so much like him.' She patted Ralph's hand, and said to me, 'And you can't see it in a black and white, but Ralph's got the same brown eyes.'

'Have you tried to find him?' I said.

Beth was caught unawares. 'N-no.'

'Why not?' I asked, pecking at an Iced VoVo—*ecch.*

'Um. Ooh. That's a good question,' she hedged. 'Hmm ...' She rubbed her chin and looked skyward. Holy crap! Beth was ralphulating. She smiled to herself before continuing. 'I think I'm too scared to. I've had David preserved on a pedestal for so long.'

'So then ... how can you move forward?'

'Ruthie—' Ralph was worried I'd gone too far.

'No, it's okay. I'll answer it. You're a wise woman.' Beth smiled at me. 'I guess I've opted for safety. The coward's way, really. And I'm embarrassed to say it, but it feeds my fantasy life.' She blushed.

Ha! 'I can understand that.' I looked off into the distance. 'Forever enshrined as a studmuffin instead of being exposed as the fat slug he might have become.'

Beth looked at me stupefied. Ralph dropped his face into his hands.

Oh shit.

But then Beth started to laugh. She whooped with laughter in much the same way Glen had. Only hers was contagious and she had all her teeth. I joined in. Ralph looked on with amusement as the two of us shrieked and screeched as only women can, doubling up, pounding the table and holding our bellies (me, hoping she also had to hold onto her pelvic floor like I did, because she was older, and it would be tragic if hers was in better condition than mine).

When our laughter subsided, Beth said, 'Oh, you have given me such a gift! David hasn't quite fallen of that pedestal, but it's a little closer to earth. Thank you, darling. May I please hug you?'

I nodded.

She got up from her seat, came around and embraced me with a firm motherly hug. It gave me the warm-and-fuzzies, but also made me feel kind of sad. My mother had never given me motherly hugs.

Beth looked at her son and said, 'Ralph. You are a lucky man.'

He smiled at the two of us with affection. 'I know.'

'Thank you,' I said to her. When she sat back down, I asked her if Ralph had told her about Glen.

No, he hadn't. So, I did.

It provoked another bout of side-splitting laughter from the two of us.

'I'm really glad I ran into him, though,' I said as our laughter fizzled out. 'It was nasty, and it made me instantly regret asking myself those if-only and what-if questions, but seeing him again put them to rest and helped me move on.'

'Mm.' Beth drew her brows together in careful consideration. 'It's funny. Asking questions is a philosopher's driving force. God knows I adore exploring mystery. But, as a human being with insecurities and fears, well, let's just say I'm selective about what I want to demystify!' She gave me an abashed smile and then started laughing. 'I didn't think I was ready to have my illusions shattered, but you've just done that for me.'

'Oh, no!' I felt bad. 'I'm sorry.'

'No, no, no. It's a good thing. Really, it is! You've helped me see that I've made what should have just been a transitional phase after my divorce, well, I've made it a way of life. But ... it's not really living, is it?' Beth became pensive, then pulled a face. 'What if David's like your Glen?'

I shrugged. 'What if he's not?'

She smiled at me. 'True. Well, you've certainly given me something to think about.'

We moved on to other things and chatted non-stop for another hour. I was enjoying Beth's company so much, I wished we could stay longer, but I had to be at Hannah and Alex's at six. I was babysitting Luca. Beth was also sorry to see us go and said she'd love it if I were a regular visitor with Ralph.

She walked with us to the front gate, and hugged and kissed both of us. She took my hand and said, 'You know, I loathe clichés—'

Falling even more in love with you.

Beth looked around to make sure no neighbours were within earshot '—but one I do believe is, "You don't lose a son when he gets married, you gain a daughter". Well, I have to tell you, I feel so blessed. I've found my beautiful son, and oh, what a daughter I'm gaining!'

Totally in love!

'I see what you mean,' I said to Ralph when we were in the car. 'She really is gorgeous!'

He beamed. 'Yeah. And clearly, she thinks the same about you.'

We sat in companionable silence the rest of the way home. When he pulled into my drive and just before I got out, I said, 'D'you wanna invite her to the wedding?'

He looked at me with love, and stroked my cheek. 'Yeah,' he said softly. 'How 'bout you ask her?'

'Okay. But, Ralph ... she needs to meet Norma.'

CHAPTER THIRTY-SIX

Simply Smashing

'Oh.' Beth put her hands to her cheeks in surprise. Her eyes shimmered with tears. 'I would *love* to come to your wedding.'

Beth had called me during the week to say how much she enjoyed our afternoon. I dittoed and invited her for lunch on Saturday. (There'd be no food shortage if I had her at my place.) Ralph, Beth and I were sitting at the dining room table in front of a 'Dear-God-what-a-fabulously-massive-spread'—Beth's words. Her elated response lasted about thirty seconds before turning to one of concern.

'You don't think my presence there might stir the pot?'

'No.' I plated a generous wedge of mushroom quiche before adding, 'There won't be any potzes at the wedding.'

Beth roared with laughter.

'Seriously, though, some of our relatives think it's disgusting we're even together. They won't be getting an invitation. That includes Ralph's brothers and his sister, and my brother.'

'And my fath—um, Albie's not being invited,' Ralph added.

'But your mother will be there, of course?' Beth asked Ralph.

His face dropped. She reached out and took his hand in hers. 'Darling, I'm your mother—I gave birth to you, but she brought you up. She's no less your mother. And I'd like to meet the woman who did such a sterling job with you.'

Pity she fucked up with her three biological dropkicks. Not her fault, she didn't have much to work with.

Ralph slowly nodded, a smile crossing his face. 'And I'd like you to meet her.' He hadn't said, *I'd like her to meet you.* It was as if something shifted in that moment, as if he stopped seeing Norma in terms of what she hadn't done.

And we learned that something had shifted for Beth's other son, Nick. She told us he was starting to warm to the idea of meeting Ralph. He'd always wanted a brother.

The three of us gabbed about many things for the rest of the afternoon, never running out of conversation. But the endless chatter wasn't exhausting. Being in Beth's presence was enlivening. I told her I felt like I'd known her forever. She said the same of me.

Ralph arranged for us to have lunch at his place the following Saturday. With Norma. Both Beth and Norma called me during the week to say how nervous they were about meeting the other.

As it turned out, their fears were unfounded. Beth soaked up all of Norma's stories about Ralph's childhood and adolescence. And when Norma pulled out a photo album from her bag and Beth '*Awwed*' and laughed and cried over the pictures as Norma explained the where's and the when's, I leaned over and whispered in Ralph's ear.

'Norma hasn't told Beth about the time your tackle fell out of your shorts. Want me to remind her?'

He pulled away, his eyes widening. *'Don't you dare!'* he mouthed.

Yeah, baby! I had Ralph by the balls that fell out of his shorts a long time ago because of good vibrations. And there were very good vibrations between these two women—ones that transcended their eternal, maternal link through Ralph.

They hugged warmly when the afternoon was over, and they swapped phone numbers with a promise to pick up their conversation during the week.

It looked like the planets were aligning across the board. The wedding planning problems we'd encountered also seemed to magically iron themselves out as our day drew nearer.

Late morning on the Saturday three and a half weeks before the wedding, I'd just got back from grocery shopping to find Ralph, Casper and Reuben in the driveway tinkering with Casper's car. Casper was moving out in the next week and moving in with Reuben. Ralph was going to rent out his place and move in with me after the wedding.

Reuben had come over to help Casper pack, but he'd been waylaid by him and roped into helping them with the car. The two brainiacs were covered in grease, and Reuben the number cruncher was reading out loud from an instruction sheet. They were attempting to replace the spark plugs. I took my load inside and was putting things away when the phone rang. It was my sister-in-law, Tammy.

Ralph and I had divergent opinions about Tammy when she first came into the family. He thought she was dumb: 'Her antenna doesn't pick up many channels,' he said. But I thought that under her naïve façade and her Tommy gun laugh—*'A-a-a-a-a-a-a-a'*—she was calculating. Over time, we came round to each other's way of thinking: Tammy was a study in cunning dopiness. I wanted to nickname her Woody Woodpecker because of her laugh. But we'd learned she'd earned a reputation at school for putting out, so Ralph wanted to nickname her Puss in Boots. Both fictional characters were stupid and shady. Ralph suggested 'Pussy Woodypecker'. It stuck.

I was surprised she was calling. She and I hadn't spoken in about eighteen months. Maybe something had happened to Myron. Her 'Hello' was curt, though, not grief-stricken. I felt relieved, but only because his demise would be an untimely nuisance. It bothered me that I thought that way.

With no preamble, no how-are-you-long-time-no-speak, she told me she'd heard on the grapevine that Ralph and I were getting married. It couldn't have been Portnoy's grapevine—hers was fast-growing. And besides, ever since I'd flexed my muscles with her, she knew better than to broadcast her poisonous seeds.

Tammy said Myron was offended that I hadn't invited them to my wedding. 'How could you do that to your own brother!' she accused.

'*Excuse* me? You've got a nerve!' I felt my face grow hot with rage. 'My "own brother" judged me for being with Ralph. My "own brother" bad-mouthed me. And hey, my "own brother" has never seen my grandson. That's his great-nephew in case you're trying to figure that one out. He didn't visit Hannah in hospital. And you and my "own brother" were invited to Luca's bris and to Hannah's wedding. You didn't come to either!'

'We had commitments—'

'Commitments, my arse! Save your bullshit excuses for someone who's interested!' I was screaming at her now.

Tammy started crying. 'Myron's really hurt.'

'Oh my God! *Get your head out of your arse!* Are you even *listening* to me? My brother is the most selfish person I know, and you ... you're on the same footing!' I slammed the phone down. *Grrrrr! Ayeeeeee!* I grabbed a plate from the dish rack and smashed it on the floor. I leaned my hands heavily against the kitchen counter and took some slow, deep breaths.

'Feel better?' Ralph's voice jolted me upright.

He, Casper and Reuben were standing next to the breakfast bar. Their faces wore concerned but amused expressions. I nodded, my shoulders sagging with relief.

'Amazing how doing things the Gweek way can ease tension,' Casper said.

Amazing how my son's facetiousness could ease tension. I laughed. 'Oh, I'm so gonna miss you!'

'Hey, I've still got my key. I can drop over anytime.'

Anytime? Shit. With Ralph's unchecked libido let loose anytime, anywhere ...

It was like they all heard my thought. Reuben looked away, Ralph gave me a dirty grin, Casper gave a little shiver of revulsion and said, 'I'll call first.'

I cleared my throat and told them what Tammy had said. They all scowled.

My anger had dissipated, but it was replaced by an undercurrent of sadness at yet another loss. 'I've got used to being an orphan. Now it's like I'm an only child.'

'Now? I think it's been like that for a long time,' Ralph said softly. 'Maybe you're just now seeing it for what it is.'

I nodded. 'Mm.'

He added, 'You know, the plate-smashing tradition in its earliest form was a way of commemorating the dead?'

I winced. 'Then I guess it was an appropriate response, hey?'

The three of them went back out to finish with the car as I swept up the plate fragments.

Forty minutes later, the four of us were sitting around the breakfast bar. They were degreased and devouring the sandwiches I'd made, and swigging lemonade with loud gulps and burps. They were crowing about the thirsty work they'd just done.

'Yeah, three people to change the spark plugs. Real he-men,' I taunted. I polished off my sandwich and had just bitten into a Tim Tam when the phone rang.

I answered it, rolled my eyes and mouthed, *'Myron.'* The three men stopped eating. Men can't multitask. I kept chewing as Myron chewed me out.

'I do *not* appreciate the way you treated my wife!'

I put the phone on speaker, shoved the rest of the biscuit into my mouth and crunched away. Loudly.

'Our parents would both be turning in their graves,' he said in a sneering tone.

'Well, that'd be the first time they're in sync, then.' I said it with a faint air of boredom as Casper, Ralph and Reuben stifled a laugh.

I heard Myron haughtily inhaling the thin air from up on his high horse. 'You always did have bad manners!'

I stopped eating and took the phone off speaker. Some things just needed unitasking, and now, I was really pissed off. 'Don't you dare talk to *me* about manners, you rude, self-serving prick!' I didn't bother rehashing what I'd said to Pussy Woodypecker. Someone with a narcissistic sense of entitlement would twist it to suit his own purpose. All I said was, 'You know, you're becoming just like Sylvia. How's it feel?'

'I'm not even going to dignify that with an answer!' Of course not. It was a trick question for someone who couldn't feel. Or wouldn't. Instead, he hung up on me.

I sat there silently fuming as three pairs of angry eyes looked on. Reuben spoke first.

'Can I just say I never thought much of your brother?'

'Join the queue,' Ralph said.

Casper put the remainder of his sandwich on the bench and handed me his plate. I was about to bark that I wasn't his slave when he said, 'Go for it. I'll sweep up this time.'

Thank God for my son. Thank God for the comedy in the tragedy. And cheers to the Gweek way!

That sense of loss I'd experienced earlier was, sadly, no real loss. And I'd moved on from the unpleasant phone calls by the time Maxi, Vette, Iris, Rhea, and I got together a couple of hours later. This time, we rendezvoused at Dawn and Harmon's place. It made sense as it was where the wedding would be held. We had a productive meeting; everything was going according to plan.

The following Saturday, Hannah, Alex and Luca spent the night at my place. They'd had their apartment fumigated and didn't want Luca exposed to the active chemicals. Alex went home early the next morning to open windows and air out the place. Ralph came over, we all had lunch together and Alex took Hannah and Luca home mid-afternoon. Hannah called me a couple of hours later.

'Did I leave my deodorant there? It's not in my bag.'

I went to the bathroom to check. 'Nope, can't see—'

'Don't worry. Found it. Alex had it in his bag.'

'Okay. But ... *what?* What the hell is this?

CHAPTER THIRTY-SEVEN

Bag of Tricks

I picked up and examined the shaggy-dog toothbrush that had been partly concealed behind the soap dispenser. I'd worked as a dental nurse after leaving school. To an ex-dental nurse, a toothbrush in this condition was sacrilege!

'I have your toothbrush in my hand and—'

'Huh? I've got my toothbrush here.'

'Well, it's not Casper's. It's pink and it's sha—'

'Oh, that's Alex's.'

'Why has he got a pink toothbrush?'

Ralph walked past, then doubled back. He stood in the bathroom doorway looking at me intently.

'What? Who cares what colour it is?' Hannah said.

'True. But why is he using a shaggy-dog toothbrush? That's not how I brought you up.'

Hannah laughed. 'You didn't bring *him* up. And I'm not his mother.'

True again. What Alex did wasn't my business. And what Hannah did was no longer my business.

'I'll give it to you next time I see you.'

'Nah. Just throw it out. I've got spares here.'

'Okay.' I told Hannah I'd speak to her later, disconnected, and put the phone in my pocket. I put my foot on the pedal of the pedal bin in the bathroom, when Ralph yelled at me.

'STOP!'

I reeled a little from the force of his voice. 'Whoa!'

'That's Alex's, right?' He pointed at the toothbrush.

'Yeah, wh—'

'*Bag it!* Put it in an envelope or a paper bag, *not* plastic. I'll be back in twenty.'

Ralph took off before I could say anything, and he was back in less than twenty. He'd gone home and returned with his toothbrush and a DNA paternity test kit.

'Seriously?' I laughed at him. 'How long have you had that?'

His face crimsoned. 'I ordered it a couple of weeks ago.'

'Uh, okay. But ... we were gonna wait until after the honeymoon to look into it. And don't you think this is the wrong way to go about it?'

'Are you kidding? No way! It's landed in my lap. Can't you see? This is divine providence.' Ralph was working himself up into a lather. I didn't feel quite as impassioned.

'Mm. I guess. It just worries me that it's a little underhanded.'

He cocked his head and gave me a quizzical smile. 'Said the pot to the kettle?'

I cocked my head and gave him a quizzical look.

'Have you forgotten that you call-forwarded to a brothel?'

'Oh. That.'

'Yeah. *That.*'

It seemed funny at the time, but now I felt embarrassed. Although ... I reminded myself I'd just followed Casper's lead and it had been a desperate but necessary move.

Ralph took a deep breath and released it slowly. 'Look. Maybe the timing's not great and I know it's not exactly upfront, but the thing is, I might have a son. I just need to know.'

I raised my hands in surrender. 'Okay, okay. But, Ralph ... these tests aren't necessarily conclusive—'

'Actually, they are. I spoke to someone at the DNA testing company and got all the information. She said their tests are a hundred per cent conclusive. It'll either show zero per cent or ninety-nine point nine nine.'

'Mm. How long does it all take?'

'From the time they get the sample—they usually do the test a day or so after it arrives—she said it'll take about ten working days for me to get the results.'

'So, if you send this off tomorrow and they get it, say, on Wednesday and then maybe do the test on Thursday ... let's see ...'—I calculated on my fingers—'our wedding is on the eighth working day. We'll be in Fiji when it arrives.' I was relieved. Whichever way it went, I didn't want to have to deal with the result until after our honeymoon.

'Uh-huh.'

'What if it's a negative reading. You prepared for that?'

'It's better than not knowing.'

'Fair enough.' I nodded. 'What if it's a positive reading?'

Ralph gave me a benign smile. 'That's a lot of what-iffing. But it's the kind that's out of my hands.' He exhaled slowly. 'Look, I can't give you an answer. I'm not sure anyone can really know how they're going to react to a situation until they're in it.'

'I guess not. If it's positive, though, I can't see you standing by and saying nothing, just basking in the joy of knowing Alex is your son.'

Ralph pinched the bridge of his nose. 'No. I can't see me doing that either.'

'I know if it were me, I wouldn't keep quiet about it. But, geez, Ralph, like we haven't made enough waves in the last few years!'

'*Only* the last few years? *Pff!* You and I have been making waves since our mothers found out they were pregnant with us!'

Ralph was right. It was never about deliberately upsetting people, though. Mostly. It was mostly about asserting our rights. And he had the right to know if he was a father. And if he was, his son had the right to know. It concerned me how he'd go about informing Alex, but still ...

'Go do your swab,' I said.

Ralph posted the test kit early the next morning.

The earth rotated fifteen more times on its axis—

—and our wedding day arrived.

CHAPTER THIRTY-EIGHT

Coming Full Circle

There was a soft rapping on the door.

'Ruthie?' Vette's muffled voice shook me out of my contemplative state. I checked the time. An hour had passed since I'd told Maxi I wanted to be alone, even before I knew I was beset with a sudden case of cold feet. I stood up as Vette opened the door and stuck her head in. Her breath caught when she saw me.

'Wow! You look gorgeous.'

I smiled at my friend. 'Thanks, Vette.'

'Five minutes.' She held up her fingers.

I nodded.

'You okay?' she asked hesitantly.

'Yep.' I was okay. Sort of. I was still in a quandary.

As Vette closed the door, I retrieved the sealed envelope from my bag on the chest of drawers. It had no logo or company name on the front, and no sender's name on the back. It was addressed to Mr Ralph Brill. (Ralph had his mail redirected to my place a week earlier and he'd spent his last night as a bachelor at his apartment.) I had a strong feeling when I took the envelope out of the mailbox in the morning that it was from the DNA testing company. They'd told him that in the interest of discreetness, his results would arrive in an unmarked envelope.

After I'd gone back inside and held the envelope up to the light—like that would reveal anything—I heard Casper pulling into the drive. I'd shoved the envelope into my handbag and put that into the large beach bag that held my shoes and stockings, underwear, make-up, shampoo and conditioner, hairdryer, and everything else I was taking to the Hyde's place. I'd be showering there.

Casper had asked me if I had second thoughts as he toted the garment bag with my dress in it and the beach bag to the car.

'No. Why?'

'Because you look shell-shocked.'

Now, I looked skyward. *What am I going to do? And when?* Give it to Ralph after the honeymoon? No. That would be a dishonest way to start our married life. Maybe when we got home tonight? Or on the plane tomorrow? If the result was negative, our honeymoon would be marred by disappointment and sadness. If it was positive, though, Ralph's obsessive-compulsive behaviour would be off the South Pacific charts! Screwed either way. But either way, for now, I needed to keep my yap shut. And my decision would have to wait until after the wedding when we were home, where I should have left the envelope.

I checked myself out in the mirror once more. Oh God, I loved this dress! A flattering A-line halter with a simple, modern lace overlay: Not fussy, not intricate—just smooth impressions of large flat flowers and leaves. It had a three-inch empire waistband and a built-in bra. Two wide scalloped lace straps extended upward from the bodice and tapered to fasten behind the neck.

Maxi, Vette and I had voted unanimously for this one out of the three optional styles Vette had selected for me—Maxi had insisted they must be red. I knew that red was an emotionally intense colour, which summed up my relationship with Ralph. 'For passion?' I'd asked.

'No, because you're a scarlet woman!'

I smiled at the memory and picked up my simple bouquet of white roses. I had to carry some semblance of purity. I'd purged so much crap from my soul that I felt I was more entitled to whiteness now than at my first wedding.

I faced the mirror again; looked into my eyes again. And once more, I asked myself if I was ready to put myself out there; if I was ready for a date with destiny. 'You bet! I deserve it.'

I left the room, walked through the house and into the family room, paused at the double doors that opened out onto the deck, and surveyed Dawn and Harmon's garden. Already beautiful, it had been transformed into a pocket of paradise with the additional pot plants, several high-back, three-seater timber benches placed around the perimeter, and rustic whimsies scattered here and there. I'd loved the homespun feel of Hannah's wedding, so the girls had suggested and organised the same theme for mine.

The guests were mingling and chatting animatedly on the left of the yard just in front of the chuppah. Most of the women shielded themselves from the sun with brown paper parasols that we'd supplied. Not the men, though. Machismo bullshit wouldn't allow it. (I couldn't see Ralph, but I was sure he held one.) On the right-hand side and taking up a quarter of the backyard was a pagoda marquee that sheltered the eight beautifully-set, six-seater round tables. The marquee was similar to Hannah's only it was smaller, open on all sides, and with four draped poles and a decorative valance. Maxi had booked the same photographer, videographer, caterer, musicians and celebrant.

The photographer and videographer leapt into action as I walked out onto the deck where Casper was waiting for me. His eyes widened when he saw me. 'Wowee, Muum!'

I kissed him, then took in the smiling faces of the people present, all of whom were important in my life ... except for Hector. Not Hector. Hector was not important. But there wasn't much I could do about his presence, or the fact that he was dressed from top to toe in white. *Bad luck, shithead. You haven't upstaged me. I'm in red!* I revelled in everyone's spontaneous applause at my appearance, and at the whispers: *beautiful, gorgeous, oh-my-God—red!*

Other than the bench seats, there was no arranged seating. No need, the ceremony would be short. Because neither of us was religious, we didn't want the whole enchilada:

There'd be no wine sipping—we didn't like alcohol.

Ralph wanted me to walk walk walk walk walk walk walk around him seven times.

'It's the only time you get to run circles around me,' he'd said. I said no. I'd wasted too many years running around in circles. He caved in. So who was running circles around whom?

He wanted to break the glass.

'Really? You actually *care* about commemorating the destruction of the Temple in Jerusalem?' I'd asked.

'Not especially. I wanna commemorate the three-year anniversary of that night I decided to go for broke, and confess my feelings for you.'

I also wanted him to break the glass.

He'd asked if my desire was about commemorating the other cataclysmic shattering it represented—that of the soul, which both of us had experienced, and which culminated in our sacred union today.

'Not especially. It's just that the glass half-full, glass half-empty saying pisses me off.' I reminded him it had been another one that my glass-half-empty mother had thrown around. 'It's time to smash that frickin' glass!'

The music started up and Casper escorted me down the three steps and along a burlap aisle runner, which was strewn with white and red rose petals. For the wedding march, Ralph and I had chosen the instrumental version of Lionel Richie and Diana Ross's 'Endless Love'. It moved many to tears, not just for its haunting melody, but also because they knew Ralph and I had surmounted many obstacles to get here, and formalise our endless love.

I gazed at my dishy groom as I neared the chuppah, where he was waiting with the marriage celebrant. His eyes glistened, half full of tears (or was that half empty?). He took my hands in his and whispered, *'You are stunning.'* I told him he was just as stunning. In his beige linen suit with a red rose boutonnière and an open-neck white shirt, my geek god was irresistible.

The touching service was over in fifteen minutes. The celebrant had spoken about our love, Ralph and I had exchanged vows, we'd exchanged rings, Ralph had smithereened the cloth-wrapped glass into ground particles, and the guests had yelled *'Mazel Tov!'* and clapped. Ralph and I were mid-kiss when the guests yelled 'Eurgh!' 'Oooaughoaua!' 'Ewww!' 'Argh!'

What? It was the kind of reaction you'd expect from teenyboppers witnessing their parents snogging. Ralph and I stopped kissing and came up for air.

Eurgh! Oooaughoaua! Ewww! Argh!

The breeze, that just minutes before had carried the heady summer scents of jasmine, murraya and gardenia, now carried the stench of horseshit.

I looked in the direction of the guests' turned heads. That lush green expanse of lawn I'd admired on the other side of the garden was a fucking horse paddock!

Two horses stood at the divider fence. The one with the motley grey coat whinnied—*nei-ei-ei-ei-eigh, nei-ei-ei-ei-eigh*—snorting and baring long yellow teeth. The other one, whose dull brown coat showed patchy hair loss, finished taking its dump. It made a *phrrrrr* noise, cast Grey a peevish look and then walked away, leaving a fresh stink to waft. Grey nickered again. I eyeballed it. It eyeballed me, snaked its head back and forth and stomped its front hoof. This made me feel ... guilty. What? *Really?* I shook my head, which shook loose a fragmented memory of an old folk song from my early school days—one about an old grey mare who isn't or ain't or wasn't what she used to be ...

Holy shit! My breath suddenly caught in my throat.

I tugged at Ralph's sleeve and asked, 'Can humans reincarnate as animals?'

He looked down at me, a slow smile spreading across his handsome face as he got my drift. He shrugged. 'Anything's possible.'

'But wouldn't that be coming back in a lower form?'

'Mm. You'd think,' he murmured as he studied the grey horse again. He looked back at me. 'But in this case, it'd probably be an upgrade.'

A mortified Dawn rushed over to us as I laughed at this witty, sexy, weird man who was my brand-new husband.

'I'm so sorry,' she said. 'Harmon's gone inside to call the neighbours and get them to clean up. I swear, the horses've never come over to the fence before. Ever.'

That they had now, fed my suspicions. Sylvia and Joe were gatecrashing my wedding! The night-mare and the stallion. No. Make that a gelding, not a stallion. No balls.

Nothing had changed. It was same old, same old in the early afterlife—him, still making methane and avoiding her; her, still whining and harping. The way my parents had behaved, the way they'd treated me when I was a child (and long past) was awful. But right now, Mr Kosta's words rang true. Life really was a tragicomedy.

The neighbours arrived five minutes later and apologised. Dawn shpritzed a whole aerosol can of room deodoriser after they shovelled the shit, bridled a truculent 'Sylvia' and led her away.

I'm married to him now. Suck it up, nag!

Everybody else was happy about my new status. After lots of congratulatory kisses and hugs and champagne sipping, we were ferried into the marquee. By the time we were seated, the smell had gone.

Ralph and I shared the table with Vette and Henry, whose complexions were translucent, and with Maxi and Nestor, who, five months into their relationship still couldn't keep their eyes and hands off each other, and were planning to move in together.

Hannah, Alex and Luca sat with Casper, Leah and Ari. Maxi had even organised a chair bow on the back of Luca's high chair.

I was worried about putting Beth at a table with my elderly relatives, but it seemed she'd taken to all of them, and they'd all taken to her. I heard them regaling her with stories about Ralph and me. Beth was riveted.

Rhea and Hector shared a table with Iris, Joel, Reuben and Ida. Hector was sandwiched between Rhea and Iris. With his bowed shoulders and his arms wrapped around himself, he looked like he'd been flattened in a Panini press. Iris could have that effect on someone like Hector, even if there was no one sitting on the other side of him.

Seated at the other tables were good friends and Ralph's colleagues with their partners.

Ralph looked around and *hmmed*. 'Interesting table configuration,' he remarked. 'If all the tables touched, it would be considered optimal packing in an octagon. You know, from a geometric perspective.'

I pretended to be impressed with his observation as I looked around. We were at the centre, the other seven tables forming a circle around ours. I *hmmed*. 'I reckon it looks like the Target logo, with our table as the bullseye. You know, from a bird's-eye perspective.' I gave him a cheesy smile.

He laughed at me. 'God, I so love the way your mind works!' He pulled me over to him and kissed me. 'But you don't need to worry. We're under a marquee. And even if we weren't, birds don't take aim when they download their droppings.'

That hadn't occurred to me, but now that he'd mentioned it, the irony of it all wasn't lost on me because I'd often thought of Sylvia as a harpy. I remembered that in ancient myth, these squawking birdlike creatures that shat on everything gave birth to a couple of horses. Thinking about what Mr Kosta had said about life being ancient myth perpetually replayed in modern dress, I got a little worried. Sylvia, the mother of all nags, used to take aim and download her droppings on me with military precision.

I fixed Ralph with a troubled frown. *'She's never gonna leave, is she?'* I whispered. *'She's always gonna haunt me in one form or another.'*

'Mm-hmm.' He knew who I was referring to. He touched the side of my head. 'She'll always be in here.' It brought to mind that old chestnut—a loved one who dies remains in our hearts forever. It saddened me that I couldn't embrace Sylvia as a loved one and that I didn't feel as if she was in my heart, and may never be. Ralph drew me close and whispered, *'Just remember, though, the more you let go, the less control she'll have over you. Like with Portnoy.'*

His words offered some encouragement. Still ... damn it! Why did she have to make an appearance at my *wedding*?

A whispered answer came from within: *'Not everything is about you. The joke's on Ralph too. He said he wanted to ride off into the sunset with you. He didn't ask for a thoroughbred as transport.'*

Baubo!

The dirty goddess's face suddenly loomed in my (Portnoy-like) mind's eye, smiling at me with her labia-lips. *Jesus Christ*—what fugliness! I started laughing.

'What?' Ralph pulled away and looked at me with a questioning smile.

'Nothing.'

Ralph—the man of my dreams. Baubo—my hero.

I felt much better. I felt even better when the waiter asked us to make our way to the buffet table.

The service might have been short and sweet, but the festive meal that followed was long, savoury and sweet. It was a lavish buffet lunch of Moroccan spiced spatchcock—butterflied, but with legs attached so Ralph wouldn't freak out; eye fillet in red wine—medium, not *bleu* so I wouldn't freak out; baked honey Tasmanian salmon; roasted Mediterranean vegetables; pumpkin and spinach lasagna; paella; and assorted salads. And afterwards: chocolate mousse; croquembouche; French crêpes; vanilla cheesecake; ice cream and crème brûlée (my favourites); and a summer fruit platter.

We'd had our fill of the savoury and I was tucking into my dessert when I realised I hadn't sampled any of the mousse. I looked at Ralph's plate. 'Is the mousse good? I forgot to take some.' Ralph scooped up a spoonful and offered it to me. I stared in wonder.

'What's mine is yours now.' He smiled at me as I accepted the offering. 'And what's yours is mine,' he said as he eyed the contents of my plate. 'I didn't take any cheesecake.'

'Okay, fine. Here!' I conceded as I spooned a bit of cheesecake into his mouth. 'But you are not allowed to touch my bloody ice cream!'

He laughed at me. 'Yes, I remember.'

When we were five, Ralph helped himself to some ice cream from my bowl. I screamed at him and called him *'Ralph Shitface Brill'*. He, who didn't give a shitface that his first name was monosyllabic and that he didn't have a middle name, started crying and yelled back, 'Well at least now *I've* got a middle name! *Na-nana-naa-nah!'*

I cried. He felt bad. He never came near my ice cream again.

Ralph finished his dessert and took to the podium to make his speech as the musical duo took a break to have something to eat. When he'd finished, there was not a dry eye in the tent. His words made me feel very loved. Sylvia's conjecture that no one would put up with me had led me to become nice as pie in my lost years, and sabotage my relationship with myself. And yet, I was now married to a man who'd been by my side through thick and thin, and sharing this special day with people whose love was enduring.

The whole afternoon effervesced with joy and love and laughter. It was over too soon. At six-thirty, the musos were packing away and the catering staff started clearing the tables. Ralph and I stood next to ours as, one by one, the guests came to say their goodbyes. Norma, Beth and Greta approached, each in turn hugging us. It occurred to me then that I had three mothers-in-law. (Despite my divorce from Reuben, his mother and I had remained close. Greta still considered me her daughter-in-law and always would, she said.) How lucky could a girl get! As they walked away, I realised my bouquet was still sitting on the table.

Beth had stopped to chat to Hannah and Alex and was fussing over Luca. With the unanswered question of Alex's paternity, I wondered what she was thinking. I called out to her. 'Beth? Think quick!' I threw the bouquet to her. It wasn't the traditional way of doing things, but not much about the wedding was. The woman had good reflexes; she caught it. Flabbergasted, she looked up at me. 'Oh, you!' she said as she came back and hugged me again.

I whispered, *'David?'*

She pulled back and smiled. *'I've started making enquiries.'*

My eyebrows shot up, my mouth dropped open.

'Shh. Don't tell Ralph.'

Without a second thought, I responded with a lip-zipping gesture. It was only after she left that the implications of what she said knocked me six ways to Sunday.

Yikes!

CHAPTER THIRTY-NINE

In the Dark

U p until now, I'd been thinking in terms of David as Beth's Twin Flame—the Lancelot to her Guinevere, the Mark Antony to her Cleopatra, the Charlie Brown to her Lucy. I'd forgotten that David was also Ralph's father.

Like a pack of Portnoy's rats on hamster wheels, a whole lot of new what-ifs began whirring round and round between my ears and gnawing at me, as Ralph and Harmon went back and forth between the house and Ralph's car, filling it up with our presents.

'You okay?' Ralph asked as he passed me. 'You've got a worried look on your face.'

I told him I was just tired.

Yes, I was tired. I was tired of worrying. But, why was I worrying? Why was I speculating about potential problems and carrying the burden of worries that weren't even mine?

I didn't need to be Ralph's pack mule so I would matter to him. I mattered to him because I was me. That was enough. And if Ralph himself was knocked six ways to Sunday from the results of the paternity test and from maybe one day meeting his father, I would be there to support him in his fall. Not try and break it. I felt like a weight had been lifted. In that moment, I knew what I had to do when we got home.

Ralph came back with the thankyou gift we'd bought for the Hydes—two large Villeroy and Boch platters. We also invited them to dinner on the Saturday two weeks after we were due back from our honeymoon. We'd arranged to take Maxi and Nestor, Vette and Henry, Iris and Joel, and Rhea and the horse's arse out that night to show our appreciation for the girls' hard work. Dawn and Harmon were stunned by our generosity, they told us. We were grateful for theirs, we told them. We said our goodbyes and, as Mr and Mrs Whatever, we headed home.

Fifty minutes later, Ralph unlocked the door to our home and dumped our bags next to the console table. Another twenty minutes later, after he'd carried me across two thresholds—the front door and bedroom door—he and I moved to the lounge. He said he had something for me, I said I had something for him. He rummaged through the bag he'd left near the door, while I skipped into the bedroom and came back with a box I'd hidden in my bedside table drawer. He was sitting back on the sofa with a ring box in his hand. My breath caught in my throat as he opened it. Inside was a stunning, full baguette cut diamond eternity ring. The diamonds were mounted in a classic channel setting.

'Oh my God, I *love* it!'

'I got it sized to fit your right hand, I know you don't like stacking jewellery.'

'You know me so well.' I slipped it on my finger and kissed him.

He unwrapped the box I'd given him and opened it. *His* breath caught. 'It's perfect!' We kissed again. 'You know *me* so well.' Well, not so well, actually. I'd bought Ralph's present a month earlier.

> I selected a simple, elegant watch. Leather band, black face, stick hour markers.
>
> 'Would Madam like it gift-wrapped?' the jeweller asked.
>
> 'Yes, please. Oh, wait. It's got a date display. Do you have one without?'
>
> He was intrigued by my request.
>
> 'My fiancé has OCPD,' I explained. 'The date makes the watch face, um, asymmetrical.'
>
> The jeweller raised his index finger. 'Ah.' He gave me a knowing smile.
>
> I left the store fifteen minutes later with a meticulously gift-wrapped, chunky, precision, water-resistant chronograph watch with stainless steel bracelet, a black face and three chronograph dials—60-minute register, 1/10th second register, 60-second register. 'Your fiancé needs something that affords planning down to the second,' he'd said. 'It trumps symmetry.' The jeweller also had OCPD.

Now, as we sat here, he, in his boxers and tee, staring at his newly fandangled wrist, I, in my nightie, staring at my newly bejewelled finger, I remembered the envelope.

'I've got something else for you.'

'Ooh! Another present?'

'Hmm ...' I stared at him. 'That remains to be seen.' I got up to fetch my handbag from the beach bag, fished out the envelope, brought it over and handed it to him. 'It arrived this morning. I think this is it—there're no markings.'

Ralph stared at it in puzzlement at first, then with trepidation.

'Look, I didn't say anything earlier because I didn't want it to spoil our wedding. I knew you'd obsess about it if you didn't open it, and it'd open up a can of worms if you did.'

He didn't respond. He probably hadn't heard a word.

With the two of us sitting there looking at it, it brought back memories of a similar scene about eighteen months earlier—Ralph priming himself as we stared at the envelope from AFIS with news about his mother. I'd been patient then, or tried to be. I tried to be patient now. I could hear the ticking of his chronograph (from the 60-second register). After two hundred and forty bloody ticks, I started getting antsy.

Hoo aah hoo aah. Let's breathe through the impatience. Hoo aah hoo aah. Let's investigate how impatience feels in my mind and body. Hoo aah hoo aah. Let's transform impatience into patience. Hoo aah hoo aah. Bugger that—what's yours is mine, baby!

With care, I pried the envelope from his grip, ripped it open and read the letter with the DNA testing company's logo and name on the top.

Oh boy.

I handed Ralph the letter and sank back into the sofa cushion anticipating the week ahead.

But then, I recalled what he'd said two and a half weeks earlier—that no one can really know how they're going to react to a situation until they're in it. Still, it was a safe bet that for the next seven days, Ralph would be saying things twice, tapping things twice and *nom nom nomming* ... for ninety-nine point nine nine per cent of the time, at least.

The End. If Only...

WHAT WILL THE BIG REVEAL MEAN FOR THIS COUPLE?

From Book 3 in the series,
My T(r)oyboy is a Twat

'Walk this way,' the receptionist instructed. Igor, Doctor Frankenstein's hunchbacked assistant with the shuffling gait, had said the same thing to his master in the comedy–horror movie, *Young Frankenstein*. Where Doc F had misunderstood (or was just a tosser) and imitated the lumbering Igor, we followed the receptionist's directive. She didn't have a hump and she didn't shuffle. But because of a pronounced limp, she waddled like a penguin.

As an adolescent, I'd have thought about mimicking her swaying gait. *Thought* about it. I wouldn't have done it, though, partly because I knew what it was like to be made fun of for being different, and also because I'd be mortified if I were caught out.

Back then, I had no control over my shameful thoughts or the impulse to laugh. Neither the passage of time nor maturity had curbed these. Even so, the urge to laugh wasn't there at the moment. Being here was no laughing matter.

I studied her as we trailed her down the hall. A penguin walk and a penguin build. She was torpedo-shaped, with a thick midsection, narrow shoulders and skinny legs. She was also torpedo-hued: gunmetal-grey hair pulled up tight in a severe bun; dressed in a pale grey, short-sleeved, polyester, O-neck tee, a charcoal pencil skirt and grey stockings; sporting boring, low-heeled pumps in a whale grey colour.

The receptionist's fifty shades of grey reflected my state of mind.

'Doctor shouldn't be too long,' she said as she ushered us into the shrink's office.

I stopped short.

The office was enormous and had a musty, old-house smell. *Ecch.* And with its heavy, murky hues, it must have once been the drawing room of this place that looked like a Georgian mansion.

'Can I get you a tea or a coffee?'

Ralph said, 'No, thanks.'

The receptionist was looking at me, waiting for an answer.

I could do with a cup of confidence. Maybe in a Starbucks insulated paper cup. Not the coffee—fuck no!—just served in a Starbucks cup to remind me that we're in the twenty-first century.

'Uh, no. Thank you.' The coffee had probably expired a hundred and sixty-five years ago. Anyway, drinking it when I was uptight gave me wind. And already feeling like I was behind the eight ball, the last thing I needed was to fart during the session.

WHERE IT ALL BEGAN ...

From Book 1 in the series,
Odyssey in a Teacup

'Hello, I'm Ruth Roth,' I said to my bedroom mirror when I was five. I talked to it often, always starting with hello because my generation was brought up with manners ... or effective social conditioning, anyway.

This time, it replied with a bitchy reminder. 'Yes, but you're *just* Ruth. Not Ruth Michelle, nor Ruth Katherine. No middle name; one syllable. Not like Myron.'

Eleven months older than me, my brother My-ron Ste-phen Law-rence Roth got two middle names and six syllables. Even to my five-year-old sensibilities, the difference in naming reeked of injustice, so I whined through my gappy milk teeth to our father, Joe (Jo-seph Ben-ja-min Roth).

'It'th not fair! Why did Myron get two middle name'th and I got none?'

'Because the extra initials will look good printed in his cheque book.'

What fucking checked book? He's only six years old! Oh, I knew these things were adult books, but still, fair's fair. 'I want a checked book too!'

'Girls don't need one.'

And there it was. Four bloody words that set a precedent for my standing in the family, and beyond.

Then Syl-vi-a Es-ther Roth, our mother, put in her two cents' worth, not only sealing the deal, but supergluing it, further contributing to my thorny relationship with mirrors.

'*Oeuf!* What difference does it make? *Pest!*'

Thanks for reading!
If you enjoyed this book, I'd be very grateful if
you'd post a short review at your favourite online retailer.
Your support really does make a difference.

Connect with Paula Houseman
Website: https://paulahouseman.com

Social Networks
https://www.facebook.com/PaulaHousemanAuthor
https://www.goodreads.com/PaulaHouseman
https://www.linkedin.com/in/paulahouseman
https://www.pinterest.com/paulahouseman
https://twitter.com/paulahouseman